# THE WOMAN POPE

# THE WOMAN POPE

## THE LIFE AND LEGEND OF POPE JOAN

### A NOVEL BY

### NELSON CLARK

*Melton Clark*
*Los Angeles*
*2009*

The Woman Pope
The Life and Legend of Pope Joan
A Novel by Nelson Clark

Published by:
**White Moon Publishing**
Post Office Box 661508
Los Angeles, CA 90066, U.S.A.
Orders at: www.WhiteMoonPublishing.com

This is a work of fiction. Events, places, and characters have sprung solely from the author's imagination. Any similarities to persons living, dead, forgotten, innocently or maliciously erased from historical accounts, are purely coincidental.

International Standard Book Number: 978-0-6151-4163-3
Library of Congress Control Number: 2007926407
Printed in the United States of America

**Library of Congress Cataloging-in-Publication Data**

Clark, Nelson.
The woman pope : the life and legend of Pope Joan / by Nelson Clark
LCCN: 2007926407
ISBN 978-0-6151-4163-3
1.  Fiction-Historical, Pope Joan, Dark Ages, Spirituality, etc.
2.  Religion-myth and legend in the Catholic Church, etc.
3.  Women's issues-perception, treatment, et al, in Latin Middle Ages
4.  Epic journeys, gender disguise, personal transformation

"Christian" Chapter art: *The work of art depicted in these images and the reproduction thereof are in the public domain worldwide. The reproduction is part of a collection of reproductions compiled by The Yorck Project. The entire collection is copyrighted by The Yorck Project and licensed under the GNU Free Documentation License.*

"Pagan" Chapter art: Eliza Yetter, used by permission

Cover Design by Dixie Press

*The world is but a bridge.*
*Pass over, but build no house upon it.*
*He who hopes for an hour*
*May hope for an eternity.*
*The world is but an hour,*
*Spend it in devotion.*
*Life is a moment upon the bridge;*
*The rest is unseen.*

Persian inscription on a gate in
Fatehpur Sikri, India
Attributed to Jesus

# PROLOGUE

T WAS ROME'S last chance.

The pope was the only man on earth who had the power to dissolve the curse on the city in this most wicked time, eight-hundred fifty-eight long years after the Lord's death and resurrection.

No rain had fallen in months. Swarms of grasshoppers covered the city, wild fires burned unchecked in the countryside and sickness lurked on every corner looking for anyone not conscientious in their prayers.

It was crucial that Pope John Anglicus VIII, John The English, walk the time-honored processional route from the Lateran Basilica to St. Peter's to exorcise the demons strangling the life from Rome.

Only he could divert the evil taken hold of the holy city.

A woman stood in the same spot she had occupied for hours. Shoulder-to-shoulder with the others, she waited, squinting down the crowded narrow street until it bent out of sight. Finally, in the late afternoon, while giving a precious gulp to her four-year-old daughter from their waterskin, she felt a ripple of expectation swell through the people.

"The pope is coming," said a man next to her. He had a discolored, turkey-waddle like growth on the side of his neck.

Around the far corner came horses. The young mother stood on her tip toes trying to see over the heads in front of her. She could feel the rumble of hooves through the ground and thought she could make out a purple banner at the end of the street.

A hand pulled at her. When she turned, she flinched at a filthy rag held in her face.

"Protect yourself from the plague, little mother."

Beyond the rag leered a bloated face flaked with thick scales of psoriasis.

"From the robe of Saint Benedict. It'll protect the child from pox."

She spat at the man's feet and walked away from the relic seller. She was young but no fool. Long ago she learned that rags, dried fingers, toes, and worse were plundered daily from corpses found on the streets, and foul men like that one sold the remains as the parts of saints and martyrs. Only new pilgrims were naive enough not to believe Rome was the home of deception as well as the resting place of St. Peter.

She edged both herself and her child toward the procession. Instantly, they were sucked into a moving tide of flailing arms. She looked over the heads in front of her. Papal guards cleared a path for the pontiff, some with long poles, some using whips. Squeezed on all sides by backs and shoulders and sweating faces, she tried to jostle her way out, but it was too late. They were both caught up and carried away in the jumble of bodies pushed toward the stamping hooves of the guards.

Through the waving elbows and fists around them she caught a glimpse of the red robes of cardinals and the purple miters of bishops on horseback. She watched their heads twist nervously this way and that. Their pointed headgear jutted above the tangled masses, and the precious stones sewn into their garments cast sparkling lights over the wretched sea around them.

As the procession approached, she sensed something was wrong. The holy men were red in the face from screaming for their acolytes, swinging their hook-shaped crosiers, hitting the people to keep them at bay. The acolytes, who fanned them earlier with palm fronds had drowned in the mob, and now the robed churchmen were afraid of their own flock.

Roman guards whipped at the crowd, lashing vicious strokes across outstretched hands, making a bloody pathway for the Holy One.

"I see him," the mother said to her daughter. The child was speechless with fear, her little mouth and eyes wide open. "Wave, Maria. Call to him. If he sees you, you'll be blessed. They say his look has magic."

She grunted and lifted Maria onto her shoulders. Beside them, the pope's envoy strained to pass through the frenzied crowd. The guards' horses reared, snorting against grabbing hands of the mob, the animals' ears twitching, and their dark eyes blinked with panic. The Holy Father, surrounded by soldiers, was not on horseback but rode instead on an old donkey.

The mother stopped her frantic waving. She stared, amazed. He was so different from the rest of his entourage. The pontiff of all Christendom could not be more than twenty-one.

He wore simple coarse robes in shades of white, and on his head was a broad-brimmed straw hat, free of jewelry, to keep the sun off. No whiskers graced his face and a soft and kind face it was, so thin and drawn, strikingly out of place above his distended paunch.

As she stared, the pope turned in her direction. Though tossed in the human cauldron around her, she could not take her eyes away. Close enough to see the pontiff's hazel eyes, the young man suddenly jerked with such a grimace that those who saw it grew alarmed. The pope panted and gulped for air as a seizure shook his body and for several seconds he twitched on the donkey, holding his belly until it passed with a final shiver. He sighed and a burst of perspiration rained off him. The pope, aware of the anxious crowd, made the sign of the cross.

"John Anglicus. Pope John the Eighth!" shouted the people, surging forward, pressing their bodies into the skittish soldiers.

"John the English. Save us. Save *me,*" said an old woman. Pushed from behind, she slammed into the back of a hairy sergeant at the pope's flank. Instinctively, he brought the flat side of his heavy broad sword around, and unable to stop the reflex, struck the woman. It broke her shoulder with a snap.

Her shriek cut through the clamor. The shaken sergeant yanked the sword back, but in his rush to pull it away from the old woman the blade dug into the thigh of the pope's donkey.

The donkey's bray and the old woman's scream were a piercing shriek in the air. Flattening its ears, the donkey bolted into the crowd kicking furiously at the air with its hind legs. The pope gripped its mane and looked barely able to hang on as the animal broke through the line of soldiers and ran into the crowd.

A dark implication spread out to everyone who watched. In that moment all faith in the pope's ability to destroy the devils plaguing Rome disintegrated. In the eyes of the multitude, this demi-god, who daily communed face-to-face with the God of the universe, had been turned into a mortal by a common beast. The most spiritually favored being on earth had been transformed before their eyes into a helpless man clinging to a donkey.

Maria and her mother were abruptly released from the clutch of frantic bodies parting before them, and the two stood wondering at the sudden open space of ground around them.

"Mama!" the child watched the injured donkey run by. It wheeled sharply and made for an alley. As it did, the mother opened her mouth to speak but was smothered in a cloud of robes.

The pope was flung from the donkey onto them.

All three tumbled to the ground and rolled in the dank earth.

Maria found herself cradled around a large, hard belly. She opened her eyes, no longer in her mother's arms. She looked up into the face of Pope John VIII. He looked down and Maria saw his surprise at seeing a little girl in his lap.

"Child," he said, drawing a soft hand across the girl's forehead. His gentleness calmed her. He touched the large double mole next to her left eye. "What's your name?"

"Maria," she said and kissed the back of his hand.

A spasm took hold and he fell back on the ground while swarms of frightened people crept close, closer than they had ever been to a living pope. They crossed themselves and mumbled prayers but no one moved to come to his aid.

A casual misfortune for an ordinary man, this fall was ominous and flooded all who witnessed it with a dark meaning.

"As he falls, so will Rome," someone whispered.

The young mother got on one knee beside her daughter, and they watched the pope writhe in pain. The wide-brimmed hat had flown off, leaving his soft features exposed to the sun.

"The pope is dying."

"Evil's come for us today."

"The devil's gutted him. Look," said a woman, pointing.

A red flow emerged from the lower quarters of the pope's robes, and when the crowd saw it, their fears quickened.

A wail like a single shrill voice rose up from the people and reverberated along the walls of the street. As if they had sensed that a diabolic age was at that moment descending upon them. Men and women turned and, spontaneously, regardless of age or infirmity, began hitting each other. It was as if blaming the stranger next to them for the oncoming apocalypse was the only power they had left.

The fighting spread and within minutes the scuffles bloomed into a full-scale riot threatening to overwhelm mother, child, and pope. The young mother tried to shield the two, but seeing there was nothing to be done in the mob, she panicked with the thought all three were going to die.

Glancing over her shoulder, she saw a crowd devour the ter-rified centurions, now unable to protect even themselves. The elite soldiers were cut down by farm tools turned into weapons by the mob.

The mother saw a man on a horse. The red of his cardinal's robes flapped in the stale breeze as he tried to move through the horde. For a moment the determination on his face made the mother's heart rise with hope. Until a hundred hands reached for his rearing horse. The animal desperately tried to turn away but stumbled. It fell with a pitiful cry and the cardinal sank with it into the crowd and disappeared.

"Help me," said the pope to the mother, squeezing her hand. "Hurry, it is near."

It took several moments before the mother registered that the pope of all Christendom, God's chosen servant, was speaking to her. The woman put her arms around His Holiness, lifted him to his feet, and with Maria clinging to her leg, all three began to walk.

After a few steps, the pope cried out and collapsed, taking the mother and girl with him to the ground. The mother draped herself over his body and waited for the rabble to dig in and crush them. She stiffened when a hand took hold of her arm.

"Let me help him, mother."

She looked up into the face of the fallen cardinal. His red outer robe had been torn off in the skirmish and along his neck was a bleeding trail from many fingernails. She noted that when he bent down with his strong arms and broad chest, he looked more like an athlete than a clergyman. Woven into the dark curls of his beard were flecks of blood and sweat, a sharp contrast to his sky blue pupils. His gaze was searing and penetrated everything he looked upon.

"Adrian," said the pontiff, relieved.

Cardinal Adrian stood up with the pope in his arms and moved through the crowd as the young mother watched, riven by an inexplicable sensation when the two exchanged looks.

She picked up her daughter. For a weapon, she chose a brick from a crumbled section of the wall and followed the cardinal.

"I'm here, I won't leave you."

"Don't ever leave me again, Adrian. Promise me."

"My word, Holy One, is sworn with my life."

The young mother tried to catch what Pope John Anglicus VIII whispered to his protector, but it was all she could do to struggle through to keep up.

With Adrian's red cardinal's cloak gone and his clothes torn in the scuffle, the man changed once again and looked more like a shifty street magician than a powerful priest with the ailing pope clinging to his neck, an anonymous bundle carried through the eye of the melee.

Adrian pushed his way to the corner of the street toward the door of a fabric shop. If he could make it through they would be safe, they could escape the madness.

Adrian had only reached for the door when two screaming men in a strangle-hold on each other fell onto his back. Adrian was thrown to one side, tripping over the body of a trampled Egyptian merchant and stumbled, hurling forward into the people in front of him.

Rolling off one man, he spun around and hit hard against a wall then fell to the ground. The fall was agony for the pope who cried out in pain, his arms around the cardinal's neck.

With Maria wrapped around her back, the young mother fought her way through the crowd until she reached them.

"Adrian," said the pope, clutching the stained robes over his belly and imploring the cardinal with frightened eyes.

The young mother frowned and put her hands to her ears, afraid to hear what might come next, but was unable to look away.

"I'm with you, Holy One," said the Cardinal. "I'll carry you to St. Peter's."

"No. It's happening. Help me. It happens *now*."

The Pope and the Cardinal clung to each other, and the young mother stood over them with her mouth open.

All sound stopped.

Movement froze.

The torrent of people faded from her consciousness.

The young mother's focus shifted from the cardinal to the pope and back. She drew in a sharp breath and saw a truth so evident it seemed incredible it was ever thought otherwise.

The Vicar of Christ, who for the last two years and four months had calmed the tormented city, was a woman.

Not only a woman masquerading as the pope, but a woman in labor. The birth contractions were literally squeezing the secret out of her. The young mother's hands passed over her own stomach, and she remembered her Maria's difficult delivery. She knelt and saw the boyish features were now completely feminine and womanly, charged with transformation.

The voices and the movement of the crowd slowly came back to her, a hissing sound growing to a roar in her ears.

"Adrian. I love you so much," said the woman pope.

"I love you, Johanna," said Cardinal Adrian, her rescuer, and he bent and kissed her full on the lips.

*Johanna.*


Maria's mother stood up with her daughter in her arms, unaware of the riot raging around them. She watched a cardinal embrace a pope as a lover and as a woman, and at the sight of it the truth of everything she had ever known fled from her world.

It could only mean one thing, and Maria's mother looked skyward and began to pray.

*The Woman Pope*

She begged for mercy on her daughter's soul and to be for-given her own sins. She knew there was not much time. Searching the sky she looked for the place where the blue ceiling above would split open. Her eyes darted across the horizon look-ing for the tear, the black rip through the blue where the heavens would crack and release devils and angels by the millions. She watched where the forces of heaven and hell would fly through the broken sky and descend to earth for the last battle on this, the Judgment Day. She knew she was witnessing the astonishments the priests promised would come at the final hour.

*Hurry, it is near,* the pope had said to her.

Maria's mother knew, of course, that this was the end of the world.

# PART 1
## CHAPTER I

JOHANNA OF MAINZ raced ahead of her father, who was laughing so hard he had to lean on his walking staff to keep from falling over. Jumping and turning, her little hands swatted the air in front of her as she ran along a forest path deep in the ancient hills along the southern border of old Germania. She looked as if she was performing an ecstatic pagan dance, leaping into the air with a squeal and when she came down her face glowed.

"I got him, father," she said, waving a closed fist.

"Who do you have, little one?" he said.

Johanna suddenly felt herself scooped up in his arms. She turned and looked into the face of Halbert of Mainz and saw a large, heavyset man with shoulder-length, nut-brown hair blending into a bushy beard that matched his fur-lined robes.

"I have the favorite of the gods," she beamed. "A bug that will follow us to the next world."

"I don't think you do, Johanna."

"I *do* think I do."

"Thank the gods bugs will not pester us when we stand before Nerthus."

He smoothed the blond, bowl cut hair from her eyes. With her short hair and scruffy appearance she was often mistaken as a boy, an error Halbert felt safe with on their travels. An oval face looked up at him and he playfully pinched a smoothly sloping nose, across it a stripe of freckles and dirt, all typical of the eight-year old he so loved.

"Oh, this one will, little one," she said, imitating his manner of correcting her. She held out her hand and opened it. A praying mantis rocked on her palm, rubbing its extremities with thorny legs. Halbert burst out laughing. He picked her up, set her on his big shoulders and continued walking.

"I can't think of any god, from Donar to the Matrones, the triple goddesses, who would not let him pass if he's held by you," he said, lifting her up over his head, setting her on the yoke of his shoulders. He walked with a springy step as Johanna bounced happily above. The branches of tall ash trees fluttered along the path of the forest glade. Beyond, at the end of the forest, was a small village.

Halbert began to sing in a resonant baritone, and a few moments later its echo came back along the wooded corridor.

"Sing with me, Johanna. You have a lovely voice when it is not asking questions."

Johanna knew her father was hungry. He was anticipating life's daily gift of their supper, whatever that might turn out to be, according to the hearts of strangers. She joined him in a plainsong they usually sang at winter solstice, but one he loved when he hoped the world might be especially generous. He picked up the pace. She put her fist close to her ear and felt the prickly scrape of the insect's legs against her skin as it struggled to free itself.

She sang with her father and the soothing vibration of their voices, plus the buzzing inside her palm, made Johanna quietly slip beneath the moment into a deeper place.

In that place she felt she was part of a great continuous line, familied to every living thing. *Look at you*, she thought, bringing the exotic green stick close and watching the mandibles work below the huge orbs of the mantis' eyes. Johanna was struck by the notion that the creature she held in her hand was essentially the same as all things that live, the same as herself. *We both live, right now, at this exact moment.*

She felt a jolt; a spark caught fire inside her lit from the Engine of all things. The feeling at first thrilled her, but then made her sad. It was part of a mystery, one easy to see, but to understand it fully required age and abilities she did not possess and had no idea where to find. She opened her hand and the mantis sprang into the air, buzzing in erratic loops to the safety of the high grass. She then squeezed the lobe of her father's right ear, a secret little signal they had used for as long as she could remember. He lifted her from his shoulders and set her on the ground. They held hands and walked.


That night in an abandoned barn, Halbert and his daughter stuffed themselves with two loaves of day old bread spread with a large hunk of goat cheese. He drank wine from a skin and Johanna stood in the moonlight wrapped in a blanket near the door. She read from grease-stained scrolls, a few sheets from Aristotle, from Cicero, torn strips of Horace and others. Halbert's bible. Smeared, crumpled, and weather-beaten, the yellowed edges of the lambskin parchments were torn at the edges from use.

He watched her and felt an uneasy foreboding at his daughter's continued fascination with the scrolls.

It had begun innocently enough, he remembered, a curious four-year-old demanding an explanation of the book's scratchy symbols. But her craving for knowledge launched them on a nightly excursion that had since lasted years. Theirs was a journey of ideas and concepts and was an immeasurable part of their relationship despite the dangers.

"Put the book away," he said. "You already know too many secrets forbidden to you and you'll be sad when you have to stop. And you *will* have to stop."

"I want to know it all, father."

"Perhaps one day when we get to Rome, little one, we'll see her glorious libraries and we'll--"

"No, Papa! Not there!" Her mood suddenly soured. "I miss Mama so much. Why did they kill her? She wasn't bad."

"She wasn't bad, no. The Christians made a mistake."

"They are evil and their faith is evil."

"Shhh. Sleep. It's men's hearts, not their beliefs, that are good or bad."

"Who says that?"

"Wise men have always known this."

"I hate the Christians and their bad god. Papa, you loved mama more than any god, didn't you?" she said, her body shaking with sobs.

"Yes, I did."

Staring off, both minds fled back into the past. Despite having the knowledge of numbers, some would say sacred while many would call it evil knowledge, they could not count the number of times they had gone back to the same afternoon three years before.

*Halbert, with five-year-old Johanna on his shoulders as always, is smiling as he gazes down on his petite wife, Gilberta, walking beside them. Wandering nomads, carrying all they own, dancing as they walk and singing a joyful pagan praise to life.*

*They rest outside a village. Halbert sits with Johanna and cuts a slice of old bread for her lunch. Gilberta wanders off looking for privacy and finds it in the middle of a wheat field. She bends, holds up withered stalks of wheat. The entire field is blighted with worms. She wipes at the menstrual blood trickling down her inner thigh and quickly buries the bloody rag in the earth. Gilberta looks back in the distance.*

*Halbert sits on the ground, draws letters in the dirt for Johanna as she chews the bread, fascinated. Gilberta watches the loving, intimate sight of her little family and sighs. She hears a noise behind her. Gilberta turns and is struck hard across the temple.*

*Two village farmers armed with clubs drag her unconscious body out of the field.*

*Halbert moves Johanna's fingers over a letter and, sensing something not right, looks up. He whistles, lets out the perfect call of a forest owl, his secret signal to her. Johanna tries to mimic him and laughs. Trying not to seem worried he picks her up and calls to Gilberta. He walks, then runs in the direction he last saw his wife.*

*Minutes later, in the middle of the village square, Gilberta jerks awake to noise and smoke. She tries to move but finds she's tied to a wood stake and a fire has been set at her feet. She looks out on the village and sees diseased villagers waving crosses, coughing and hacking at the smoke and cursing her. A priest, a hood pulled down so low his face cannot be seen, sprinkles holy water on the flames at Gilberta's feet.*

*"You wandering demon. Devil whose blood brings death to our fields and plague to our people, take your curses back to Satan. Tell him we live by Christ."*

*It is then that Halbert, holding Johanna, breaks through the crowd. Gilberta sees them and the little family screams for each other.*

*The crowd goes after Halbert, another foreign demon who has caused the righteous so much pain and trouble. They raise their clubs, then stop when they hear the creature bellow, enraged. Halbert raises his staff and charges, beating every person, man or woman, who tries to flee before him.*

*Johanna watches the flames consume her mother. Gilberta, her agony complete, slumps into the fire and succumbs. Johanna looks around for help from anyone, anything. She sees the hooded priest slip away, afraid for his life before the fury of the bellowing pagan.*

*Watching the priest escape, the cowardice of the anonymous man responsible for all of this horror transforms the little girl. Her terror and hysteria fade, her little face relaxes and only her eyes show emotion. Hate.*

*She watches the flames roar and listens to Halbert roar and swing, pounding his staff into flesh, breaking teeth, shattering bone with no mercy.*

*Johanna stares. Her eyes burn cold.*


A long while later her breathing returned to normal and she settled in the comfort of her father's arms. Halbert's rocking calmed her, the memory passed and soon she drifted through the door of a dream.

On the other side of that door she was walking along a sandy beach. She stooped to pick up a shell when a tremendous, sparkling wave rose up on the water's edge. It filled the entire dream horizon and swelled higher than a mountain. The wave crested and then tumbled down in a perfect transparent blue curl.

*The Woman Pope*

Instead of destroying Johanna, the water drenched her with a gentle touch, a touch made of sound. The sound was an incomparable rush of voices. Smiling at the sensation, Johanna thought she was being carried away on a wonderful dream until, without thinking, she opened her eyes. Halbert still held her, his head bent forward, the rumble of a snore in his nose.

She blinked and looked around the room, wide awake and gulping air. The wave continued to wash over her and flooded the barn, engulfing everything. She knew something had come for her.

She closed her eyes and opened her mouth and tasted the song-that-was-more-than-sound. It was sweetly aromatic with a roasted nut-like flavor. She savored the taste and felt a tingling spread through her body. Johanna reached in front of her and felt the vibration of the wave, its softness, its texture like feeling the wind on her fingertips. The song told her to cast her burdens aside, the voices whispered to her to rest, as if she had come from a long journey. She relaxed and let the sensations rush in and lift her up into their arms.

# CHAPTER II

THEY WANDERED FOR years and walked hundreds of leagues through the wilderness of Europe long before it would be named so.

"Run with me, father!" said Johanna, and trotted down the road. They traveled along a well-used road toward a village Halbert knew.

"You go on ahead," he said. "I'm too old."

Halbert watched his daughter and saw the reflection of his own large boned features in the long swiftly pumping legs. But her size was mellowed by the delicate softness of her mother, Gilberta, with fine blond-streaked hair blowing back in her wake. Halbert also saw in his child his own sharp intelligence, magnified.

Halbert had always been big and as a boy was expected to excel only in matters of strength. But his was an intellectual appetite. Quick to learn Latin and Greek from the monks who took him in, the shy orphan read all their books and surprised the brothers and priests with vigorous debates in an agile, scholarly tongue. This verbal agility would be needed later -- after he met his soul mate, pagan Gilberta, and was thrown from the church and became a father -- to keep up with a little girl who gave him good chase from the time she could speak.

"Come, you turtle," said Halbert running by, startling Johanna with a swat on her rear. "Can't beat a fat old man to the village?"

"Not fair!" she laughed, and took off after him.

Always alert to every stage in her childhood, Halbert made her think and dig for the answers she relentlessly ran after. Johanna met his every challenge then surpassed each one. The only information he ever kept from his daughter, upon the death of her mother at the hands of Christians, was his education and once-close relationship to the church and religion she hated so much. The pain it would cause was not worth the hate he knew would fill her little heart.

"You win," panted Halbert after she had caught and passed him. They approached a village near the southwestern border in the land of the Western Franks. Halbert rested on a boulder at the edge of the road. Johanna was about to tease him when he held his finger to his lips. She listened, strained to separate the sounds of the forest from a plaintive din beyond the trees. Wailing voices came across the far distance.

"What is that?" she asked, her eyes wide. He shook his head.

They walked warily through the forest and into the village.

She was eleven-years-old that day and her father had reluctantly promised to go over the Greek alphabet as part of her birthday present. A boy was the first to see them enter the village and pointed to the many-colored pouches hanging off Halbert's staff, the sign of a traveling herb seller. He ran off and shortly after, led a large shirt-less man to them. He asked Halbert to come to the funeral of his father and spread herbs to keep sickness at bay. In a rough dialect he promised two days worth of food and a pair of outgrown wooden shoes for Johanna. Halbert sealed the agreement with a handshake.

The man led the way.

Johanna frowned and crossed her arms, kicking the dirt as she walked. Not happy to have to wait until that night for her lesson, she needed to know everything *now*.

They followed the man through the village and Johanna noted the roofs of the cow dung houses were already girded with fresh layers of thatch to meet the autumn. A short way beyond the houses stood the village cemetery where the grieving family and entire village gathered at a funeral pyre. The body rested on top of the stacked wood, laid out in the dead man's finest clothes.

"The pox?" Halbert asked.

"How did you know that?" asked the son, fearful. "Have you heard tales of our village?"

"No. But why would he want to be burned rather than buried?"

"Burned with all his possessions," said the son's wife, a dour, stick-thin woman at the pyre. She spat. "Damn him."

Halbert knew the outrageous request must have devastated both family and friends not only hoping to gain from the well-to-do man's passing, but the sacrilege of having the village watch a family member burn like a common witch. Never in memory had anyone heard of such a request as it went against all their Christian burial customs.

"I have no choice and you know it," said the son. He slapped his wife across the face and sent her away yowling. "You want to loose the house and land? Father said if I refuse his wishes it all goes to the village as charity."

"Heat some water," said Halbert to the son. "I'll make a drink to protect you and your relatives."

Johanna sat on the ground away from the proceedings and played with her old rag doll, but had no interest in either toy or ceremony. Her eyes were on the pyre. Her mouth dry from the day's warmth, forehead glistening with sweat, Johanna had seen plenty of corpses but only one, her mother, purposefully burned.

The dead man's possessions were stacked in tall piles around the pyre. Winter clothes, hardwood chairs, objects of finely carved woods, iron trinkets in the shapes of men and animals, plus oiled skins of snow rabbit, red fox and deer. Wood barrels were filled with odds and ends, but as Johanna looked over the goods, a peculiar shape caught her eye. The object stuck out of the last barrel at the very rear of the stacks. A cylinder of some kind or a roll of parchment inside a quiver or a tube, she could not be sure. All she could see were tiny black designs.

Johanna made her way toward the barrel.

"The learned man believed the pox clings to his possessions. Imagine that! Oh, he wants to spare his family and all of us from it," snorted a thick-necked woman, her stubby hands covetously fingering a rich tapestry depicting flying birds and wild boar.

"He read books and was wise, but this is superstition," grumped a red-faced man, the sweat of a new fever on his forehead. "He just wants to take it with him."

"What's it to you?" snapped the woman. "You wouldn't get nothing anyway."

"Tell you what I get. I get to be first in line to curse his soul on its way to the fire in hell."

"Blame his wife. She and the son are the ones making the family burn his goods. Dead man, son and widow are all fools."

A scream startled Johanna and everyone turned. She caught sight of the dead man's wife fainting as the pyre was torched. Family members began to toss articles into the blaze while Halbert mixed herbs for the broth.

Johanna's eyes locked again onto the cylinder and concentrated. Soon the mystery of the flowery designs faded; she knew what they were. Not tiny paintings or decorations at all, but letters. Greek letters. The letters Halbert traced on the ground that morning came racing back. The bold shapes were symbols, symbols for sounds that rose up into walls of words. The walls were then joined as sentences and each sentence wall was roofed with thoughts until in the final construction a dwelling was painstakingly built out of words. It stood where only parts had been, a structure made of thoughts and ideas, filled with the treasure of knowledge. And that house was about to turn to ash.

Johanna edged closer until she was in front of the leatherbound tube, the pillars and arches of the symbols clearly visible. The letters commanded her; everything about them radiated power, secrets and called out with a mystical beckoning.

She knew she could not let them be destroyed.

Johanna trembled at the act she was about to undertake. Not only did she take her life in her hands if caught, but just as harrowing was the thought of her father's wrath for stealing, not for food or need, that was the covenant of beggars. But to steal out of greed or lust was, next to murder, a most terrible crime.

"Forgive me, father," she whispered to herself, and casually ran her fingers over the lines of the letters. She touched the quiver as if merely tracing the black shapes for their pretty geometry. Yet when her fingers reached half way down the scroll they gripped the cylinder and lifted it out of the barrel.

"You," said a voice behind her. She pulled her hand away. Profusely sweating and naked to the waist was the son of the dead man. He stood above her stripped of his shirt and his inheritance, his mouth sucked into a grimace and his skin striped with soot from a fire it was his hateful duty to feed.

"You little scavenging rat. What are you doing?"

"Nothing, sir…I…I…"

"Thief! You want forbidden property? Here. Since no one else can have it, feel free to share my father's wealth -- including his flames," he said and reached down. Incredibly strong fingers dug into the soft flesh of her underarms. The man lifted Johanna high in the air a long moment, his eyes burning into hers with a hatred that chilled her little heart. He walked to the fire holding her out in front of him until a scream slapped him still. Other screams sprang up. He dropped Johanna and ran.

She hit the ground, flat in the dirt, and watched the man run for the bonfire and his mother, the dead man's wife. The widow had climbed onto the raging platform. She entered the fire and hugged the body, instantly engulfed in the orange curtains of flame.

The man and his family called out to her, reached into the blaze only to pull their arms back out, singed. The old woman waved her hand to ward off those who would follow while she embraced her husband with one arm. Halbert restrained two of the daughters from leaping after their mother into the flames. The entire village, hands to their heads, shuffled around the raging pyre in a dance of panic.

Johanna realized she was not the one cast into the flames and got to her feet. The son, arms blistered, tore at his hair, tilted his head back and shrieked at the calm evening sky. All eyes were on the victims and Johanna was forgotten. This time she did not hesitate.

She lifted the heavy leather tube out of the barrel, tucked it under her arm and fled from the roar of the pyre. She ran in terror for what seemed like miles.

Johanna cut through fields, tripped and fell again and again. She hid beneath a gnarled oak until late that night, crying, hugging the scroll, rocking it back and forth like a baby in her arms.

*Who would do such a thing?* she said to herself. Risk her life, for what? Risk everything for paper, for symbols? For something she did not even know its meaning?

"Wicked girl. Thief," she said. This perverse behavior flew in the face of her father's teachings.

"I'm sorry," she wept. "I could not let them burn you."

Johanna shivered. She felt the world despised her for what she yearned for, fixed her with the same feral hatred as the son who would have surely tossed her into the fire as one more bauble destroyed because he could not go against his father's wishes.

"I won't let them hurt you," she said, stroking the soft leather tube. She smelled the musky scent and fingered the leather strips tied around it. Her tears wet the hide, softened it, and her body heated the tube, heightening the thick animal aroma to such an extent that it seemed the thing was about to stir, wake, to actually come alive, a beast of ideas. And now it was her beast. She promised herself she would break its wild secrets and ride its kicking spirit until she tamed it as her own.

She clutched the heavy tube to her chest and walked out from under the oak feeling as though she carried the means of both her life and her death.

"Johanna," said Halbert when she returned that night. He was so angry she thought he would strike her, something he had never done. She almost wished he would to exorcise her torment. The man loomed over her like a giant, hands on his hips. He raised his hands and she waited for the blow.

Instead, he took her in his arms and wept. So relieved and confused she did not say a word and clung to him the rest of the night. Halbert was so tired from the tragedy of the funeral and worry over Johanna that he fell asleep before she could confess her crime.

When they left the village in the morning and were on the road, Johanna ran to the tree and retrieved the quiver. Without explanation, Johanna set the heavy leather tube in his hands. Turning it slowly in his hands, Halbert's eyebrows shot up quizzically as he undid the straps.

"What have you done now?" he sighed. He pulled out several sheets of parchment rolled around each other in a thick log.

Halbert looked at the tangled halo of sun-bleached hair, the green eyes wide with fear, her mouth parted with a question.

"Do you have any idea..." He opened his mouth to yell, and stopped. He went back to the scrolls, unrolled sheet after sheet. His anger was overpowered by each length of tightly curled paper. Johanna saw the excitement bubble up behind his eyes. He wanted to be angry, to make her realize the depth of her sin and show her she had gone beyond a whole range of moral and social boundaries.

"Johanna," he began, then sputtered into a dumbfound silence. She had set a treasure in his hands, a mother-lode they could excavate each time he took it from its leather cave. Every page a was jewel-laden mine that would not be exhausted for years.

Halbert promised himself he would scold his daughter later. He would threaten, he would plead, he would lecture her for hours on end about the seriousness of her crime.

But at that moment he hurriedly replaced the rolls in the quiver, tucked the quiver under his arm, grabbed Johanna by the collar of her dress and then ran as fast as he could. Halbert bolted down the road with Johanna held at arm's length, her little feet running alongside him, barely touching the ground.

# CHAPTER III

"WE MUST HURRY," said Halbert, motioning for Johanna to put the scrolls away. A boulder high as a house stood as a giant wall over their hillside camp. Johanna sat with her back against it, huddled over a mathematics scroll spread out before her, her sturdy fingers holding down the curled edges while the length of her long hair hid her face. With a flip of her head, the blond-streaked hair whipped over one shoulder and she smiled knowingly at her father.

"We have plenty of time to get there," she said. "I hear many ships sail from that harbor."

"I only feel like we're making progress when we're moving," he said, stamping out the remains of the night's fire.

"We're not that far away," she said. "A week at most."

She slipped the scrolls back into their leather tube, then stood and slung the heavy cylinder over her shoulder like a quiver of arrows.

Halbert gazed at his child while she prepared for another long day of walking. Now, at nearly sixteen, she was as tall as he, but thankfully his round largeness had been curtailed by the thinness on her mother's side. She reached her fists toward the sky, stretching, on her tip toes with her solid but long legs together. He watched as she tightened the muscles in her calves, thighs, back and arms. The childhood freckles had disappeared across her nose, replaced by smooth skin and a wide, full mouth curling up at the edges. A mouth with a perpetual, insolent turn resided on plentiful, sensuous lips. Her face was an open boulevard, saved from being too round by the delicate oval of her chin and the slendering length of the face itself. The whole portrait was centered and brought into sharp focus by two piercing hazel eyes. A mix of greens and browns and blues set beneath slightly arched eyebrows, at the moment fixed on him as he packed.

"Imagine," said Halbert when they were walking again. "Sailing to Rome. No more talking, no more dreaming. We are on our way, and I thank you, daughter."

"I am simply tired of listening to you about it," she said, facetiously. "There is nothing keeping us from your 'Eternal City,' so let's go see what the fuss is about."

They headed toward the coast of the newly created Western Frankish Kingdom and planned to catch a ship sailing south.

"Remember, when we get there, I carry the scrolls," said Halbert.

"But I always --"

"No arguments. No one can even suspect that you read, understand?" he said, and ran a hand through the thick brown tangle of his hair. "You have no idea how dangerous your knowledge is."

"I do because you've told me. Repeatedly."

"But you don't believe me, do you? Do you, Johanna? I'm telling you, you had better be discreet."

After the incident at the funeral pyre, Halbert guided the way through the intricate maze of the scrolls rescued by his daughter. But even at twelve years of age, Johanna had quickly mastered the labyrinth of Greek symbols, understanding each level of meaning with a tenacious grasp.

"When we live in Rome," she said. "I'm going to ask the Emperor himself about the things we've read about in the scrolls. He'll settle our disputes."

"Johanna. Look at me. Don't breathe a hint that you can read, either to emperor or stable boy."

"I'll ask him to explain why I cannot know as much as a man."

Halbert rolled his eyes. He feared going beyond rudimentary stages of teaching because it set her, set them both, dangerously apart from the world they moved through every day. But his amazement at the mystery of the scrolls kept them coming back. Even the mystery that they should not have been scrolls, but codices or books, copied by monks, taking years to transcribe a single volume for each of the works gave them hours of debate.

Why scrolls? Halbert could only guess that the individual sheets were meant to be copied but never were, and he could plumb the reasoning no farther. Johanna suggested that they were kept on hand in case any disaster should happen to the books so that their source would not be lost.

"I think how far we've traveled should be measured by the work of our brains, not by our feet," observed Halbert that evening at their camp, firing the kindling with flints. They walked several leagues that day and were so engrossed in a discussion of geometry that when they looked up, they were surprised to see the sun at the horizon before them.

"Pythagoras charted similar kinds of measurements," said Johanna and squatted next to him.

"Don't bring him into this discussion," said Halbert, dismissing her argument with a wave. "The man thought himself better than Zeus and was the head of a cult."

"You're not serious?" she laughed, feeding the little fire they had built with leaves.

"His was a cult of numbers, of lines and space. As if by constructing a perfect triangulation one could look into the face of the gods. What arrogance. Perfection is not an equation we have yet to work out."

"I know, father. Pythagoras was just a man, and like all men he was mistaken. He created a beautiful world but failed when he tried to make a single world larger than the universe. Still, that does not deny his remarkable devices."

"It's remarkable his head wasn't met with a device," said Halbert and gave Johanna his sideways glance, one eyebrow raised. They laughed, and he put an arm around her.

≈ ≈ ≈

Johanna waited for her father in the village square, playing with the children near the well. She kept an ear out for Halbert's return from selling herbs for coins. They had almost enough for a ship's passage.

"Draw the cat again, please," pleaded a little six-year-old girl, and tilted her face up to Johanna. The girl had no left eye, the darkened eyelid slack and sunk in. Scabs and bruises marked the rest of her body. Johanna knew her physical weaknesses would keep her from seeing adolescence. Her playmates saw how adults treated the runts, the sick and lame. They had begun working to isolate and persecute her.

Johanna placed the stick in the child's hand. "Now you do it, just like me."

"I can't."

"She's no good," said a chubby six-year-old boy. "She got no eye."

"Ollana is very good," Johanna said. She kept her hand over the child's and drew one half of the cat's full front face. She took her hand off midpoint in the drawing and whispered. "Make it the same by going the opposite way."

"It will be bad," said Ollana ..

"Nothing you do will ever be bad, child," replied Johanna, coaxing the girl's hand. "You can do it, I know you can. There you go."

The girl, squinting and sweating with effort, traced the other side of the drawing, stopping, correcting the curve. She finished her work and stood back, ready to run.

The little crowd moved in closer, ready to make Ollana pay for what was sure to be as misshapen as she. The children stared. They looked down on a perfect reflection of a cat's face.

"Show me, Ollana," said one girl who was so filthy that dirt caked muddy veins and rivulets on her arms and legs.

"No, help me to do it," pleaded another girl.

"My turn, Ollana. Please," whined the chubby boy. He turned his head, coughed up a mouthful of bloody phlegm. "If you do, I won't hit you no more."

Dozens of animal portraits were created with the sweep of Ollana's hand. Johanna turned away and began to practice her writing.

"What are those?" asked a boy whose ears curled forward in gristly flowers.

"What do you think they are?" Johanna asked as she worked the stick. The children were intrigued by the strange squiggles.

"A snake, right?"

"A tree."

"That's a house."

"Flower!" they shouted, clapping and jumping up and down.

Later, Johanna lingered in the sun on a bench near a church. The bored children once again turned their attentions to Ollana, chasing her with wood switches down the street.

"You leave her alone," Johanna called. *Oh, little one*, Johanna sighed to herself, *I'm afraid you will die while still a child.*

The children stopped the chase, but Johanna knew it was only until she looked away. The last of a late autumn breeze was pushed from the village by wilder air and Johanna smelled a wetness that would soon spray the countryside with a cold rain.

Muffled voices came from the church. Johanna went to a high window at the side of the building. Johanna cocked her head but could not hear clearly. She spied a broken barrel close by, Johanna rolled it to the open window, climbed up on it and peeked in.

It was a meeting of priests, arguing about what she could not tell. Johanna fancied herself inside the church with the men, debating the monks, using the wisdom of the scrolls to argue against their evil god.

Suddenly, the barrel was kicked out from beneath her feet. Johanna grasped the window sill and hung in the air. A vicious lash ripped into the back of her right leg and she fell and rolled in the dirt clutching her calf.

"Witch," hissed a man. He held a leather horse whip and had a wine-stain birthmark on half his face and neck, like a half-mask. He was flanked by two village matrons and another man.

"I am not a --" began Johanna. The man swung again. Her arms took three stinging blows to protect her face.

"Those magic symbols you drew convict you, witch," said the other man. Johanna glanced over at the village square where several parents stood crossing themselves and spitting on the ground. Turning back, she took a surprise blow that opened a gash on her cheek.

"You cast spells on our children," cried one of the women.

"I did nothing except play with them!"

She tried to run but they barred her escape, trapping her against the wall of the church then grabbed her arms, dragging her from the side of the church.

"Father! Help me!" Johanna screamed.

"You can't fool us, witch."

Her hair was pulled hard by the two women while the two men pinched the skin on her arms and neck. She was dragged to the village square and thrown onto the spot she had drawn the letters.

"What's that if not magic symbols?" demanded the man with the whip. Johanna stared down at the partially covered Greek omega.

"It's not magic," Johanna said. "It's only part of a word."

"A magic word from the devil," said the whip-man.

"You bewitched my children," said a toothless woman, a greasy yellow scarf tied around her head. She looked past forty, though she was just out of her teens. "My boy has taken sick with a bloody cough. It happened right after he saw the evil pictures you drew."

"He's had that cough for months," cried Johanna. "He said you pay so little attention you never noticed it."

"They want answers to riddles we don't know," said the other man.

"How do you know it is a word?" asked the whip-man, so close she could see a large vein pulsing out from the scarlet side of his neck. "Tell me how you know what a word looks like?"

"It was told to me by my father."

"You know it's a word because you know how to read. You cast spells on children. You read and draw magic symbols. Take her to the river. We'll see if she's innocent or if she sleeps with the devil."

Johanna was dragged into the street. Villagers watched.

"Father!"

"We'll teach you."

"Let me get a piece of her," said a man and twisted her left nipple.

"She won't kill my children with spells."

*The Woman Pope*

"Let me have her," said a woman as the crowd began to froth with anger, yelling and reaching out to torment a devil among them.

"Kill her."

"Wait till we get you to the river, witch," a girl taunted, slapping at her leg. Johanna looked down. It was little Ollana. The child caught Johanna's look and did not pause, but hit Johanna with her little fists.

"You're going to die in the water," Ollana said.

Johanna looked at her, knowing for the first time in her life Ollana was on the other side of persecution. Her one eye glistened with excitement and relief.

"Why the river?" Johanna screamed.

"If you're a witch you'll stay under several minutes and live," said a hag whose chin sprouted a patch of beard-long whiskers. "If you survive, our accusation is justified."

"I can't live under water," said Johanna.

"Then your death will prove your innocence."

At the river's edge Johanna's hands and feet were bound.

"I've done nothing."

The old hag placed a rope around her neck to keep her from drifting downstream, then pushed Johanna into shallow water.

"Repent, witch, before you die," said the toothless woman. She stepped into Johanna's face and spat in it, then grabbed the front of Johanna's dress, pushed her backwards into deeper water. Johanna splashed and tried to keep her head above the surface.

"She floats like a witch," said a woman. Johanna gagged, swallowed water. She sank, once, twice, three times. Each time she managed to bring her head to the surface.

"She needs more weight to her."

The toothless woman reeled Johanna back to the shore and the whip man tied a heavy rock bound with rope around Johanna's waist.

"Float *now*, devil," smiled the whip man. The crowd laughed.

The toothless woman leaned in to push Johanna back in the water but instead, the hag was yanked off the ground by her hair.

She traveled backwards several feet and landed in the dirt, screaming.

Then one end of a thick walking staff crashed through the crowd, striking the man who held Johanna's left arm with a sickly *crack*. The bone in his forearm snapped. The man looked at his unnaturally bent arm and passed out. The whip-man watched as a ferocious madman with a staff came at him. He stepped back as Halbert reached out and snatched the whip from his hands.

"Brother. This girl possesses the black arts of a witch."

"This girl is my daughter and is no witch," roared Halbert.

"She wrote magic emblems and enchanted our children."

"Never," said Johanna, protected by Halbert's arm. "I showed them a letter, father. The one I saw you make."

She gazed at Halbert hoping he would take the prompt though she knew how he hated lying, but this was different. His eyes stared into the crowd, glazed with an anger she knew would revisit her if they lived to escape.

"Her only crime was to watch me write," he said. "I read every day. I read in languages none of you have ever heard of nor will ever understand in all your ignorant lives. My child only recreated what she saw me draw, the omega, last letter in the alphabet, and also the symbol of your god's wrath on Judgment Day when he comes to damn you all."

Several crossed themselves at the pagan's curse. Halbert untied Johanna and threw the ropes down.

"She's a witch who reads. We saw her work," said the whip-man.

"You are a fool who would kill innocence in the name of your god," Halbert said and turned to see the extent of his daughter's bloody face, welted neck and shoulders. He spun around, furious.

"You are all dead," he yelled and snapped the horse whip across the whip-man's face and sent him to the ground. Halbert held the screaming man by his hair and whipped him with continuous blows.

"Father, stop," said Johanna. Halbert struck the man with such fury that the mob's bloodlust for a witch turned to dread, suddenly fearing retribution for their part. The crowd quickly dispersed.

Halbert continued without let up, and Johanna saw he was going to beat the whip-man to death. Johanna leaped onto Halbert and held his arm.

"Show him mercy, father, please."

She could not get his attention and the whip-man had lost consciousness. Johanna finally slapped Halbert and yelled. "Stop now!"

Halbert came to his senses, stopped in mid-swing, let go. The man dropped into the dirt, soaking wet with blood. Johanna led her father away as villagers watched from a distance, fear and hatred in their eyes.

"You caused this," he said. "Your gluttony for learning came for its payment today."


They were quiet as they left the village. Halbert's face was grave, his shoulders slumped. The sun set behind a grove of yew trees filled with jabbering martens in the branches. The long shadow of the trees stretched across the road, striping father and daughter as they walked beside the forest.

"I hate them."

"Quiet. We'll make camp in the trees, and tomorrow we go down to the harbor and leave all this."

"I hate them for what their beliefs have done to mother, to me. And to you. With all my heart."

"Shhh. Put your hate into your feet and walk," he said. Loud voices turned Halbert and Johanna back toward the village.

"I see them."

A dozen men hurried after them with swords and knives.

"The witch's father killed Clarn."

"And the smith is dying from his curse. Get the witches."

Halbert grabbed Johanna's hand and they ran from the road into the safety of the darkening woods. The shouts of men and clanging metal followed them into the ancient trees.

# CHAPTER IV

JOHANNA STARED AT the horizon. Near dawn, she watched the black sky over the ocean grow a thin seam of red. At the south end of the shore she could make out Halbert speaking to an oarsman standing beside his little rowboat. The oarsman shook his head.

"Hurry, father," she whispered out loud to herself.

She turned toward the north end of the shore where sleepy men were waking at their camp. The same villagers who had chased them into the woods. The men had searched for her and her father, calling out to them with threats of death. Johanna and Halbert had separated in the wood, remaining within eyesight but hidden from the hunting party. Halbert whistled. Johanna had seen the men frozen at the sound of a complex series of bird calls  the party knew were most definitely not from this land. She had whistled back to her father and both watched fear wash over the superstitious men believing they heard wood elves calling back and forth in the dark. The search had been called off, but camp was set up at the shore to ensure the witches could not escape by sea.

"But I have no use for herbs," said the oarsman, shrugging.

"Herbs *and* a coin, I told you," said Halbert, who held himself back from striking the thick-headed man. He turned, saw Johanna at the edge of the woods waving, pointing down shore. The search party was moving. Fast. He had been seen. Halbert signaled, and Johanna ran out from the protection of the woods down onto the rocky shore.

"The captain will not accept herbs for payment," began the oarsman, who found himself lifted into his rowboat, oar in hand.

"I'll gladly speak to him myself," Halbert barked. Johanna rushed up, furthering the man's confusion. He was about to protest, but found his collar gripped tight. "Now row."

Father and daughter pushed the dinghy into the choppy surf, hopped in. The oarsman saw two glares fixed on him and put his back into his work. The party of villagers ran to the water's edge and cursed the pagans, but did not dare set foot in the living sea, more powerful and deadly than any wood elf.

Johanna clung to her father and pointed to the ship, larger than any vessel she had ever seen, anchored in deep water.

A long stone's throw from it she could hear the creaking of its wood frame. Johanna watched the ship rock on the swells and was met by a putrid smell, a sour reek of human waste, sweat, oil, and long decayed food.

"It's so big," she yelled over the wind.

The ship loomed before the little dinghy as it maneuvered beside it. The craft rose ominously then dipped deep into the turbulent swells, tossing up billows of foamy waves that crashed so hard against the high hull it looked impossible to board.

Several deck hands scuttled like crabs over the railing along a grid of ropes and reached their arms out for the dinghy.

"Stand and be ready," called a crewmen in a harsh Germanic. "I said stand if you're gonna sail with us, you stupid bear."

Halbert sat frozen, clutching the sides of the rowboat. Johanna pried his hands free as the rowboat rose up on a swell.

"Give me a moment," said Halbert, panicking as the boat came along the side of the ship.

"Now, father. Go," she said and pushed him.

The sailors grabbed Halbert, passed him roughly up the rope grid lines, and at the top threw him over onto the deck. When another swell came, she stood up and was lifted from the boat. She looked down at her feet and saw the dinghy fall away down into the swirling water while she remained airborne, held by several arms, pulled up the grid of rope as if flying.

But as soon as she clung to the ropes the assisting hands were all over her. Hands supposedly hoisting her bottom upward were squeezing it. She tensed, tried to look behind her and felt hands on her breasts, cupping them, kneading the soft flesh with the hunger of scavengers.

She tried to protect herself from a gauntlet of anonymous hands and fingers. Kicking and striking at them, she tried to fend off dozens of faceless hands crawling everywhere on her. On deck Halbert was a world away, her screams swallowed by the wind.

"Father, help me."

But she was alone with the groping hands.

One set of fingers from below crept up her leg, scuttled their way over her calf, under her dress, and raced up the back of her inner thigh. The hand forced itself between her thighs from behind. She gasped when she felt the hand take the whole of her sex in its calloused fingers. It squeezed the soft lips they found, tugging at them, rubbing in a circular motion with hard strokes. Johanna struggled, arms reaching for the rail. One of the fingers probed frantically, trying to separate the folds guarding her entrance.

"Stop it. Stop!" she said, terrified by its raw insistence. No one had ever ventured there and the sensations shot a blinding lightheadedness and a wave of awareness rippling over her body. Then the thick persistent finger located the seam and pushed, trying to enter her. She tried to scream, but Halbert leaned over the rail at that moment, took her arm and pulled her over onto the deck.

They staggered several paces on the rolling deck, tripped and fell. Their wobbly land legs could not comprehend the unruly sway. Laughter from deck hands greeted them when they tried to stand.

Johanna watched the men climb back over the rails and knew Halbert was unaware of what transpired, assuming it was the clumsiness of their first voyage making the sailors laugh.

The boat pitched again and threw them off balance, sending Halbert to the mast to cling to a rope. Johanna looked over at the men once more. One bald deck mate whose remaining hair created a stringy, dirty white curtain along his neck, held a finger under his nose. He inhaled deeply for his mates who guffawed. Others challenged him, and he responded by passing the finger under each nose of his shipmates and inspired breathy sucking noises and cooing.

A prickly heat rushed to Johanna's face. The violation invoked unfamiliar sensations that were immediately boiled in shame.

She turned away and saw a young monk coiling rope across the deck. When his gaze met hers, she knew he had seen what happened. Her shame redoubled, shot down so deep inside her it was met with another sensation hurtling its way up: anger. It burned through Johanna with a commotion so reckless she had to pant to control her breath.

*I'll kill them. I'll toss their carcasses into the waves after I slash their bellies with their own knives. I'll make every man who touched me watch his guts ladled out of his stomach by my bare hands!*

She moved toward them not realizing what she was doing. The men's smug expressions brightened and some licked their lips at the prospect of exploring her again, with or without her consent.

"Come to me, lass," taunted the bald deck mate with open arms.

Johanna was about to reach them when a hand took her by the elbow and guided her to the ladder leading below deck.

"Sometimes it's wiser to let the tide recede first," said the monk softly, "before trying to swim into the crashing surf."

She glared into his eyes and was met with the pale skies of an astonishing blue. She gulped air and tried to hold back tears.

"I won't be handled by those dogs or by you," she said and pulled her arm from him.

"Johanna. Come here."

Halbert haggled with the captain, tried to pay while he stumbled on the deck, dropping the silver coins. Johanna gave a final glare to the young monk and went to her father.

≈ ≈ ≈

She settled Halbert in a corner space below deck near a smoky brazier, the only source of heat. Halbert lowered himself onto a pallet of mildewed straw and was overcome with seasickness compounded by a depression after his conversation with the captain.

"This ship does not sail for Rome," Halbert said. "What have I done?"

"You kept us from being hanged," Johanna said. "Now rest. Where we are going?"

"To an island. A place called England. A vile, barbaric land I've heard. But that's as far as our money will take us."

"And from this England we will sail to Rome. It will be fine."

She dared not tell him what happened with the sailors. He'd try to kill them all and would end up dead, leaving her a slave. She realized the monk who stopped her knew as much. What eyes he had. Johanna rubbed Halbert's hands and watched nausea wash over him with every sway. Studying him in the shadowy light, she became frightened by what she saw.

Her father looked old. In his early thirties, flecks of gray in Halbert's hair and beard marked him deeply. He had been a father for years by the time he reached her age. He had never been like this before. Always the protector, he charged into every situation with the confidence of a man who believed the gods guided his every move.

How many times, she wondered, had he manipulated situations to keep her from what she had just experienced? Like the time she was nine years old and that friendly man took her swimming while Halbert consoled a grief-stricken woman. They had taken off their clothes to go in the water and the man's eyes were so wide, staring at her little body. Halbert had grabbed the naked man, slapped him senseless, then tossed him down a rocky ravine where he rolled bleeding into a stream. Halbert kept the stranger's clothes, using them as rags, but never gave her an explanation. Other puzzling circumstances began to fall in place.

"Johanna," her father said. "I'm going to be ill."

She found a cracked wooden bowl and brought it to him. He hadn't seen the sailors and there would be other situations he would not see.

Laughter came from above, clomping footsteps on deck. She looked at Halbert and felt a pang of protective love burn through her.

"Johanna?"

"I'm here, father. Right here with you. Shhh."

She squinted in the half light and her heart was tempered with a revelation. To navigate the oceans of the mind would still be her passion, but now she was going to have to be the watchful one. She would have to keep herself planted squarely on the shores of this world if they were not to perish.

"Don't worry, father," she pulled a blanket from their bag, covering him with it. "I'll take care of you."

≈ ≈ ≈

A shrill scream woke Johanna in the middle of the night. The creaking ship brought her fully awake and she sat up and looked around. They were quartered in a small makeshift cubbyhole midship, separated from the crew, though she could hear their snores and night sounds. Unable to sleep, she held out her right hand.

"It is so large," she said, as if seeing it for the first time. She turned it this way and that. She had her father's hands. In fact, she had grown into a large boned body with only a few delicate features of a sixteen-year-old maiden. She lifted the hem of her dress, pushed her legs straight out, tightened her thigh muscles and wriggled her toes. Big, but not a mannish body, she reasoned. Muscular and sturdy yet long and angular, not like the squat frames many peasant women possessed. She put her hands over her breasts. Nicely rounded but small and easily fit in the cup of her palms.

"What is it about flesh that drives men so hard to it?" she wondered and absently massaged them. Her nipples responded, hardening between her fingers. A tingling sensation bubbled over the skin and sent pleasurable waves down her stomach and flooded the delta between her legs. She took her hands away. Is that what they felt? She put her hands above her breasts and felt the thick sinews of muscle braided beneath. A matter of inches, yet one was a simple touch while the other shook a place she had rarely given thought.

She went above deck and was refreshed by the morning breeze. Any worry of another sailor attack dissolved with the gentle mist spraying off the swells. She faced the hills half a mile away on the shore, burnished in magenta and ladled with light from the rising sun. The hills seemed like gigantic gems haphazardly piled along the horizon. She turned windward and was taken by a rush of excitement. She felt she was sailing over more than water; this passage would lead her beyond the old world into realms unimaginable. She resolved to be brave in the coming days and was grateful for a life more unique than the thousands of souls in the towns the ship passed. Souls who would never know, never want to know, what she had already experienced. She, Johanna of Mainz, looked into the bluing sky and promised herself she would never take a moment of her precious life for granted again.

≈ ≈ ≈

In the afternoon she cajoled Halbert to come above deck, and once in the sun and wind he brightened and color returned to his face.

"It's cold," he said. She took off her black wool shawl, put it around his shoulders. Johanna had on her other clean dress, a worn, pale brown frock, frayed at the square neck, the hem blowing in the wind at her ankles, her hair whipped like a banner. She took a leather strip and tied it back into a single tail.

"It helps to keep moving," she said. They walked around the deck, heard strange tongues and several dialects of Norman, Gaul, and Frank.

The two had come nearly around the ship when they passed a man huddled beside a crate. The bald sailor who touched her secret place was on his knees, in agony, re-bandaging a crushed hand. The same hand, she noted, which had violated her. She thought of the cry that woke her. His bald head was burned by the sun and threw into contrast the tattoo of a coiled snake on his forehead. He looked up, saw her and turned away. Good, she thought. Suffer for what you've done.

"Let's get out of the wind," said Johanna. They found an alcove at the stern of the ship and sat down. She took a scroll from the leather quiver and began to unroll it.

"What are you doing?"

"I'm going to study, of course."

"What did I tell you," he said and snatched it from her hands and stuffed it back into the quiver.

"No one can see us."

"I don't care. That was my biggest mistake. Teaching you to read."

"Your greatest gift. The wonder it has given me. I will always love you for it," she said, trying to soothe him. Johanna had rarely seen fear like this in her father and it worried her. She tried to change the subject. "You've never told me how you came to read. How did you learn?"

"You love the beauty of truth, don't you?" he asked.

"Almost as much as I love you, father," she replied, feeling his anger barely held in check.

"Is that so? Well, I learned to read, my young Hater Of All Things Christian, because I was a monk. There. It is said."

She felt as though she had been hit in the stomach and the air in her lungs sucked out. "I'm quite sure you were anything but a monk, father."

"Think, Johanna. How else could I, could anyone gain knowledge that only the church has? You think this knowledge fell onto me from the sky? I was given to the church as a boy, an orphan, raised in it."

She could only stare. As she did all their years together, everything they had done and everything he was to her, suddenly began to make an uneasy, but perfect kind of sense.

"The brothers were kind to me and opened up the world when they taught me to read. Christians who loved knowledge and were generous? Yes. But when I was younger than you, I lost it all. I was turned away from the monastery when I met your mother."

"Why?"

"She was a pagan. There was no Christ, no Virgin Mary or saints in her world. And I could not change her heart. Looking into her eyes, I didn't want to. I gave up that life for the most beautiful woman in the world. We stole away with a few scrolls as all I owned."

"You never told me. You never said a word."

"After she died I was ashamed to add fuel to the fire of your hate."

Halbert exhaled a long sigh. At last, the burden of his secret was lifted. He glanced at his daughter and could see the shock.

"How do you feel now about truth, knowing that all that you love comes from all that you despise? Do you despise me as well? Will you judge me the way you judge others? Or is only your 'truth' worth knowing?"

He turned away. Johanna stood and walked out of the alcove onto the deck, unable to fully understand what she had been told.

Johanna was torn by anger, revulsion, pity and relief. It certainly made sense once she calmed down. There were no pagan libraries or scholars. They had never met another pagan who could read or write. The more she thought about it, the more she was glad her father got to let go of what must have been an unbearable weight. She was about to go back and apologize, when she felt a presence. She turned and saw the blue-eyed monk who had steered her away from the sailors.

She almost flinched when her eyes landed on the young man. He looked to be near eighteen years old, his first dark brown beard not quite filled in. She thought he had the gaze of a man searching for the most secret place in every thing he looked upon. He wore a clean monk's uniform; a brown robe that was blown upon the wind to his thighs to expose their sinews, roping down past his knees into powerful calves. His sleeves were rolled up to keep from being soaked in the sea and revealed the muscles of his arms etched clearly against the bone. His was a very honed and browned body, lean and fiercely muscled from endless chores. His face was an innocent map, easily amazed. However, the lines of tension around the eyes acted as an arch holding up the crease across his forehead and suggested a taurean stubbornness, always anticipating a challenge. His open face had no way to conceal emotions. She remembered the look on it when he took her arm and knew she was too harsh on a gesture that probably saved her life.

He lowered his eyes when he saw her, shy. Both looked away.

Halbert had fallen asleep. When Johanna turned again the monk was gone. She rose and walked along the railing to the bow. The sea kicked up and rocked the ship despite a cloudless sky

The monk knelt at the tip of the bow with his hands together in prayer, staring out to sea. His prayer ended, and Johanna unconsciously held her breath as he turned and looked upon her with his penetrating eyes. He opened his mouth to speak as the ship dipped in a deep swell. A huge wave crashed over its nose and hurled a massive sheet of ocean onto him. It flattened and washed him along the deck for several paces.

Laughing, she went to the young monk and bent to take his arm.

"Are you all right?"

As she gripped his arm, Johanna's hair came free from its binding and blew around her head. The touch of hand to arm froze both a moment before he got to his feet. A current raced through their skins from the touch, enhanced by the connection of their eyes. Johanna was used to looking into eyes, looking for truth about their owner. Usually eyes stopped at a certain depth, but the eyes before her continued opening up, bringing her in and letting her fall into them like an endless well of blue.

"I'm fine," he replied. She pulled him to his feet with such force the monk took notice of her strength.

"You should take your own advice and not try to swim into the crashing surf."

"Yes, my advice has left me cold," he said, shivering.

"You need to dry off some of that foolishness," she said and turned away so he would not see her smile. "Come. I'm Johanna."

"Adrian," he said and followed her. "My name's Adrian."

≈ ≈ ≈

Below deck he huddled over Johanna and Halbert's smoky brazier. Johanna wrung out his drenched shirt and stole a glance at his wide shoulders when he wrapped them in her blanket.

"I see one of your shipmates was injured." She squeezed out his wet shirt.

"Cleph met with an accident last night," said Adrian. "I understand his hand went where it shouldn't have."

"So he was injured twice. Once for the intent of his mind, and again for the action of his hand."

"You are perceptive, Johanna."

"And you are wrong to take action that's mine. It is my place to confront him."

"You would have had to do that last night in the dark. I met him on his way here. Cleph has no use for words and uses his rude hands to win debates."

"And now he has only one rude hand left," she said. He reached out for the shirt. She shook it out, handed it to him.

"I apologize for defending an honor not mine to defend. I must go."

"Please do," she said as Adrian started for the ladder. "But I...I don't believe your apology is sincere."

"Why is that?" he asked, turning back to her.

*What should I say?* she screamed at herself while he stood waiting for an answer. After several seconds Adrian shrugged, started away.

"You would truly honor your apology by...by joining me and my father for supper."

"I beg your pardon?"

"An honorable man joins his intent with his actions," she smiled, connecting the thought.

"Fine. I'll bring fish to show my sincerity," said Adrian, making a mock formal bow.

"Fine. And since we can only offer you bread," returned Johanna with an exaggerated curtsy, "we'll thank you for having us to supper."

"My pleasure."

Before his footsteps faded, Johanna was filled with an immense surge of energy and found herself pacing the cabin.

She had never been awkward before a man or woman despite their rank. Everyone was approached without distinction, except this monk who made her breath strangely uneven.

"No," she said aloud, hands on her hips. She would not have feelings for this boy.

*What if he's as vile as his shipmates but more cunning in his strategy?* she argued. *Perhaps he plans to wait in some corner where he can advance without a witness, like Cleph. Perhaps his hands would not be content to touch for a few furtive seconds.*

"Stop this," she said.

She wished she had the insight of her father when looking upon the hearts of strangers. Johanna shook out the blanket. Her mouth was dry and she was ashamed of the bizarre leap she had taken into fantasy. She started to fold the blanket, but paused to smell the rough wool. An essence of him clung to it, permeating her with his closeness. For a moment she let herself linger in the smell, a woody, ephemeral musk with the scent of hair, skin and a warmth she could not identify.

"What is that? I know it well, why can't I name it?" she wondered as she inhaled breath after breath of him. Halbert came down the ladder and she put the blanket aside.

"I need to rest," he said and put a loving hand on her cheek. With this gesture she put an anxious hand to her face, to her hair, appalled at how she must have appeared to Adrian; smudged face, hair tangled and ragged in her patched dress like some wretch.

"What is it, Johanna? Are you ill, too?"

"No, of course not," she replied indignantly. She chastised herself for her vanity and helped Halbert onto his pallet.

"Who is he to impress?" she mumbled as she put the blanket over Halbert.

"What was that?" he asked. "Who is what?"

"Nothing," she said, tucking him in. *He is just a youth, ignorant of things I know, illiterate beyond his passably smooth speech. He's probably seduced many simple girls with the charms of his eyes and smile alone. And he is very aware of that,* she thought.

Halbert gave his daughter a puzzled look and patted her arm. "Perhaps you should rest, too."

"I'm fine, father, I told you."

Halbert shrugged, turned over to sleep.

She promised herself he was going to face more than some idiotic farm girl when he came to dinner. Johanna went to her sack of belongings, found her clean slate gray dress and shook it out. She was appalled. It was so old, so childish! Where was her mother's pretty sash? She had so much to do before she confronted his sly wickedness. Johanna wanted to look her best when she put him to the test. If his purpose was anything but honorable, the young monk was going to be met with a tongue of such sharp and deadly dexterity that any depraved intent would be put to death on the spot.

# CHAPTER V

THE SMELL OF fish upset Halbert's stomach, though the wine Adrian brought calmed his nerves.

"Thank you, son."

"Are you all right, sir?"

"Fine. I just need to rest."

Halbert excused himself with the wine and retired to his darkened corner to listen.

"I'll see to this." Johanna took the sea-bass fillets from Adrian.

"Perhaps I should come back," Adrian said. "When your father is better?"

"Sit," said Johanna. She set to work salting the flesh of the fish and pressing herbs from her pouch beneath the skin. Adrian looked around but there was no place to sit and nothing to sit on. He remained standing, an earnestness radiating from his piercing eyes while she skewered the fillets and set them skin side down over the coals.

"What about your family, Adrian?" she asked. "They must miss their son so far away on dangerous seas."

Standing next to her at the brazier, he breathed a long sigh on the coals, brightening them almost to flame.

"I miss them, too. But I'm on a mission. Our village was attacked and taken by Saracens. Instead of sacking the village, they stayed to live on our land and rule us. We became their slaves. I was called upon to escape, and in Rome I'll raise an army against them."

"Rome? You sail the wrong direction, monk."

"The route overland could take a year and the captain was kind enough to let me earn my board to get to the Holy City. Once there I'll ask the Pope for his help."

"I'm sure your Pope will be happy to kill as many as you like."

Adrian did not respond, but watched Johanna work on the fish.

"You're not like other monks I've seen," she said. "Most are soft and sly with tongues more slippery than this fish."

"I was a soldier from a family of soldiers. Until I watched the eyes of my brother, in agony when he was dying, with a sword in his neck. God spoke to me through his eyes, called me to Him."

"I lost my mother because of your god. All my prayers are for his blood."

"God saved my life."

"He took everything precious from mine. Yours is a cruel god who kills what he can't have."

"No. He only wants our hearts."

Johanna held up the brazier's sharpened stirring stick. "Wants them pierced on a stick for dinner."

She dug into her waist-pouch and when she sprinkled sea salt onto the fish the coals crackled from the cooking juices and the light from the brazier cast their faces in amber. Sadness descended on Adrian, and he blew again on the fire.

"You are lucky your father is with you. I hope my family survives the time I'm gone."

Johanna was moved by Adrian's love for his family and regretted her combative barbs. She reached over and touched his hand for comfort. Johanna took the stick from Adrian and lifted the wine skin next to the brazier.

"I can't imagine being away from my father," she said and dribbled wine onto the fish. "I hope you return home soon to free them."

Adrian watched her tend the food with the stick, adding more wine to the fillets. He smiled. "And when I return I'm going to tell him the tale of the maiden and drunken fish."

She playfully poked the cooking stick at his chest, the subject gladly changed. "I'll have you know this is a delicacy on some finer tables. Don't you mock me, sir."

Adrian held his hands above the coals and rubbed them, looked across the fire at her, his eyes crinkled impishly.

"Mock you, one person? Never. Mock man in general? Always."

"And what blasphemy is this?"

"Not blasphemy. I see all mankind as a child who creates a game for the stick he's found, his toy."

Adrian took the cooking stick from Johanna, it was a long piece of charred wood, and he held it up like a weapon.

"This child invents, says of the stick, 'This is my sword and I am king!' And the more he plays with other children the more the child makes up rules to keep the others from becoming bored and going home. 'All must follow me, do what I say.' Then he claims the rules he has made up come from God. 'And if you do not follow these rules, you go against God Himself and will burn in hell forever!'"

"You have the roots of wisdom, Adrian. Fuller than the roots of your beard," she teased.

"That's not true," he said, touching his face, embarrassed. Johanna laughed, and Adrian had no choice but to join in.

Impulsively, she grabbed his beard as if to yank it. Adrian braced but she held her hand to his face, loosened her grip and gave his whiskers a soft stroke instead. It struck Johanna that this was the first time she had ever touched a man like this, gently and with another meaning.

Adrian's face was frightened but determined and he bent his face toward hers. Johanna stood chained to the greatest fear and at the same time was bound to the greatest longing she had ever felt. Adrian's eyes held her frozen in place and closed the distance between them. His mouth parted slightly in the moment before a kiss.

"Johanna," Adrian whispered.

"Adrian. I've never done…I've never kissed anyone."

"Neither have I. But I want to. More than anything."

Her eyes never left his, and his words freed her from her fears. She boldly reached her hand around his neck and pulled

Adrian down toward her mouth, knowing they had nothing to compare this moment to, and so could not fail. Her lips were not sure how they should work, should she open them a bit, should she wait for him, if they should...

"Johanna? Are you still awake?"

"Yes, father," she replied with a start. "I'm right here."

"Get me some water."

Johanna and Adrian turned away from each other and looked down on fish far too blackened to eat. She went for the water while Adrian pulled the fish from the coals and burned his fingers in the process.

"How are you?" said Johanna, rushing a water-skin to Halbert. She looked back at Adrian, sucking on a blistering thumb. Sheepish and awkward again, they passed shy smiles to each other, and Joanna knew they both silently acknowledged a second, deeper hunger far beyond the loss of dinner.

≈ ≈ ≈

Johanna spent every moment with Adrian. She felt a keen awareness that the few days left on the sea were the only things between their parting and never seeing each other again, a prospect she didn't dare think about. She could sense Adrian felt the same.

"I can lift that," she said, grabbing a bucket from him.

From morning till night Johanna followed Adrian around the ship as he performed tasks no other seaman would endure. Johanna noted how the other crew men avoided his company.

"For a girl, you are strong."

"Thank you. For a monk you are not half as foolish as your shipmates think."

Adrian removed buckets-full of fetid, vermin-infested water from the bilge, made repairs while hanging precariously off the side of the ship. They talked as he worked, and Adrian gave no thought to the dangerous labors. Johanna asked about the coldness the sailors treated him to, though their attitudes contained a large portion of wary respect.

"When I began, I had to defend myself every day. Before I came aboard, I was warned never to let a slight pass without a swift reply. These men watch closely and prey on the weak, whether one does the will of God or not."

Cleph had been the latest crew member injured or beaten. They all shunned the man-boy monk who never turned the other cheek but was quick to retaliate and difficult to defeat.

"You are a bright girl, aren't you, Johanna?" he said in a playful, but irritatingly superior way. She pulled tight on one end of a torn canvas sail with the other end tied to the rail, giving Adrian a taut surface on which to sew the damaged material.

"I am not ashamed of my intelligence," she said, her eyes narrowing. "If you are, tell me now."

"Well, you must agree that a woman with too much in her brain is evil, since it makes her turn from her duties of motherhood," he said and ran the long bone needle through the tear. His hands worked quickly, long tapered fingers stitched a ropy thread through fabric.

"You cannot possibly be referring to that old belief held by dead churchmen and fools? That view is dying and was never true."

"And you have the true doctrine, I suppose?" he asked, facetiously, pulling tight on the stitch. "Johanna of All-Wisdom?"

Johanna stood up and glared.

"Good bye, Adrian," she said and walked away.

"What? Johanna, where are you going?"

"You want to bully your way out of arguments? Fine," she said, turning back to him. "Bully someone else. I imagine Cleph is eager to exchange ideas with someone of his own mind. I don't have time for it, nor do I care for your ignorance. Good bye and good luck to you, sir."

She walked to the steps below deck. Before she could disappear, Adrian jumped up, took hold of her arm.

"Truly, I am a fool," he said. "I am used to women who giggle and are without a thought in their heads."

"I won't be treated that way."

"I apologize," Adrian said. "Please. I'm so sorry."

"I know it's how you are taught to see us. But it is not true and you, you with such a fine mind should know better. I thought you were a man, monk or not, who recognized another seeker."

"I beg you to forgive my ignorant presumptions. Please, Johanna."

Standing before her, Adrian was so sincere and his manner so earnest that her anger fled. She reached over and took his hand from her arm. Adrian appeared crestfallen, until she grasped his hand in both of hers and squeezed.

≈ ≈ ≈

"How long until we land?" Johanna asked, standing beside Adrian at the rail. He knew she really meant how long did they have left.

"Perhaps another day or so before we turn westward and leave the coast," he said, squinting into the distance. "Depending on the winds it will take a day to make the island."

He looked out at the shore for several minutes and tried to dismiss the growing importance of the moment they would have to part.

They had had so many intense discussions on every subject it reminded Johanna of the hours she and Halbert spent scrutinizing each other's logic. This was the only topic they had avoided.

"Get back to work, sailor," called a crewman. Adrian simply turned and gave the man a look. Johanna took his arm and pulled him to her. The sudden closeness of their bodies made them freeze, each transfixed on the other.

Adrian slowly bent his face to hers. When their lips touched, Johanna was charged by the soft comfort of Adrian's mouth, so warm and gentle and at the same time a new hunger was born.

Another sailor's call startled them. They stepped apart.

"See you tonight," said Adrian, his arm at her elbow.

Johanna's knees shook so hard she reached for the rail and stood for several long breaths to compose herself, her fingers pressed to her lips trying to recover the sensation of his kiss.

≈ ≈ ≈

"What is it you seek, Johanna?" Adrian asked that evening as they stood below deck at the dimly lit brazier.

"You won't laugh at me?"

"Never."

Adrian listened to Johanna describe her love of knowledge and her desire to understand everything. Her eyes glimmered as she equated her passion for wisdom as Adrian's passion for his God, in fact Wisdom was the god she worshipped.

"I've never meet anyone like you," he said.

She looked away. No one he had ever met fought so hard or yielded so gracefully. They had known each other three short days, yet Adrian knew he would never find another spirit like this, able to articulate her heart like a priest and her mind like a philosopher.

Halbert, from his corner, watched his child walk a path he could not follow, could not call her back and could not even bear to watch as she, with bounding strides, took the road leading away from him.

Early the next morning Johanna sat and read to Halbert in their corner. She translated a difficult Greek phrase from Aristotle, when without warning Adrian stepped from the shadows, earlier than they had agreed. He held up three dried apples hoping to surprise them with his gift. His smile vanished when he heard Johanna and saw the scrolls open in her lap, the words unmistakably in her command.

"Johanna," he hissed, disgust in his eyes. He looked at Halbert. "How could you allow this! Are you a sorcerer disguised as a man?"

"Judge nothing until the end," said Halbert, ominously.

"Adrian, listen," she said.

"I've been deceived," he spat. Adrian threw the fruit at their feet and left. Johanna reeled across the floor to the ladder.

"Let him go, Johanna."

"He doesn't understand."

"The boy will not endanger us."

"That's not what I fear."

"I see the fondness you have. The more you nurse it, the more your hearts will ache when we make land."

"He hates me."

"No," said Halbert as she started up the ladder. "But save both yourselves from anguish. This will make the parting easier. Listen. Do not let this infatuation steal your heart."

"That's impossible."

"Until a man steps between you to cloud the light of reason?"

"No man casts a shadow that long."

"Especially me, daughter?"

His words seized and held Johanna in place on the stairs. The red around his eyes, the wear of extended sea sickness on his face, her father had been left alone almost the whole time. She had treated the voyage as a frolic even as he was plagued by illness and doubt. She had been selfish, absorbed in the pleasure of a stranger's company and had abandoned the only man on earth she ever trusted, revered, and loved, and who loved her back with the same intensity.

"You are part of reason's light, you help me see it," Johanna said. "I love you. I'll never leave you."

≈ ≈ ≈

Johanna stayed with Halbert and did not leave his side until that night when he drifted off to sleep. She had pressed him long into the evening with questions about subjects they had never discussed. Not about books or intellectual concepts of this world, rather Johanna put Halbert through a far more difficult task of answering questions about her mother. At first he tried telling her stories she already knew, anecdotes of their life as a family, but Johanna was not interested.

She wanted to know about love.

"How did you meet?"

Her questions rolled out in waves.

"Was the spark between you immediate? Did you feel some connection, a fate?"

Had he known any other women, had her mother any other beaus? How old were they? How were they able to see each other if he was a monk? Did her mother feel the same or did she have to be won over?

"Too many questions," he said. "You never stop."

"They're the same ones you'd ask, father, and you know it."

Her interrogation rekindled times as long buried as the woman he had so long kept from his mind. Johanna's questions took Halbert to a precipitous ledge overlooking both happiness and grief, and it was a long fall onto either one. He thought of Gilberta, her beautiful face as close to his as Johanna's. He told his daughter about the day, the very minute, when Gilberta finally said she loved him. He felt again the warm sun on his shoulders, recalled it was just after noon, the summer day had baked the ground and sent heat waves from the water up into the air along the riverbank. He was coming out of the shallows of a river, drenched from head to toe in his monk's robes after playing with children, imitating animals, showing them how to whistle bird calls.

Gilberta had watched his loving hands hold the little children, making them laugh as he laughed along with them. She had rushed into the water up to her knees and kissed him, her lips and tongue all over his as the current tried to pull them downstream.

"I love you," she said.

*I'm holding the most beautiful woman in the world,* Halbert said to himself, not believing his great good luck.

The ghost Johanna invoked seemed to stand before them in the drafty hold of the ship as Halbert spoke to his daughter of their life before Johanna.

"You loved her so much," Johanna said when he paused. "And you knew right away? That you were lovers forever?"

"Yes, but as you guessed, she had to be shown the way."

"What? You mean she was like me? Willful? No."

"Willful?" he laughed. "If I said left, she went right. She had a keen mind and was stubbornly eager to prove it."

"And you aren't stubborn?" she said. They laughed and were quiet.

"We had to be together," he said.

"Like me and Adrian," Johanna said and sighed.

"No. You don't know him, Johanna. Your mother and I --"

"You knew it the first time you saw her."

"That was different. We had time."

"We have no time, and yet I know it just as surely."

"You forget, Adrian thinks otherwise after what he's seen."

"Adrian knows it, inside. He's still ignorant of the superstitions that hold onto him."

"Some men never escape the foolishness that holds them."

"Adrian will."

They did not speak for a long time. Finally, it was impossible to contain the sadness filling her heart. Johanna put her head into her hands. Halbert reached over and pulled her close.

"I don't know what to think," she said, sobbing. "I don't care if he hates me, I love him. We leave soon and he'll sail out of my life with this ship forever. Father, what should I do?"

Halbert could find no words of comfort or wisdom. He could not bear to see her hurt, and this was the deepest ache he had ever seen on a girl who had witnessed so much squalor, misery, injustice and death. None of it affected her the way this boy had. Halbert, the farthest away from his dream of seeing Rome, could not be farther away from rescuing his child from her suffering. Halbert could not answer the most important question she had ever asked:

"Father, what should I do?"

They fell asleep holding each other. Johanna woke late that night and left the space that had grown thick and suffocating with more than its usual clamminess and stood above deck in the brisk air. A pale emptiness inside her seemed to be reflected in the crescent slip of moon rising on the eastern horizon.

She walked to the stern where the helmsman, a small dark man from Gaul, was bent forward with his full weight on the tiller, asleep. Johanna slipped by him and dropped to her knees on the deck. She looked up and took a deep breath.

Gazing at the edge of the sea she caught sight of the arc of a huge meteor. It raced down the horizon, its comet-like tail cutting a swath through thousands of shining stars, blinking from so far away, so mysterious and ancient, as they had always been.

She paused and gathered herself beneath the starry cosmos, its true face hidden beyond the dots of light. Johanna intuitively knew the universe's great shadow was all that was ever seen, a cloak draped behind the constellations. She sighed and came to the point, compelled to speak aloud to the night.

"God of Adrian. If You exist, hear me, Johanna of Mainz. If You are Lord of all, over the Infinite Heavens, answer me. You have taken so much from my life already. What do you want? Tell me what You desire of me."

Several minutes passed. They turned into hours. Still she waited on her knees until her patience failed, and she stood up.

"Your silence tells me all," she said bitterly, turning her back on the night and heading below deck. "As I knew it would."

# CHAPTER VI

JOHANNA ROSE EARLY and went topside. She saw Adrian try to enlist a crew member into conversation, but the man scowled at the monk and walked away.

"Adrian."

He saw her wave at him, but headed below. Johanna walked to the ladder leading to the crew compartments and looked down into the hold. She thought a moment about crossing the threshold of the men's private world, and then abandoned hesitation.

She passed two sailors who had accosted her. They were naked and picking lice from the other's rank body and cried out at the sight of her.

"Woman below!"

"Get out!"

The looks on their faces were horrified with violation as they jerked away from her eyes, hands over their parts, incensed that a woman dare intrude on their privacy. One was the bald Cleph, his bandaged hand pressed to his genitals. The men watched her fiery gaze silently scoff at the parts she saw.

Adrian was at his pallet pulling out books wrapped in skins when Johanna entered.

"There's no debate," he said, holding up a scroll. "You are evil if you can read these."

"I can, but I know you don't believe that," she said, reaching to touch his arm. "Don't treat me like you do."

"It's one thing to toss foolish ideas back and forth in a game," he pushed her hand away. "But you are not a noblewoman, nor are you high-born. A woman without rank who reads has slept with a devil."

"Is that the extent of your logic? Is that all you have learned? If it is, you are the biggest fool I have ever met. You deserve the company you keep down here."

He brushed past her and hurried above deck. Right on his heels behind, she ignored the outraged shouts of the sailors.

On deck Adrian picked up a barrel, carried it to the rail next to an old sailor casually stitching a deep gash in his forearm with a metal hook and fishing line, sewing two thick flaps of flesh back together. Johanna stood beside Adrian, and whispered.

"I am not a devil, witch or a spirit. I am a seeker of knowledge, a lover of wisdom just like you would be if you were not so ignorant. You told me you were beyond this."

"It is unnatural. Where I come from, God gave woman her knowledge and man has what's given to him. We dare do nothing but take our natural places within that law."

Adrian went to the stern of the ship. Johanna followed and stood behind him as he coiled a line.

"Who wrote this law where you come from?" she asked.

"A stupid question. Leave me."

"No. Make me understand. Who wrote this law?"

"Wise men, saints. From God's Mouth to their writing hands."

"I see," she said, putting a facetious hand to her cheek. "Your god speaks only to men."

"God speaks to us all, as you well know."

"How can that be? If He spoke to women they might be called to spread your god's word. They might be moved to write it in books. A woman might even know what a man knows and seek what he seeks."

She grabbed his arm, hard.

"The two might come together in their search to find that god you think is so loving."

"It is the law, Johanna, and you break it," he said with a flat finality. "You deceived me with knowledge not yours to own."

"And you, monk, follow children who make rules for their toys, saying they come from on high," she said and reached over, took a cooking stick from a brazier and placed it in his hands. "Here, child, go obey the laws you made up. They have nothing to do with any god."

She walked away and left him staring at the stick.

≈ ≈ ≈

That evening the ship turned away from land, heading for what seemed like the terrible ledge of the horizon where oceans fell away into nothingness. The ship passed from clear skies and sailed into a billowing fog that, before the sun set, engulfed the ship in a stale thickness.

The ship was without the comfort of shore at either horizon and below in the rancid darkness, Halbert and Johanna could not escape the cold. They huddled close for warmth.

"It's better this way," she thought as she shivered beside her father. How could she even think of loving a man who cherished such ridiculous beliefs? If he could not see who she was beyond his foolish superstitions, how could they be lovers?

"Oh. Oh, Gilberta," groaned Halbert in his sleep.

Johanna looked at her father, his teeth chattering in the cold.

She tossed and turned, fighting imagined battles against Adrian, going over every word they ever exchanged. She stood Adrian before several imaginary tribunals and at every trial he had no choice but to accept her brilliant assessment of his faults, agreeing with her verdict.

"I've been deluded," Adrian would weep. "By doctrines of foolish men long dead. Forgive me."

Before sentencing him, his contrition was so complete that she took Adrian in her arms and forgave him. Johanna found that in forgiveness all their differences faded and holding him tight all anger fled. It was so natural to lift her face to his, meet his lips...

"No!" she cried, sitting up in the dark, infuriated at her twisting mind. The night passed in endless arguments and she was unable to get the voices out of her head.

At dawn a surprise wind blew in from the north, the seas churned and the fog swirled and began to scatter. Excitement spread through the ship as the smell of land filled the air and everyone knew the voyage was nearing its northern-most destination. Sailors lined the rail straining to see across the water.

Johanna came above deck and stood with her father although her eyes wandered over to Adrian, who was on the opposite rail.

"Land! I see it!" called a sailor from the bow.

"There! Sweet, sweet land!"

"Oh, Christ," yelled the old sailor, his stitched forearm held heavenward. "Once again we are delivered from sea-demons."

A cry went up from the entire crew as anxious hands pointed into the distance, marking land. Johanna and Halbert peered through the dissipating fog and looked across the choppy water to a raw and forbidding English coastline. Several young sheep, braying and frisky, wandered across the craggy faces of the cliffs above the crashing surf.

"Devils and satyrs roaming free," said Halbert bitterly.

"Let's leave our old lives here, father, aboard ship," she begged, hand on his shoulder. "And go ashore with new hearts."

"I have no heart left. But I will try."

The captain called out, "Ready the shore boat."

"Here?" asked Halbert, amazed. "This is not a port."

"I'll get our things," Johanna said. Halbert turned to the captain.

"You will take us to a proper port, sir!" he demanded. The captain looked at him with contempt and spit over the side.

"Your coin has brought you farther than you deserve," he said. "And your daughter has disrupted every one of my crew and is nothing but bad luck. I want you pagans off this ship before we are further cursed. However, if you leave your daughter with me in my quarters for an hour, perhaps we can arrange –"

Halbert reached over and gripped the man's neck with one large hand. He pulled his face within an inch of his own and squeezed.

"You will be food for the fish before that ever happens."

The man's eyes bugged and his skin blossomed from red to purple as his mouth worked silently like a landed fish, but it was impossible to wrench from Halbert's iron grip. It was only after Cleph spotted the flailing captain's life being choked out of him that he called several deck hands over and pulled Halbert off.

Below, Johanna gathered their sack of goods and checked the area a final time. When she turned to the ladder to go she froze. Adrian stood at the door. A tense moment passed in which Johanna could not tell if he was planning to expose her as a witch or if he was there to curse her and finally cast her from his heart. She instinctively looked for a weapon and a way out.

"Johanna," he began. She held her breath.

He rushed across the space between them and before either one could react she was in his arms.

"Say I am a fool!" he cried, squeezing the breath out of her.

"You are a great good fool!"

"I couldn't sleep. My mind and heart have been torn to pieces, and I'm left with nothing but rags."

"They make a fine cloak on you," she said to make him smile, touching his face, unable to take her eyes from his.

They could not stop. They kissed long and hard, sending the message of their minds through the passion in their lips. She loved this man the way she knew he loved her, despite the fate before them.

The clatter of footsteps on deck rose and they broke away.

"I can't leave you," he said. "Come with me to Rome."

"Adrian," she began. "We have to follow our fathers."

"Where is this rule written?"

"That law grows from our hearts."

"Please, don't turn away," he pleaded, kneeling before her. He took her hand and placed her index finger on the side of his head. "I've come such a great distance from here to be with you. Everything I know I gladly leave behind. Stay with me. It has been only a moment since I first saw you, but I need you with me for all my life. I already know this. Johanna, I love you."

He took her hand from his head and kissed her palm.

"The dinghy sails for shore!" cried a voice above deck.

"I cannot leave my father."

She turned and rushed up the ladder onto the deck where she was caught by Adrian and pulled close. Halbert, with panic in his eyes, was forcibly held at the rail by deck hands, unable to find Johanna among the faces looking landward.

"I can't lose you now," Adrian whispered.

She looked into the face of a man who had just given his heart away for the first and last time in his life, a face as passionate as her own.

"You will not lose me. Listen to me, Adrian, we will meet again. When my father and I find our way to Rome--"

"Oh, Johanna," he said. "I cannot live this sad little life till then, love. Are you telling me you can?"

Halbert looked over the railing and spotted her.

"Johanna, we have to hurry! They're forcing us off the ship!"

"Come or be damned, you," the boatman cursed from the dinghy bobbing in the rough water.

Johanna took Adrian by the arms and, hopeless, she had no choice left. So she lied.

"I will find you."

"Find me, how? The whole world moves between us."

"When we will get to Rome I swear I'll find you."

Adrian was devastated: a reunion was impossible. What was she saying? He knew she felt the same, knew the yearning of their souls drew them together, but why was she driving a blade into his heart with what they both knew was a lie?

"Continents will separate us and millions will wander in our path," he said. "We'll never find each other again."

Halbert, pulled off the rail by sailors, called again. "Johanna, please! They will sail without you."

"Get in the boat or swim to shore," yelled the boatman.

"In the middle of nowhere?" said Halbert to the captain. "Take us with you to port."

He looked for Johanna, saw her across the ship, reaching out to Adrian, both unaware of the excitement around them. Halbert was suddenly lifted up and thrown over the side.

"Johanna."

"Use the faith your god gave you, Adrian," Johanna demanded, close, grabbing a fistful of the young man's hair and pulling his face to hers. "Know we will meet again."

She kissed him, mixing the salt of sea mist and tears. Johanna did not believe a word she said and knew neither did Adrian. He understood as well as she did that the world was too big. It would be the end of them once they parted. Inwardly she railed at herself for giving false hope, forcing it upon him and blinding him in the manner she wished to be blinded.

As they pulled back a last time, she saw that each gazed at a face that now would be held only in memory.

Johanna broke free and hurried to the rail. She climbed over then turned back, wanting to run to Adrian's arms. Halbert, down in the boat, called for her, his arms raised. She looked back at Adrian, hating her weakness and her selfishness, yet unable to stop the charade. The words flew out of her mouth even as she tried to stop them. "I will find you, Adrian. Know that."

She went over the side of ship. Adrian went to the rail, watched her climb down. The boatman pushed off. Johanna and Halbert held onto each other, looking up at Adrian, who wept.

"Good bye," she whispered, waving.

Adrian disappeared from the railing, and when he returned to the rail he held an object. He called out but she could barely make out the words as the dinghy's oars pushed the little boat toward shore.

"Johannaaaaaaaa!"

He held the thing aloft, tossed it into the air where it caught the off-shore wind and hung there, twirling end over end, suspended between sky and ocean. It came down and splashed in the water near the dinghy. It was the cooking stick she had handed to him. He had used it to illustrate the story of a child inventing rules in the name of God, and Adrian knew he clung to many of the same rules, until now. It floated near the little boat.

"I don't need it any more," said Adrian, touching his heart.

"Adrian," she screamed across the distance.

After a while he no longer had a face or waving arms, but had become a small form indistinguishable from other people and shapes on the receding deck of the tiny ship.

Oh, my God, she thought, suddenly struck with the unthinkable: She wanted this man more than knowledge, more than her father or life. But she released him to the ocean, alone with cruel men as his only company.

She never noticed Halbert's arms around her, keeping her in the boat, keeping from hurling herself into the water and drowning to prevent the distance from growing between them. An hour later they still had not made the shore, but bucked and swayed in the churning waters.

"I said take us all the way in, damn you," threatened Halbert. But the boatman would not cross the breaker line, though Halbert slapped the man so hard his nose and lips bled.

"Look at the rocks, pagan," the man cried. "Look."

Halbert saw it was the truth. Any attempt to make the rocky shore would be disastrous in the boat. They had no choice but to ease themselves into the frigid, neck-high water. It made no difference to Johanna.

Tossed and thrown ashore by crashing waves, the cold foaming rage of seawater was invisible compared to what she felt inside. Halbert dragged her coughing from the surf and carried her away from the rocky beach.

They climbed a hill as an icy wind blew on their backs so hard it was difficult to walk. At the hill crest they stopped to rest. The sky was overcast; for miles around the countryside was hilly and wild and took on an eerie sour green in a diffused, dull light.

Johanna watched the ship fight the swells as it beat north up the coast. The sheer exertion returned her senses, though the soberness was grim, like a bowl of water set out in the snow to freeze. Johanna waved a last time, watching the ship disappear around a bend, not comprehending why she had done such a terrible thing to her heart. She had fallen in love with her beautiful monk, then let her love sail away.

"I let him go."

"What?" asked Halbert. "What did you say?"

She shook her head, numb.

They walked away from the sea holding hard onto each other, heading down a road through a verdant but foul-weathered land that stretched out of sight over green rolling hills. The sun's light retreated at their backs, the last of its rays eaten by a sky thick with clouds and heavy with rain.

# CHAPTER VII

AFTER MANY HOURS they approached a farm house set forlornly at a crossroads. It was little more than a large wattle and daub hut protected by a fence of an impenetrable high hedge. But smoke poured from the chimney and gave a feeling of warmth in the last minutes of dusk.

The gate had a crude wood carving fashioned across it of the Anglo-Saxon goddess Nerthus, the Harvest Queen, and Halbert and Johanna's spirits rose a bit when they saw it.

"Perhaps they are kind to strangers," Halbert said and opened the gate. It set off a clanging iron bell warning of their approach.

Three steps onto the property and the door was flung open. A beast the size of a large wild boar lunged across the yard with bared, snarling teeth from a bull-like head. They had never seen anything like it.

They turned and ran but the beast was a black blur and at Halbert's heels before they could make the gate. It ripped into his robe, its jaws snapping onto cloth. The jaws opened and snapped again, clamping deep into Halbert's calf. He cried out and stumbled as Johanna reached the gate. She had to pull Halbert along with the animal attached, dragging behind. It would not loosen its grip and shook its head viciously back and forth, ripping at his leg.

"Get off him!" she screamed at it. "Get away you devil."

Johanna reached the gate, frantic and fumbling with the latch. She got it open, pulled Halbert halfway through the entrance but was held back by the grip of the beast. Halbert swatted uselessly at the thing as Johanna looked around, panic-stricken, no one to call, no weapon in sight to strike the monster. Then she realized she was holding onto the open metal gate. The beast continued to growl and shake its head with Halbert's calf locked in its jaws. With both hands she swung the heavy iron gate and slammed it as hard as she could into the thing's head. A massive blow, still it only stunned the beast, but the thing let go of Halbert, backed away with a yelp, gagging and shaking its head. Johanna pulled Halbert through and shut the gate. It was then that she realized the beast was a dog, a breed she had never seen before. It rushed the fence, stood on its paws and hurled a coughing bark at them.

"Put your arm around me," she said.

They limped into the dark. No movement came from the house and the enraged dog howled and jumped at the gate, running madly back and forth along the length of hedge-fence.

They hurried down the path in a darkening forest, Halbert panting and Johanna too frightened to stop. She wondered about this evil land, if it was populated only by terrible storms and predators. And where were the people? They saw signs of humans, cultivated fields, cattle, sheep but had not seen a soul all day. Thunder rumbled in the low skies and echoed around them.

"It's going to come down hard."

Lightning suddenly streaked across the trees with a loud *crack* that stopped them in their tracks. The explosion of light came over their heads and lit up the forest in a blinding white flash. The rain fell as they ran for refuge, drenched and chased by the shapes lightning created amongst the stark shadows of trees.

They huddled beneath a large oak but were not spared from the driving rain. The lightning concocted tortured, demonic shadows in the whipping branches and the whole forest howled with a hard-blowing wind while the sky above roared with thunder.

"It's all right, Johanna," said Halbert without conviction. "We will live through this, too."

The storm raged around them with a supernatural intensity and Johanna and Halbert hugged each other as tightly as possible, as if the power of their bond could counter the dark magic of the storm.

$$\approx \approx \approx$$

By morning the rain had let up and they walked almost two leagues in the same gray, overcast light. The air was cold, but still. For hours they staggered along the muddy road and Johanna, eyes on the mud and trying to stay on her feet, finally looked up.

"Father?" she said, not trusting her eyes. They neared a village. She tugged at Halbert and tried to hurry him, but he had not spoken all morning, and when he took two steps his strength gave out. He took Johanna down with him into the mud. The evil night, the loss of Adrian, the cold harsh land, and now the mud from head to foot were all she could endure. She sat beside him and wept.

"Please, England," she said. "Show us your heart, not your fist."

Her plea was met by a sound so cold it brought a chill to her. An eerie cackle came from a high embankment on their left. Johanna turned toward the sound and saw a monk riding a donkey, his features obscured by a brown, hooded cloak. The brother was laughing at them.

"You find pleasure in misery?" she called, amazed. The man laughed harder, spurred his donkey on and said nothing. Johanna scrambled to her feet.

"Our filth will seem like a paradise when you die, sir," she said, and chased after him. "You evil thing, I will make you feast on this pudding."

He stopped laughing and turned to look at her, pulling up the animal. Johanna dug up two fists full of mud as she ran.

"Swallow this, and choke on your laughter," she lunged, throwing the mud and splattering his cloak. "I pray your evil god will see you die in agony."

She pounded at his leg with her fist. His foot came up. The heel caught her squarely in the chest and sent Johanna tumbling

*The Woman Pope*

down the embankment, sprawled in the mud. The monk rode off, beating the donkey to a trot.

She rose, staggered to Halbert and helped him off to the side of the road.

"Let's rest here," she said. She sat beside him on a rotting log, looked around. A cottage stood near the entrance of the village. Clothes hung out to dry in front of it and a woman stood on the front step and plucked an emaciated chicken. Johanna left her father and approached.

"Have mercy, Mother. My father is --"

The woman turned, slammed the cottage door shut without a word.

Johanna glanced back at her father on the road. He was beyond the point of caring, as if he were ready to die here. She bristled and a rush of anger straightened her back.

"You will not do this to us," she called at him. "We have work to do."

"What?" his slack mouth asked, uncomprehending.

Johanna went to the side of the house and slipped around back. A sack hung on the inside of the window sill and Johanna could see it contained loaves of bread. She hopped up on the sill, reached in and slid a loaf out.

Johanna then brazenly walked up and tore a wool blanket from a line of drying clothes on the side of the house, threw it over her shoulder and defiantly looked around, inviting a challenge. A pair of eyes peeked tentatively from behind a window, but no one came out.

"Bless your charity, England," she said loudly, then walked back to Halbert, the blanket draped over her shoulders like a shawl, the bread tucked under her arm in plain view.

"Get up, father," she said standing over him.

"My leg."

"I will help you, but you must get up and move now."

Once she had gotten him to sit beneath a tree several meters from the road, Johanna tore a strip of material from the blanket, knelt by her father and uncovered his calf, gouged with several red, blue and gray tooth punctures. She wrapped it the best she could and felt him shiver with fever.

"I should not have let you come ashore," Halbert said, wincing. "You and Adrian --"

"Shhh. Rest and eat."

The day warmed only a little as they sat beneath the tree while Halbert dozed uneasily. Johanna chewed the tail of the bread loaf, unable to think, to move, to do anything but obsess upon a faraway ship and Adrian's face.

She went to wipe her hands and saw how dirty she was, how the dried mud weighed her down, caking her mood as well as her body. She forced herself to stand and look around. Her gaze fell on a pond at the edge of a forest. She stepped away from Halbert and hurried toward the trees.

Wading up to her thighs, she took off the muddy dress and a moment later the sun pierced the clouds for the first time since their arrival, lighting up the water and warming her chilled skin. She smiled wanly and slipped beneath the surface.

≈ ≈ ≈

On the opposite side of the pond, behind a tree, the girl was being watched. If one looked hard, someone's breath could be seen, expelled in frozen streams from the shadows. The voyeur observed the girl, midway into her teens, as she ran her hands over her breasts, down her stomach, around to her back and behind. The hooded Watcher viewed the young woman come to life in the sunshine, splashing in the water, becoming refreshed. He listened to the girl-woman hum while she scrubbed the mud from her dress. Her small, rounded breasts swayed gently with the movement, the hardened nipples brushing the surface of the water as she worked. Her nakedness in the sunlight revealed a muscular body. The outline of taut muscle was clearly defined in her arms and across her back. The watcher saw boyish hips and a flat belly, yet a feminine softness remained about all her parts. The voyeur looked on, gulping hard on breaths before his long, thin hands slipped beneath his robes to search out his own parts.

The girl being spied upon sensed something and glanced up. The voyeur quickly pulled back behind the tree, concealing him-

*The Woman Pope*

self in the folds of his mud splattered brown cloak, hoping his donkey tied nearby would not bray and give him away. His face was only a shadow inside the monkish hood, but the shallow breath coming out of it in jagged misting puffs described an unmistakable lust.

# CHAPTER VIII

HUDDLED NEXT TO her father that night, Johanna was consumed by wild dreams. Swimming across warm, gelatinous waters, she was suspended in a liquid thick as mud yet clear as a stream. Johanna slowly turned around in place and saw nothing but an unbroken line of horizon over the transparent oceanic gel. She looked up at the sky and saw impossibly large wings above, blocking out the sun, their iridescent colors so bright they startled Johanna awake.

She shivered under the trees in the yew grove; the campfire was long cold and, though it should have been dark, she found herself squinting into the flame of a lantern. Instinctively she leapt to her feet and grabbed Halbert's walking staff.

"Who are you?" she demanded.

The lantern was held by a red-haired boy of about ten. He stood over her with an old donkey nodding drowsily behind him.

"M-my master sent m-me," he stammered, stepping back, his lip quivering under the weight of the impediment.

Johanna pushed her hair from her face. She was not surprised by the defective speech, but that she was able to comprehend the boy's stilted English.

"Who is your master, boy?" she said, slowly, so he understood. "How does he know us?"

"He's a p-priest and saw your p-p-plight."

"When did this priest see us?"

"I do not na-na-na --" he stopped, gave up and shrugged, completing his sentence.

"My father is ill."

"We will h-help," said the boy. He patted the donkey.

Johanna steadied Halbert on the animal while the boy led the way. After an hour's walk through a close forest the land opened up. In the distance under the fading moonlight appeared a walled estate. Johanna had seen many castles on their travels, but her pulse raced at the sight of the palatial apparition perched like a crown on the peak of a hill.

"Is this where the priest lives?" she asked.

"H-he is our lord and m-master."

"He owns all this?" The boy nodded. "How can that be? I thought priests owned nothing."

She grew uncomfortable at the thought of entering such a grand place and brushed at the gray cloth of her un-dyed coarse cloth dress. She carefully arranged her black shawl, the single piece of heavy clothing she owned, and wrapped it around her head and shoulders. By the time they crossed the grounds of the estate, the only light came from the sputtering lantern, the moon having fallen behind a ridge of hills and left them in near pitch dark.

The donkey stopped outside the door of a long, squat building, and the boy helped Johanna lift Halbert down.

"You c-can sleep h-h-here."

"Help me get him inside."

They dragged him through the door and set him on a straw cot. The boy got Johanna a bucket of fresh water and she helped Halbert drink. He brought blankets while she took off Halbert's wet robe and wrapped her father in the soft wool. The luxury felt peculiar. The touch of the downy wool and the warmth of the space did not seem like the meager lodgings of a priest. The boy produced bandages and a bowl of herbs. She uncovered the wound and sniffed for the smell of rot, but there was no infection. After a thorough cleaning, she dressed the calf then Johanna turned to thank her helper.

"Boy --"

He was gone.

Johanna lay beside her father, pulled the wool blanket over them, and put her arm around him to keep him warm while his body shook and jerked in unconscious fits. If there was a god she would have prayed for his life. But she was suddenly so tired she could not even look around the room. Johanna fell asleep holding her father.

She awoke inside a warm shaft of sun light. They were in an empty section of what Johanna guessed to be servant's quarters. She went to the door and opened it, catching her breath as the true dimensions of the estate announced themselves to her sleepy morning eyes.

She looked out on emerald green grounds well tended and considerable. The manor was surrounded by a high stone wall topped with shards of sharpened rocks and metal spikes. This place did not easily let the world inside and was more like a fortress than an abbey.

"Father, wake up," she said. "Look at this."

But he was asleep and soaked through with cold sweat. She bent and put her hand on his forehead. The fever had broken and he no longer twitched, but was adrift in a peaceful void of sleep. Fresh herbs and a pile of neatly folded clothes had been set by the door.

She picked up the topmost cloth, held it out and was surprised to find a well cut woman's tunic about her size, in a light green so pale it brought out the color of Johanna's eyes. She stepped out of her old dress and found herself beaming at the fit and how comfortable it was. Perhaps England did have some worth, she told herself.

She cleaned Halbert's wound again, bringing the new herbs and a bowl of water to his straw pallet. The swelling had shrunk, responding to the previous treatment and Johanna packed moistened leaves, sprigs, twigs and dried berries into the fresh dressing. She lifted them to her nose and sniffed. It tingled at the pungent smells which made up the poultice. Aside from the green, spongy lichen, she recognized none of the others. Halbert remained asleep, and when she finished she went back to the doorway.

"It's so green here," she whispered to herself.

In the next moment Johanna was drawn out of doors, walking across the grounds on an expanse of cropped grass. No one was in sight and she found herself beside the main building, a great stone castle with a single citadel towering above all else. She hurried past its intimidating entrance.

At a side entry she came to a massive wood door. It was ajar and she peeked inside.

"Hello?"

Johanna's echo came back without a response. She had a fleeting thought that crossing this threshold would be a larger decision than simply entering a building, but let it go as she took a step into the room.

And with that single step she entered another world.

She had to lean against the doorway. From floor to high ceiling the walls were packed with books, manuscripts, codices, scrolls and scripts. They ranged from the tiniest leather packets one could place in the palm of one's hand, to giant tomes secured with metal clasps and leather bindings that would take two men to lift and open. She stood in the midst of a library beyond anything in her imagination.

The room was a treasure chamber filled with jewels of knowledge. There was not a single place left to put another book; tables, chairs, floors, every surface was piled high with them. Johanna walked around the walls touching leather-clad volumes. A table stacked with dozens of different-sized and shaped books was lit by a wide shaft of sunlight streaming down from a window near the ceiling. The golden light was so bright she could see a thick screen of dust motes swirling upwards in random patterns inside a slow-moving draft of air.

She approached and opened a large, leather-bound book directly under the shaft of light. She thought she would faint. They were the brightest colors she had ever seen in one small space. A religious illumination shone up at her, bounding the gilded borders of sacred text. The Latin letters were so intricately feathered with flourishes she could barely read them. She turned a page and a world populated by angels sprang up at her. Finely wrought portraits of haloed saints gazed heavenward in rapture. She turned the pages, following scenes from the Christ bible, all drawn with what appeared to Johanna to be pure gold, royal amethyst, green-speckled malachite, sunset amber, drops of frozen red pomegranate juice. And every translucent color shined up at Johanna from the parchment in a brilliant surprise.

It was like gazing upon a kind of miracle, one that could have only been created by some supernatural power. Tears welled up in her eyes.

She heard a noise and jumped away from the book. A silhouette filled the doorway in black robes, chilled her heart and she fell at once to her knees.

"Forgive me, I did not mean to trespass. I was only looking to find someone about."

"You were looking for knowledge," said the figure gently but with a knowing accuracy. He spoke the English tongue with a high-born accent, was tall and thin as a starving ghost with razor sharp features and a silky, mellifluous voice. "You can read."

"No, Sire. I only look at the pretty shapes on the paper," she replied. "Is the master here?"

"I am he," said the figure. "I am Sergius."

She went and took his hand, kneeled and kissed it. "You are our savior."

"I am but our Savior's servant. Rise, beautiful flower. Welcome to my home. You are?"

"Johanna of Mainz. My father might have died without your help."

"I heard of your circumstances from a servant," he said, his eyes narrowing as the corner of his mouth curved upward with a smile, "who wears your mud on his cloak."

"Bless your kindness, master Sergius," she said, blushing. "And your books."

He gave a quizzical look as he passed by her to the table.

"Their wisdom must have informed your goodness," she explained.

"Perhaps," he said. Sergius touched the book she had been looking through, his silhouette dissolving into a form she could see clearly for the first time. He was not the demon she thought in the doorway, but a strikingly handsome older man in his fifties, steel gray hair shorn close to his scalp, the round shaved skin of his tonsure magnifying not only his head's thinness, along with thin lips and high eyebrows framing a long face, but it also brought out its aquiline nobility. Added to the austerity of his features was the extraordinary chin-hair he grew, like no other Johanna had seen. Though he was clean shaven, there was a single queue braided from three wispy clusters, long white billy-goat whiskers from the tip of his chin reaching down half an arm's length, with the end of the braid secured by a blood red ruby clasp set in gold and as large as a small rock. He motioned her beside him.

"This is what you wept over. A book of illuminations made by my Irish brothers centuries ago. Is it not magnificent? As precious as innocence itself."

Gazing at the inspired pictures, she nodded. He closed the book and crooked a finger at her.

Johanna followed him through a maze of corridors inside the castle, climbing a long winding staircase with only the tap of Sergius' sandals and the swish of his robes to accompany their ascent. She inhaled a mysterious fragrance he left in his wake. Sergius smelled of dusky incense, like an ancient and slightly spoiled nut-like wine.

They reached a large, circular room where the walls were draped in tall tapestries and the whole space was bounded by windows. They were atop the high citadel she had seen while crossing the estate. Sergius went to a window and looked out.

"Come here, flower," he said. "See what I see every day."

Johanna peeked around his shoulder at rolling green hills dotted with wandering cows and sheep grazing over a landscape which, from the vantage of the citadel, looked not only inviting but like a peaceful paradise.

"I did not know Christian priests had wealth," she said, hesitant. "Or owned property."

"Not all God's servants are born in poverty. Some are called bearing the weight of riches," he replied. Then, in Latin. "*And to follow Christ, that burden is a heavy one.*"

"*May your chains help you find truth,*" she replied in same, instantly regretting the slip. She not only gave away part of her secret, but she let loose a presumptuous remark.

"You know more than you confess," he said.

"Forgive my impudence, sire," she said, head bowed to the floor. Johanna felt a hard twinge of regret that she had revealed herself so easily. "I am a fool, as my father often says."

"Stay, Johanna," he said. She looked up into kind, gray eyes shot through with bolts of browns and greens. "Your father will heal, and you will learn many things here."

"Oh, thank you," she said. Finally safe and with the promise of care -- from no less than a Christian priest -- she broke down, sobbing at his feet as Sergius softly stroked the top of her head.

≈ ≈ ≈

Days passed and remained mild while Johanna tended to Halbert and watched as he regained strength. His color returned, as did his appetite, and even a bit of his humor slipped back in one morning as she was tightening the cloth on his leg and he cried out, then smiled slyly and stuck out his tongue at her.

"We will be able to leave soon," Halbert said as she changed the dressing. The deep punctures had grown into brown scabs thick as shells, protecting the flesh healing inside.

"Oh, yes, I can tell you are anxious to get going," she said facetiously. She did not want to leave, either.

Johanna spent the time walking the grounds while Halbert sat in the doorway absorbing the weak sun or limping alongside her with the help of a crutch. Both wondered aloud at their fortune. What were the chances of finding such luxurious solace in this primitive land?

They did not speak to Sergius during their recuperation outside an occasional wave as he paced high above them in the citadel, sending and receiving exhausted messengers who ran across the grounds or rode through the manor on frothing horses.

They also did not communicate with the manor serfs, whose difficult tongue had Saxon similarities to their own, but were secretive and unfriendly. Halbert sensed an unspoken malady festering beneath every person they met.

"Excuse me, friend?" called Halbert to a servant. Johanna walked across the estate with her father as he exercised his leg that morning. The haled servant hobbled by on the stump of a foot and kept going without a glance.

"A strange and clannish breed," said Halbert.

"If it is their natural way we should respect it," Johanna said.

"I have never seen a way like this that was natural."

"These queer folk don't seem put upon. They live a quiet life with the priest as their master."

"Is that how you see it?" Halbert cast a skeptical eye on her. "These are truly a hard bunch if they've had no provocation to turn this way."

The exception was the stammering red-haired boy. He often watched her on her walks as he drove his donkey laden with harvested vegetables from the fields to the manor's store rooms. They smiled and nodded to each other, but one day he surprised her when he spoke.

"T-t-there is a f-feast tonight," he said and turned his freckled face shyly away from her.

"How nice after the famine of silence," she said, smiling.

"T-t-tonight you will be the mm-master's guests."

"How do you know this, my young friend?"

He started to answer, shrugged, and snapped the reins of his donkey and left.

Johanna looked after him, puzzled, but she and Halbert were in fact invited that evening to join the rich cleric. A dour maidservant stood in the doorway of their quarters that afternoon, announced their required presence, then left without waiting for a response.

"Can you mend my robe, Johanna?" Halbert asked, holding the less ragged of his only pieces of clothing. He wagged a finger at her through a tear in the seat.

"Wear the one our host gave and show your gratitude," she protested.

He gave her a sheepish grin. "These English monks are tiny things."

She laughed and took the old robe from him.

"Maybe I can work a small miracle if that's what it takes to make you presentable at his table," she said. "And if it means we get to taste some fancy foods tonight."

"Ah, Johanna," he said. "Sergius is a simple man beneath his inherited gifts. A plain and simple meal will greet us as it has every night since our arrival."

"You are right," she said with a sigh. It was true, they had only eaten bread and dried fruit and the occasional gruel, the same diet as the servants.

That evening they were led to the dining room, Johanna in her muted green tunic and Halbert in a greatly modified version of the gift robe, and were met with smells so powerful they had to stop and look at each other. They saw meats being roasted on large, squeaking fire spits as they passed the kitchen. Aromas of wine, honey, almond and other marinades rushed in and out of their nostrils without definition.

They were ushered into a high-ceiled space and saw Sergius sitting at the far end of the massive dining room. He was illuminated by the flames of several torches tall as children, at the end of a table that could sit thirty. Johanna and Halbert were seated while servants entered and the table was soon filled with roasted meats, loins and thick cuts of beef and veal. Long skewers of wild pheasant and other fowl had been cooked at the flame until the tender, herbed meat fell from the bones. Warm bread loaves topped with crushed nuts and tangy goat cheese were served alongside boiled vegetables, salted and herbed and piled high on platters of solid gold.

"Where are your other guests, sire?" Johanna asked from the far end of the table as trays were brought out by a line of servants.

"The Holy Spirit will be the only other guest joining us this evening," replied Sergius.

She could not believe it. There was food enough to feed twenty servants.

"Amen," said Halbert, after Sergius said a blessing. He could not contain himself and voraciously dug into the food.

Johanna ate in silence, as did the two men. When she was done she sat back and watched a long-legged spider crawl over her plate. She gave a look to Halbert who continued long after she and Sergius finished. Halbert drank gulps of a foamy mead between bites and provided all the sounds, loud and echoing,

*The Woman Pope*

within the great hall. Sergius picked at the mound of food in front of him, barely touching any of it.

"Your health returns, Halbert," said Sergius, wryly, sipping wine from a long stemmed gold goblet. Her father caught himself gorging from his often refilled plate and stopped, laid down his spoon, and pushed the plate away. Johanna suppressed a smile as she watched her father tuck a medallion of roasted beef into the folds of his robe.

"Thanks to your generous mercy, master Sergius."

"Your pilgrimage has been harsh. May England be gentle with you."

"May the English people have a gentler bite than their beasts," Halbert raised his glass. He and Sergius laughed.

"England has much to commend it," said Johanna. "A green beauty and a wealth of knowledge."

"Your daughter desires the sustenance of my library rather than my table."

"How did you find so many books," asked Johanna. "Let alone have the good fortune to collect them?"

"Many came with my inheritance. As for the others, they seem to be like migrating birds and prefer to stay together."

"I wager there is no other library like yours in the whole world," she said.

"It is nothing compared to the ones I knew in Rome."

Johanna and Halbert spoke at the same time. "Rome?"

"You have actually been to the Eternal City?"

"The simplest libraries in Rome make my humble hall look like a hovel."

"No, sire. Yours is wondrous place. A treasure."

"It is a dangerous place for a girl child," Sergius replied, softly. "Books were written for man."

"But were not the wisdom in books written for all?"

"Johanna," said Halbert, warning with his eyes. He turned to their host. "Even crawling as a child she'd leave no mystery alone."

"Learning can turn a curious maiden into a conjuring woman," said Sergius. "Surely, even as a pagan you know this."

"We do not share your faith, true. But can't learning do the same to a man?"

"Knowledge is a forked road for any who dare take it," he acknowledged. Johanna saw an opening, but instinctively felt it was safer to frame her opinion as a question.

"And many who dare will fall by the wayside if their hearts are foolish or dark, whether man or woman, is that fair to say?"

His reply made them sit up in their chairs.

"I know you deny it, but the fact is this, and may you mark these words as true. For a noble woman it is different, but as a peasant your life will end violently should your knowledge of the written word be revealed outside these walls. It is witchcraft to all but men and the high-born. If you ever forget this, the flame, the rope, or the stone will come to remind you."

He sat back and let the message sink in. "You argue well on a full belly," he said, softly. "My mind is lazy after food. I must be hungry to debate."

He stood and they followed suit, Halbert fumbling with his crutch. Sergius took a flaming rushlight and led them from the room down a long and high-ceilinged corridor, pitch black except for the flickering flame of the torch.

"You are troubled?" asked Sergius gently, as if sharp words had never left his mouth.

"Your kindness helps," said Halbert. "If we had paid enough to sail to Rome, my heart would be soaring right now."

"Rome, yes, I long to return. Even now I wait for my call to serve. It may come any day, if my prayers are answered."

Halbert looked at Sergius with a renewed awe, in the presence of one who had actually stood on the hallowed grounds of the Eternal City. "Please tell me about the city."

"May I take my leave, sir?" Johanna was several steps behind them. Halbert admonished her with a look. "I wish to sleep, if I may."

"Certainly. My stories have little use for youth. A servant will lead your way."

"Thank you, but I know the way, sir," she said and took a torch from the wall.

"Good night, love," said Halbert and kissed her forehead.

"May you both enjoy Rome, if even in your mind's-eye," she said and curtsied. She walked down the corridor. Sergius held the taper above his head so that she might have more light to find her way.

"Rome is much like a woman, beautiful to observe, lithe and propelled with life and filled with fiery energies not unlike flesh itself. She is often rude and quarrelsome and yet supple, sensuous in spite of herself. She is a mystery one desires to seize upon, to press her breasts to one's own, to cover her with kisses until she submits."

"And the libraries?" asked Halbert.

"Come," said Sergius. "I have some excellent mead from the Frankish monks that will smooth out my ragged tales."

The men continued down the hall, Sergius' sputtering flame barely lighting the way.

≈ ≈ ≈

Johanna blew the candle out and glanced behind her. She walked quickly through now-familiar passageways, feeling her way along moist, slippery walls in the dark and easing her feet out in front of her to search for the tricky step, moving in silence, alert for servants.

At a large door she slipped the bolt up, careful to hold onto the cloth she had earlier placed between it and the latch to keep it from locking. She entered, quietly sliding the door closed behind her. A long fireplace ran the length of the north wall, and at the hearth Johanna bent down to the glowing remains of the fire. She took the thick candle from her robe and placed the wick on top of an ember, blowing on it until a flame appeared. She held the tip out toward the room, casting light on the sleeping library.

"Virgil. Pliny. Horace. Plato," she said, astonished as her fingers caressed the book bindings. Like a child in a pastry kitchen, she went from shelf to shelf, marveling, tasting and browsing before settling down with the main course.

Soon she was completely engrossed as she had been every night of their stay. Exploring the ancient texts were the only times she was spared from thinking of Adrian. Safe in the depths of concentration and away from the hurt in her heart, she did not notice the figure slip into the room and crouch behind the tapestry at the far door. The night wore on and she was too consumed in the philosophies of the Greeks and the brilliant mathematical treatises of the Persians to be aware of the presence lingering close by in the darkness. The Watcher stayed in the far shadows of the room, observing what had become her nightly excursion. Johanna had charted a course through worlds whose cartography few except the most learned had ever mapped and whose borders extended beyond physical shores. But as she plotted her way along new landmarks, the seeker of secrets was about to discover a land so dark that no map or book could reveal its whereabouts.

# CHAPTER XI

JOHANNA JOLTED AWAKE in the middle of the night to a violently ill Halbert. She poured a bowl of water from the pitcher and pressed a wet rag to his head. His teeth chattered, his lips were purplish and a fiery heat emanated from him.

"Too much mead," he said. "I will never drink it again."

"I remember those very words the last time you drank it," she chided nervously, wiping the cloth over his forehead. Both knew it was more than drink ripping through Halbert's body.

"The gods! Like knives slashing my guts!"

"I have to find a physician."

"No, Johanna. Stay with me, please? Don't leave."

She stayed holding Halbert. He groaned but did not get worse. The sun rose and he slipped into an uneasy sleep, while other sounds registered above her worried heart. She went to the door and was met by the ringing of bells across the grounds.

Servants rushed by carrying crates stacked with equipment and supplies. Wagons and pack mules were led from barns to the center of the grounds. Johanna came out and caught sight of the stammering boy struggling with his stubborn donkey.

"Boy. What's happened?" she said, running up to him.

"H-h-he has b-been c-called."

"Called? Where?"

"To Rome!"

Startled, she turned. Sergius, waving a scroll, hurried toward her from the manor. "I've waited years for this day."

"I'm glad your prayers have been answered," she said. "But my father --"

Sergius turned away when he spotted four men pulling a wagon to the library door. He stepped up and struck a young man across the face so hard he fell to the ground.

"You fools. The largest wagons for my books. They are more valuable than a hundred of your lives."

"The floor should be lined with fabric," Johanna offered. "Or skins, better still."

The suggestion cut through his anger and was exactly what was needed.

"Yes. Line the bottom with the thickest skins from the winter room," he commanded.

"We will depart at your wish, sire."

"But your father is not well," he said. On her surprised look, he explained. "He drank much last night. No matter. Come."

Sergius walked across the grounds and into their room. He went straight to Halbert.

"Halbert, I leave for Rome tomorrow," he said and kneeled beside the ill man.

"Rome?"

"And you must join me."

"I . . ." began Halbert, confused.

"Listen," Sergius said, close to Halbert's face, his chin whiskers a white rope on the cot. "A year from now, by the grace of God, we will arrive in Rome and I will be confirmed as a bishop. I will give you a post in one of the libraries. What say you? The only wandering left for you will be to spend your days in the heart of learning."

"So much to consider," Halbert replied, overwhelmed. Johanna was behind Sergius, her mouth open at the proposition.

"For the sojourn, Johanna will be my library's guardian."

This second news struck as astounding as the first.

"I need someone who loves my scriptoria as much as I do. No one in my household but Johanna is fit for the job. I know of her love for them, and she knows their value."

"My father," broke in Johanna. "Is not fit for travel."

"I will leave my personal physician to attend you. The rest of the household follows in a week," said Sergius, his gaze wholly on Halbert. "Recuperate, then you be in charge of the second caravan to Rome."

"Let me stay back with the library. We'll leave together when he's well."

"The library is my greatest treasure. It must travel with me."

"Perhaps you could wait until he is better?"

"I've waited five years. There are no tomorrows left."

"I need ...I have to consider," Halbert began.

"What more is needed?" said Sergius and stood. "I have laid at your feet the most incredible opportunity of your lives, and you humiliate my offer? I withdraw it. Tomorrow I leave at dawn."

He wheeled, his cloak circling the air, and was gone. Johanna and Halbert searched each other's eyes.

What was the poisonous gamble they were even thinking about? She knew that if they turned this chance aside without consideration they were doomed to forever regret not attempting Halbert's dream of Rome. With a nod they could escape this sour and mystifying land. She could find Adrian there and her father's heart would finally have peace. But to separate? Johanna's neck chilled at the possibility.

"An impossible risk," said Halbert. "We cannot take it."

"Yes, you need to get well."

"It is not that. It's too dangerous."

"Yes, Father. Much too dangerous."

Could he face life without Johanna? He looked into the intense blue-green of her eyes. Could he survive not knowing if she was alive or dead? He stroked the plain of her flushed cheek, his thumb tracing the last of her girlish freckles, fading with her childhood. She kissed his palm. No. Never. They cannot part.

Johanna thought of Adrian crying at the rail of the ship and knew she could not live if she lost both men. No. They dare not contemplate such a risk.

"Johanna," he began, shaking his head. "The dangers."

"I will not leave you alone here, father."

But the treasure of what might be theirs kept coming back. What a colossal prize. If they took this one chance, they could be finished with this wretched island forever.

She looked at Halbert. The skin on his face had a gray pallor, but she could see his mind turning over the possibilities. *We should not do this,* her mind screamed. What if he doesn't recuperate? What if he follows and is met by bandits or storms or a disease that strikes him down on the road to Rome? She already lost Adrian and would never forgive herself if she lost her father.

"I don't want to lose you," he said.

But Rome was such a powerful vision it bloomed as one thought in both their minds. A present so beautiful and wrapped in hopes, trimmed with so many promises that neither father nor daughter could actually guess what was inside the package.

"Johanna," he began.

"Yes?"

Halbert did not speak again for a full five minutes. Bells from the manor's chapel rang out with an irritating metallic peal. The sound rose alongside the frantic voices of servants scurrying across the grounds. Father and daughter listened to the discordant chimes ring around the room, as loud and raucous as the thoughts ringing in their heads.

Halbert leaned back, sighed, then closed his eyes.

"Go," he said, finally. "Go catch up with our dreams."

Before she let herself have a second to think, Johanna dashed out the door and ran as fast as she could across the estate. Flinging off every argument with each step, she called Sergius' name, disregarding the crowd of suspicions chasing behind her, running at her heels, pursuing her across the green lawn, their warnings grasping at her back, her hair, her dress. All trying to make her stand still and listen to them.

Johanna spotted Sergius and raced toward him. He was chastising the stuttering red-headed boy who held tight to his donkey.

"Sergius!" she called, her voice so high it was a shriek.

Sergius heard her voice and stopped admonishing the boy. He cocked his head slightly to one side, though he remained turned away, as the footsteps ran toward him. He waited for her to rush breathlessly to his side, knowing Johanna could not see the smile spread across and crease his face.

# CHAPTER X

THE FOLLOWING DAWN the courtyard of the estate was filled with over forty covered carriages, carts, and wagons readied for transport. Each vehicle was stacked high with tables, chairs, furnishings, crated equipment, rakes, scythes, hammers, wine, wheat, and mead, with all the food in burlap sacks for the animals and people who belonged to Sergius. The Herculean effort kept nearly one hundred servants up at a frenetic pace and filled the manor with voices shouting orders and threats the entire night.

"Thief," cried a cook, her fat body covered entirely in a greasy sheen from her labors. She held a thin scullery maid by a lank yellow hair and pulled the chicken out from under the girl's arm. "If I tell master, this bird'll be picking at yer eyes when yer head rolls across the yard."

"An' believe me I'll have your head as a playmate," said the girl, wrenching free from the big woman. She turned, pointed a finger and fixed the cook with a glare. "After I show master the food bin you made to horde supplies away these two years."

The two squared off. Arguments continued all night throughout the manor and pushed the exhausted household to its limit. Room after room was cleared until the estate was hauntingly empty. The floors were trashed with debris and the hollow rooms sat silent in the brittle light of morning.

But everything was ready when the sun crept wearily over the forest, its weak rays unable to heat the dark bottoms of the clouds.

"You're sure that's the last of it?" asked Johanna.

Her young assistant, the stammering red-haired boy, nodded. She supervised the last books to leave the library, the last stack of books into the wagon, then they both led the vehicle toward the caravan, now stretching from end to end of the manor. She could stand it no longer. Johanna ran across grounds strewn with litter from the frantic night.

Johanna rushed to her father. She had given him herbs to soothe his gut, but Halbert still fought a raging fever.

"Father."

"I love you so much, daughter." he said, holding her tight.

"I can't do it." she cried. "I cannot leave you."

"You will never leave me, sweetheart. No matter how many miles or days we're separated, you'll never leave me and I will never, ever leave you," he said and lifted her face to look in her eyes. "We are joined forever through our souls and will meet in the next world. I will love you forever, long after this life, Johanna."

"I cannot live if we separate. It is too dangerous."

"And our only chance," Halbert began, but stopped, his eyes over her shoulder. She followed his gaze and saw Sergius' silhouette in the doorway. She rushed to him.

"Please, let me follow in a few days when he is well," she pleaded, and fell to his feet and kissed the hem of his robe.

"The library's value surpasses ten kingdoms, ten thousand treasures."

"I will guard it with my life," she promised.

"It cannot stay," he said, shaking his head, his voice full of sympathy. He gently stroked her hair. She turned back to her father, her arms around Halbert's neck, tears wetting his face.

"My physician assures me he will recover soon," said Sergius. "He will follow and join us in a few days."

"I'm staying," said Johanna. "I've changed my mind."

"If you so choose, fine," said Sergius. "I will find someone else."

"And we can follow when he is well?"

"I am afraid that is not the bargain. But how about this, Halbert? We'll have to wait three days on the far shore to gather more supplies. If you feel better tomorrow, take the ship that crosses over and join us."

"I will stay with you, father," said Johanna.

"Go," Halbert said to her, finally. He forced a smile at Johanna. "I will follow you tomorrow, I swear. Don't worry."

"That is good and best," said Sergius.

"Father, I love you, I don't want this."

Sergius bent and took her arm, pulling her gently to her feet.

"We must reach the shore before nightfall. Halbert will be fine."

Sergius walked her to the door. It now seemed inconceivable that they could ever have agreed to such a proposition. Why in the world did they say yes?

Daughter and father locked gazes in a final look.

"Father..." she began, but Sergius gently pulled her arms from the doorway and led her off.

$$\approx \approx \approx$$

The long caravan of wagons, peasants, animals, and possessions rolled slowly through the gate. Johanna's wagons were at the end, the last to leave. Sergius led the procession on horseback, stopping out of sight of her at the main gate. He signaled a mounted guard who came forward with several indentured servants in the livery of Sergius' household. They followed the mounted guard, approached his horse and got on their knees before their master.

"You who remain are hereby released from my service. You are free to fill your hearts with the love of Jesus Christ." Sergius paused to listen to their murmured amazement. "But not to fill your pockets with my property. An armed party arrives tonight, and if your actions are otherwise, if one rag is missing, you will be taken in irons and will follow my ship to Rome, bound to me for another seven years. That is if you survive the journey below in the ship's hold with the vermin."

He paused to watch several in the group visibly cringe at the thought. "God bless your sinful souls."

Then, seemingly as an afterthought, he said, "Oh, and see that the pagan is treated well, he has my blessings for giving his daughter to me as a gift."

He raised his hand and signaled the caravan. A horn was blown, high-pitched and shrill, piercing the cold morning air. The wagons moved out amid yelling, slapping fights and the prodding of asses, horses, pigs, cows, sheep, chickens, and other animals, plus over a dozen crying, irritated babies jostled from sleep.

Long after the weak sun had passed mid-day, Johanna's wagon finally passed through the estate's main gate. The caravan stretched down the road before her, wending around forests and meadows all the way to the edge of the coastline.

She looked back, eyes red, and whispered. "Hurry."

Hours later, miles down the road at the crest of a hill, the mounted guard who was party to Sergius' warning to the remaining servants, watched the last of the caravan cross the rocky beach and load their cargo into waiting dinghies to sail for a ship moored in the bay. The guard turned his horse and raced back, digging his heels into the animal's sides.

The sun had set by the time he reached the estate. He rode the horse into the courtyard at a full gallop. The anxious servants ran up to him for news. The guard took out his sword and rode up the stairs of the manor's entranceway. He whirled the blade over his head and smashed Sergius' coat-of-arms, striking it off its mount where it clattered to the ground.

"The evil one takes his curse to Rome! Praise God we are free!"

He reared the horse and when it came down it trampled the shield. A heartfelt cheer went up from Sergius' remaining household. Many wept openly while others broke out in a spontaneous dance where they stood, as if the hand of hell itself had been lifted from their souls.

Halbert drifted in and out of a black sleep the whole day and into night. When he finally awoke he found himself slightly dizzy, but cool and the stabbing pains in his belly were gone. He

*The Woman Pope*

got up, splashed his face from his bowl and marveled at his good health, and suddenly thought to catch the ship.

Halbert had feared their decision was a greedy illusion, but this miraculous turn proved they were not foolish to serve their dreams and he would soon be with his daughter again.

He reached for his sack of belongings, vaguely aware of the noise and commotion in the doorway. He turned and was met with an avalanche of hands grabbing him, pulling him from the room.

"Bring him to the fire!" boomed a voice behind Halbert.


A bonfire blazed in the courtyard. Servants staggered around it drinking from cases of bad wine Sergius had thrown out, guzzling the vinegary brew. Two drunk stable men raced to consume an entire bottle apiece to the encouragement of the crowd and immediately one sprayed the contents of his stomach across a row of howling onlookers. Wild Celtic music played at a gallop on pipes, drums, horns and gut-stringed harps.

Dragged across the grounds, Halbert saw many servants in the grass at the edge of the fire's light, coupling openly on the manicured lawn. He saw women bent over while standing, hands on their knees, skirts flipped up onto their back, or on all fours on the ground, digging their fingers into the earth and yelping with abandon, panting in ecstasy while drunken men worked be-hind them, grunting and braying as they clasped themselves against the hips lustily bared before them.

Halbert looked upon the scene and knew he was going to die. Every scrap of furniture, remnant of clothing, anything of value Sergius had left behind had been stacked at the fire, ready to be taken away by the freed servants. They now understood that his last words were more lies; he was never returning and the people were suddenly without a governor for the first time in memory. A delirium ran through the estate as Halbert was pushed toward the fire.

"The good priest has left you in our care," yelled a man, who then yanked on Halbert's nose and laughed. Four men carried a large, crude cross to the fire made from timbers twice as tall as a man. Halbert was thrown down on it and his arms and legs lashed to the wood with leather strips.

"Why do you do this?" Halbert yelled.

"Why do you sell your daughter to a whoremonger?" a woman spat back in his face.

"Whoremonger?" No, we follow him next week! Johanna is the keeper of his books."

He was drowned out by laughter. Once secured, he was lifted up by several men and, borne aloft, strapped like Christ to a cross of wood, Halbert was carried to the flames.

"Prepare the way to hell for your master," said another man. Halbert understood that his life was their vengeance. The crowd bellowed its delight, whirling with the music like madmen and women in the hot bright light of the crackling bonfire, waving their hands and dancing in a harsh and jerky way, not a joyful celebration, but filled with bitterness. Without knowing why, Halbert sent a prayer -- not to any of the gods Gilberta had introduced him to, but to the first god of his youth, Jehovah. *Lord, Whom I have forsaken, please do not let me die without seeing Johanna again*, he prayed.

The crowd began to chant.

"Haul him up! Haul him up! Haul him up!"

Two men tied rope at the sides of the cross, then moved to either side of the fire. Two other drunken cross-bearers tried positioning the end of the cross in the midst of the roaring flames, but the fire was too hot and made the cross impossible to maneuver, as it was for the rope bearers who got too close to the heat to hoist the stake.

"You idiots. Should have let us put him up before you lit the stupid fire," cursed one of the drunken cross-men, stumbling on his feet. "Give us lads some more rope!"

"I am dead," cried Halbert. The flames leapt at his feet, his legs, singeing his habit, the smoke and fire blazed in high, lapping orange fingers.

In the dark, near the front gate, a woman was on her hands and knees, being taken from behind by her sister's husband

*The Woman Pope*

when, over the groans of the man, she heard the sound of approaching horses and a wagon. To her partner's dismay she pulled away and scrambled to her feet, frightened.

"Sergius' guard," she said, thinking the priest had kept his word and sent an armed party to inspect the property.

Four men galloped into the courtyard followed by a man and a horse-drawn wagon. The woman ran naked into the dark, leaving the man holding his unfinished business in his hand as a rider pulled his horse up to him.

"You, what's going on here?" the rider demanded. There was shame on the half naked man's face. He pulled at his leggings and ran into the dark clutching himself.

"What are you doing?"

The leader was a young knight armored with a dented breastplate that had been painted with a subdued forest green coat-of-arms. He took in the sight at the bonfire and his bushy eyebrows rose and his black eyes widened in outrage.

"Stop this!" he yelled at the people nearest Halbert.

He kicked his horse, its hooves throwing back clumps of grass and earth as it ran. He grabbed a rope from a cross-bearer as he rode by. Easing the stake back down, he laid Halbert on the ground to the immediate howl of protest from the drunken revelers. The knight pulled out his sword and chased away the drunken rope men. He rode into the crowd, then leapt from the horse unafraid of the bloodlust in the eyes of the people.

"The son of Louis the Pious," a voice said. Others recognized the rider and backed away. All went quiet.

"You'd crucify a man? What evil have you taken to your hearts? Why have you replaced one tyranny with another?" the mustachioed soldier demanded. His long dark hair was damp with sweat, his high, balding forehead glistening in the firelight. He swung the sword and hacked Halbert's bindings off. The crowd murmured as he called for water and when one of his men brought a filled bucket to him, he took the ladle and helped Halbert drink.

"We renounce Sergius' faith," ventured a voice. "The faith of Lucifer!"

"The pagan sold his daughter into slavery," came another. The crowd's anger rose again. The soldier's guards got off their mounts.

"Never," said Halbert. "Sergius said we'd follow him to Rome. He said the rest of his household would leave next week."

"Who'd believe a fool lie like that?" scoffed a hawk-nosed woman. Calls of disbelief flew around the fire, their hatred of Sergius revived.

"Nothing follows that evil priest but darkness," said the knight. "He sold this land, sold his servants and sold his title to my family, and we were glad to see the demon go."

Halbert's face blanched upon hearing his worst fears spoken.

"But he's taken my daughter. He's cheated our lives! Please. I have got to find her!"

He tried to raise himself up but was stopped by the soldier's gentle hand. The knight called to his man driving the wagon.

The old man looked up at his name, doffing his wool hat in respect.

"Simon. Carry this man with you on your wagon when you sail to the monastery."

He signaled his men and Halbert was lifted, carried over and set down in the wagon. Halbert felt the cool wood of the wagon's planks against his skin in sharp contrast to the heat of the cross. The soldier got up onto the wagon bed beside him and faced the crowd.

"Listen to me. You know who I am. I came because I received word that your tormentor is finally gone. You are now under the protection of my family. Take this time to live as a free people, to treat each other as you wish to be treated. Have you forgotten what the Gospels proclaim? It's the only way to escape the bondage that has held you."

The soldier knelt down to Halbert.

"Simon will get you to the shore where Sergius landed. I apologize for these people but their lives have been cheated as well. They have been enslaved by him for years."

"Thank you for my life, friend," said Halbert, clasping the man's arm in gratitude. "What's your name that I might spread word of your kindness?"

"My name is Louis, and I am the unrecognized son of Louis the Pious. I was not a fit heir to my grandfather," he said. Then he looked out on the crowd. "Until tonight."

"Who was your grandfather?"

"The greatest soldier since Arthur," he said, eyes flashed proudly. "Charlemagne."

The name was legendary, even to Halbert. Louis jumped down from the wagon, called by the crowd hungry for more. Knowing no other way, the people wanted to be led again. The old farmer Simon drove toward the gate and Halbert watched the crowd gather around Louis. Several knelt at the soldier's feet in awe, as if he were a holy man. Halbert turned away from the scene and looked anxiously to the night ahead.

# CHAPTER IX

IN THE HULL of the creaking ship, Johanna put her shoulder next to the stammering donkey boy's, and together they heaved a final wood crate of scrolls into place in the corner. When they stood up he made a funny face to get her to smile, but she could see nothing beyond anguish.

"D-don't worry," he said, tossing his red hair out of his face. "You have much d-d-destiny b-before you."

"How do you know this?" she asked. Though puzzled by the comment, she felt strangely comforted by the freckled-face boy, who simply grinned at her.

"Protectress of knowledge," said Sergius in the doorway, startling them. "Come to my cabin for some well-deserved refreshment."

"I should finish here, my lord."

"Let the boy do it," said Sergius and reached a thin hand out. "We have business."

Sergius led her on deck and paused as he gazed out to sea. His two other ships followed behind in their wake. A full moon had risen on the eastern horizon, a phantasmagoric orange globe furiously lighting the ocean. The lunar craters appeared so large it seemed possible to reach into the pocky canyons and touch their contents. The moon's reflection shot a second time to the three ships by way of its sea mirror, a shimmering beam across the water in a deep, rich amber. The wide rippling stripe stretched over the ocean to the very frame of the vessels and lit up each ship brighter than a hundred lamps.

"Look," said Sergius, pulling her close and putting his arm around her, his eyes widening at the sight. "The moon goddess at the beginning of her reign, aiming her chariot across the night."

Johanna extracted herself and looked at him. "That goddess is from the old religions and not from your faith, is that not so, my lord?"

"You have so much to learn, Johanna."

Once in his cabin he handed her a goblet of mead. She regarded him warily, glancing around the spacious quarters, the stateroom of a royal passenger. It was warmed by a well-stoked brazier beside the bed and by thick rugs on the floor and hung from the walls and ceiling. A large oak bed covered in blankets and richly patterned pillows took up most of the space.

Sergius fingered the ruby clasp at the end of his long white chin whiskers and touched his thick goblet to hers.

"Let us celebrate the wind at our backs," he toasted. "We'll make shore before dawn."

"You spoke of business?"

"Yes. Your meticulous caring for my books. The books you have seen to by day and the same books you have absorbed until late every night since your arrival."

"I've read without ambition, wanting only to reflect upon their wisdom," she replied defensively. She thought she had been so careful.

"I watched you in the library every night. Wisdom would have kept your eyes away."

"I wish you'd speak plainly to me of your business."

"I want to protect you. We share a secret that leaves you vulnerable if discovered."

"I have no fear of that."

"If one word escapes, you die a witch."

"Would you hold that word against me?"

"No. But we must stay close in order to keep the danger of discovery at bay."

"Your silence is all the weapon needed."

He stepped close and stood next to her. She fought what was rising inside, tried to keep the panic down.

"Drink. It is excellent mead, as your father knew."

"I am sure it is," she said and raised the goblet to her lips. But as she looked into the liquid, several horrible truths suddenly reared up out of the depths of the glass: Halbert's illness was that of a man poisoned -- Halbert had drunk with Sergius last night. Without seeing him, Sergius had known of his sickness, then Sergius' refusal to let them follow later when he was well. She set the glass down on a stool and shook her head, backing toward the door.

"I'm very weary. I must take my leave."

"Your leave is here. This is where you sleep."

"I sleep alone, thank you," she said weakly, turning the door handle. It was unlocked.

"I have been patient until now, but you understand me quite well. Come, I want you ready for bed."

She whirled around, all fear drained away and replaced with anger.

"If you think I --"

His hand came across the side of her face. It struck with such force her head whipped to one side and filled with a mad ringing, like the screech of a giant hawk in her ear. Sergius took her by both arms, dropping his cup to the floor.

"I own your secret," he said as his long fingernails dug into the soft flesh of her upper arms. "And it will be paid for tonight or you will be dead before we reach land."

"Don't do this, please."

He smiled and pushed her back hard, slamming her head into the wall. Colors flashed across her eyes and she could barely hear over the din in her head. Sergius remained serene, his only arousal the steady gaze of his eyes fastened onto her, studying her every reaction.

"From the day you attacked me on the village road -- yes, I was on that donkey, laughing at two filthy stumbling beggars -- I had to see you broken like a young mare and to ride you, to make you unfold your innocence unto me."

He swung his fist into her stomach and the punch dropped her to the floor. He took her by the arms and lifted her to her feet while he whispered in her ear.

*The Woman Pope*

"Johanna of my books, listen carefully. You are about to revel in what I will teach you. You will learn and grow far beyond what I give you tonight. You are going to become the consort of the man who will one day become pope. You will see that my bed is a small price for your life. You have been chosen for the grandest luxury and to enjoy more knowledge than a thousand men ever collect in their lifetimes."

She gasped for breath with all her might but was unable to bring it into her lungs. Sergius carried her to the bed and tipped himself over on her and again forced the air out of her as they toppled onto the pillows. He pulled up her dress and placed his body between her legs. Sergius exerted little effort in avoiding her weak blows and went at her with the detached curiosity of an indifferent surgeon with a saw.

"You will not take me," she gasped, finally sucking air into her lungs. His face was just inches above hers.

"Johanna, I have already taken you."

He suddenly swung his fist and struck her across the head so hard she lost consciousness.

Sergius eased back and raised himself up onto his knees on the bed. He pulled his robe up to his waist. Wearing nothing underneath, he exposed his uncircumcised penis above her limp body. It was taper-thin and long like the rest of him, pulsing faintly yet still down-turned, partially flaccid as its pointy tip wagged along his thigh. His pubis was a gray tuft close to the skin like the cropped hair on his head.

Johanna came to, woozy, nauseated, her mouth bleeding.

Sergius took hold of himself and squeezed the slow-responding shaft. He coaxed it shrewdly until the head crowned the foreskin. His eyes glazed over and he was unconcerned with Johanna, focused only on the sensations he brought to himself.

She roused slightly. Her eyes focused and fixed on a brazier at the bedside. The hot coals glowed in the metal bowl and warmed a bottle of wine. She reached for it.

Sergius' hand came across her face and struck again. Her head was thrown in the other direction.

"I will be the first to widen your shores," he said as the thrill of his violence rushed to his penis. It inflated it to a purplish red and rose to fullness in his hand.

"When you are ready," he said, his breath thickening, "others will take their enjoyment from you, and I will be there as witness to your pleasure of them."

Sergius readied himself, holding up his robe. In the dim light he was a black-hooded silhouette above her, only the flash of eyes pierced out from a skull.

"With this knowledge, you will never look back."

He lowered himself, pressing his belly to hers and positioned his penis to enter her. With experienced fingers he located the sealed mouth of her hymen and placed the tip of his cock to it. He pushed. She screamed and arched on her heels to resist the penetration. Flinging her arm to the side of the bed, she reached again for the brazier and this time grabbed a fist-sized red-hot coal. Sergius saw the move and tried to stop her arm, but with all her strength she forced her hand between his legs and pressed its burning contents to the sack of his scrotum.

His scream ripped across the room.

He tried to leap away, but she took hold of his braided chin whiskers with her other hand and pulled his face close as she pressed her coal-hand to his genitals with all her might, searing the flesh on them both.

"Burn, devil," she hissed in his ear.

He rolled away, and Johanna clung tight to him. They tumbled off the bed in a heap. He screamed again then struck and knocked her into the wall. He rolled on the floor kicking his legs in a fit, his hands buried between his legs. A thin smoke rose up around him and the smell of charcoal and seared flesh hung in the air. Johanna got up, stumbled against the wall and looked at her hand, black with ash and mottled with blood.

Two servants burst through the door and rushed to Sergius. Johanna ran out of the room. He rolled over and pointed.

"Bind that witch before she kills us all!"


She reached topside and ran across the deck, passing sleepy servants awakened by the screams. She arrived at the stern and looked around and knew there was no place left to go. Over the side in the moonlit waters, Johanna saw an object floating on the surface of the water and she strained to make it out.

A dinghy bobbed far behind the ship, held by a lone rope. Quickly, the fingers of her unburned hand found where it was tied at the rail and she worked to unfasten it. She got the first knot loose, pulled at the second final one, loosened it to free it from --

She was spun around. Enraged with pain, Sergius stood before her as four hands came on either side and took her.

"She cast a spell and called sea demons up from the deep to devour us. Captain, have her brought to the main mast."

He took a broadsword from a servant-guard and pulled it from its sheath. The blade flashed like a silver bolt of lightning in the moonlight.

Sergius staggered toward the mast but half way there dropped to his knees in agony. Servants rushed to help, but he roared curses at them. Johanna glanced at her captors. One was Sergius' servant monk, Gaetani, and the other was the stammering boy.

"Help me. Let me die, but not from his hand. I beg you. Kill me. Kill me now," she pleaded.

"S-s-she's innocent," whispered the red-haired boy.

"She's a witch, fool," said Gaetani. "Don't listen to her."

"B-be brave, girl. All your sorrows will p-pass soon," the boy said.

"Bring her to me," bellowed Sergius.

They approached and the servants formed a wide semi-circle in front of her, afraid of the witch. Johanna faced Sergius and stopped struggling, became still.

"Hold out her arms."

Gaetani and the boy spread her arms open. Sergius scowled in pain and lifted his robe, his skinny legs parted to let the breeze cool his blistered parts. He breathed in short, wheezing gulps. The Captain of the ship, a grizzled Norman, stepped forward.

"Sire, wait. This is my ship and I give orders on the lives on board," he said and turned to the gathered crowd. "This is a decision for –"

The man suddenly dropped to his knees, his mouth a stunned question, then he fell to his face on deck, his spine sliced from the blow of Sergius' sword. The crowd stepped back and watched the Captain convulse and die before them.

"And I tell you this is Satan's ship. A devil has taken this woman and if you want to live you will listen!"

Every eye went to Sergius and felt the chill of his words.

"Her charms lulled me. She read spells from a book to inflame a black lust in me. Look at me! Do you see? She took my manhood into her devil's mouth and burned it with hell fire. I almost died. But the spirit of Christ called out. He revived me. Jesus Christ Himself spoke to me, said, 'The power of God prevails. Make His Strength come through your blade and you will save your people!'"

"Liar," muttered the boy. Sergius raised the sword over his head. Johanna felt warmth spread within her, as if a lantern the size of a bonfire had been ignited inside her chest, illuminating her blood and bones, her brain and soul. Despite her imminent death, Johanna was filled with a serenity that overwhelmed her fear.

She gladly gave in to the sensation. It filled her so full she had to open her eyes and smile at Sergius. It was a smile of such complete and disarming tenderness he was momentarily unnerved by it. He paused, shaken. Then he made his final pronouncement.

"In the name of Jesus Christ, to whose Power you must submit, I command you to die, devil. Die and leave my people alone. Die and flee back to the black bowels of hell from where you came."

He raised the sword over his head with both hands, then swung straight down to cleave her in half.

The instant the blade began its downward arc, the boy yanked Johanna's arm, pulling her from the grasp of the other man. The sword sliced air and dug deep into the deck.

"She's no witch, just as you have never been our master! All of you know it's true!" yelled the boy. He spoke without the trace of a stammer. "Run, Johanna."

He took Johanna's hand and raced for the stern. The stunned crowd stood there.

"She has bewitched him. Get them," said Sergius, pointing. The servants were baffled and looked at one another until he screamed again. "Go or stand in her place!"

He swung the blade a second time.

This time the heavy broadsword met the neck of the scrawny blond scullery maid who had fought the fat cook over the stolen chicken. The blade passed through skin, flesh, tendon, artery, bone and barely slowed, lifting her head from her neck with the ease of a scythe cutting a stalk of wheat. The scullery maid's surprised head teetered on her neck a moment, then tipped forward and hit the deck and rolled. When it came to a stop the eyes were blinking, the mouth was open and the teeth chattered as if feeling a sudden cold from the separation. Servants screamed and leaped out of the way of the girl's trunk which stood in place, a fountain of blood gushing from her neck, motionless except for the hands at her side opening and closing into fists that clutched at the air before her body collapsed onto the deck.

Johanna and the boy ran to the aft railing then turned back to the main deck. The crowd followed Sergius slowly, fearing the extent of Johanna's supernatural powers. They had seen her smile at Sergius and had never witnessed such an expression, worn as a shield at the moment of execution. It had more power than Sergius' blade and the look on his face proved it to every witness there.

"The dinghy," Johanna said, remembering the little boat. The boy followed her where she had untied the rope.

She had done her work too well. It was gone. The dinghy would be floating far away by now. The boy saw her slump and knew any escape was lost. He touched her shoulder.

"We go to God tonight. But by our own hands. Hurry, girl," said her young deliverer. She took his hand and winced when he squeezed. Blood smeared their palms as if joining them in a bond.

"You'd die for a stranger? Who are you, boy?" she said.

"Not afraid to die is who I am. My name is John. Go, while God gives me courage."

"John. It shames me to say how much I've hated Christians."

"Judge nothing until the end. I am told that God calls us both. Farewell, Johanna," he said and kissed her cheek.

"Farewell, John. You are a true Christian," she said, returning the kiss on his cheek. "May your god give you rest in his heaven."

She turned and jumped from the rail.

Johanna fell through the air so slowly it was like gliding on a feather down, down, down for the longest time. She looked up at the night and stars and noted that Orion had moved in its path since she had last seen it. She wondered where that spectacular full moon was. Had its orange skin been peeled away upon its rise? How had it gotten so late? What did John mean when he said he was told god called them both? She suddenly gasped, embraced by a wet explosion as Johanna was swallowed by the cold dark sea.

John put his foot up on the rail to follow, and stopped short. He looked down at his belly and watched in surprise as the entire length of a long broadsword shot out from his stomach. He saw moonlight gleam up at him from the bloody blade.

Behind him, Sergius pulled the sword out of the boy's back. John turned, fell across the railing and faced Sergius and the crowd. The pain was so great on the boy's tortured face that it was a chilling tableau for all who saw it.

Sergius plunged the sword in again, this time between the child's ribs. John shook with convulsions, then stopped. He died clinging to the rail in wordless agony.

"Two demons dead," said Sergius. He turned his bloody blade toward the servants. "But there are more aboard this ship."

The three ships sailed into the night, lit by the fast-descending moon. The freed dinghy bobbed along far astern, drifting away, rocking in the sea, nonplussed by the sounds of horror that came from the lead ship and echoed off the two following vessels.

The dinghy floated with its nose pointed at Sergius' ship as if quietly observing the madness on board. Lanterns on the ship's deck swayed with movement and cast long, exaggerated silhouettes of the terrorized servants across the sails, making them look like giant shadow puppets. The main mast shivered, then the entire ship yawed violently from port to starboard and back. The servants, chased across the deck by Sergius, were jagged shadows of raised arms and jerking heads projected against the sail in the lantern light. They ran screaming from one end of the ship to the other trying to avoid his broadsword. But it kept striking again and again and would not stop. The little dinghy drifted behind the last vessel for a few moments, then slowly left the light of the lanterns, slipping into the darkness, bobbing restlessly.

# PART 2
## CHAPTER XII

TWO MONKS WERE returning from the village market and walked the rocky shore along the rugged coast of France. One carried a sack filled with crabs and mussels, the other monk a net bag stuffed with fish slung over his shoulder. A breeze blew onto shore thick with salt and the smell of kelp. One brother, seeing a usable piece of driftwood at a tide pool, picked up the wood then noticed similar pieces floating in the wash of water. He climbed gingerly behind the rocks and saw they belonged to the wreckage of a small boat. When he got into the swirling tide water, he dropped his bag.

"*Mon Dieu.*"

He watched a body facedown on the sand a few feet from him, half in, half out of the water. He called to his companion and the two men hauled the figure onto the beach.

"This poor girl," sighed the first monk. "She's dead."

"The abbot will want to know who she is," said the second.

They crossed themselves, blessed her, and hoisted the body onto their shoulders, leaving their bags on the rocks. They headed for the monastery in the distance, a large ancient villa built high into the steep hillside above, overlooking the ocean.

≈ ≈ ≈

Several monks gathered around the table where Johanna had been laid out. They looked gravely on the form hidden beneath a woolen sheet. The Abbot entered and was deferentially acknowledged by the brothers. A serene man with a tonsured head of wiry, bowl-cut hair, he had an unlined, wide face. The leader of the monastery owned the saddest, most gentle brown eyes any man there had ever seen, lingering beneath two wild bushy hedges of eyebrows. He briefly peered under the sheet. His lips tightened and he shook his head.

"She's not from the village and is unknown in the outlying hamlets," said the monk who found her.

"Prepare her to rest in the cemetery," said the Abbot. A young monk, his cheeks ravaged with deep red pits from a long bout of acne, stepped forward.

"But we know nothing about her, father," he said, incredulous at the nonchalance around him. The pimpled skin flushed an even brighter red. "What of the transgressions or maliciousness in her heart? She may have taken her own life, or the lives of others. She may have performed demonic acts."

The Abbot smiled and put a fatherly arm around the excited young monk.

"If we did not know you, son, and you were found without your robes, would you have us assume that of you? Would you have us bury you with the outcast? Or would you hope we would err on the side of mercy and let you rest with the saved? Bennito," he said, turning to a middle-aged monk. "Put this poor child to rest."

The monks nodded at the elder's wisdom and followed him out, leaving brother Bennito alone with the corpse. The little monk rolled up his sleeves and pulled back the sheet.

"So young," he sighed. He viewed a bluish, still Johanna, naked on the table. Bennito had to turn away, clasping his hands in prayer and closing his eyes.

"Lord, help me," he prayed. Her youthful beauty and nakedness, her smooth skin preserved in the cold water were at odds with his calling. Embarrassment flooded Bennito's long, good-natured face and reached beyond his black hair until it reddened the scalp in his tonsure. He prayed for several minutes before being struck with an inspiration.

"Of course! Thank you, Lord. Why didn't I think of that?"

The simple elegance of the inspiration confirmed everything Bennito believed. He was reminded once again that God provided all that was ever asked of Him. Bennito poured a bowl of water from the pitcher on the preparation table, took a measure of cloth and placed them both on the body table. He dropped a palm-full of aromatic herbs from his robe into the water. He tore several long strips of the cloth and tied the last strip around his eyes. Nodding to himself, satisfied, he dipped another strip in the water and began a ritual bathing of the body, blindfolded.

Starting with her feet and working his way up, Bennito sang his most favored Gregorian chant as he labored, his hands feeling their way along the body like a blind man.

He rinsed the cloth and washed her neck and down the shoulder toward her elbow and back up to her breasts, where his hand paused.

Self-conscious and afraid, still he lingered, feeling the firm roundness in his hand. Three panting breaths later and his fingers were scalded by guilt. He quickly proceeded down her arm to her hand and passed over the burned palm.

Johanna's blistered palm reacted. It clutched the monk's hand. Bennito froze, though a prayer flew from his lips.

"Thank You, Almighty God! Thank you for making the retribution of my sin so swift! Thank you, oh Lord of All!"

Thankful tears fell as he took off the blindfold, ready to submit to the avenging angel who would now take his life.

"Father," Johanna whispered, looking up at him.

"Father!" Bennito screamed at the same time. He pulled his hand away and ran from the room. Johanna's eyes rolled up in her head and she again slipped from consciousness.

≈ ≈ ≈

Johanna lived in a land between dream and consciousness for several days. She was hauled from other-world to other-world with fantastic scenes posted before her in an endless parade.

At the beginning of this state she flew like a great bird over treetops, soaring above a green and unfamiliar countryside. Below she saw a man who could have been Halbert but when he looked up his eyes were as large as melons, clear as glass. She flew high up through a puffy cloud and heard the thunderous buzz of flying insects. Coming out of the cloud she was no longer flying but riding on the ground, jolted and bounced along on the back of a kicking donkey. The beast turned its head to look at her; it had Adrian's face, but older, squinting helplessly into her eyes. He opened his mouth to speak and disappeared.

Suddenly the blue sky before her fell away and was ripped in half down the middle of noon. A wind of gale force sucked her off the animal and Johanna was propelled up into black space, thrown with more velocity than if she had been shot from a bow. She flew through a night sky, a void with stars in the far distance inside an infinite room of the cosmos.

Flying along, it dawned upon her, *I am dead.*

She looked over her shoulder and, even though she was millions of miles from Earth, saw herself drifting slowly down through the murky waters of the English Sea toward the bottom.

She turned from the scene and calmly wondered about her destination as she sped through a realm where every thing, living and inorganic, radiated a higher self.

A colossal red rock crossed her path hundreds of leagues in front of her. As large as the earth, it tumbled slowly in space beside her. She realized the glimmering red on its surface was not just a color. Glowing from inside was an emotional field with a complex life of its own and the color known as "red" had been released from the constraints of human understanding.

She sailed along, aware of being carried and surrounded by beings she could not see.

*Perhaps they are demi-gods*, she told herself. *But I cannot see them, only feel them, and they are nothing like what I was told gods and angels should be.*

She thought about what a god should look like and became frightened. Suddenly, this world she was being carried through meant that everything she had believed could prove to be wrong. *What if these are Christian angels? If this is a Christian heaven, where is Jesus?* she wondered. She looked out on the otherworld before her and saw no golden cities she had heard about nestled in the clouds. *Where are their saints and disciples?*

Instead of the Virgin Mother or archangels, Johanna watched vast sheets of icy white, like frost forming on glass, roll out and streak across her path. These crystalline shapes shot out for hundreds of thousands of leagues, forming geometric, dimensional images on the canvas of space. Johanna felt these images had a life beyond the patterns they made, that they were living things. As they raced by her, each one had its own size and distinguishing marks, colors, family, history, and intent.

*Just as I picture an idea forming,* she told herself. These ice-sheet creatures were so old Johanna instinctively knew they came from the murky beginnings of the universe

The sheets continued to frost themselves across the vast room of space. She remembered the ideas and concepts Plato and Pythagoras described in the scrolls, but these knitted sheets were different. They stretched farther than the distance from earth to the moon hundreds of times over, and as the crystals burst and flowered in the space before her, Johanna knew that each one held more ideas than a world populated by millions of Platos and Pythagoras could have imagined in countless lifetimes. It was too much to absorb, and she closed her eyes.

Johanna felt a force. A power so vast and so pervasive it completely removed the distinction of space and time. She looked up and saw only endlessly twinkling constellations above her. She reached toward them.

She sat up in the bed, drenched in sweat, her bandaged hand reaching toward the ceiling. She staggered to the doorway and saw a monk walking down the corridor carrying a bowl of water.

"Help me. My father is ill," she said to Bennito, who turned. The monk was now the owner of a streak of pure white hair in the center of his forehead which marked his experience with Johanna on the table.

"Mother of God," he said, his face draining of color. He dropped the bowl and ran past two monks. The monks went to the feverish girl and returned her to bed. The Abbot was called.

"This spirit was not meant to leave us yet. Rest from your long journey. Rest and have no fears," he said, smiling, smoothing the hair from her face. Comforted by his gentleness, she slipped into a peaceful sleep that was thankfully void of dreams.

≈ ≈ ≈

*The Woman Pope*

Halbert said goodbye to Simon at the gates of the monastery.

"Come inside with me," said Simon, who doffed his hat. Though he was an old man he had the wits of a kind child.

"The brothers are nice and will feed us crab cakes and cardoons," he continued, excited. "They make crunchy bread that's soft on the inside, brother Halbert, with delicious oil made from olives to dip it in. I know they'll help find your daughter."

"I am sure they are compassionate, Simon, but Sergius might be just over that hill. I might even find her today if I hurry," said Halbert, and clapped Simon on the shoulder. "Thanks for your kindness, my friend. I shall remember you as one of the good Christians. Farewell."

He hurried away using the staff Simon gave him and ran for a wagon driven by a farmer and his young son. They were leaving the monastery with a heavy load of fresh vegetables. Halbert hailed the man and tried three different languages he thought might fit the region.

"Friend. Are you traveling far?" he asked.

"Across those hills," said the farmer, finally, in a northern Frankish accent. He gestured toward distant slopes in the east.

An hour later the farmer's six-year-old boy was still staring at the grizzled pagan. Halbert winked but the boy got under his father's arm, frightened of the wild-looking man. To the child's amazement, Halbert puckered his lips and called out a perfect imitation of a bobwhite. The boy peeked for a look. Halbert did a raven, a goose, a blue jay and finally the song of a bird whose name Halbert did not know but repeated exactly its seventeen different trilling loops. The boy, coaxed out of his shyness, smiled this time and passed his half loaf of bread to the big man.

# CHAPTER XIII

IN A CHAIR set out in the sun, Johanna recuperated and spent many days watching the monks work in their garden, laughing, talking beneath a sunny umbrella of peace that hung over the monastery.

*They are so happy, so tranquil here,* she thought.

The monks saw her and waved, treating her with a kindness she came to cherish. Her heart had been devastated, but in the days her body grew strong. They were surprised by her agile responses in Latin, even more when she quickly picked up their tongue, pointing to everything around for the right word in their rolling, lush, breathy language.

"What does a Benedictine order mean? I thought all Christians were the same," she asked, planting herself down among the brothers in the garden. It was the first of many questions about these men and their mission. The monks received her daily interrogations with interest.

Every day the Abbot, on his hands and knees, laughed and worked alongside the other monks before and after their rigorous regime of prayers. Every day she made her way to the chapel where she watched the rituals of mass and listened to the brothers sing their mournful chants. Every day she spent hours in the garden digging and planting with the brothers, discussing points of theology and agriculture.

"'A wise man has no place in him for hatred,' Boethius says," commented the Abbot's secretary, brother Julius, one afternoon.

"Boethius was a fool," Johanna replied, ripping at a weed beneath a bushy carrot plant. The brothers and Bennito and

Julius looked to the Abbot, expecting him to take her to task since Boethius was a favorite philosopher.

"All men are fools," the Abbot said, smiling. "Some are naive and some are devious. Which was he, do you think?"

"Oh, naive beyond words, and a liar," Johanna said, flicking the weed away. The brothers shifted uncomfortably at the outburst. "He wrote that a harsh life brings us closer to God, a proven lie. I've been chewed and swallowed by life, and no god has dared show his face."

"I believe what he meant was that difficulty alone does not call the Divine Heart to us," said the Abbot, tying off a drooping grape vine with string. "But those tests allow us to examine what's valuable in our lives."

"I knew that lesson as a child."

"Johanna, if we left this garden on its own, sat and watched it in hopes of its feeding us, instead of toiling under the sun, straining our backs to clear it, to plant it, harvest it, would it yield for us?"

"Yes, it would," she said petulantly and continued weeding. Then, after a stubborn moment. "For a while."

"Until it was choked by weeds, parched from lack of water. Until the fruits and vegetables died on the vine. It gives us nothing unless we toil for it, as anything of value requires."

She was about to argue, but stopped. "Your god has taken everything from me, including the happiness I had with one of yours."

"I'm afraid it's you, my child, not God, who has closed the door. He is there, He has always been there. He does not leave."

"I don't believe in any god, yours, my father's, there is none."

She rose and ran off to her room, crying. That night she begged the Abbot's forgiveness and praised his kindness and the monks' compassion toward her. The Abbot forgave her and she thanked him and headed for the door.

"Your forgiveness does not come from me," he said. "It comes from God, Who loves you."

"Thank you," she said, looking at the floor.

For nine days, wrapped in a blanket and standing on the monastery's western-most wall, Johanna watched the sun slip into the ocean. She searched the horizon for signs of a ship.

Halbert should have arrived already. He must have become ill again or…Every possibility she encountered had a bad end to it.

A fortnight after coming back from death, Johanna rose from her cot, carried a sack of belongings given to her by the monks and approached the Abbot working in the garden.

"Dear Abbot, the goodness you have shown me I'll share with the world. I am sad to go, but I have to find my father."

"Child, it's not time," he said, standing and removing the straw hat from his head.

"I must be at the coast when he crosses to follow Sergius. Or I must sail back to England to find him."

"That name," Julius said.

"Brother Julius?" asked the Abbot. "Have you heard of one who has come from the island?"

"A new man takes our vegetables to market, yes," said Julius. He called to a man loading crates onto his wagon. The smiling old man came to them and doffed his hat.

"Simon, you've come to us from England? Know you a priest named Sergius?" asked the Abbot. The man nodded. A wave of apprehension washed over Johanna.

"Did his household follow him to Rome?" she asked.

"That's what that man thought," said Simon.

"Was the man's name Halbert?" she said. "I'm his daughter."

Old Simon became frightened, fearing he had done a wrong.

"They almost killed him. Sergius lied, no one follows him. My master, Louis, had me bring him on my wagon. H-Halbert told me about you."

"What happened to my father?" She stepped close to the man-child.

"Let him speak," said the Abbot, hand on her shoulder.

"We came here," Simon said, trembling. "Got to the gate and he refused to enter. Said he had to catch you."

"When was that?"

"He said his daughter was with Sergius. I didn't know."

"How long?"

"A fortnight," said the simple man, bursting into tears.

The Abbot put his arm around Johanna for comfort, thinking her about to weep. She drew herself straight and the Abbot watched an intense resolve bloom in the young woman's eyes.

Johanna took his hand with both of hers and dropped to her knees.

"Thank you for your unending kindness, Abbot. The love you've shown me has been a salve on my heart, but I must find my father before he catches up with Sergius."

She kissed his hand, rose, hugged the man and ran off before the Abbot could speak. The three men watched her head for the gate.

"Call Bennito to me," the Abbot said. He turned to the tearful Simon and blessed the farmer. "Come, my good friend, you've done no wrong. All is just as it should be. Brother Simon, shall we go see what brother Raimond is making for lunch?"

Simon looked up, saw the Abbot's conspiratorial smile and felt a twinge of hunger at the prospect of walking through the monastery's kitchen, dipping bread into various bubbling pots, sampling the sauces and soups the brothers took such great care to prepare. Simon stopped crying and smiled at the good father. The Abbot patted Simon's back and they walked toward the kitchen, arm-in-arm.

≈ ≈ ≈

Johanna ran along the road leading down the long hill, the monastery receding behind her in the distance. When she finally stopped, out of breath, she dried her eyes.

"He's not dead!" she said to the trees, shaking her fists, laughing for the first time in weeks. "He lives!"

She knew he was pursuing her with the same vigor he used to protect her from harm. She also knew the wound of hubris her father carried must be as painful as her own. Tricked by a priest who was no priest, she vowed a dark revenge on Sergius.

An hour later Johanna picked up her pace, fearing Halbert would catch the caravan before she found him. He would try to kill Sergius and she knew it would bring his death.

She felt a vibration beneath her feet. Looking back she saw a wagon with two horses approach at a swift gallop. The wagon slowed beside her and Bennito, now with two streaks of white hair pluming his head, smiled at her. She did not stop walking.

"Brother, I am on my way to Rome and cannot linger with you," she said bluntly.

"That's too bad," he said brightly and snapped the reigns and brought the horses to a fast walk to pass her. "The Abbot sends me home early for a visit and I was hoping for company on the long journey. Ah, well. Good-bye then."

She gaped as he rode by, the words sinking in. He turned back and winked.

"You live in Rome?" she called out, incredulous. He nodded and laughed, patting the bench beside him. "Bless you and the Abbot both!"

She ran and hopped up onto the wagon next to the brother.

≈ ≈ ≈

That night in camp, Johanna picked at a roasted apple while Bennito pulled a skewered partridge from the fire. He kept staring at her as he ate.

"Where did you come back from?" he blurted out. "I've seen many dead before you and there was no doubt you were dead, yet you returned. Why?"

"We die when it is our time, Bennito. I guess I still have much to do, such as rest. We leave early, so, good night."

Bennito continued to watch her long after he finished his dinner, waiting for the secret to reveal itself. Possibly a spirit would rise up from her as she slept.

Johanna could not sleep. Bennito's questions brought back memories of her encounter with death. A special knowledge had been granted to her from some unknowable place. She felt that place was a dimension closer to a god, possibly the One God, though it could not be described nor was it anything like what she had learned from reading, or from her father or from the monks. She had glimpsed a world beyond this one and knew it was only the first step of the journey.

≈ ≈ ≈

For six weeks Johanna walked ahead of the wagon as they passed through fields, plains and mountains. Bennito was a good-hearted man, an excellent traveling companion as well as a guide who had a humorous, self-effacing disposition yet was not above the occasional prank. He once took a large pair of sheep shears from his kit to cut a length of rope.

"Johanna," he said. When Johanna turned she was horrified to see his hand missing from his arm.

"What happened!" she rushed to him, only to find the hand re-appear from the sleeve of his robe along with laughter.

He was a font of knowledge regarding his birthplace, Rome, and Johanna absorbed everything he said about the layout and customs of St. Peter's resting place. She practiced Italian with him and Bennito responded with a history of the church. He also continued to ply her with questions about her miraculous restoration but was never fully satisfied with her answers. He secretly believed she withheld some essential part of the story.

"You have a most agile mind," Bennito confessed after a month on the road. The days flew by faster than the leagues and Johanna now spoke only Italian with Bennito, pretending not to hear when the monk slipped into Latin.

"I hear some strange bird chirping in my ear," she jested, looking back at Bennito as she walked ahead. "It speaks a language I cannot understand."

"You understand more than you reveal," said Bennito.

"Ah, the little bird flew away."

A month and a half along the road to Rome, they traveled through a mountain forest and Johanna, as usual, walked in front of the wagon. The day had ebbed into a cool fall afternoon and shadows had grown across the narrow road. The countryside around them had changed quickly. The sturdy oaks and elms gave way to evergreen bushes and sharp-tipped pine as they climbed higher and watched as snow-capped mountains took up most of the sky before them.

One afternoon, Bennito, vigilant even through his playfulness, squinted into the distance of the road ahead.

"Why walk when you can ride, Johanna?"

"I have to build strength. All that time in bed softened me," she said, walking backwards to smile at Bennito. Suddenly, three ragged men stepped out of the woods and blocked the path.

"Johanna," said Bennito. She saw the strangers and quickly got onto the wagon. Bennito passed her the whip.

"Brothers. Bless your days," he called to them. To Johanna he whispered. "Be ready with the horses when I give word."

The leader had a huge pink belly spilling out of his trousers, the taut skin of it looked like the engorged neck of a frog. The man had little pink eyes to match, with jowls hanging over the collar of his food-stained shirt. He held up a short, rusty sword and Bennito slowed the horses.

"Friar *merde*. We only want the girl and the horses. You may thank us for not cutting your miserable throat," said the fat man in an oddly high voice. "Quickly, leave or die."

The two other men came onto the road and grabbed at the horses. But Bennito, moving faster than Johanna had ever seen him, whirled around with a thick walking staff.

He swung it down on the head of the fat bandit with a *crack*. The blow dropped him to his knees, his pink eyes rolled up into his head, his ears bled, and he fell forward until he bounced on his belly on the ground.

"Now, Johanna."

"Huh-yah!" cried Johanna and whipped the horses. They reared, shook free of the men and galloped down the road.

The two remaining thieves ran and leapt onto the sides of the wagon. Bennito turned and climbed into the bed of the wagon as the second bandit pulled himself up.

"God bless you, sir," Bennito said and swung, hitting the bandit across the hands. His knuckles smashed, the man yelled and dropped into the road.

But the third bandit was quicker and jumped onto Bennito's back with his knife out, pulling it back to slash his throat. Johanna saw and without thinking let the horse whip fly. It struck the man across the eyes, removing several layers of skin and splashing blood across his face. The bandit stepped back and put his hands over his face.

"My eyes," he cried as Bennito turned to him.

"Something in your eyes? Let me get that for you."

The monk performed a rapid-fire one-two cross-punch across the man's head as the horses galloped at full speed.

"Goodness," continued Bennito. "I missed a spot."

Bennito made a final thrust into the man's gut and flipped him off the back of the speeding wagon. The bandit hit the ground and tumbled over and over in the dirt.

"As good as new, sir," Bennito called. "Good day to you all, brothers, and may His light shine upon you."

He sat next to Johanna and took back the reigns, slowing the horses to a walk. The two travelers laughed and whooped, drunk with their victory.

"You are skilled with that whip, Johanna," he told her.

"And you've skill with that staff, Bennito," she said, clapping his shoulder. "Teach me, please."

"Perhaps we can make a trade? If you will tell me what it was like to go through death and back."

"I think we might be able to strike a deal," she smiled and put out her hand. They shook. A light whistling sound came from behind, followed by a deep *thump* that jolted Bennito upright in the seat. The horses stirred nervously, snorting and shaking their heads. Bennito's eyes widened and he opened his mouth as if he were going to speak, but instead turned to the horses and snapped the reins hard.

"Bennito?" asked Johanna, suddenly frightened.

"We must hurry again," he said weakly.

The horses bolted down the road once more as the monk slumped forward, the shaft of an arrow sticking out of his back.

# CHAPTER XIV

"BENNITO!" SHE CRIED as the wagon sped down the road out of control.

Johanna looked behind and saw two more bandits running after the wagon as they re-armed their bows. Johanna took the reins from Bennito, who went limp and slumped across Johanna's lap. She forced herself to ignore the blood seeping onto her and spurred the animals on, running the nervous beasts hard for miles.

"We've lost them," she said. She turned off the road into a grassy area near a stream. They were in a long valley bounded on either side by open fields.

Bennito could not move his arms or legs, and she knew that there was no feeling left in his limbs. She was so frightened she lifted him off the wagon as if he were a child without thought of his weight and carefully laid him down on his side and put a blanket over him.

"I'll ride for help," she said, her eyes unable to look away from the shaft sticking out of his spine. Nausea swept over her when she saw the blood soaking his robes.

"Stay. There is no help," he said, managing a smile. "Rest with me on the grass."

She could not believe it. "Rest? Bennito, I have to go!"

"Please?"

She began to protest, but stopped. There was no use. She sat down, took him in her arms and lightly rocked him.

"Now," he said, trying to relax. "Talk to me, do not cry, Johanna. When you died did you go to heaven or purgatory?"

"Bennito," she said, wanting to run for help and not discuss her silly dream. She looked into his eyes, saw the life in them fading. He strained to remain playful, but Johanna saw how important her reflections were to him. She smoothed the coarse black hair from his face.

"It was a far journey, brother. I went to a place that was larger than heaven or hell where I saw everything as it is. I saw that this life is a short and narrow illusion," she said, then hesitated. "But I'm afraid I cannot tell you the name of that place."

"You don't know? Was it filled with angels or with flames? That would give me a hint!" his laugh turned into a liquid-filled cough. Blood bubbled at the corners of his mouth.

"Everything is different from the stories we've been told in this life," she said. "In the next life our eyes open completely. I have seen it. And now you will, too."

He was comforted and relaxed with a sigh that rumbled, and Johanna heard a watery burble in his lungs. His eyes darted back and forth and he became agitated, lifting his head.

"Look! This is a beautiful valley. What's that I smell? Lavender. Johanna, I'm going to come back, like you. Yes, that's exactly what I'll do. Only this time you'll be standing there and *your* hair will turn white. This time I will be the one who laughs. I will be the one who has to explain to you about...about...ab --"

Johanna saw the natural light in his eyes dim, lose their translucence and become opaque. He blinked several times in rapid succession and, like a candle extinguished behind the pupils, the light went out. Still smiling up into her face as if he was just about to laugh, brother Bennito let go and died.

With Adrian, her father, and now this sweet man gone from her life, Johanna's heart froze.

"What else can You possibly take from me?" she hissed at the sky. She closed Bennito's eyes and sat with him a long time. It calmed her to stroke his hair and listen to the buzz of insects and watch a promenade of yellow butterflies. She had not noticed before, but when she finally looked up, she saw thousands of them fluttering everywhere. Each yellow wing went on with its daily duty; hopping, flying, crawling on the wind-waving grasses and along the ground. A young hare, mottled brown with long twitching ears, stopped near by, sniffed the air, and wondered at a scent which usually foretold danger. It turned its eyes to the humans and stared. The rabbit bolted into the underbrush, its hind legs kicking up a puff of dirt.

"You're right, it is beautiful here," Johanna smiled.

She took a breath, exhaled and felt a bit better. She relaxed her eyes, let them take in the colors of the wild flowers beside her and the expanse of the early fall field where Bennito's journey had come to an end. The valley spread out for miles and was painted in early autumn reds, yellows, golds, rusts and violets.

Near sunset, Johanna stood next to the shallow grave. Her anger had died with the exertion of digging it and it felt good to work hard with the earth.

"Gentle man, I pray your god takes you into the loving heart you say he possesses," she said as she patted the soil that held his bones. Johanna picked up Bennito's robe and walked toward a tiny stream hidden among the high grasses.

Entering the stream, she washed the blood from the robe, scrubbing the cloth, slapping it on a large boulder in the water. The dark red turned pink and the particles broke up and drifted downstream.

That night Johanna sat at her campfire surrounded by Bennito's possessions. She had unhitched the tired horses and filled bowls with water she found in the wagon to let them drink. While in the wagon, Johanna found the sack with Bennito's effects.

She flipped through the worn codices he had borrowed from his order, examined the sheep shears he told her he would use on his family's sheep and how his mother would make Johanna a woolen dress for the coming winter. There was a pair of sandals he brought as a present that fit her perfectly when she tried them on. She felt down deep into the sack. A razor for shaving his tonsure was laid alongside the remaining supply of dried fish, fruit and grains. She held up a needle and thread, returned them to their leather kit, and set it beside a large brass water vessel.

Johanna picked up the heavy jug and looked at her reflection stretching around it.

"Shiny as a mirror," she said out loud. She set it on the ground close by the fire and aimed its shiny bottom where she could see herself. Her eyes were red and puffy from tears and the curve of the brass jug rounded her narrow, freckled face. She had lost the softness of a young woman and the thin face that looked back at her could be of either sex. She nodded to herself, took a handful of her long sun-streaked hair. Adrian held all that hair in his hands once. She remembered his touch, his face, the love in his eyes. She examined her hair with an objective scrutiny, the strands shining back at her in the brass. Then, she picked up Bennito's shears and cut it off. There was no sting, no pain. So she lifted the next hank of hair and did it again.

$$\approx \approx \approx$$

The villages and towns she rode through had few people on the streets as most labored in the fields for the autumn harvest. The summer made its last burst of heat before the cold winds swept down from the north to transform the feel, look and smell of the world and prepared the land for winter. Johanna passed a deserted village while a dusty humid wind blew through it.

Two men, their faces blotched with lesions and so skeletal they had to hold each other up, observed her wagon from a doorway. As she passed close by and nodded to them, the men watched in silence. Johanna felt their gaze all over her and kept checking the men for signs of her deceit. When she saw nothing there, she hoped their only thoughts were on a closely-cropped, tonsured young monk walking alongside his wagon, guiding his horses and holding a staff almost as tall as himself. She hoped they would note to themselves that the little monk wore the brown robes of his Benedictine order, however, she also hoped they could not see the curious hole sewn shut in the back of the robe with the outline of a large, dark stain.

One of the men suddenly reeled on his feet and put his face into the neck of the other man. Johanna watched the man cry softly, and could only think that it was because he saw her as though viewing his own past, as if he were watching his own life before him, the ghost of himself walking with youth and vitality and fearlessness through the town, and the precious memory of it, so long ago and far away, was too much for him to think it was gone forever.

Johanna smelled the charnel scent before she saw the pile. Hurrying to the wagon, she tied a rag around her face, got up on the bench and whipped the horses. She pressed them into a hard gallop. They passed a tall stack of bodies in the deserted street, piled up, waiting their turn for burial. A flag warning of a small-pox plague waved eerily in the hand of the last corpse lying atop the high stack.

"Hurry," she urged the animals. "Go."

Johanna whipped at the horses and raced them a long time to put as many leagues as she could at her back.

≈ ≈ ≈

Two days later Johanna stood beside the horse team in the road, sweating with the last of the late summer humidity. She struggled with the cinches, trying to tighten their yoke when a wind picked up. The sudden gust was dry and bracing, blowing the thick stillness from the air, shaking the treetops and shrubs for hundreds of meters around in rippling waves. It was autumn's first rush and the cool tang made the horses perk up, shake and snort into the air, refreshed. Johanna got into the wagon and brought them to a trot, knowing that within a few weeks the pleasant wind would turn cold. She had to be well on her way to Rome before winter stopped her travel.

At dusk she led the nervous team through a darkening wood, her eyes shifting back and forth on the sides of the road.

"It's all right," she said. "There's nothing here to hurt us."

She passed beside large clumps of pansy, foxglove, while above mistletoe and spider moss hung from the trees, on the ground emerald lichen stretched tight as a blanket and only a few daisies, henfern, toadstool or the occasional violet poked its head through the forest cover. The horses were skittish for no reason and their ears twitched, hearing something she could not.

Up ahead, beyond a bend in the road, she heard shouting. She led the horses off the path and turned the wagon around, ready to head back. She held Bennito's staff and sat on the wagon bench and had an anxious debate with herself whether or not to flee. Finally, gripping the thick wood with both hands, Johanna hopped off the wagon and followed the voices.

Easing around a tree, she slipped the rag around her neck up over her nose and mouth to disguise any girlish features. Johanna peered down to a dip in the road. Three men with clubs circled a young man who clung to a sack of possessions. She told herself she could not get involved. *It's too dangerous and there are too many of them.*

"Give it up and you can go," shouted the first robber. "Come on, fool. Drop the sack and run."

The victim shook his head and one of the men feinted with his club, drawing the young man forward while the second and third thieves jumped from behind, taking him to the ground.

The second thief tugged at his sack without success while the first yanked it away from both victim and partner and turned to run off with his prize. But before he could take two steps, Bennito's staff came down on his head. He dropped face down into the dirt. The third man saw an oak staff raised his way and ran off into the forest.

The second man, club in hand, rolled on top of the young man and was poised to bring it down. Johanna stepped up and swung, striking his club arm. Horrified, she watched the blow completely sever the man's hand from his wrist. Club in hand shot out into the air, rolled on the ground several lengths before coming to a stop.

The robber stood and screamed at the sky, the hood of his cloak thrown back from his face. It was eaten away with leprosy, he had no lips and his nose and chin were only cavernous pockets in his face, making sense of his withered, fragile limbs. The leper ran off holding the remains of his arm before collapsing in a heap off to the side of the road.

The dazed robbery victim walked to the second man and squatted over him. This was a leper as well, and his brittle skull was caved in. Johanna approached, the rag still across her face, and looked down at the diseased man.

"This leper is dead," said the young man.

"I'm so sorry," she said. "I didn't mean to kill him!"

She looked at the pathetically crunched face of the dead man in disbelief and shame. Johanna turned to the robbery victim, beseeching him with her eyes to forgive her this crime. Their eyes met, and she felt a massive blow strike her in the gut. She got to her knees, tried to suck in air. She tried to scream and instead fell on the ground, unconscious.

The victim got his water skin, knelt beside the monk, uncovered the rag from his face and daubed water on the young monk's forehead.

"This is not your fault, brother. They were desperate and hungry."

He stopped and looked closely as he washed the dirt from the monk's cheeks. His expression changed. This was no monk. This was no boy. He sat back on his heels, numb.

"Johanna?" he said. "Is that…?"

Johanna opened her eyes. "Adrian. You are here?"

"Johanna. Johanna," he said, was unable to say anything else, his entire vocabulary slain, reduced to one word, one thought, one answered prayer.

They held each other in the middle of the road, clinging as if they would never let go, both of them afraid this terrible dream would end and return them to wakefulness.

"Shhh," said Adrian. "I hear something."

"What is it, love?" she asked. Voices came down the road and moments later several armed lepers feebly hurried in their direction. Johanna and Adrian ran to the wagon. Hopping onto the bench, Johanna took the reins and guided the horses back onto the road, toward the approaching lepers.

"No, Johanna, we should take another path," Adrian said as he swung onto the bench.

"I am not turning away from Rome," she said, cracking the whip near the horses' ears, setting them galloping toward the lepers.

The men dove from the road as the wagon hurled past.

≈ ≈ ≈

The night was clear and warm as Johanna huddled with Adrian together at their campfire, never leaving the reach of the other's arms. They continually kissed each other on the lips, face, eyes, hair, hands. Smelling, touching, gazing in speechless wonder at their good fortune. Johanna draped herself across his chest and whispered her story with a melancholy contentment which freed her heart and gave her permission to feel, something she had been afraid to do since Bennito's grave.

"We will catch up with Halbert, don't worry," said Adrian, his hand smoothing her hair. "And that evil priest will repent."

"Yes, love. Now. Tell me what happened to you."

"Right after leaving the ship, not a hundred feet away from shore," Adrian said, "I was jumped by my shipmates."

"Why? Was it Cleph?"

"Cleph and almost everyone else. They all wanted revenge, so they robbed and beat me."

"Bad?" she asked, holding his face in her hands.

"I was lucky. The crew of another ship passed by and kept them from killing me outright."

"I am thankful to them."

"They stole everything. I had less than when I started."

"What a hard time you've had of it. I'm sorry."

"Sorry? Johanna, I am here now. With you. I hold everything I'll ever need again in my arms. Sorry. Love, this is a miracle. That beating forced me to stop and recover, like you did at Sergius' in England. By the time I started again you must have been at the monastery. You got a good start on me with the horses, but if I had not been hurt . . ."

"And if I had not stayed with the brothers . . ."

"I'd have gotten a lot farther, and we'd never have met."

"Yes," she said and nodded. "It is a miracle."

He lovingly stroked her short hair, sad and grateful all at once.

"But my ambition has done this," said Johanna. "I deserve the heartache of losing my father. I'm the rightful owner of misfortune."

"Shh," he quieted her. "No. Our youth has turned from spring to an early frost. But it's only one season. We'll make it to the next."

"This is my punishment. I coveted Sergius' library. I was greedy with the illusion that I could not only have its wisdom, but travel with it to find you in Rome. Then I dishonored my father by putting my greed above him. You should leave me to perish," she said.

"I will never leave you again," he replied. "I love you with all my heart and more than this life. This is a sign. God has given us back from across the entire world. Now we can find our fathers."

"Adrian," she said, cupping his face between her hands again, feeling his beard through her fingers. "I cannot believe our good fortune. I cannot believe I have you again."

"*Pater Noster*," Adrian began.

She held him close and listened to him pray. Then he softly kissed her burned hand. It had healed, but on her palm remained an angry red scar that erased a portion of what fortunetellers would call the life and destiny lines. They held each other throughout the night for fear that the world might come to separate them again, as if to let go might mean they would lose the other forever.

# CHAPTER XV

SERGIUS' GENITALS HAD almost been destroyed two months before and he had thought of little else since.

The three hired river boats pulled away from the bank of the wide river and sailed down its slow, southeasterly course. Sergius stood at the rail of the first ship and scanned the shore.

"Bring my mead," he said to his aide, Gaetani. "Heated, not scalded this time."

"Yes, my lord," the monk replied, backing away.

Sergius turned from the water and caught sight of one of his serfs. A woman walking away, her eyes cast nervously back at Sergius with her arm thrown protectively over the shoulders of a figure with a blanket over its head. They hurried toward the ladder leading below deck when the woman's coveted object tripped, fell to the deck and came out from under the blanket into view. The mother quickly tried to cover it again but it was too late.

"Why, a surprise. A beautiful little present," Sergius said. He caught a glimpse of the pretty twelve-year-old girl as she was pushed down the stairs. Her mother glanced back and sent a pleading look to the priest. Sergius smiled and made the sign of the cross, blessing her. The mother burst into tears.

"No," she cried, clutching her palms together. "Dear God in heaven, please, no!"

She disappeared below, bereft, as if Sergius had damned instead of blessed them. She had obviously been so successful at hiding the child at the manor but the cursed accident in these close quarters made concealing her daughter impossible. The mother's wail came wafting up from below deck, sounding like someone who had just lost a child to a horrible death.

Sergius felt a tingling thrill that made this arduous journey suddenly almost bearable. He whispered to Gaetani who handed him a cup of mead. The monk nodded and left the deck, heading below.

"Ah," Sergius gasped, wincing. He faced the wind, his smile short-lived. All at once the fiery burning began and he had to quickly reach beneath his robes. He adjusted his ruined parts, moved as they were to stir despite the unbelievable pain when touched. He lifted his robe above his waist, bared himself without modesty to the air knowing not a single eye would dare look upon his yellowed and thickly scabbed genitalia. He dipped a ladle into the barrel at his side and withdrew the cool water he kept for this purpose. He poured the liquid over himself and groaned with agony and relief.

"Not yet, not yet," he whispered to himself, trying to keep the anticipation of his new flower from reaching his scorched manhood.

He dribbled another ladle full over himself and was vaguely distracted as he watched a figure on the shore run into the river, calling out to the passing ships, before he returned his attention to the cool sensation on his flesh.

≈ ≈ ≈

"Wait for me!" Halbert ran into the river waving at the boats, but they were too far away.

After all this time he knew he had remained only two, perhaps three days behind Sergius and hurried without rest to catch the caravan. By the choicest luck while begging for food at a village, he heard that a caravan traveling to Rome was headed for the river. He ran all the way.

Halbert caught sight of a group of wealthy merchants boarding a dinghy for a chartered ship moored in deep water. He ran to the dock and across its wobbly planks, tugged at the arm of a silk-robed merchant whose floppy velveteen cap was trimmed with a canary yellow feather.

"Help me, sir," said Halbert. "Take me with you, please. I must--"

The man struck him on the side of his head before Halbert could finish, throwing him headlong from the dock into the water.

"Since when does a beggar make demands?" said the man down at Halbert. He smiled at his companions. "Friends, are you familiar with this new custom?"

He turned back to Halbert. "Know your place, vermin, or God will watch you dragged behind my boat at the end of a rope."

His companions laughed at Halbert, spitting at him, then pushed off in a rowboat. Halbert dragged himself onto shore and ran along the bank with an eye on the river boats, trying to catch up.

≈ ≈ ≈

Johanna stopped the wagon at the well in the square. The village was a lonely collection of dung and thatch huts on the edge of a forest. Beyond, a snow-clad mountain range rose on the eastern horizon. Adrian got down, stretched and looked at the peasants standing in line for water.

"We'll let the horses drink and rest a bit," he said and reached up, touched her face. She flinched from the contact. "What? What is it?"

"Nothing," she said, moving away. "I'll get water if you'll find food for the horses."

Johanna took the brass vessel and water skins to the well and waited with the villagers to draw water, keeping an eye on Adrian as he went into a building. She could not believe it. He was right there. She feared to let him out of her sight, still astounded they had found each other. Johanna could tell Adrian had regained all his natural strength during his recuperation from the beating. He still wore the brown monk robe, but it was shorter and belted at the waist with a dagger in a scabbard. Leather straps of his sandals wound up his calves to his knees, and as he moved his step light and sure. The curtain of his hooded cloak trailed behind him and the loose curls of his brown hair fluttered at his shoulders. She smiled that such a beautiful man loved her.

Johanna felt an uncomfortable sensation and looked up. On the other side of the well a wild-looking woman was staring at her. Armed with a bow and a quiver full of arrows, she carried two long, bone-handled knives tucked into her leather belt. The wild-woman was dressed in painted skins, had wavy black hair thick as a mane. She was the owner of an olive complexion and an animal beauty borne of a strenuous hunting life, yet also had a fragile, aristocratic quality to her longish face and aquiline nose. These features contrasted with her mahogany body; muscled arms hard as a man's, long bared legs that were powerful springs from running through woods in constant chase. *How strange a monk must look to this woman.* After a long wait, Johanna filled the water vessels.

"Your god is dying and soon to be buried," said the wild-woman grimly. She spoke in a strangely accented Saxon.

"He is the god of love, uh, sister."

"You don't even believe it. Look around you, monk," she said, and gestured at the destitute village peasants. "Your god of love hates us all. We want our Old Ones back."

Johanna turned from the angry woman. Right into a smiling Adrian, his arms full.

"Food, wine and a present," he said, and handed her a folded cloth. Johanna unfurled the cloth. It was a woman's dress.

"It's time for my old Johanna to return to me," he said.

"Adrian," she hissed and, horrified, crumpled the dress in her hands and walked away. At the wagon she set the bowls down to let the horses drink.

"I know it is not the best cloth," said Adrian behind her, hurt. "But it's fine for travel."

"It came from your heart and I thank you, love," she said in a low voice. "But until I find my father, I must stay this way. Please, let's go. Too many eyes and ears around us."

They got in the wagon and drove off. They did not speak for a long time and the silence built a wall each was afraid to look over.

"You do not feel safe with me," he said, finally.

"It is not you but the road I fear."

"I will take care of you. Don't you believe that?"

"This is best for now," she said with finality. Johanna pointed toward a pond before a grove of trees. "There. A lovely place to rest."

They ate a mid-day meal in silence near the water.

"Have my bread, love," she said and fed Adrian the last of her share even after he shook his head. Johanna was tender, she held and kissed his hand, stroked his cheek. Then she suddenly took his beard in her hands, pulled him to her and kissed him. They reveled in each other's lips and mouth a long time. All slights were forgotten, erased by their tongues moving in and out of the other's mouth, exploring, raising sensations as both quickly heated to a boil.

"Adrian, wait" she said, and broke away when he reached for her breasts and briefly held them. Both let out a small gasp when he squeezed them, fitting so perfectly in his hands. His control was gone and left only the single destination of passion to follow.

"I want you, Johanna."

"And I want you. But our desires are all we can have right now."

"Why?"

"For one thing we are not married," she said. "And for another we have promises to fulfill. To find our fathers."

Johanna stood up and paced in front of him. She ran her hands through her short, sweat-dampened hair to pull herself back from the hunger. She looked to make sure they had not been spied upon, took his hand and helped Adrian to his feet. She bent and picked up Bennito's staff and threw it to him.

"Come on," she said, a mischievous look on her face.

"What?"

She raised her staff and crouched into what she thought was a fighting position.

"Oh, no," he said and shook his head..

Minutes later, at the edge of the pond, Johanna mimicked the way Adrian held his staff and approached him. Adrian held the staff out in front him, his eyes locked on hers. Johanna lunged in a mock feint, then quickly moved to one side and jabbed at Adrian with a maneuver she hoped would take him by surprise. Adrian blocked the move then stepped in close, pushed the staff against her chest, threw her back and easily knocked her to the ground.

"Don't stop," she pleaded, scrambling to her feet.

"You don't have a man's strength," he said and threw up his hands. "All the maneuvering in the world is no good if I can split your head with one blow. You should stay a woman."

"We must travel hundreds of leagues. How many more thieves will see us as a man and a maid, marking me as a prize and you as a fool? How many times can we escape after tempting highwaymen? I know how hard it is for you to see me like this and, Adrian, I love you for it."

"I love you so very much."

"You know I can do this. You remember the lepers," she said, sweetly, and wrapped a hand around his neck. "Give me the knowledge I need."

"I cannot," he said and pulled away. "It does not exist."

"You cannot or is it you will not?" she said. He turned and started walking away. "You stubborn…"

Without thinking Johanna swung her staff and caught him on the ankle. It tagged the bone and he yelled and automatically swung his staff, hard. Johanna braced with hers, breaking the blow. She was knocked back and stumbled, but stayed on her feet. Adrian seemed shocked at both of them.

"I did not mean that," he said nervously. "You know I did not mean --"

"That's my warrior," she smiled coquettishly and crouched into position. "My big, stubborn warrior. Come. I'm ready for you."

He rubbed his ankle and they began to circle each other, bent and alert, as opponents.

≈ ≈ ≈

The days became colder, leaves blew from the trees and flew across the road. The nights were spent closer to the fire beneath wool blankets, discussing strategies they should take when they caught up with the caravan, if Halbert was not located before then.

"If Sergius hurt him," she said, so tense Adrian thought something would physically break on her.

"We'll find him first. Your father is fine."

He cooled her vengeful desires and reminded her again of the miracle of their meeting.

"I love you, Adrian," she said as Adrian draped his cloak over her.

"And I love you," he said, stroking her cheek with hands that were at once slender and strong. "I praise Almighty God for this miracle."

During the day Johanna walked ahead of the wagon, her strength growing with every league. She often held the staff above her head.

"Do you expect enemies from the sky, brother?" Adrian laughed, the wrinkle across his broad brow deepening. At first his blue eyes flashed with the use of 'brother' and his voice was tinged with sarcasm. But after three weeks of continuous use he pronounced it with deeper affection. Johanna calling him brother back became part of a secret language they were creating.

"For my arms, brother. They need strength in them."

"Make them strong with what you know. Feint. Feint," he called and made a feinting motion. She imitated it.

"Now, lunge! Cross. Yes. Now cross back. Jab. Retreat," he said and she followed his commands, a soldier in training, exactly how she wanted to feel.

"I want to be ready for anything," she said with a jab, then pulled the staff back into place for the next command.

They stopped at a hillcrest, Johanna perspiring, her breath frosty puffs from the drill. She looked radiant and was pleased with her performance. She glanced at Adrian for confirmation but he wore a concerned expression as he looked down into a clearing.

"What's wrong?" she asked.

"Trouble."

A large group of savage-looking people gathered in what appeared to be a noisy ceremony taking place around a monk tied to the trunk of a leafless, lightning-struck tree.

"The ancient people," said Adrian. "I passed them when my ship was at port in the north."

"Who are they?"

"Wanderers. Pagans who keep the Old Religion. They stay mostly to the forests."

"Those are not my father's people nor his religion. What's that man wearing?"

"It's too far away."

"Wait. A robe. A Benedictine robe. Adrian. That's the Abbot's order," she said as a terrible scenario sprang to her mind. She hopped up on the wagon and took the reins from Adrian. "Run, you."

In the clearing the ceremony built to a frenzied pitch. Scores of men and women dressed in the skins of deer, fox, bear and cow, feathers dyed in blues and greens, all manner of forest-found accoutrement, shell necklaces, bracelets, wooden slatted vests. They all danced, drank, stumbling and hanging off one another. A blast from an elk horn went up, scorching the air.

The wild-woman from the village well lowered the horn and waited for her followers to quiet.

"We give this man to our gods, who we've shamed," she said in a loud, clear voice. "We turned our backs on Donar, god of war, on gentle Friausius, and the Matrones, the triple goddess, and all the gods of land, sea and sky. We foolishly looked to the angry Christ god, who ignored us."

She took a dagger, curved and razor sharp, and ripped open his robe and exposed his chest.

"Take his heart, oh gods," she prayed, eyes skyward, the knife aloft. "And look kindly on us again."

The pagan queen held the dagger out, put it to the skin on the monk's heart. She began to push it between the man's ribs. There was a commotion at the back of the crowd. The clatter of a horse's hooves scattered pagans in their wake.

"Noooo!" cried a voice. The crowd turned as Johanna and Adrian pulled the galloping horses up, stopping the wagon in their midst.

"No god asks to spill the blood of his child," Johanna called out and stood up in the wagon. "Only men demand it."

"The Old Ones are hungry for our attention and you, little monk, will be fed to them next," said the woman.

A roar of agreement went up from the crowd, hands and weapons and howls were raised, rattling the air. The roiling mass of yelling savages moved in on the two intruders and surrounded them. Johanna and Adrian pressed close together and could not only see the barbarians come toward them, but could feel the weight of the crowd through the ground, rumbling through the earth like a stampede.

# CHAPTER XVI

THE SAVAGE MOB had blood in its eyes.

Adrian was struck at the ferocity of the crowd, but instead of being terrified, Johanna was electrified in the moment. Her eyes flamed with emotion as she stood in the wagon and pointed at the masses converging on them.

"Yes, take my life. Spill my blood." she said loud, for all to hear. "Your own lives will follow as surely as darkness follows light."

This sounded like a curse to the superstitious mob. Some stopped where they stood, unsure, looking to the wild-woman leader for direction.

Before Adrian could stop her, Johanna jumped down and waded into the crowd toward the wild-woman.

"Kill for your gods today and you will find yourselves killing for pettiness tomorrow," she said and looked every person she passed in the eye. One woman put her hands in front of her face to keep the spell from reaching her. "And finally, you will kill each other for the smallest slights, until every argument requires death."

"If that is required," the wild-woman said. "So be it."

"That is what *you* want, sister," said Johanna. She stepped directly up to the woman and fixed her with a look. "Because of the pain in your heart."

The pagans saw the monk was unafraid and stood eye-to-eye with their leader.

In that moment, Johanna's manner changed before the bewildered mass. She took a breath and did not take her eyes off the wild-woman. She nodded with such certainty it was like she had gazed into the woman's soul.

"I-it--" the wild-woman stuttered, thrown off by Johanna's intimation. The followers watched closely and quieted to an eerie silence. "It's for the gods."

"No. Not for any god. It is only for *you*, so filled with pain, sister," said Johanna, softly. "You cannot hold it inside anymore, can you?"

The aim of the accusation struck the wild-woman's confidence. Her expression revealed a fear so deep it was as clear as a thief caught red-handed. Every member of the tribe saw the little monk had called a truth out of the depths of their leader, raised it up into the woman's consciousness and there was no way she could now escape it.

"N-no," the woman protested weakly. "It is our duty."

"It is for the spirit you have lost," Johanna said and turned to the crowd. Then, in a whisper that each savage bent in and strained to hear: "*Every last one of you.*"

A murmur rippled through the people. A ragged man stepped forward.

"We ask for so little. We only seek small comforts in life and cannot even get those."

"Where do you seek your comfort?" Johanna asked. "Do you seek it in the misery of others? Where is the comfort you seek, brother? Is it in blood?"

Suddenly, she took hold of the arm of a huge, ruthless-looking man and looked him in the eye. So taken with her intensity, he pulled from her grip and scrambled away.

Johanna walked through the crowd wearing a luminous smile for the barbarians who parted before her. She moved to a drunken man holding a liquor jug.

"Is there comfort in there?" she asked and put a hand on it. He cried out and clutched the jug to his chest like a child hiding his toy. The crowd laughed. He patted the jug.

"My god," he said, sarcastically.

"Then you worship a tiny god with no power," she said. "A god that has nothing to quench your thirsty soul, brother."

Johanna rose to her full height, reached her arms out toward the people. Every eye saw Johanna look more fearsome in her serene passion, without saying a word, than they had seen in their leader's bloodlust. Johanna began to sweat, her eyes widened.

A profound change came over her.

Adrian watched Johanna with the others. She seemed to be taken over by a force not of this temporal life. Adrian looked out at the mob of pagans: They saw it, too. As much as he thought he knew her, Adrian could not imagine the sea change he was witness to: Her body language shifted, she seemed to glide above the earth through the crowd, and her facial expression was that of some creature not of this world.

She walked to the wild-woman who tightened her grip on the sacrificial monk and put the dagger to his throat.

"I do this," she began. "For our gods."

Johanna stared at the wild-woman, peered deep into her eyes. For that instant all was silent. Then a chime, from some eternal distance, rang, though only Johanna heard it.

Johanna leaned in and whispered. And hundreds of pagans strained to hear her words.

"So full of pain you can't hold it inside. You have to share that pain with someone, anyone. Isn't that your truth? Isn't that all of our truths?"

"I...it's," she stuttered. "It's our duty."

"No. I know this. I have been in this place. I was you," she said and turned to the crowd and yelled. "I am you. All of you."

She staggered back as if struck by a club. Her eyes fluttered up in her head and only the whites showed. The pagans saw the change and were thrown into a terror. This was not a monk. This was a young man being taken over by a great power.

Images exploded before Johanna eyes in the moment she looked out on the barbarians, and she was powerless to do anything but watch:

The city of Rome glimpsed from a hilltop.

A pouch of money spilled out onto a floor.

Sergius' face twisted into a taunt, mocking er.

A body falling from the sky directly above her.

The images stopped as suddenly as they began and Johanna stood weaving on her feet. She regained herself but all who saw her face knew she had been transported to a place they could not see.

Several looked skyward, expecting to be struck by the lightning of the little monk's words. Adrian, too, was spellbound by this person he had never seen before.

"Seek your comfort in the arms of the One God, the Father of all His children. Let Him comfort you," she said. She put her hand on the shoulder of a man with palsy. He trembled as if he inhabited the tremors of an earthquake and could barely look at Johanna from the shaking. "Ask Him. Right now, all of you. Turn to Him, ask for your True Comfort. The True Comfort you need."

She continued on to a tall forest woman who stood in the midst of the horde, sobbing. Johanna touched her arm and heard gasps rip through the crowd.

She looked over. The man with palsy, his eyes locked onto hers, smiled in amazement. The trembling had stopped.

The man gazed down at himself and stared. He looked at her again, clasped his hands, fell to his knees. *What was happening? What is she saying? What is this pagan girl doing?* Johanna's mind cried out to herself and watched herself speaking and doing things completely removed from her earthly body. She moved through the crowd, blessing them, encouraging them to pray. In awe before her, pagans dropped to the ground as she passed.

"He is here. He never left you," said Johanna, and clasped her hands in prayer. "Let Him find you. Let Him hold you."

Adrian watched her wade through a sea of praying men and women. Long wild hair and the fur of skins blew in the cold breeze, rattling weapons hushed and not a one of the violent, fearful tribe of hundreds remained on its feet.

Hours later, deep in the early twilight near a forest, Johanna and Adrian rode on the wagon, the beaten monk between them. The man drank from a water skin, still in shock.

"Your miracle saved my life," he said. "And the man with palsy –"

"It was no miracle," she said. "The man needed an invitation to leave his sickness."

Adrian looked behind the wagon.

"We have company, brother."

Johanna turned back. The wagon was followed by a ragged pagan army stretching into the distance, going around a far bend in the road.

# CHAPTER XVII

SERGIUS' CARAVAN ROLLED onto the windswept Italian plains eight long months after it had set sail from England. All who survived the treacherous crossing were scarred by its severity. The number of wagons left had diminished from forty-one to eight. The remaining servants were weak from infrequent food and ravaged from a forced march from sunrise to dark.

"We cannot do this" cried one of the chosen men, a tanner at the estate. He was on his knees. "We'll be dead before the day is over. Please, have mercy on us."

"Get in the leather and die then or die by my sword now," said one of Sergius' aides, his blade raised over the kneeling man.

Sergius stood at the side of the road and watched as his aides harnessed eight feeble men to one of the wagons stuck in the mud. He rarely spoke directly to the servants, only to his trusted monk Gaetani who commanded the guards to carry out his orders. The servants, prodded by swords, cried out from their yokes..

They made several attempts. One yoked man suffered a heart attack and had to be replaced. Finally, the heavy carriage was pulled from the muddy rut. The man and four donkeys that had given out were left where they had fallen, dead.

"Are you ready, flower?" Sergius asked as he got on the wagon. He sat next to the thirteen-year-old girl from the ship, now orphaned and under his wardship. A week before she had watched her dead mother stripped of clothing and flung down a steep ravine the caravan passed in the mountains.

The girl nodded numbly and Sergius smiled, drew his hand across her wind-burned face. He whispered in her ear and she got into the bed of the wagon, closing the curtains behind her. He signaled and the caravan moved on, urged by the snap of whips in the hands of servants promised money and more food to keep the weak going.

"You there, come," Sergius called to a limping servant. Sergius signaled the surprised man to join him on the wagon's bench. The mason for the manor hurried on his bad leg, hurled himself up and sat alongside Sergius, thanking Almighty God for his luck. He knew Sergius had no idea who he was or what duties he performed as a mason. He was handed the reins. Sergius got into the bed of the wagon, not bothering to close the curtains.

The mason's happiness at not having to walk soon faded as groans and heavy breathing came from within. Try as he might, he could not stay turned away. Slowly, he swiveled his head, unable to resist. Finally no choice but to look back into the carriage bed.

Sergius was on his knees in front of the whimpering girl. His robe was raised and she was ministering to his burns with a wet cloth, though how he directed her to do so could not clearly be seen. He was not looking at the girl but at the mason. Sergius let out a climactic moan, as if he had been waiting the whole time just for the mason to turn, waiting for him to quench his curiosity.

The mason instantly knew where Sergius' pleasure came from. Sergius had coerced him without a word, forcing him to participate in the scene, feeding his curiosity, making him a voyeur to the priest's lust. Sergius groaned, took short panting breaths, but whether it was pain or ecstasy the mason could not guess. The mason's head snapped back to the front. His shame was such that he set down the reins, slipped off the bench and let the carriage move on, driverless.

"Gaetani," called Sergius. "Send the guards to dispatch that demon. My ward and I could have been killed."

The mason walked a good ways from the caravan before he was spotted. He continued to limp through the field, praying to God to forgive his weaknesses. He could not keep from looking

*The Woman Pope*

and he could not save the girl. It was the last straw. Life, the world, everything was finally and unequivocally evil. He could not save any of them, any of the others who perished so horribly in front of his eyes. It was an inhuman, insane journey across the continent. He simply did not care anymore, even as the guards gained on him with their swords raised.

The exhausted servants who bothered to watch the pious mason with the armed guards in his wake, could not raise enough energy to care. It was just another moment of death that would likely overtake them, too.

The mason never stopped praying out loud, even as several blades came down on his neck, hacked into his head, his arms, and pierced his back with the wet cough of metal struck into flesh.

An hour later the sun was still high, but the long shadow of a mountain range reached the caravan, engulfed the decrepit train in its extended dusk, and blew an icy draft down upon the caravan's back.

≈ ≈ ≈

On the same mountain road Sergius had passed over a week before, Halbert trudged knee-high in snow through a high valley. The painful glare of day dimmed into a bluish twilight as storm clouds rolled in. The valley was wide and sprinkled with snow-wrapped trees, frozen ponds. Surrounding the valley, rocky ledges hung with frozen swords and daggers of gleaming razor sharp ice. Halbert made his way through the tremendous blue-white palace.

*This would be the most inspiring panorama, were I a bird flying over it*, thought Halbert. But trapped within the dazzling great hall, rags wrapped around his head, ice clogging his beard, Halbert was so cold and tired he longed only for the unyielding heat of the plains.

It began to snow again. He pulled his old cloak closer, and walking through a ravine, he passed what appeared to be a single leafless branch sticking out of the snow.

But something about it made him stop.

"I beg your pardon," he said to himself blankly, breathless and lightheaded in the thin air. His closer look at the limb revealed it was not wood at all, but an arm extending out of the snow, its hand outstretched in a pathetic gesture, as if to halt death. He knelt, brushed away the snow. Halbert looked upon the remains of a middle-aged woman, her clothes taken for their bit of warmth. She was left with nothing, not even a burial at the road's end.

"You poor soul. He left you behind, too?" Halbert did not recognize her from the manor, but knew for certain Sergius had passed here and that she was the latest in his trail of death.

He pried his blue fingers loose from his walking staff, unwrapped the rags covering them and blew on his hands to circulate the blood.

He walked on, training his mind on a happier time to distract him from the cold. Halbert thought of eight-year-old Johanna running ahead of him down a sunny path on a summer day. Everything in the world was possible along that trail. A warm breeze puffed lazily at the trees in looping gusts, insects buzzed and whirred in the tall grasses, bees bounced over flowers, and the forest was redolent with honeysuckle. Halbert listened to two blue jays argue in an ancient oak and watched a jubilant little Johanna skip down the path as she sang to herself.

A bitter gust of wind cut sharply into the memory and brought Halbert back. He got angry at himself, knowing that this was the way to die, by not paying attention to the deep snow as the valley's treacherousness rose quickly now that the sun had gone.

Halbert tried to keep his spirits up by attempting to practice his bird calls. The wind stopped, as if waiting to hear his bird song. Halbert blew, but his mouth froze into the purse of a whistle and nothing came past his lips save for the white plume of his breath in the quiet stillness of dusk.

≈ ≈ ≈

The pagan army followed Johanna and Adrian for two days. From their ranks came raucous singing during the day and at night their camp echoed in abandon. Only the wild-woman leader, Veleda, dared come to their camp fire at night and sit with Johanna and Adrian.

"What tribe are you, Veleda?" Adrian asked, passing her a cup of willowbark tea. She stared at Johanna, still awestruck. The monk whose life had been saved sat away from the fire, his gaze fixed a thousand meters out into the dark.

"We are the last of our kind and have lost our real name," she replied. "We are hated by most and stay to the woods now, though ours was once the only religion here, and our gods the only gods."

"Where did you come from? Where is your home?"

"In lands far northwest of here. It has some new name I do not know how to say."

"What happened to your people?" Johanna looked over Veleda's shoulder and saw rows of attentive eyes watching beyond the fire.

"The Christ came and killed our gods. We practiced the old ways in secret. Our people were everywhere, the islands in the north, in Germania," she said, gesturing in each direction. "Over the years the bards and teachers left and took our magic with them. We forgot the ceremonies, how to call forth our gods and goddesses. So they left us, too. We have been left by all the gods, until yesterday."

Veleda raised her cup and smiled at Johanna.

Johanna and Adrian stopped the wagon beside a wide river bank, near where Sergius had sailed from weeks before. It was late afternoon and they said good-bye to the beaten monk, who refused to travel any farther with them. At the river's edge the frightened man limped north, glancing nervously over his shoulder at the pagan multitude waiting in silence, all eyes on Johanna.

The quiet was eerie. Johanna got up in the bed of the wagon to face the ragged lot. Mostly dark haired yet fair skinned, a hundred fifty men, women and children waited.

"I must leave you here, my friends," Johanna said, speaking slowly, enunciating the rough Germanic most knew. "We have shared two precious days, but now I continue on to Rome."

"Why Rome?" asked Veleda.

"I have to find my father."

"We will follow you! We want to find our Father, too," said Veleda. The crowd called out in a cheer and Johanna realized her error and started to speak again. The wild-woman turned to the others. "Do I speak for us all?"

They roared their agreement.

"We follow the monk to Rome!" the pagans yelled.

The wild-woman turned to Johanna. "What is your name, brother monk, so we might praise it?"

"No, Veleda! Praise God only," she corrected. "I…I go by the name…John."

The name came spontaneously to her lips, a surprise. As soon as she said it the memory formed in her mind. Johanna again lived the moment when John, the red-haired stammering boy, stood at the rail of the ship that night, gently kissed her cheek and told her his name before she jumped overboard, saving her life.

"We follow John!" Veleda yelled. The pagans commenced with a skewed chant,

"John! John! John!"

Johanna raised her hands and instantly the noise died.

She felt a chill at the immediate silence, at this new power. She could not be responsible for so many. Johanna felt for them but did not like these roughs or their primitive ways, ways that were rude and unpredictable. She could not locate why they repulsed her since they were similar to many uncivilized tribes she and Halbert had encountered. They must get away, escape this brutish crowd that would be a distraction every step of their way.

"Friends, I do not even know how to find my way down river, how can you follow me?"

"Ask God!" came voices in various tongues. The barbarians swarmed around her, whistling, shouting, waiting for another miracle like the palsied man.

Johanna looked at the faces before her and was afraid. The power that had come over her two days before was gone, a strange memory. Johanna did not want to lead anyone. She was a woman disguised as a man, not a leader.

Several pagans marched to the river bank, tromping back and forth at the edge, blowing goat horns and calling out their demands to the heavens.

Johanna looked for Adrian. *These hardened children think they are at a magic demonstration, waiting to be astonished by the next trick*, she thought. They wanted to find God through miracles and trances. Johanna felt ashamed. She misled them back on that road. The passion in the forest came back to haunt her as a monumental error in communication. Adrian stood near the horses, letting them drink from buckets of river water.

"Brother *John*," he said, facetiously. "I think this might be a good time to pray to the Lord to be shown the way. The way out of here."

"Excellent idea, brother," she replied, and raised her hand for silence.

"Friends, I must make this journey by myself," she said. The entire party looked confused.

"We want to follow you, John," said Veleda.

"No, you cannot," she said, and wanted her voice to sound firmer than it did. "I must go. You stay here. Good bye."

"But what do we do, Brother?" Veleda looked tearful.

"Do what the One God says when He speaks to your hearts."

She sat by Adrian, who had gotten up on the bench. He snapped the reins lightly and the wagon moved out.

The pagans did not know what to do. They followed the wagon as it rode along the river. They looked expectantly at the little brother; he could not possibly leave them now, could he? Now that he had shown them the True God?

The monk had told them to ask. Ask they did. Where were the answers to their prayers? mumbled the pagans to each other. Adrian and Johanna passed apprehensive glances, and quickly led the wagon away from the river.

Whispers passed through the tribe which both Johanna and Adrian could hear from the wagon. Was this a charlatan who fooled them? Perhaps this little monk laughed at them, thinking they were dumb. The grumbling turned to anger.

"Adrian, what have I done?" whispered Johanna next to him.

"Get ready," he said, and looked for the best escape route. Nodding toward a southern pathway, they made ready to run for their lives.

The horses were suddenly pulled up short, the reins taken from Adrian.

"Tell me, brother, where you think you are going?"

Adrian turned to the voice and flinched. Though he sat high on the wagon, he looked eye-level at a giant of a man, huge and towering with two close-set, black, soul-less eyes peering into his with a scowl. The pagan had shaved half his bullish head smooth, while the long hair on the other half stood on end by means of a foul animal paste so putrid it made Adrian want to gag. The man was hairy as a bear, his face, neck and arm hair blending over his body into a single contiguous black felt. He held tight to the reins with one hand, in the other rested the blade of a sword as tall as a man on Adrian's left shoulder, one sharp edge against his neck.

Adrian felt the blade press his jugular vein. His eyes went from blade to owner and saw the giant's crooked smile, waiting eagerly for Adrian to move so he could cut his throat.

≈ ≈ ≈

"Hand me the reins, *brother*," demanded Adrian, and reached for the leather. The pagan giant simply put his hand over Adrian's face, covered it from ear to ear and prepared to slice his head off with his sword. Johanna jumped from the wagon, got in front of the man and looked into his face.

"Stop!" she threatened. "You listen to me!"

Before she could continue, a barrage of animal horns sounded, trumpeting the air and causing the river bank to hum with expectation.

Several pagans near the water began to howl.

Dozens of hands waved and pointed upstream. The giant swordsman took the weapon away from Adrian's neck and turned in the direction of the noise.

"Look what message comes from heaven." said Veleda.

"God answers John again," shouted a bald woman in the crowd, and the phrase was passed along like a chant. Johanna and Adrian looked out on the water and witnessed a sight that would stay with them forever.

Rounding the far bend on the river, like the vessels built by forgotten ancient gods, three seagoing Viking longboats sailed into view. Blowing downstream in the slow-moving current, their red-striped sails unfurled, billowing in a strong tail wind. The exotic crafts were at least fifty leagues from any ocean and most of a continent away from home.

"We hunted with them months ago," said Veleda. "They continued the search for the house of Odin, their father god. They said he hanged himself, but perhaps his ghost spirit is here."

"You know them?" Johanna asked. More barbarians.

Veleda smiled. "Good fighters from the north snow world. Vikings are a fierce people who look for oceans to cross."

"I've heard of Vikings," said Adrian. "But nothing about their gods, and nothing good."

"That is all right," smiled Veleda. "I am sure they will tell you about them, and then our little brother will explain where their gods have gone on our way to Rome."

Johanna looked out at the oncoming ships. Pagans rushed to the water and lined the banks of a sandy beach, dancing and shouting, their prayers miraculously answered.

Johanna and Veleda watched Viking and pagan call to each other in war-like challenges, both tribes shaking their weapons, cursing in their respective languages as the longboats sailed along. Adrian walked to the river bank for a better view, the strange splendor of the ships drawing him closer.

"We'll cut your heads off and use them as torches on spears!" cried a pagan in crude Saxon.

"We will skin your hides and wear you in winter!" returned a red-haired, silver bearded Viking. He waved a tremendously long, double-edged lance. Pagan and Viking continued to threaten each other, stacking one outrageous claim atop another until there was nothing left to climb.

Johanna stood on the wagon to see better, shading her eyes from the glare of the sun, fearing a battle was about to take place.

"We will, we will, uh, will eat you! Then fertilize the fields with your spore!" called the pagan giant from the bank.

"Well...how about if we...we...we will just fertilize your heads with our spore," responded the Viking with the silver beard, his red hair tied in a knot at the top of his head.

Both sides could hold back no longer and burst out laughing. The big sails of the ships were lowered, gliding smoothly into the shallower waters of the river. A surprised Johanna looked at Veleda.

"It was all bluster and wind," Johanna said, relieved.

"The games of warriors," Veleda shrugged.

As the three longboats neared, Veleda explained that the Vikings had broken from their violent clan at the mouth of the ocean in northwestern Germania. These Norsemen wanted peace, did not want to raid the wealthy monasteries and villages along the coast and were gladly sent from their brethren so that more spoils could go to fewer plunderers.

"Where are you heathens going?" called a blond-haired Viking from the lead ship. A short tattoo was blown on an elk horn and lines of long oars came out from the ships, making them look like great centipedes on the water.

"We go to find our Great Father in the south," replied the pagan giant at Adrian's neck.

"Join us," cried the Viking, speaking for the others. "We heard good things about the south. We will hunt together again."

The oars were plunged into the water to drag the ships, anchors tossed out when the longboats came as close to the banks as they dared.

"We will show you how to ride the wind and the water," silver-beard continued. "That is if you weaklings are not too afraid."

"Warriors walk," the pagans shouted back when the giant and the few other pagans translated, puffing out their chests, laughing. "Lazy women ride on the water."

"Come aboard and show us what lazy women do."

The taunting continued and in the course of the game the Vikings invited the pagans aboard with gestures and challenges to sail south. It occurred to Johanna, as she stood on the wagon for a better look, that of course these two disparate tribes would find assurance in each other.

Both were outcasts, traveling through regions where they were feared and hated. Both tribes longed for a connection, a place to settle where they would be welcomed. When their treatment was otherwise, as it always was, their humiliation sparked violence.

Dinghies were launched from the longboats, and pagans began swimming out to the anchored ships.

"Hey," Johanna cried.

She was pitched backward and rolled into the bed of the wagon. Trying to sit up, Johanna thought the motion was the horses being spooked. Instead, she saw that while watching the longboats, the horses had been unhitched and led to the water.

The wagon was lifted into the air and carried on the shoulders of thirty yelling pagans. They walked it to the river as the Vikings cheered.

"Put this wagon down. You fools put it down right now!"

Her heart was stricken when she saw Vikings throw more ropes to several pagans swimming along side the ships. The pagans paddled back to the wagon with the ropes in their mouths and tied them on. The wagon was then pulled across the water to the ship by oar-strengthened arms of the Vikings.

"Stop! What are you doing! Adrian!"

"Johann-- uh, John!" Adrian called from the shore, elbowing his way through the crowd at the river's edge. "Brother!"

Hand over hand, with massive grunts matching the arms pulling at it, the wagon was hauled like an over-sized water-sled across the river and right to the side of the lead ship. Johanna had trouble catching her breath; the memory of boarding her first ship to England dug like a claw in her throat.

She struck at the hands as they came over the side of the wagon for her. Johanna tried to leap into the water, but was grabbed by a blur of arms, lifted across the space of wagon to ship so quickly, and set on the deck of the lead Viking longboat with no time to react.

"Don't touch me," she whirled around as hands let go of her and backed away. She looked over the deck and faced the barbarous northmen. More than three dozen men, women and children were on this first ship, all staring at her. A fair-skinned people in furs and hides, some wore pointed leather caps with nose bridges, others were bareheaded, and every mane was long and blew in the river wind. Each head had different colored hair -- blond, black, brown, white, yellow, and red-headed -- a sight that impressed Johanna because the variation was not like the familial likeness she had seen in villages where people had the same color eyes, hair and skin. The ship was clean, well-maintained and she could smell the strange, piquant odor of the wood it was made from, plus other smells of dried meat, a fiercely sharp tang of fermenting fruit alcohol, and the salt water smell of a far away ocean.

"Brother!"

A frantic and drenched Adrian climbed aboard spitting river water. Pushing aside the Vikings he rushed to her and forced himself not to take her in his arms with relief.

"I'm fine," she assured him, touching his arm.

"One moment you're next to me, in the next the wagon is flying over the water," he said, looking around the strange boat.

The calls of people started again and the rail of the ship was crowded with everyone yelling back and forth. Soon the river bank was deserted and Veleda's entire party clamored aboard the three longboats. Johanna's wagon and the two horses were hauled onto the deck with ropes and the brute strength of both tribes working in concert.

"At least they head in the right direction," observed Adrian, wryly, squeezing out his cloak.

"I do not plan to swim to Rome with these roughs," said Johanna.

"I wonder how we're going to get the wagon back on land," he sighed. Johanna watched the crease in his forehead deepen as he assessed their situation. His pensive expression, concern for her welfare, reminded Johanna of how much she loved this man and she reached over and squeezed his arm.

"We'll have them set us ashore," she said. "Believe me, I'll make sure they'll be glad to be rid of us."

The silver-bearded Viking, the captain, stood at the prow and blew a long note on his elk horn. The huge triangular sea sails were raised. The colorful billows luffed noisily until trimmed in the fresh gust and the ships moved into the current. Johanna and Adrian watched two other swift Viking vessels follow, cutting river water with their sharp, upraised prows arced skyward almost as high as the main masts.

Johanna faced those on board. The massive Vikings worked the oars and sang in cadence despite the wind at their backs. Men, women and children in animal skins mingled with the pagans and Veleda, all gesturing, trying to communicate.

Johanna sat with Adrian on the covers of two large water barrels lashed to the railing. The shock of the last hour faded and Johanna remembered how much her feet hurt. Removing her leather sandals, she massaged them.

"On a ship once more," said Adrian. He pulled his wet deep blue cloak around him against the wind. "The Lord must know best."

"I have to be truthful," admitted Johanna, putting her feet up on the railing, letting the wind caress them. She took in a breath of breeze, looked out at the land going by. "My poor feet are grateful for the rest, even if it's only for a day."

Together they watched the swift river carry them away.

≈ ≈ ≈

Sailing was so much easier than walking that Johanna and Adrian were quickly lulled into a relaxed and recuperative state while they floated by forest, village and hillside. In the days that followed, Johanna observed camaraderie as well as tension building aboard the ships. Viking men looked with desire upon pagan women and tall Viking women eyed sturdy pagan men. Johanna knew there was going be bloodshed or marriages. Or both.

The ships sailed down a stretch of a river whose name the pagans pronounced in the Gaul tongue. Near the foremast a game of skill was offered by three Vikings as a diversion to the water-nervous pagans.

"Observe, brother John," said Larst, the silver bearded Viking. He took four running steps, reared back and threw a large double headed hatchet. The weapon whirled through the air across deck, digging in to the leg of the target, a chalk outline of a man marked on the door leading below deck.

The voyagers approved with whistles and applause. Veleda walked up, kissed the man full on his lips, plunging her tongue deep into his mouth and kept it there to the hooting calls of the crowd. Larst reeled backwards, blushing and gasping as everyone laughed.

"That woman's blood," Johanna whispered to Adrian, "is always set to a full moon."

Johanna's arm was taken and she was led to the center of the ship. Loud coaxing from the entire crew drew Johanna hesitantly up to the mark. The big Viking put a small hatchet in her hand, a boy's first weapon. Larst guided her in the correct arc of motion over her head, then stepped back. Johanna took a few practice gestures, then ran and threw with all her might. The hatchet sailed over the door, passed over the railing and splashed into the river.

Laughter rocked the boat. Seeing the look on Johanna's face, Adrian tried to hold back. He put his hand at his mouth, but it got the best of him and he turned away, shoulders shaking. Johanna walked away, humiliated. The mortifying laughter bored into her. In a flash she reached over, pulled a small hatchet from the belt of a Viking. She made the four-step run again.

"Haaaaaaaah!" she cried with effort, throwing the weapon through the air with all the strength she possessed. It sailed over the heads of several people who wandered into the path of the game, and they ducked and cried out.

The hatchet dug smack into the forehead of the chalk target.

Both tribes were stunned into silence. Then they jumped to their feet with a deafening yell. Even the Vikings were impressed by the accuracy of the little monk.

"Laughed sooner than you should," said Johanna smugly when Adrian shook her hand.

"And I believe you will remind me of it for a long time to come."

"You may be certain of that."

"You can add this skill to that of your staff. You'll make a fine warrior yet."

"We may have need of both skills before we leave these ruffians," said Johanna as she waved to the crowd.

The three ships drifted downstream during the day, sailing past long stretches of wide river with mountains in the distance, high cliffs along the river bank. They sailed past towns where frightened people ran screaming into their huts at the sight of the war-like longboats.

And every day Johanna watched Adrian witness his faith to Viking and pagan alike.

Alternating between three languages and several dialects, plus the common sign language, Adrian spoke to small groups and individuals. Few understood his words, but the comfort of his voice calmed and made every passenger contemplative. Yet every night his efforts collapsed under the endless merrymaking, the occasional drunken brawls and the continuous sexual assignations.

Neither tribe could keep its hands off the other.

Every night Johanna followed Adrian to the sounds of panting, of moans and frenzied caterwauling to secluded areas of the ship.

"Get off her," he cried, walking up and slapping a Viking's bare behind in motion. "Both of you. Get back to your beds right now."

The man roared, stood up holding himself, ready to kill for the interruption. But before his hands lifted from his manhood, Adrian's staff came down on his head and dropped the big man to the deck, out.

"Perhaps you should leave these strangers to their own ways."

"That's not how I've been taught, Brother John."

He prowled the ship, prying couples apart like dogs. Adrian was known to throw buckets of cold river water on naked writhing bodies, the yelps heard around the ship, chastising them only to hear the fevered grappling renewed as soon as he left.

The third night, a frustrated Adrian returned to his bed and ignored Johanna's look of yearning.

"I am so tired of these lascivious goats," he said from under his blanket. "Their lust sickens me, angers God."

"Ah, yes, I'd forgotten you know His heart so well."

"Johanna," he said. "You know what they do is sinful."

Up on her elbows, she turned to him.

"They're a simple folk and look for simple things to fulfill them. Sometimes I wish I could forget the little knowledge I have and be content with innocence like theirs. They're children. They don't know what sin is and have to be instructed."

She watched him pull his blanket close and turn away. Who were they to judge any soul on this earth? *Judge nothing until the end*, she remembered her father used to say.

On deck the next morning, Johanna made a slow, exaggerated sign of the cross on herself. The gesture was not comfortable and doubt spread through her. What happened with the pagans? Was it a mistake?

"Watch how I do it," she said to the gathered Viking and pagan children. They giggled and followed suit, but mirrored the movements so that they genuflected backwards. She laughed and showed them again, though she was increasingly bothered by the feeling that the more she spoke, the more she knew nothing about religion beyond giving praise to the One God of all.

"Try it again," she smiled. "That's right."

She watched the world float by in pastoral scenes of countryside, farms and forest. The doctrine she learned from Adrian about the mother church stalled on her lips. The words about Jesus, Mary and the saints arrived empty in her mouth.

"Speak to God from your heart," she said to one confused pagan man grieving the loss of his long dead wife. She left him at the rail, his head in his hands. Johanna walked across the deck crowded with men discussing techniques in making weapons and hunting, women trading secrets in beading and jewelry making, and children playing everywhere. It dawned on her, sadly, that she had not been called to the Spirit since the first meeting with the pagans in the forest.

Johanna knew her experience falling from Sergius' ship and her possession in the forest was beyond description. To attempt to strain them through the tiny mesh of religion was as futile as having a blind man describe the splendor of a mountain from the touch of its shadow. She was reminded of her smallness, of how small the word religion is when set against reality. She felt unfit to lead anyone anywhere, much less point out a direction for these souls to follow.

Johanna stopped walking when she saw Adrian come up from the hold. Two cold days had passed since their argument and she watched warily as he came on deck with Bennito's shears and a razor and strode across deck. She looked away, afraid of what he might say.

Without a word he took her by the arm, walked her to a crate beneath the huge triangular sail and sat her down.

"Can I be of some assistance, brother?" she asked, trying to be aloof, distant. But when she gazed into his eyes her expression thanked him for the silent reconciliation.

"Sit still, John."

He stood behind her and cut her hair again, as had become his habit. He carefully reshaped, then shaved the tonsured circle at her crown. Johanna sighed at his gentle touch. It was a gesture beyond apology, showing his support. Johanna reached a hand behind her, and discreetly touched his calf while he worked. The day was cool and pleasant as they watched the two tribes play games, all the while flirting with each other. Adrian bent to her.

"I'm sorry," he whispered. "I love you. Nothing else matters to me."

Johanna was about to speak when a voice was heard above the din. The ship stopped still and listened as a Viking man sang a song.

To Johanna, his far north speech sounded like vowels and consonants sung backwards, words dipping and dragging in reverse. The pagans smiled at the strangeness of the voice, but remained respectful. Johanna's dark gold hair, bleached by the sun, was clipped and flew in the breeze around her. As she listened, she was overtaken by compassion for these people. It was useless to fight against it. She listened with the others, sharing a moment with a large blond man who, for all his outward ferocity was transformed into a small, vulnerable boy by the haunting wistfulness of his song.

His song ended on a high, extended noted and everyone remained quiet for several seconds. The man was startled and jumped back a step when applause and yelling erupted around him. The Viking had been transported to another place, surprised by his song's reception.

"There is warmth inside that big brute," commented Adrian.

"That's what I've always said about *you*," replied Johanna, mischievously, looking up at him as he massaged her shorn scalp.

The Viking made an awkward bow, and in the next moment the world aboard the ships changed.

The deck was hit with an enormous jolt. As if a great monster from the river and heaved itself into the prow. Everything and everyone on board was thrown off their feet, up into the air, forward. Water barrels, children, cows, squealing pigs, horses, crates of goods were all sent rolling across the deck into frightened heaps at the prow of the ship.

Johanna got up and ran to the rail. She looked out on the end of the navigable river. Craggy foothills before them led up toward the biggest mountain range she'd ever seen. The river was broken up into pieces by smaller streams coming down the hills. They had landed where the great river was born. The proud carved prow was crushed, its wood splintered deep into a rocky beach of an island in mid-stream.

The voyage by water was over. The long walk began.

# CHAPTER XVIII

ONCE THE WAGON was on shore, Johanna and Adrian quickly hitched the horses. They knew that now, in the confusion of disembarking, was the time to escape.

"Are you ready?" she whispered.

Here was the chance to retreat before any more of their coarse charm dug its way into her heart. The Vikings would not leave their boats, she reasoned, and both tribes had mixed many of their men and women, lovers who would not separate.

Adrian got on the wagon beside her, took the reins. Johanna glanced back, then shook her head.

A long line of semi-orderly followers, pagan and Viking alike, waited for her command. Beyond the crowd, the three ships were abandoned where they had run aground, left behind as easily as a cold camp fire. The sailors were ready to march.

"We seem to have more company, brother," said Adrian. He shook the leather straps of the reins and drove the frisky, boat-weary horses down the road

≈ ≈ ≈

At the same moment Johanna heaved a sigh, giving in to the fact that she was the reluctant leader of a brigade of barbarians, Sergius' wagons rolled through the enormous gates of Rome.

"Look there, Flower," Sergius said from the wagon, pointing beyond the main iron doors towering five stories above them.

The girl looked blankly at the great wall under construction around the perimeter of the city. "A wall around Vatican Hill. What a marvel."

The girl paid no attention, but braided the cloth hair of her doll while she softly sang to it. Sergius' eyes narrowed at her childishness. He clicked his tongue and signaled Gaetani.

"Make sure all stay close by now that we have entered the city," he whispered. "This is the most dangerous part of the journey and they do not even realize it."

The servants who survived did not have the strength to be apprehensive. The entourage had dwindled from an original forty-one wagons to four broken and barely usable vehicles. What started out as ninety-four healthy Christians numbered less than twenty wretched souls with the sick and maimed stuffed into two wagons and lessening that number every passing hour.

Many servants had left the caravan along the way, sneaking off at night, though most who attempted escape were killed in front the others, a gesture to keep their loyalty. Some were lost in skirmishes with bandits, but the rest succumbed to boils, fevers, adder bites, bites by diseased wild dogs, falls, drowning, chills, gangrene, despair, and assaults from fellow servants. Once, a rogue boar ran off with an infant. A dozen other maladies through a punishing wilderness diminished their numbers.

Finally, when the city was within sight, there was only one person who cared at all that they had reached their destination.

"Look at the grand basilica they've re-built!" said Sergius. The sole owner of joy among them as the wagons clattered over stone avenues, invigorated by the wonders of the holy city opened to him once again. The party limped past an ancient fountain with dirty brown water dribbling from the beautiful mouths and buckets of water nymphs. With this second chance, Sergius nodded to himself, there would be no more mistakes on the path to the Chair of St. Peter.

≈ ≈ ≈

Johanna walked beside her wagon along green hills rolling across the high mountains. She carried a three-month-old baby in her arms and walked over a pine tree landscape, the ground a lush grass carpet in a half dozen shades of chartreuse, lime, frog, mold, forest green.

"You beautiful little animal," she said, cooing at the baby. "Where is your father?"

"The father has no interest in her, nor I in him," replied the Viking mother along side her. "I'd just as soon find a man who loves us both."

The infant had the dark, curly hair of a pagan and the pale hazel eyes and fair skin of a Viking. Its Viking mother, plain-featured but with flashing brown eyes and a muscular build, smiled. The child was one of the fruits of the two tribe's first meeting before Johanna's arrival.

"You really do not care who he is? Or you do not know?"

"We make our own way," said the woman and aimed an inviting smile at a beefy pagan nearby who returned her gaze with eyes on the solid sway of her walk. Johanna put an arm around the woman.

"You need a husband."

"As you need a wife?" the pagan replied with a smile.

Johanna looked over the woman's shoulder and had to take a breath. The size of the colony had grown. And with the larger size came slower momentum. She could not believe how slow they were going. It had been two months on this section of the road alone. The frequent camp, the waiting for the ill and injured to get well, all conspired to drag her and Adrian farther and farther behind.

"Veleda?" she called. "Has Burlish returned?"

"Brother, give him a chance," said the wild-woman as she walked ahead of Johanna. "He only left this morning."

"We need to send more than two men at a time," said Johanna patting the baby's back absentmindedly.

"How many would you like?"

"Five," she said. The child burst out crying, startling her. "Sweetheart, I'm sorry!"

Scouts were sent not only to feel out danger ahead, but were given precise instructions regarding the large caravan of a wealthy priest. The reports always disappointed.

The pace was a boulder on Johanna's neck and nothing she did could speed them up.

"Can you please get the horses hitched so we can get going?" she said to Adrian the following morning.

"Here we go again," he muttered under his breath, then mimicked Johanna without her knowing, moving his lips as she called out her familiar routine.

"Time to move," she cried, clapping her hands and getting up on the wagon. "If you can not keep up do not hold the rest of us back!"

Two more months had gone into this grueling continental trek already eight months long, but the journey was a holiday for the four hundred people who made up the colony.

Every one of them a child, Johanna said to herself as she led them from the night's camp. At least, she considered, grudgingly, they were happy children. There was always laughter, and romance bloomed every day between the tribes. The followers of the little brother inhabited a large village that drifted from town to town as a slow-moving, human hive.

"You two," Johanna called. "Get down from there."

She spotted two eleven-year-old boys trying to sneak a ride on the side of the wagon late one afternoon.

"We're tired," one protested in his Norse tongue. They could not help laughing and pinching each other. They had leaves and sticks and bits of the forest stuck in their wild hair and when Johanna sniffed the air as they approached they smelled sour and sweet at the same time. "We want to ride."

"How about you ride on the end of my staff," she said, laughing and shaking the rod at them. "Two strong boys like you. You should do something useful, like learn Latin."

"We are warriors," said the dark-hair. A child, he had already picked up the language of the men.

"We want to fight," concluded his blond haired friend who was missing a front tooth.

"You want to protect your families?" asked Johanna as they hopped down from the wagon and walked beside her. They had swaggering gaits, sharpened stick swords tucked into their sashes and their little chests were puffed out like they had seen the men do.

"We want to kill bad people who want to kill us!"

"And we want to kill them first!"

"I have an idea," said Johanna, and she bent and whispered conspiratorially. "I will make you my guards, protectors for the whole colony."

"Do we get to kill people?" blond boy asked.

"You get to *save* others from being killed," she said. "Wouldn't you like that better?"

The boys frowned at each other and shook their heads.

"We want to kill people."

"If you watch carefully," she responded, "keeping an eye out for trouble and reporting to me, we will see."

"You will let us kill them?" blond boy asked, his tongue sticking hopefully between the gap left by the missing tooth.

"We're going to run into bandits, boys. When we do, you'll get your chance to be warriors. Keep a sharp eye out around the colony. Now, go, run off that wicked energy."

Johanna smiled and watched them run, whooping at their new grown up roles.

The arbiter for every dispute, Johanna knew she was respected and obeyed without hesitation by Viking, pagan and newcomer alike. The little brother made most her decisions while on foot as they traveled. At night at the fire with Adrian, she decided issues from petty thefts of food to the forbidden appetites of a Viking woman and a pagan woman, two mothers who were found in an lingering embrace, to deciding the health policies for the colony.

"You stink of liquor, back away," she said to the little pagan one morning as they walked. The same man who recoiled when she touched his liquor jug that first day she met the pagans. Excrement and vomit mixed with sour liquor came off the filthy little man. Several colonists put hands to their noses.

"Gilk harms no one but himself," the man protested, weaving as he walked.

"Many complain against you," she reminded him. "You are lewd with women and ask for sex. You expose yourself when refused, then run away."

"Gilk has never touched anyone but himself," he said, holding up a finger for emphasis. Everyone laughed.

"Set aside that jug or be set aside from our company," she said. "Decide now."

"There's no decision," he said, trying to be dignified and at the same time remain on his feet. "Gilk says good-bye."

He turned off the road, clutching the jug, his only possession. The followers jeered at his back, glad to be rid of the perverse nuisance as well as his reek.

The colony believed little brother was the most just and merciful of men, excelling in making people understand their actions and responsibilities. The little brother loved her duty. It was the only thing that kept her from waking at night and running off.

Johanna took the Viking baby from her mother. Petitioners waiting for her walked patiently behind.

"Who is next?" she asked.

"We are," said two men, waving their arms. "We are."

"No hitting," she warned. The pagan men began to argue when a cry came from the back of the caravan.

The pagan Gilk ran out of the woods, his liquor jug gone. He clutched a gaping wound in his side. He turned to the forest to point, and was struck squarely in the eyes, head, arms and stomach from a flock of arrows shot from the woods. He was dead before he hit the ground as a piercing howl, like a hundred rabid wolves, came from the forest.

One hundred Saracen warriors on horseback broke out of the cover of trees and swarmed over the rear flank of the colony.

"Adrian," Johanna called. She handed the baby to its mother, grabbed her staff and joined several shouting Vikings and pagans, men and women. All drew their weapons and tried to block the screaming attackers who, in their black burnooses rippling behind them in the wind, rode like black fires on horseback out from the forest.

*The Woman Pope*

# CHAPTER XIX

HALBERT STOOD UPON an open plain at the fork of a crossroads. Two paths, one wound lazily to the south, the other rolled north up into the mountains. The face of an ancient stone marker in the middle of the crossroad once gave the destination of the routes, but had been long ago defaced into oblivion by passing vandals.

Resting his weight on the walking staff he had made, Halbert looked down one path, then the other. His eye caught an odd shape. He walked off the road and came upon a body nearly covered by the high grass. It was another of Sergius' servants.

"What's happened to you, friend?" he asked, kneeling beside it. He examined the corpse, blown with flies, worms and insects. He then stood and hurried down the fork nearest the body, confident he was on the trail of the caravan.

"Mother Nerthus," he prayed as he ran. "Let her at least be with Sergius and not discarded like these poor souls."

≈ ≈ ≈

From the second story window of his temporary rooms, Sergius looked down upon the remaining survivors. The dozen or so left alive huddled next to the last two wagons filled with the sick and dying. Sergius had taken quarters in the city for himself, the monk Gaetani, his young 'flower,' Marozia, plus three of the healthiest and loyal men left.

"I fear this crop has come to market spoiled," he said, digging into his purse. "We must cut our losses and continue."

The men looked eagerly at one another. Sergius pointed to the first man, whose dagger-tattooed cheeks had thrown fear into every servant's heart.

"Approach," Sergius said.

One at a time the men knelt before him. Sergius whispered a final proviso in each man's ear then waited for him to nod.

At sunset Sergius' three men herded the last of the servants through the streets. Heading in the direction given by their master, they left the reputable parts of the city. Through narrow ancient boulevards and winding alleys, the half-dead foreigners anxiously looked around and clung to the sides of the two wagons as if they were lifeboats at sea.

A local man, a miller, called out to the group, waved his arms. He stepped close and spewed a rapid, non-stop warning in Italian. The foreigners reacted like chased dogs and hurried away. Other citizens watched dispassionately or clicked their tongues at the foolish strangers who dared enter the slum of Hell's Quarter as night fell. Surely they must know the inhabitants of that part of the city, scurrilous thieves, the insane and the murderous, were just beginning to wake. They must know what they are doing or they themselves must be crazy or evil.

"This is far enough," said one of Sergius' men, hand on his sword, his eyes glancing furtively around. His other hand poked a finger into the place where his ear had been, worrying the exposed hole in his head and rubbing the scarred-yellow burn area around it. They halted the wagons in a cul-de-sac of crumbling buildings abandoned almost a century before. In the middle of the square an untended fire burned with the acrid stench of marble.

Everyone in the party kept glancing beyond the perimeter of the fire, feeling eyes watching them from the shadows. The shadows cast by the fire upon the walls of the buildings were weird, flickering shapes over reeking piles of rubble and filth.

*The Woman Pope*

"Master has not only brought you safely to Rome," the one eared aide said. "But in his kindness has decided to give you freedom."

The servants looked blankly at the men.

"Don't you see?" asked the aide, his eyes darting to the darker corners, not really able to make out shapes that slipped from shadow to shadow. "You are released from your indenture, your debts have been paid. You are no longer bound to Sergius."

"What about our pay?" asked one man. "We don't have a scrap of food for our bellies."

"Pay? Your freedom is your pay," the ear-less man said.

"What about the sick?" asked Cook, and pointed at the two wagons. Her once fat body had been reduced on the march to a skeletal thinness, with grayish flaps of wrinkled skin hanging from under her chin and upper arms as proof of her former frame. "What about them?"

"Where will we stay?" asked the stable master, who went into a fit of consumptive coughing and filled a blood-stained handkerchief.

"Stay wherever you wish," the other aide said. His tattooed face flickered in the dim light of the fire. All three men eased away from the wagons, shoulder-to-shoulder, back-to-back, like a crab scurrying across sand; their eyes sensed a conspiracy spreading in the dark like a contagion. The survivors were startled by the sounds around them outside the fire light; discordant whistles and bird calls and drum beats.

"But we have no work in this city," said a laborer.

"We do not know the language," said Cook. The aides broke from their crab formation and fled as fast as they could, their weapons drawn, expecting an attack at every darkened corner.

"Don't leave us here!" a chambermaid screamed, her voice a hollow echo bouncing off the empty buildings. The servants shuffled around the wagons.

The last surviving members of the priest's household came to the end of their long journey that night, left alone in the most ruinous sector of Rome with the eyes of human predators fixed upon them. Hungry groups gathered in the shadows, just outside of view, and disembodied laughter came from beyond the fire-light. The servants could not run, did not have the strength to escape their new captors and knew if any dared to bolt they would perish.

All that was left to do was wait for the sputtering fire to burn itself out and for the night to cover the two decrepit wagons.

"Bishop Martus' passing was a sad day for us all," said the elderly churchman. His grey face suddenly scrunched up into a horrible, wrinkled frieze. He let loose a tremendously loud and wet sneeze directly at Sergius without the slightest attempt to cover his mouth. He paused to wipe his nose across the folds of his robes.

His huge and cloudy eyes were as puffy as the neck of a bull-frog. At the apex of the sneeze his eyes bulged to the point of popping out, bringing the picture of an ornately dressed frog closer to Sergius than he cared to imagine.

"I hear he was the most pious of men, Archbishop Clement," said Sergius. He knelt on the carpet before the Vicar of Rome, who was dressed in purple robes and a high, gem laden tiara. It had taken a week of bribes and promises but Sergius was finally granted an audience with the archbishop. He hoped the man's reputation was not a fiction and prayed that Bishop Martus had not given too good a description of Sergius to the late archbishop before he died.

It was the death of Martus which had allowed Sergius to re-turn to Rome. What Sergius had done in his first life in Rome he hoped the good Bishop Martus had taken with him to the grave. Sergius winced at the memory of old man Martus walking in on him and the two orphaned girls in his chambers all those years ago. The private 'catechism' he was caught performing on them had been on Sergius' third day in Rome. The unimaginable shock of what the Bishop witnessed almost sent Martus to the next world right then. Sergius, bribing his guard in the Vatican prison, slipped out of the city that night. He left nothing behind in Rome except his name, which he changed on the spot to Ser-gius, taken from a hallowed pope centuries ago. He fled back to the safety of England.

The Bishop's death was the message received at his manor and with Martus dead, Sergius' exile had been quietly transmuted.

"It is true," said the archbishop, his nose twitching with another sneeze. "Bishop Martus loved God above all material things, as do I."

Sergius eye's narrowed slightly at this unwelcome news.

"Even if you could find a loving, honorable soul," Sergius agreed, pressing lightly ahead. "The Bishop would be a difficult man to replace. I have been praying such a man lives in Rome."

The archbishop rubbed his nose, yawned and looked disinterestedly at the priest at his feet. The long white chin hairs sweeping the floor before him as he knelt was a strange sight, even though the archbishop was used to oddities from all over the world finding their way to Rome.

Clement wondered who this cipher had paid to get this far. Certainly this ferret of a man could not possibly be hinting at wanting Martus' office. But what was his real agenda? He ran down a short mental list of the most obvious Vatican bribes which might give a clue, but his concentration dissolved when the aroma of his favorite dinner, about ready to be served, came to his nose.

The thick smell of boiled, heavily salted pork livers and late season sour cabbage wafted through the door of his private dining room. His mouth watered and it was time to dismiss this nobody.

"I hope that your prayers will be answered but I am afraid the Bishop's role on earth has gone with him to heaven," sniffed the archbishop, the twinge of another sneeze working through the aroma of liver and cabbage. "There is no need to fill his shoes any more."

He held out his ring to be kissed. Sergius sucked in his breath and paused before his leap. The seriousness of the risk had thrilled his insides all day long in anticipation of this moment.

Sergius did not kiss the proffered hand but put a scroll in it instead.

"What is this?" the Bishop glared as he unrolled the paper. His lips moved as he read. Sergius studied the priest, knowing in the next moment he would have to prostrate himself before the archbishop and beg for his life, or kill the old man and attempt a second escape.

The old man locked his gaze onto Sergius.

"You would give all this to the church?" the archbishop asked.

"Your holiness, my wealth is a burden that is better to serve the poor. You will distribute this small donation to the deserving, perhaps on your travels to the winter basilica. Or however you see fit."

The archbishop looked closely at Sergius' hands, humbly clasped. He returned the priest's obsequious expression with a jaded smile.

"The wagon with my poor gift awaits outside," said Sergius, his head bowed in submission. "If you so desire."

The archbishop touched Sergius' shoulder and bid him to rise. Sergius smiled and felt the man's anticipation. They walked to the window and looked down into the alley. Sergius clapped his hands and his three men beside the last wagon snapped to attention.

The aide with no ear flipped up the muslin curtain. It revealed a wagon stacked with rich tapestries, gold goblets, plates and two sturdy metal chests. He opened one of them and the archbishop leaned so far out the window Sergius had to keep the man from tumbling three stories to the ground. The chest was filled with gold coins, ingots, bracelets, necklaces. A small fortune shined back at the Archbishop of Rome.

"I am certain Bishop Martus looks down from heaven at this moment, well pleased with the man who will wear his robes," the breathless archbishop exclaimed, his eyes bulging at the bounty. He turned and embraced Sergius, holding him as close as a lover.

"Reverend Signore, the graciousness of your benefaction outweighs my meager offering," said Sergius, gently trying to squeeze out from the man's sweaty arms.

"You are much too kind, dear brother."

"Let us celebrate my arrival to the holy city and the good fortune of Rome's destitute. I pray they will benefit from what I offer."

"Don't sell your endowment short," admonished the archbishop, wagging a finger at Sergius. "Those who receive your gift will be greatly enlarged."

"I pray it will be so," said Sergius. "Your Grace, I have some excellent mead, the taste of which you might find enjoyable."

"I might indeed!"

"You might even be able to coax a bottle or two from me for your trip to the country, archbishop," said Sergius. The men laughed and walked arm-in-arm toward the dining room door.

≈ ≈ ≈

"Get to the wagon!" Adrian yelled. He swung his staff and blocked the blow of a scimitar as it came at his head.

"I'm staying!" cried Johanna. She swung her staff and clubbed Adrian's attacker to the ground.

At the foot of snow-topped mountains, the lovers fronted a line of Vikings and pagans who fought a cavalry of black-turbaned Saracens.

Axes were flung at backs, scimitars slashed shields, arrows hailed across the sky in dark clouds, arcing then falling as they rained around the monk, striking colonists running to get away.

Johanna saw Jonyal, the hairy pagan giant who had almost cut Adrian's throat, swing his sword wildly despite the fact that more than half a dozen arrows stuck out of his arms, legs and head. Two mounted Saracens charged him from either side, waving their scimitars.

"Come, let me help you find your God!" Jonyal yelled and swung, cutting one of the men off the saddle of his horse. But the giant was not quick enough for the second rider who slashed a deep blow into his back. Jonyal staggered, turned and was met by a third charger thundering past him. The point of the Saracen's long lance ran completely through the giant's stomach and out his back before it snapped off. Jonyal dropped to his knees and merely slumped his head forward. His body remained upright, propped up by the broken lance.

Pitiful screams of horse, men and women filled the air. Johanna's oak staff worked furiously, meeting heads, backs and faces as the colony was overrun from every side.

The black riders came in screaming waves to disperse the colony. Once done, it would be an easy task to eliminate the clusters as they fled, which was their classic strategy. But the marauders were met with such savagery from pagan and Viking, fighting shoulder-to-shoulder without fleeing, their resistance threw the horsemen off their plan.

Ten minutes into the raid, Larst, the Viking captain, leapt onto the saddle of the Saracen leader and split his head open with an axe.

Larst left the axe there, held the corpse in place and rode the man's horse around the colony to show both sides his victory.

A horn was blown. The swirling mass of Orientals turned in retreat. The colony cheered and redoubled the fight while the attackers tried to pull back into the forest.

Johanna looked around for Adrian and blanched at what she saw. "No!" Johanna ran, as a Saracen, his turban splashed with blood, rode with his blade raised and swooped down on a fleeing Viking, one so small his helmet bounced on his little head as he ran from the rider, crying, armed with a stolen enemy scimitar, much too big for him.

"No!" she cried again. "He's just a--"

A single slice from behind and one of Johanna's eleven-year-old protectors rolled in the dirt nearly cleaved in two, dead.

Johanna sprinted out of the fray and charged the Saracen.

"You would murder a child? He was a child, damn you!"

The leader pulled up his horse and saw what he had done. About to get off his mount and go to the boy, he saw a hysterical monk running at him. The robes changed the Saracen's demeanor. He raised his bloody sword and yelled, as if it were the monk's fault the boy had entered the battle and died.

He galloped for the infidel running towards him. The Saracen charged, leaning to one side, lifting his scimitar over his head.

"Allah Aqbar!" he cried. "Allah Allah Allah Allah!"

He swung at the infidel, the blade swishing the air.

Johanna ducked, felt the breeze from the razor sharp metal within a hair's breath of her neck and at the same time whirled around. She hurled the staff with both hands.

The oak rod struck the rider square in the back, throwing him from the horse. The warrior hit awkwardly, his leg twisting with an audible *snap*. He bellowed in pain, caught his breath and saw the little monk standing above him holding his own bloody scimitar, a murderous look in his eye. A shout from behind caused both to turn.

"Allah Allah Allah Allah Allah!"

The Saracen second-in-command galloped at Johanna and was about to cut her in half. She felt the thunder of hooves bear down, beating into her ears and watched the rider bring his sword back.

The Saracen suddenly jerked his head to one side.

He dropped his weapon and galloped passed Johanna. He slumped on the horse, tried to remove the arrow deep in his Adam's apple. Johanna looked over her shoulder in the direction the arrow came.

Veleda, re-arming her bow, gave Johanna a grim smile.

Adrian rushed to Johanna and beside him the Viking Larst went to plunge a rusty sword into the Saracen squirming with pain at her feet.

"He's mine!" she cried, and pushed the Norseman aside. The Arab hissed a curse at her and raised a dagger clutched in his fist.

"Brother John," warned Adrian, seeing her mad look.

"Thief of innocence," she said. "Murderer!"

"No. Jooooan!" said Adrian and reached out to stop her.

She brought the scimitar down hard as she could and, with his own blade, sliced off the Saracen's sword arm at the elbow.

Adrian called her name, but his voice was lost in the battle. The Arab screamed, rolled and convulsed, the hand of his severed arm gripping a fistful of dirt in a spasm. Holding the heavy weapon with both hands, Johanna came out of her frenzy and stared at her work.

"Adrian?" she asked, and looked up at him with a quizzical look. She turned, dropped to her knees and vomited. A great howl went up from Viking and pagan alike. With a renewed energy the whole colony chased the retreating marauders into the woods. The battle was over.

The agonized face of the unconscious Saracen haunted her that night as she tended him. Earlier, she had two Vikings reluctantly hold him down while she cleaned and cauterized the stump with a heated sword blade, then stanched the arm with herbs and dressed it with bandages. After she splinted his broken leg, Johanna stood up. The front of her robe was a solid burgundy. She went to a dying pagan woman whose final moans called out for the little brother to come with his magic touch before her imminent departure from this world.

# CHAPTER XX

HALBERT WALKED THROUGH the immense gates of Rome. He counted to himself; it had been ten long months in arriving and he wondering how long Sergius had passed through the same gate before him to make the city his home again. Exhausted, he had made a mistake the month before. He followed the wrong fork at a crossroads, and it took weeks to get back to the source of his error.

After backtracking the many wasted days, he finally hurried down the correct path and on the road Halbert met an Italian merchant heading for Tusculum, eleven leagues from Rome. He traveled with Giovanni Bercovicci on his wagon, loaded to its limit with huge wheels of aged cheese. Bercovicci, grateful for the company and a pair of strong arms to protect his valuable cargo, immersed Halbert in the language of Rome along the way. A month later they said good-bye at his villa at Tusculum. The merchant gave him a cloth-wrapped wheel of the pungent cheese as a gift, telling Halbert he could sell it in a Roman marketplace for enough to feed and house him for a week if he haggled well.

Halbert arrived at the city gates late that afternoon. He sighed, hands clutching the cheese to his chest, weeping and smiling as he passed beneath the high walls of Rome.

"Tell me, friend," he asked a man carrying a tall basket on his head stuffed with green anise stalks. "Are we truly entering the Eternal City or do we dream?"

"Get away, beggar. You will know it's a dream when you find yourself dead."

"Why would I find myself dead, friend?"

"One way or another, all you pilgrims find your way to the foreigner's cemetery or the bottom of the Tiber."

Halbert laughed and his spirit rose despite the remark. He looked around at the grandeur of Rome.

"Such a beautiful city, is it not?" he asked an old woman moving among the crowds shuffling along the street. Everything moves so fast here, he thought, even this old mother has speed in her step.

"Beautiful?" she said, surprised. She placed a penny in his hand. "Poor blind beggar. Hurry from here. Go."

After walking for several hours in a blissful haze, Halbert bought half a loaf of week old bread with the penny. He set the cheese beside him and ate sitting on a crumbling marble base, all that was left of a grand ruined column, looking on the busy street. In his gladness upon arriving at the city he had dreamed about for so long, all Halbert saw at first sight was a Rome made entirely of art. Glorious artwork fashioned into buildings by painters and sculptors, master-builders. A cosmopolitan, sophisticated people passed Halbert from every corner of the world, stylishly dressed, speaking languages from the new Frankish kingdoms, Greece, Syria, Egypt, Byzantium, the Saracen empires and a dozen others. He turned, startled by a ghostly image beside him.

"That's mine, child," he said.

A filthy little girl of nine with a soot-blackened face and the steely glance of an old woman had wrapped the big wheel of cheese to her chest with little stubby fingers and was carrying it off.

"Stop before I hurt you!"

She disappeared into the crowded street with Halbert close behind. Thinking the emaciated child could not possibly get far hauling such a heavy object, Halbert pushed his way through the crowd.

With a dozen quick steps she was gone. The frail-looking urchin vanished with a wheel of cheese as large as her head.

Halbert pushed people aside, concerned for her safety, expecting her to be crumpled on the street, exhausted from the weight of the cheese. There was no sign of the girl or his only means of support.

Much later, finally, he had to admit that the child was the new owner of an excellent source of income and once again he had nothing. His only consolation was perhaps the little girl might be able to leave the streets with her new wealth. But if he had found her, cheese or not, she would not have been able to sit down for a week.

Remaining buoyant, Halbert walked through streets blessed by the hands of the gods.

Yet the more his eyes took in the city the more Rome revealed her real self. An ancient urban municipality, it was filthy, harsh and crumbling at every turn. Walking through throngs crowding the streets Halbert saw despair on every corner.

"Forget the city. Forget the cheese. Let's return to the heart of the matter," he said out loud, shaking his head and vigorously rubbing his hands together as he walked.

He turned his focus toward finding Johanna.

What happened to their convoy? Did they take a wrong road? Were they waylaid and taken as hostages? Halbert considered every possibility, then returned again to the city's main gate. No one he questioned recalled a grand train of wagons, only the usual small bands of wandering merchants and ragged pilgrims.

"Are you sure?" he asked, repeating himself for fear his poor Italian was not getting through. He directed the question at a woman who had set up a stand across from the gate with her strands of poorly made bead bracelets.

"I should know, I live here," came her response, the same as all the others. "I watch that gate every day."

He walked for hours, stopping everyone he saw.

"Don't run away. Listen. Have you seen a girl, she's eighteen, tall and with light brown, blondish hair, new to the city?"

"A whore? I might have taken her once in the underground."

"No, she is not a...you." Halbert had to stay his hand. "No, she is a good young woman. Let me tell you what she looks like, perhaps you have seen her?"

Late that first night, with only drunkards, criminals and the insane left on the streets, Halbert paused outside a row of shabby buildings. He slumped against a wall and slid down to the street.

Unable to take another step, Halbert fell asleep on his knees leaning against the wall.

He awoke with a tickling sensation on his side and the smell of feet in his nose. Halbert opened his eyes, crying out at the sight before him.

"What are you doing?"

The thing touching him backed away and Halbert got a better look, making him wince at the full impact.

A tiny, barefoot troll-like creature stepped back and glared indignantly at Halbert.

"Unbelievable," the thing said, speaking to no one in particular, shaking its hairy head, disgusted. "Not one single solitary thing of the slightest value on this ragged lump. This is some kind of first."

"You were trying to rob me?" asked Halbert, incredulous. "*You?*"

"Had you anything worth stealing," the little man grinned, cocking his head at Halbert like a raven. "I assure you I'd be long gone, and you'd be left with nothing but the smell of my feet as evidence."

"How is that possible?" asked Halbert, standing, looking down on the impudent little thief. "You have no...uh, you haven't got..."

"I have no hands, oh Wise Observer of Men!" taunted the troll. He held up the stumps at his elbows and waved them obscenely at Halbert, making him back up, wary. "A singular man like yourself sees what others often miss."

"Your hands hacked off for stealing," observed Halbert, determined not to let this little bug best him. "So now you steal with your feet."

The troll dropped to the ground, rolled onto his back and, to Halbert's surprise, applauded loudly with his feet.

"Bravo!" said the troll, looking more like a strange animal than a man. Dark skin, thick black hair, coarse as a wild horse's mane shot through with gray tendrils. His bangs were cut crudely over his narrow and perpetually squinting black eyes. Eyes small and cunning that barely fit on either side of a tremendously downward sloping nose with wide flaring nostrils.

The nose blocked the sight of most of his mouth and baby-like teeth hiding behind thin, snarling lips.

He stopped clapping, bent his knees to his forehead and with an extraordinary kick, leaped from prone to feet without using his arms.

"Good show," said Halbert, applauding back, smiling at this odd creature, who made a short bow.

"What is your name, stranger," demanded the troll, knocking at the dust on the back of his clothes with his stumps, "so I might avoid wasting my time on a destitute beggar like you again."

"I am afraid you are stranger than I, Halbert of Mainz, and will always have that peculiar honor. What is your name so that I might pray the next appendage you lose from theft will be your tongue?"

"Mullung lose his tongue?" The troll looked at Halbert with genuine surprise. "May your little-used member be whittled to the size of a gnat's prick before Mullung tur Alandim is at a loss for words."

Halbert laughed and bowed in return. "You may be right, Mullung, sir, though for my organ to become the size which yours is now is not a problem for a learned scholar as it is for a bawdy troll."

Mullung made a chortling sound under his breath. "And speaking of tongue, Monsignor von Mainz, have you breakfasted yet?"

"Not yet, Signor Mullung. My servants must still be asleep to keep me waiting so long."

"It is so hard to acquire good help, believe me, sir. With your permission, I would ask you to join me in a slight but delicious repast at a generous butcher shop I know. Beef tongue," said Mullung, winking at Halbert and strolling toward the front of the alley.

"Thank you for your offer, but I am most full of tongue," said Halbert, holding his stomach as if he were stuffed, walking alongside the little man. "My stomach needs something with more bite to it."

"That could be arranged," said Mullung dryly and they walked out of the alley eyeing each other side-ways, sardonic smiles held at bay.

"I need my strength as I continue my search."

"Search, sir?"

"I've come to Rome to re-claim a vast treasure of mine."

"I see," said Mullung, his smile widening. "May I offer my humble services? Before you stands the finest guide in Rome with the most complete knowledge of this principality since the Justinian age."

"Impressive," said Halbert as they walked. "I will consider your offer, sir."

They were already friends.

Halbert spent weeks wandering Rome with tiny Mullung as his guide. He never bothered to ask for food and was surprised when Mullung begged or stole a morsel with feet as agile as the quickest hands, and always gave Halbert an equal share. When the homeless dwarf learned of the real nature of Halbert's treasure hunt, he joined the search for Johanna and became the only person Halbert trusted.

"No, Halbert," said Mullung one afternoon as they drifted from the main arteries of the city. The troll kicked the absent-minded man's leg to get his attention. "Even I do not venture down there. That's Hell's Quarter and the last place you want to visit. This way."

The Eternal City, Halbert realized, was mostly a slum.

Mullung pointed to the ancient aqueducts above their heads.

"They once provided plumbing and running water to all Roman citizens, but look at them. Useless arches running above open sewers."

The smell of raw sewage plus another constant stench was in Halbert's nose. "What is that infernal smell?"

The dwarf indicated the fires they passed, burning around the city.

"Marble. It comes from the remnants of the great pagan coliseums and circuses and monuments to the old gods. They are scavenged for the marble and pieces are stolen and burned down to make lime."

"Lime? What on earth do they need lime for?"

"It is made into plaster to build the flimsy hovels we stay in. The cheap huts are put up, sold, and rented to naive pilgrims and foreigners moving to the city."

For two months the men walked night and day through Rome searching for Johanna. Using their sharp tongues on each other, jabbing and slicing in Italian and Latin as they wandered in and out of slums and suburbs, they did not know how powerful a medicine their friendship was for both. Halbert loved the little man's withering wit and knowledge of Roman landscape, both physical and historical, and Mullung, though he would never admit it, loved the big man who saw beyond his size and his severed hands, respected his mind despite the constant reminder that marked him as a thief. The troll's hardened heart had softened knowing a man like Halbert existed.

As days, then weeks passed, Halbert became desperate to find some kind of evidence of Sergius and his party. But Mullung could find nothing. It did not help that few offered information when a hand-less scowling dwarf and a bear-sized beggar came asking questions. And Mullung could see that Halbert was not only fast losing hope of finding his daughter, but after trudging through the poor sections and daily witnessing the savagery and destitution, Mullung feared his friend was losing hope of any kind.

"Take note of what I show you next, my friend," said Mullung one late morning. He led Halbert down a wide set of stairs into the dark.

Halbert followed the little troll down a long set of stone stairways into the underworld of Rome. Passing catacombs, stepping into a lurid darkness, the friends pressed their way toward a subterranean marketplace buried several stories beneath the city. Halbert squinted in the dimness illuminated only by torches on the walls of the stairs leading into pitch darkness.

Halbert heard voices and knew that once again the troll was up to mischief. They reached the bottom of the stone stairs and passed stalls set up along the walls. Everything forbidden above ground was for sale here. Implements used in rituals, row upon row of charms and magic potions to attract or entrance a lover, books of spells for occultists and the mystery sects.

"What devilment are you brewing, little evil one?" demanded Halbert in Latin, though mesmerized by the people as his eyes adjusted. A group of six men walked by in masks. Two women passed in the opposite direction, their breasts covered only in some kind of see through gauze, followed by more masked men and women with more jewelry on their arms, necks and around their groins than clothing on their backs. Halbert was amazed. In a world where harsh punishment was meted out to anyone, man or woman, who bared any flesh or showed any inclination of lascivious behavior, this hidden world celebrated and threw it in the face of restraint and modesty.

Just then one of the most beautiful women Halbert had ever seen swept by. Tall and voluptuous, with golden hair piled in slick swirls atop her head, she parted the crowd with two bodyguards before her as she regally walked through the marketplace.

"A courtesan no doubt," remarked Halbert, trying to be nonchalant, though no one on the street could take their eyes off her.

"At one time. Now she is senator Theodoric's wife," said Mullung. "Lady Althea."

The senator's wife was naked except for a long translucent tunic. She wore a veil over the lower part of her face and let it trail behind her in a train. Halbert was three feet away when her perfect white body glimmered by. Full sensual lips painted bright red and set in a smile as mischievous as the sparkle in her blue eyes. He could smell a musky sensuousness in her wake. Every inch of her was covered in a sheen of frankincense-perfumed oil, making her skin look like wet white marble. Halbert could see the pink aureoles and nipples standing proudly out on her round, high-riding breasts. Her jeweled sash hung with delicate arrangements of rubies and emeralds emphasized the undulant sway of her hips. The crowd bowed, craned their necks, licked their lips as if she were a walking banquet. Applause broke out as she passed. Smiling, nodding to all, lady Althea paused briefly to examine a bangle at a stall. Then, before the hungry crowd could squeeze in too close, she disappeared down set of stairs. Guarded by her men, she slipped into the recesses of the underground baths reserved for the high born, the wealthy and perverse who, above ground, served as the city's pious leaders.

"That woman," said Halbert, dazzled, "could be Venus if she were human."

"See what I have been saying? The old gods still live here and exert a powerful hold," said Mullung. He dodged a pretty woman's fist after he caressed her passing thigh with one of his stumps.

Halbert took two seats at the edge of the main marketplace while Mullung went to a man at a brazier and paid for a mound of grilled meat piled high on a wide leaf the meat seller used for plates.

"Suddenly you are rich, my little thief?" said Halbert, looking hungrily at the food.

"My feet itched for coin last night while you were snoring up a gale," said Mullung, his mouth full of seared strips of thinly sliced venison. "A small purse came our way in the guise of --"

"Don't tell me," said Halbert, waving off the story.

But his mouth watered so much at the smell of the food he could not ignore Mullung's sarcastic smile when the plate was pushed between them. Halbert dug into the mound. They finished it in gulping mouthfuls, the first food consumed since the day before. Both licked the leaves and wanted more, but had to content themselves with the parade of revelers passing by in the underground world.

"Atlas looks at home here," said Halbert. He pointed to a statue of the god across the way, bent beneath the weight of the Earth. With his downward gaze and heavy load, the god could have been a peasant passing through the market with his labor on his back.

"Another empty spirit carrying his world into the city," observed Mullung. He belched loudly as punctuation. A woman passed by and gave him a look for his rudeness, to which he replied with a series of gestures with his tongue. She hurried away, but not without a curious look behind her at the little man.

"Come on," said Mullung, and rubbed the stumps of his wrists together. "The night is young and I've only begun. If you want any more of that venison, we have work to do."

Mullung took him through every section of Rome though Halbert never gained a clue to the whereabouts of his daughter. He grew to know the city enough to look sadly upon the remains of what once was the greatest metropolis in the world.

"Don't you see, my argumentative giant?" observed Mullung that evening, holding his stumps over their fire, crowded around it with other poor and homeless pilgrims. "Even as it remains as the throne of the Christian world, Rome nears its final breath."

"It is being raped," sighed Halbert. "And left for dead."

They walked the streets and with every step their spirits sank a lower, feeling that the Rome was on the verge of collapse.

"Perhaps the new wall will keep evil out," said Halbert. The Leonine Wall, the ten-man-high wonder that bounded the entire city, named for the current pope who financed it. Though the wall was high enough to keep Saracens, Tartars and Lombards outside, Mullung was fond of saying it could do nothing about the scourge inside the walls.

One morning Halbert awoke to crowds hurrying past the doorway in which he had fallen asleep. He and Mullung followed the scurrying poor around a corner where the street opened up onto a boulevard as a large procession came down the stairs of St. Clement's Basilica. Escorts of mounted Vatican guards surrounded the holy party, while liveried trumpeters heralded their approach. Rows of pages carried colored banners with Latin prayers written on them. It was a dramatic spectacle in glaring opposition to the slavish conditions of the decomposing city.

"A royal procession?" wondered Mullung. He sat on Halbert's shoulders, shaded his eyes with the stump of his forearm and tried to get a better look.

"What is it?" Halbert asked a woman in front him.

"They buried Archbishop Clement today."

"Was the archbishop a good man?" Halbert asked, and the woman nodded. Mullung clicked his tongue and spat.

"He was taken to heaven by some terrible sickness in his stomach. I could hear his screams from my home. The new archbishop has just been confirmed," she said and pointed to a grand carriage. "He was a close friend of Archbishop Clement. A warm and generous man who loves the people."

"Of course," said Mullung with a smile. "And I am the Archangel Michael, at your service."

The new archbishop, beneath a tall miter on his head, stood up into the open carriage, blessing the crowd. He turned in Halbert's direction.

Halbert stood on a crate to get a clearer view of the new Christian holy man. His face drained of color when he saw him. Sergius waved briefly at the crowd then signaled the coachman to hurry off.

"Thief! Where is my daughter! Where's my little girl!" Halbert hollered.

Yet in the same breath he felt hope that Johanna was alive.

"Hey!" cried Mullung. He was thrown from the big man to the ground, left amidst the towering waves of people around him. Halbert pushed his way through the crowd to get his hands around the throat of the devil and squeeze the truth out of him. But within a few meters Halbert was swallowed and sank beneath the sea of followers as Sergius' coach disappeared down the street.

# CHAPTER XXI

JOHANNA WALKED BESIDE the wagon bearing the wounded from the battle. Those who survived the previous month were well enough to travel, but it took weeks of convalescence before the colony continued. They had buried close to seventy men, women and children.

Johanna adjusted the awning of the wagon shading the injured.

She studied the Saracen. He sat away from the others and cursed her in an unending stream of vituperative Arabic. She nursed him despite the venom he spat at her and was at his side every day. His one arm went for her throat at every opportunity.

"Let it go, brother," said Adrian walking beside her. "Christ will have mercy on him, but he deserved death and when he gets strong enough he will try to kill you if he can."

"I could not stop, Adrian," she took his arm. She rarely touched him around others and he saw how afraid she was, how deeply she had been shaken. "I was overtaken by something."

"You were overtaken by the fact that he murdered a child. You wanted blood."

To be possessed by a force so dark terrified her. Where did that impulse spring from? Not from the battle itself. Johanna and Halbert had walked through too many fresh battlefields and learned far too much from them.

Halbert.

Her father was so strong and exuberant, a father like no other on this earth. What other man would look for the secrets of life where no other dared to go? *To learn something new and make it your own often has a high price,* she remembered him saying.

The swell of missing him surged through her. She remembered other words of his and tried to be brave. *The death of another is a way for us to find out why we are here.*

Johanna looked at the hate-filled Arab to see if she might discover an insight to her transgression. Was it his faith that filled her with black hate at that critical instant? He's so strange, dark and different. Was it his foreign-ness?

She turned back to the caravan. It had grown: Several hundred strong plus wagons, animals, refugees and every day it collected more as word spread of the boy monk on a pilgrimage to the holy city.

Another family came running down the foothills, through the fields, carrying all their possessions on their backs. The larger the caravan grew, the slower it moved, weighed down by those who had no hope left and were ready to believe the pilgrim's promise to all who watched it pass.

"Tonight?" Adrian whispered from behind as she walked through the quickly cooling afternoon. His voice startled her.

"I'll try, Adrian," she said. He shrugged, but the smile on his face disappeared when others clamored for her attention.

"The bandages come off tonight," she said to her aides. That evening at camp she removed them while three Vikings held the Saracen so he could not strangle her with his good arm.


Johanna did not speak to Adrian about her feelings. A nagging doubt lingered when she thought to broach the subject of the Saracen, but to bring it up would burden a relationship already weighted with other unspoken dangers.

*What is happening to us?* she wondered.

The more responsibilities she took on, the more Johanna had to restrain herself with Adrian, letting their secret only bloom briefly at night when everyone slept.

"Court continues tonight, little brother?" Adrian asked.

"If I can get away," she whispered. "I'll come to you."

Her fear of being discovered colored every aspect of travel. Both knew there was no choice but to keep their meetings limited. But weeks passed and still they did not re-join at night. They walked silently side-by-side, a kind of hysterical strain beneath the pressures of the long road to Rome.

"Do what you will, your Honor," said Adrian.

Adrian lost patience and avoided the subject with her. At night while Johanna listened to case after case between bickering neighbors, he found another fire to sleep beside. Every night she planned go straight to Adrian and every night some new aspect of her judgment was tested and she was absorbed in the process of making decisions that had to reflect the words she preached by day.

By the time she finished, fires were cold and Veleda was the only one left awake.

"You have come a far distance," said Veleda one night, as she sharpened her arrowheads. She chewed on a leather strip, softening it, whittling the tip of a wood shaft. She wrapped the wet leather strip around a stone arrowhead sharpened to a razor's edge and tied it to the cleft in the shaft.

"We all have, Veleda," returned Johanna. Yet another night she was too exhausted to look for Adrian. She lay back with her head against a roll of cloth.

"Not in leagues, brother," she said, glancing up from her work. "I meant in your disguise."

"Disguise?" said Johanna, stiffly. She fought an impulse to stand, but instead put her hands behind her head, stared up at the night sky. Veleda's hawk eyes were always watching. Veleda was her first supporter, the first to praise, but also carried the deepest scrutiny, looking for weakness.

Had she discovered Johanna's secret when her monthlies took her by surprise on the road a few weeks back? Johanna was quick to hurry for the bushes, but noticed red drops behind her on the road. Was it while she took a late night bath when the moon was bright enough to reveal her in the water? Or was it just Veleda was a woman and knew Johanna was not a man?

"You hide nothing," Veleda said, "yet reveal little. The mark of a good disguise."

"Say what you are hiding," said Johanna, but when she looked over Veleda was gone.

*The Woman Pope*

Several days passed without a sighting of Veleda. When her friends were questioned they told Johanna she vanished into the woods with the intent to return to her wild ways. Johanna nodded, slightly relieved but also concerned by the news.

"I will return," Johanna said, stepping off the road. The followers left her to her privacy.

She made a ritual of leaving the caravan when it stopped to make camp, excusing herself from the constant barrage of questions and problems demanding attention.

"She stole my food!"

"He slept with two women at once."

"Why won't God to heal my son?"

"Why should we confess when we can speak directly to God?"

"Why do we need Jesus to have God to listen to us?"

When the voices overlapped and became a continuous, aggravating shriek in her ears, Johanna had to get away. She walked through the woods to clear her head. Everywhere she turned it was Answer this, Why is that, Decide now!

The moments she took for herself in the forest were precious.

As Johanna walked with the slow caravan she noted to herself it had been more than a fortnight since she had seen Adrian at her fire. She turned and left the buzz of clamoring voices behind and walked once again into the trees. She tried to relax, let the birds and the crunch of leaves beneath her feet erase the sounds in her head as she walked down a path lined with waist high fern. She stopped when the caravan's voices died away. Johanna let out a heavy sigh.

A glinting flash of movement in the forest made her focus on it. She watched as Adrian, bag over his shoulder walked away from the colony.

"Adrian, where are you going?"

He stopped, looked around and saw her. Then kept going. She ran after him as fast as she could when she saw the look on his face and felt a chill that froze her heart. She knew he was leaving the caravan for good.

# CHAPTER XXII

SHE RAN AFTER Adrian for what felt like hours. But he knew the ways of the forest too well to ever be found. She finally gave up when the afternoon sun fell behind the mountains.

"Has anyone spoken to Adrian?" Johanna asked anxiously. She passed through the colonists, away from her usual place at the head of the caravan. She tried to find someone who might have a clue to why he left without a word to her.

"Who is Adrian?" asked a voice in the crowd.

The response made Johanna cringe. The fact that Adrian was not even known to some in the colony was proof of how bad the situation had become. He had been missing for several days and before that he stayed away, not even saying goodnight at the fire.

The more she asked around, the more nervous she became. Johanna sent out messengers. Why had he left her? Panic rose like a knot in her throat.

"Veleda?" she called to the wild-woman. When Veleda stood before her, Johanna made up her mind what to do.

"I no longer want this duty," she said, taking the wild-woman aside. "I relinquish being leader of these pilgrims as of today."

Veleda gave her a knowing look. "What is it you want?"

"Peace. Calm. And to get to Rome, quickly."

"What do you want from me? I will not take your place."

"I know that, but can you help me find someone else who will? I cannot bear it any longer, I have other duties I must attend to."

"What duties could be more important, John?" the wild-woman asked. Johanna felt foolish and desperate. She had only one answer and she knew the danger of revealing it.

"I have to find Adrian."

"Adrian? Is that all?"

"Do not question my motives and I will not question yours."

"If that is all you need then we will find him. But let me ask you this. If you have Adrian, will you lead us?"

"I don't want to."

"We have no one else, brother. You know that."

"This role was never my idea."

"And now none of us has a choice in this matter, do we?" said Veleda, exasperated. "So what do you want?"

Johanna gave up and walked away.

"We will find him," Veleda called. "You take us to Rome."

≈ ≈ ≈

Adrian was located that night by Veleda's men as he sat deep in thought beside a stream. He was brought by force before Johanna and thrown to his knees.

"Don't treat him like a prisoner," she said and rushed to him.

Adrian pulled away and stood up.

"I am a prisoner who is not bound, is that it?" he said, dusting himself off. "I have my freedom, but should I try to escape, my way will be barred and I will be dragged before the king?"

"Never," Johanna said, stung. "You are bound by no such rules."

"By what am I bound, *brother*?"

"By faith only and you know that."

"Faith in whose word? In whose promise?"

"You know whose word was given to you when we found each other again."

"That word faded long ago on this road," he said.

The others around Johanna and Adrian shook their heads at the obtuse speech.

"This is not your business," Johanna ordered the crowd away.

"You are someone I don't know anymore," said Adrian when they were alone.

"Please, listen. As I've said before," she reminded, and took his reluctant arm. She walked him through the crowd to her camp fire where a pot of herb tea hung above the flames. "Don't let your faith in me run away, no matter how hard the road."

"My faith lacks patience, little brother," said Adrian. They faced each other like two opponents instead of lovers.

Johanna poured him a cup of valerian tea, lifted it to her lips and blew on it gently, then put it to his.

"No, your faith does not lack patience," she said. She smiled when he took the cup and sipped. "It only lacks feeding. And I am here to feed it, Adrian, I promise."

He studied her. A long time had passed since they had shared a smile.

"Let us talk about the way it can be best nourished," he said and drained the tea in a single gulp. "And let me tell you what I desire."

≈ ≈ ≈

"You may see our little brother next," Adrian said to a teen-age Viking boy and a Druid girl who had asked to be married.

Adrian spent the next two weeks at Johanna's side every moment, but now in a new role. He had asked to be in charge of those who wanted to see the little brother. Instead of a mass of voices and arms tugging on her for attention, he organized a process to be heard. He made it his job to listen to each griev-ance first, weigh its merit, then pass it along for John's consideration. It worked better than either could have imagined. Adrian was exactly what was needed to keep order in the chaos of colonists vying for her time and also keep them close to-gether.

One afternoon as they neared the crest of a ridge of hills, Adrian sent a gossiping woman away, and listened to a man whose donkey had been crippled by another colonist's cruel joke. Johanna walked ahead as usual, leading the caravan. Her hand hung above her eyes, shading them from the sun, as she peered over the slope of hill they were about to descend.

She screamed out suddenly. "Adrian!"

Adrian reached for his knife and ran to defend her.

At her side, knife out, Adrian looked for the danger. Johanna pointed in front of her. A gleaming line of man-made jagged spires and columns rose up at the edge of the horizon. The buildings of a tremendously vast and ancient city lay in the far distance.

Rome.

# PART 3
## CHAPTER XXIII

JOHANNA STOOD LOOKING out over the famed seven hills more than a year after saying good-bye to her father. Behind her, over four hundred weary followers cheered and wept at the sight. The relief of nearing Rome broke like a fever as the city rose up before them.

Johanna hugged Adrian, went to the wagon, took a loaf of bread, a skin of water and walked to the Saracen. The man limped beside the wagon, his missing forearm hidden beneath his black burnoose.

He did not meet her eyes, but neither did he object when she led him from the caravan off the road. She handed him the food and water. He stopped trying to hurt her two months ago. Something had broken inside, his eyes went dull, his one arm continually draped over his chest and fingering the nub at his elbow. He still felt the aches and itches of old scars on fingers that were no longer there. She spoke to him in the broken Arabic she had managed over the months to coax from the sullen man.

"You need not enter the holy city," she said. "You are free. Go home."

"You do not wish to parade your prisoner before your generals?" he asked, confused.

"You were never my prisoner, but I was yours. I kept you close to make sure you healed and to keep others from hurting you," she placed a dagger in the belt of his caftan. "I beg you to forgive my cruelty. I can do nothing but bid you farewell and wish Allah be with you."

"Why let me live?" he asked, suspicious. He had dreaded this day, but was prepared to be tortured for his faith. Every night he vowed to the Prophet that the infidels would see one of Mohammed's soldiers leave this insignificant life with praise for Allah in his heart and a curse to his enemies on his lips.

"Perhaps your merciful Allah is my God, and my merciful God is the same as your Allah," she said. "Might that be His great gift?"

"It is not possible," he said and looked away. Johanna bowed low and touched her fingertips to her forehead in his custom.

"All things are possible with Allah," she said in the same tone of finality he had used when speaking to her.

He watched Johanna walk back to Adrian and lead them down the hill toward the city, still miles away. The Saracen soldier stood for the better part of an hour and watched the colony pass by without anyone's attempt to stop or kill him. Then he turned and walked due south in a haze of disbelief, overwhelmed by a compassionate gesture that was outside every known rule of warfare.

Nervous guards got into battle positions along the turrets of the Leonine Wall. The soldiers watched as yet another battalion from a foreign army marched toward the city. However, the kingdom of this aggressor could not be identified from this distance.

Four cavalrymen carrying banners of Rome galloped out of the city gates.

From the well-traveled road leading down into the city, Johanna signaled the colony to halt. Everyone watched eagerly as the horsemen approached. She and Adrian walked ahead to meet the soldiers. The riders stopped short, waiting for the unknown army's commanders to come away from their troops to a neutral point off the road.

"Who sends you to Rome?" demanded the captain after an abrupt salute. His polished copper helmet gleamed in the sun and the red brush of its plume looked like a blood flower above the grizzled man's head.

"No one sends us," said Johanna. "We're pilgrims who seek God in the holy city."

The captain smiled back at his aides. The tension from possible trouble was replaced with relief and contempt.

"Then you are strangers on this land, without use or recommendation," he sneered. "Be off."

"Sir, we have traveled hundreds --" said Adrian.

"I have direct orders from the new Archbishop of Rome. We are to keep all parties over fifty from entering without invitation or trade."

"We must enter the city. I have to --" began Johanna.

"Go back. Or face the force of the finest army in the Roman Empire if you try," said the captain and glanced over the small arms of the spent warriors. "Our city no longer entertains the wretched. Mobs who think they've come to the Promised Land yet have nothing to trade but misery. Go or die by the sword of Rome."

The men wheeled on their horses, galloped back, laughing out loud for mistaking this ragged horde for a well trained army of invaders. Johanna ran after them, coughing their dust. She stumbled and fell as they rode off without a glance behind.

"What have I done to these poor people?" she said, crying and furious in the same breath. Adrian helped her to her feet. She looked back at the caravan; their number reached beyond sight, disappearing over the hill. How could she have possibly thought herself competent to lead anyone to the Holy City? She was simply a deceptive girl not fit to be one of the followers much less to lead. Her deception had turned about face to strangle her with her own hands.

"You led us safely where our fathers are," said Adrian. He walked her back, but at the caravan Johanna refused to answer the tumult of questions put to her. Instead, she got onto the wagon bench and sat.

A crowd surrounded the wagon, all talking at once. Pleas to get her to speak were met with a blank silence. Apprehension swiftly flowed back to the ranks of confused men, women and children.

Johanna sat on the wagon and stared at the city.

"Brother John, speak to them," Adrian said in a harsh whisper. "The people are nervous and I'm afraid they might hurt themselves."

She did not respond. Adrian enlisted Veleda to call a camp on the spot. They moved off the main road away from spying Roman eyes, and kept everyone busy all to prevent hysteria from rising.

Night descended but still Johanna did not move. Adrian, fearing the caravan's mood, built their fire away from the wagon so her stricken expression could not be seen. When he looked at her he did not see a monk, but a young woman. Not a soldier, not a leader nor a judge. Just a girl who had witnessed a dream killed before her, and with its death a glimpse of how the world worked.

The strain of the march across a continent visited every part of her body. She sat slumped on the wagon, run through by the spear of misfortune.

It grew late and the camp settled in. Adrian spoke to so many anxious followers his voice became hoarse. He watched Johanna a long moment, then stepped onto the wagon beside her, placed a blanket over her shoulders and looked out over the environs of Rome.

"The air is much warmer, thicker here," he said quietly. "And have you noticed the stars take a different path in the sky? Not like on the ship when we met. Those stars were chilled by the sea. They were so far away, like they had to strain their ears when they listened to your prayer for God to speak to you that night on the deck."

"You heard me?" she asked, coming out of her torpor. She recalled that night, on her knees on the deck of the ship as it sailed to England. She had asked Adrian's God to show Himself.

"You were angry," she said. "I've never seen you so angry. And so was I."

"We were beyond anger. I thought I lost you and I wanted to die, to leap overboard. Then I saw you on the deck. That you asked God to come to you made me love you, Johanna. I knew I'd love you forever at that moment. Even though He was silent, I knew God Almighty was touched by your gesture and that He would come to you some day. As He did. And He brought us both here."

Johanna watched Adrian stare up at the sky. She realized she looked upon the most beautiful man in the world. So constant was his faith, in God, in her. A man she could trust with her life.

"Adrian." She reached around his neck. Johanna wept, let go of the intensity of the journey. To herself, she praised God for His gift of this man.

Johanna took his face and kissed Adrian. It was the first time in months they had been close. With her lips on his, Adrian was driven on by her passion. He held her tight, his trembling hand reached down through the top of her robe. He felt beneath the cloth binding around her chest which kept her breasts a secret. He found her left breast and held it, felt the heat and pulse of blood from her pounding heart and felt the soft weight of it curve in his hand, round and topped with the erect halo of her nipple.

Her hands swept over him, feeling the strength of his arms, the arch of his back and with his hand on her breast, she moaned and squeezed him tighter. His hand moved slowly over her breast and she desired him so much she reached below his waist to feel his hardness. She put her hand around it, and felt the quickened pace of his heartbeat come back through the material of his tunic. It matched the tingling moist intensity between her legs. But Adrian broke away, panting, pushed her back and took her hand from him. "Johanna, we cannot."

"Please?" she begged. A fiery lust blew over her like a brush fire.

She pulled him to her, sealed her lips and tongue to his. He shifted his legs to escape but she reached under his robe anyway and took hold again, her fingers wrapped tight around him.

His hand responded in kind, and went beneath her robe and, moving his fingers over her legs, felt the firmness of muscle on top and where they melted into softness along her inner thighs. He could not stop himself despite his desperate prayers. His rational mind disintegrated when his fingers moved to her secret place. Once there it was impossible to retreat. He cupped her sex in his hand and both tensed with an involuntary jolt.

Johanna felt the heat of his hand explode through her.

Adrian felt the complex softness of the textures and folds and creases tucked beneath a downy tuft. He could not stop touching, holding her. His fingertips gently squeezed the length of the boroughs, hills and valleys he found everywhere along the lips of her sex.

The wagon groaned beneath them. They stopped a moment fearing they would wake the camp, and got down from the bench. They rolled beneath the wagon. The horses, tethered close by and sleepy, paid no attention. Johanna pulled at Adrian's clothes, and felt him tug at hers, tossing them aside, rubbing frantically on each other. Adrian got on top of her and she wrapped her legs around his hips, impatient for his entrance. She kissed his face and rubbed his arms, but he did not move.

The frightened confusion on his perspiring face told Johanna he had no idea what to do. She reached between them and took him in her hand. Feeling the length of him caused them both to shudder. Johanna put the tip of him to her gate and felt Adrian hold himself there, poised, like a tender first kiss.

Then Adrian lurched his hips forward.

"Ah. Wait. It hurts."

His look was suddenly miserable at being the cause of pain, and he stopped moving.

She was astonished. "I didn't know it would hurt so much."

"I'm so sorry," he started to pull away, but she held him tight.

"Come back. It's alright. Here, I want you to come in."

But her pain frightened him, pulled him back to his senses and he rolled away.

"Don't stop," she said.

"We cannot," he said and grabbed her hands in his. "We cannot become lost in our spirits and in our flesh. Not now."

"You're right," she said and shame bloomed on her face. She tried to turn away, but he held on, taking her shoulders, pulling her close.

"I love you so much," he said. "I want to make love to you and I am not ashamed of that desire."

"But I am."

"Let's promise each other. The fire will wait for us until it is our time to lie together."

"Yes," she said, weakly.

They put on their clothes in an awkward silence. Adrian hugged her and, despite having to deny himself the desire he had thought so often about, he was quite happy.

"It's time to leave all this, Johanna. We'll have to get into the city another way, by ourselves. It is time we found our fathers."

"Leave our people?" she asked. "What would they do?"

"Find their own destiny."

"How can you say that?"

"Yes, they helped us here. We were safe in their number, but we've arrived now. The promise is fulfilled. We'll find our way in and they'll find theirs. You've done all you can and the longer we stay the more time we lose," he said and walked toward the horses.

"We have to bring them inside the walls. I cannot just leave them."

A warning flashed too late in his mind: They had come too far, through so much with her. The feelings she had for these people were clearly described on Johanna's face. There was no question she loved her innocent brutes no matter what Adrian told himself.

"I will not be stopped now. Adrian, do you honestly think I've come all this way to be turned away at the door? All of us, every one, or none will pass through that gate."

"Think about it. You heard the soldiers, they'll kill us."

She folded her arms, defiant. Seeing this, he knew she had fully recovered from the ordeal with the Roman soldiers.

They heard a noise and turned. Veleda leaned on her staff. Behind her, hundreds of faces stretched out beyond the light of the camp fire. They sat or crouched on the ground, waiting silently for her. Waiting for her word.

A chill quivered through Adrian. How long they had been there, what might they have seen? But Johanna was not put off by the company, she was inspired.

"You saw today that the holy city does not give its love unearned. Rome must be wooed, she must be taken like a lover," she said loud enough for all to hear her. "Have we come all this way not to court our beloved?"

She stared at Adrian until he understood. He had quietly savored the idea of being kept out of the city because of the colony. It was the perfect opportunity for the two of them to sneak off, leave the responsibility of the colonists behind and find their fathers.

Perhaps if they had made love they could have fled. The shared carnal knowledge might have removed Johanna from her role. The act might have made her see they should be man and wife and that their mission was not only to find their fathers but to build their lives together. But it was too late. Everything had changed now.

Johanna stood on the wagon and faced the crowd. Adrian watched his lover look out upon a sea of faces crowded together in the night. She was their leader once more.

"Brothers and sisters," brother John, the little monk said and waved them closer. Adrian could not prevent a sigh from escaping. Hundreds scurried toward them in the dark to get within earshot. "Come closer. Yes. Listen to what we must do."

# CHAPTER XXIV

IN A VINEYARD, long bushy rows of grape vines stretched for miles, away from the outskirts of Rome into the rolling hills along the path of the Tiber River. An old vintner squatted on the ground and scrutinized a dusty purple bunch of grapes on a gnarled vine.

"You beautiful waste," he said and picked a single grape. He squeezed the dark bulb between his fingers and let the juice run down into the cup of his hand. He sipped from the sweet reservoir it made and shook his head. His gaze passed over row after luxuriant row of glistening fruit waiting, swollen, perfect. All of it untouched and about to turn from ripe to rot.

*Damn the foreign bishop*, thought the vintner. Forbidding the superstitious laborers from picking his vineyard, saying the land had been lately cursed by a pagan spirit. The old man, moving down the rows, knew the archbishop was the only evil spirit on the land. When the vintner had refused to sell him the land for any price much less the outrageous pittance he was offered, the abundant acres his forefathers harvested since Pope Hadrian were fated to spoil.

The vintner turned to move to the next row and nearly fainted. A savage group of men stood in the lane before him and blocked the path.

"What do you want?" He backed up though he knew he was too old to escape. "Has the archbishop sent you to finish his threat?"

The old man drew himself up to his full height, took a little dagger from his sash. Little more than a fancy jeweled decoration, he held it out. "Come, I'll mix your blood with the juice of my grapes and send you back to your Grace."

One of the barbarous strangers stepped forward and the old man braced. The man went to the vines, snapped off a bunch of grapes. He held it out for the vintner to see, then knelt at the pile of harvesting sacks the entrance to the row. The barbarian made a show of placing the bunch in the sack, then putting it over his shoulder. He looked at the old man and waited.

The old man did not understand. The savage indicated his band of men, picked another bunch, placed it with the other in the sack, pointed to the vineyard and swept his hand across its expanse. When he faced the old man again, he made a gesture the vintner understood. He briskly rubbed his thumb and fingers together.

*Money.* Pay. Relieved, the vintner laughed.

"By the cocks of the old gods, yes! Pick everything!" he nodded and enthusiastically gestured. The pagan and his men whooped and hurried to the sacks, passing them along until all were handed out. Johanna's colonists went down the rows of vines, picking the grapes, stuffing them in the sacks, happy to be the only laborers for the vintner's harvest.


At the foundation site of what was be a large house, the construction foreman handed a metal trowel to an older man with a grizzled beard, more silver than its original red. The foreman pointed to a pile of bricks at one corner of the foundation, then returned to a set of plans spread out on the stone wall. A moment later a tremendous noise made him turn.

He saw several Vikings at the corner of the foundation along with Viking Larst, rapidly putting down bricks at the base. Tier by tier grew before the foreman's eyes as many hands expertly lay brick and mortar and a long, high wall rose up almost magically from the ground.

In the open marketplace outside the main gate of the city, a company of women from little brother's army swooped into the market. Invading the stalls, spreading throughout the bazaar, selling exotic jewelry, colorful woven materials, crafted pots, carved utensils, beads, shells and polished stones from far-flung territories the local market people had never seen before, caused a flutter of excitement.

Veleda strode into the bazaar alongside a group of Viking and pagan hunters bearing a buck, its legs tied to a stout branch, swaying between the men as they walked. Veleda had two large hares and three game birds, gutted and cleaned, tied to the ends of a long bough she bore across her shoulders. She set her catch in front of a butcher's stall and began to haggle for a price.

In the camp that evening, a roaring bonfire sent flames high into the night lighting up a line of men, women and children. Johanna watched the rugged people lay down the fruit of their labor on a huge pile, food and goods enough to feed and equip a battalion, no, more than a battalion, a community. At Johanna's encouragement from the back of the wagon three days before, this diverse group, with individual talents, pooling their skills, scoured the countryside and returned with plentiful results.

"I am so proud of you all." Johanna stepped up to the towering pile. She took a loaf of bread, raised it over her head. The gesture was met with a loud cheer. She broke off a piece, chewed it, then passed the loaf along as a symbol for everyone to partake.

"A toast to the bravest people I know. A toast to my family," she said and drank from a wine skin, then passed it into the crowd.

Animal horns were blown. The combined cultures from across the continent began playing indigenous musical instruments before the great bonfire.

"Little brother," they shouted

Arms reached out and she was lifted into the air and hailed. All through the camp played Viking lyres, goat horns and pagan wood flutes and pipes, crossing over each other in a lively concerto around the rhythmic beat of drums. More drums than Johanna and Adrian had ever seen in one place. The air was filled with the sound of drums, signal drums, gourds, skins;

deep, tall and loud and all pounding out over the camp. Johanna was set back down to earth.

Men, women and children danced around the fire, seized by the sweet ephemeral luxury of life, at being safe and fed and the possibility of remaining so even if tomorrow proved all of it to be an illusion.

"You better put that glum face away," Johanna teased. She pulled a brooding Adrian to his feet. She got behind and pushed him into the musical frenzy. "I will dance that stubborn face back where it belongs!"

She laughed and pushed him into the midst of the other celebrants. Holding onto and swinging his arms, she turned him around until his mood broke and he let go and finally enjoyed the taste of their little victory. They sang, danced and feasted most of the night, gorging themselves on all their senses. Who knew when a moment like this would come again?

Johanna and Adrian madly swung each other around and around to the music. They threw their heads back and howled. Their hands, so wet with perspiration, slipped and Adrian was flung backwards, rolling in a reverse somersault. Johanna ran over and sat beside him to rest a moment. They laughed at themselves as dancers gyrated around them.

"See, brother," she said as she wiped her hand across his glistening brow. "I plan to wear out that stubbornness and make it pour out of your hide."

"If I did the same to you, brother," said Adrian, wiping his hand across her forehead, "there'd be nothing left of us but two big puddles."

The touch heightened their secret yearning. Adrian got up, pulled Johanna to her feet and guided her back into the dancing fray.

≈ ≈ ≈

"We are tired of roaming," said a Viking at the evening meeting. He held his infant daughter in his muscular arms while his teenage pagan wife stood beside him, arm through his. She nodded wearily.

Winter had come and gone and with it a series of achievements and an occasional rout. When spring made its appearance, the tally from the colony's work showed their successes far outstripped any setbacks. And after months of moving the camp from place to place, the hundreds of men and women wanted to stop. They wanted to settle, somewhere, anywhere, Rome or not, it did not matter.

"Does everyone feel this way?" Johanna asked as she rubbed her hands together briskly at the fire.

"We all have seen Rome," said Veleda from across the flames. "We have walked her streets alone and in groups. There are marvels and holy places, but most of the city is foul and sick. We can visit when we feel the need, but we do not have to live there."

The colony roared its assent.

The nightly discussions, which Adrian instituted to air tensions, uncovered the growing malaise. The majority of colonists yearned to settle down and it forced Johanna to set about putting another plan into action, one she had thought about for some time.

"Brothers and sisters, let us work through the summer," she said. "Then I will present my plan."

The plan in her head would not only cure the malaise, but would change the colonist's relationship with the little brother. That summer every one worked hard and whispered eagerly amongst themselves about the possibilities. What was the little brother up to?

"Adrian, call them closer so they can hear," Johanna whispered. It was a mild autumn day nearly a year after the colony had camped on every hill and valley around Rome.

"Any closer and we will be crushed," he replied.

A fine early fall afternoon breeze laden with a crisp pine scent was carried down from the mountains. The day had a propitious feel to it with puffy white clouds scudding over the tops of the hills.

Adrian stood to one side of Johanna as the contract was formally struck. The entire colony eased forward to listen, hundreds of silent people in a rippling ring spread across the grade of the hill. Adrian coolly eyed the transaction, hearing the clink of metal as Johanna counted out gold coins from a cloth purse into a thick hand adorned with many rings.

The purse emptied and the counting was done.

Johanna stepped back and regarded Theodoric, a powerful Roman senator now officially their landlord. In his forties, he looked decades younger, like a child despite the curly white hair held in place with a laurel wreath in the old-fashioned style. He was a short man with the powerful body of a bull and the smooth, ruddy red face of a cherub trickster, a face that owned a wicked sweetness forever lingering around his eyes and lips. Even at his most innocent, Theodoric looked like a beautiful child guilty of intent to commit some puckish fraud.

The Senator looked around the camp and beamed. He put back the coins, held the purse high for all to see, jingling its contents. His privately paid entourage of mercenaries, one hundred of the finest soldiers made up of Italian, Saxon, Frankish and Norman warriors, plus his five-year-old son in a miniature soldier uniform, were lined up behind him on the grade at the entrance to the camp. His forces faced the settlers on horseback in shining armored rows.

"May you prosper on this land as I have," said Theodoric in a loud voice for all to hear, making an extravagant, slightly comical bow to Johanna.

"Yes, you have profited much from us already," she said in kind and returned the exaggerated bow. He stopped his bow, gave her a look. He was used to playing the powerful fool but it was a role he took to the stage alone and he was never, ever mocked. Johanna returned his look with a steady gaze that penetrated the crinkle of his eyes. The expression told Theodoric he was not among his usual circle of sycophants. Though this ragged 'little brother' held no official religious rank, Theodoric looked across at a presumptuous boy-monk who proclaimed himself an equal.

"Do you mock me?" he asked, the tip of a snarl whipping at the end of his words.

The words tightened everyone who heard them and tension instantly rippled through the soldiers, felt by their horses who stirred nervously beneath them. Theodoric's entourage put their hands to their weapons and immediately Johanna's ranks did the same. The rumble of unrest turned palpable, ready to explode from a single signal given from either leader.

Johanna raised her hand without taking her eyes off Theodoric. The entire colony quieted. Theodoric mentally noted the total response to the little monk's gesture.

"I do not mock you, Senator. I only suggest that gold cannot be planted, nor can one raise children on the soil of gold. It requires real earth, so we will in fact profit much more from you than the few coins you take from us."

The look she gave Theodoric suddenly melted into a smile. She put out her hand, fearless. In that moment the most powerful senator in the Roman Empire was won over. He threw his head back, laughed, took the offered hand and shook it vigorously with delight.

"You'll make a fine tenant, little monk, and I pray we'll both have good harvests," he said and the handshake released the surrounding tension.

A long and thunderous cheer erupted from the colonists. The monk and the senator sealed the bargain with a gulp of wine brought in golden goblets from Theodoric's dark Assyrian slave boy.

"May you live well on this land," he said and mounted his horse. He winked at her, turned his huge white horse and rode off in a thunder of hooves from the settlement to the roar of the colonists.

Johanna looked at her barbarian family spread out over the hill. Hundreds hugged each other and many wept at having a home at last.

Adrian, agitated, was unable to remain silent any longer.

"That man controls us now like he does the senate," he said as the cheer followed the horsemen over the hill and off the property.

"He'll protect us, don't worry."

*The Woman Pope*

"We're in his debt before we've even settled in," argued Adrian. "You made a pact that holds us hostage the first time we fail to pay."

"That will not happen, brother."

"You are so certain, *brother*. I hope that certainty does not cost us too dearly."

"I know what I'm doing," she snapped.

"And your judgment is so perfect it does not need to consult with anyone?" he said loudly, throwing up his hands. "Could not even one of us poor, ignorant barbarians help with the biggest decision ever facing us? Or are we all your foolish children meant to follow blindly into indentured slavery?"

"No, of course not."

"I follow you, but I am not one of your followers," he said. Adrian turned and walked away through the celebrating crowd.

≈ ≈ ≈

The monk Gaetani hurried along a secluded corridor. He was in the darkened innards of the Vatican, walking along a carpeted path known only to a few. He squinted in the dim light to accommodate his poor eyesight, which reinforced the deeply engraved wrinkles in the center of his brow. Those creases of skin dug more than a quarter of an inch into the flesh between his eyes, growing like branches of a leaf-less tree, sprouting three thick crevasses that reached into the center of his high forehead, highlighting the balding wisps of remaining hair. At just twenty-eight, these remarkable premature wrinkles aged his countenance and gave him an aspect of profound worry.

He stopped at a chamber door and put his ear to it. Muffled sounds of crying came from within. He knocked the two-and-three signal then waited for the call to enter.

Gaetani crossed the floor of a palatial room. Sergius, in the center standing on a sheepskin rug, washed his hands in a gold water bowl on a stand. Gaetani hurried to it and held out a white cloth to dry his master' hands. When Sergius gave the cloth back, Gaetani disposed of it in a basket in the corner, discreetly noting it was tinged red.

"Thank you, my son," said Sergius absently.

Sergius' ward, Marozia, her face made up so that she looked much older than her thirteen years, squatted in the opposite corner of the dimly lit room, weeping. She was naked and wrapped both arms around her legs. A muscular soldier, his hairy back to the priest, swayed on his feet above her, glistening with sweat. Naked below the waist, wearing only sandals and a metal breastplate, he wiped his penis with the girl's dress. He yawned, finished it with a belch and tossed the dress to the floor. Sergius stepped away from the bowl to a table and decanted the bottle of metheglin, a kind of fortified mead heavily infused with spices.

"Has Theodoric accepted?" Sergius asked.

"No, your grace. He has not," replied Gaetani. Sergius sipped the drink, enjoying this challenge his assistant brought back.

"The next price I offer will be much lower, did you tell him that?"

"He..." Gaetani fumbled for words, then sucked in his breath with resolve. He must be direct with his master or face his harsh but loving discipline. "The senator has leased the land and will not sell."

"He's lying. No merchant in Rome would rise against me."

"It was not a merchant, my lord archbishop. The land was leased by a band of zealots who paid the Senator to live on and work the land. These savages follow a monk who led them across all of --"

"A *monk*?" Sergius interrupted, his interest suddenly piqued. He held a finger to his lips for silence, wanting to intuit the possibilities before any information was revealed.

Sergius walked over to the girl and gently took her arm, bringing her to her feet. He bent and picked up her soiled dress. He shook it out for her as if he were a doting servant, held it over her head for her to slip on. She obeyed, meekly raising her arms. Gaetani observed two thin red lines roll down her inner thigh, streaming in twin rivulets toward the curve of her knee as she pulled the dress over herself. The monk looked away. Sergius took the girl by the arm, led her to the chair and sat her down. He poured a second glass of metheglin and handed it to her, encouraging her to drink. He nodded at Gaetani to continue.

"Last year this monk was turned away from the city with hundreds of his followers. They roamed as a roving work force, finding wages in the fields and vineyards, selling goods they made."

"The old vintner Pantagruel had a fine harvest this past year despite the curse on his land," interrupted Sergius again, smiling to himself, a mystery solved. "Remind me. We must visit our friend and bless his crops again for next year. Continue."

"Their labors brought in enough money to purchase the lease. The barbarians are building a sizable village on the land."

Gaetani waited for his master's comment. When it did not come he had little else to say.

"It is said that at night the monk secretly enters the city and ministers to the sick. He has won many disciples in every sector of the city. The poor regard him as a saint."

"What is this saint's name?" asked Sergius. He ran a hand gently through the girl's hair, straightened the tangles from her face.

"They call him John, your grace."

Sergius sipped his drink and kept his eyes on the girl, memorizing her, absorbing her features as one would a beautiful portrait whose likeness one wanted to remember and enjoy at some later private time.

"John is a good name. Surely a reasonable and prudent monk, a man who will understand that he has been deceived," said Sergius, putting his thin lips on the girl's exposed shoulder. He kissed a large round scar where he had branded her with the Seal of the Archbishop. "He will obey the church. Leave me now, my son."

Gaetani nodded and went toward the door. Sergius stood and helped the disoriented girl from the chair, leading her to stand next to the monk. He then took a pouch from the folds of his robe and placed it in Gaetani's hands.

"Gaetani, my brother. That land is the door to Rome and the key to the papacy. I must have it. By any means, do you understand?"

"Of course, your grace," the monk bowed.

"Now, take her away," Sergius said and placed her arm in Gaetani's, joining them together. He touched her cheek. "I am afraid she has no aptitude for the kind of pleasure required here and has learned little in these halls. This girl needs to understand the value of luxury. Marozia's reluctant heart needs to be tempered by the street."

Minutes later, Gaetani opened a door leading into a dark alley and the streets of Rome beyond. Marozia suddenly turned and held onto the monk out of sheer terror.

"Have mercy on me, brother." she pleaded. "I have nothing and nowhere to go."

Gaetani pulled her from him and looked her in the face.

"And you will never find another master so worthy as Sergius. Go," he said and pushed her out into the night. The teenage girl, her face a smudge of paint and tears, wrapped her arms around herself and walked from the archbishop's palace in a daze.

Without a second look Gaetani closed the big door and bolted it. He walked quickly down the hallway, and as he did he felt for the pouch Sergius had given him. He stopped, then turned and ran back to the door, frantically unbolting and opening the door.

"Marozia!" he yelled. But the alley was empty.


Sergius watched the door long after they had gone, lost in thought, stroking the long whiskery rope down his chin. Only the sound of snoring accompanied the archbishop's meditation. An hour passed when, metheglin in one hand and a lit candle in the other, he walked over to the soldier who was passed out in the corner of the room. He took a length of rope kept beneath a chair and stood over him, studying the drunken man.

"As vacuous in slumber as when chasing hollow pleasures," Sergius said. He set down the drink and candle.

Without stirring him from his stupor, he tied the man's hands and feet to the thick metal rings he had installed on the floor until the man was stretched out. Sergius picked up the yellow silk sash from Marozia's dress. He ran his fingers over its length,

*The Woman Pope*

reveling in the smooth, cool texture, and inhaling the youthfulness of her scent. He squatted close to the unconscious soldier.

"Beautiful young man with the flesh of Adonis, but with none of his discipline," he whispered, staring appreciatively at the muscular body. He slowly wrapped the silk sash around the soldier's genitals.

The wrap turned into a knot that went from the head of the man's flaccid penis and testicles to its neck at the pubic mound. Then he took a sip from his goblet and slowly poured the remaining contents over the material.

Sergius steadied himself on his haunches and firmly grasped the ends of the sash, checking to make sure the soldier would find himself unable to move when he awoke. Sergius took a deep breath, let it out in a sweet anticipation.

"Every action requires its own perfect moment," he spoke over the man, like an incantation, a spell. He then took the candle and held it just above the alcohol-soaked sash. "If the moment is to have its own perfect effect."

He touched candle flame to sash.

# CHAPTER XXV

"DIRL FINISHED MARKING off the lots," said Johanna to the crowd milling around her. They stood on a slope overlooking the leased acreage. "Everyone will get a chance to draw for a piece of land."

Johanna happened to look up from the flurry of questions thrown and saw Adrian walking off. She handed the site plans back to the gray-bearded Viking Dirl.

"Adrian?"

He did not turn or acknowledge her. She broke from the group and followed him. Johanna feared the friction between them and how deep it had become. Ever since the land was leased they had done nothing but fight. She wanted to take him aside, beg his patience until they were settled, but every time they spoke every word came out angry. She called again, but he simply continued on his way. He passed through the colony and all its configurations of families, now completely mixed into evenly distributed clusters of pagan, Viking and other cultures picked up along the road to Rome.

Johanna hurried by men and women at the cordoned off sites they hoped to win at the drawing, discussing what herbs and vegetables they would plant. She passed other settlers on what would be the main streets, debating the positions of the grids laid out for what was becoming their own village.

"Adrian, please stop," she whispered to herself.

He left the settlement with Johanna's eyes on his back and stepped purposefully into the forest. She suddenly realized where he was going and held back, letting him go.

Adrian reached the crest of the hill at the edge of their land and walked down a trail toward the next valley. He picked up a rock, threw it as hard as he could into a stream to vent his frustration.

The role he had created for himself was at odds with his desires. He was angry for becoming Johanna's assistant. Angry and, no matter how hard he tried to deny it, ashamed to be in love with a woman who lived as a man. And angry to be forced to hide every glance, never free to openly love her.

*And I cannot even bear to think about Rome,* he thought to himself. He must get to the pope and make the Holy Father listen. The pope must give him soldiers to save his family from their slavery. But how could he get to him?

Every strategy had failed. To gain an audience with the pope had been kept from him, tantalizingly held outside his grasp. How many times had he been turned away? Manhandled by the guards, even beaten at the door? After the difficulty of the journey it should have been a simple task to stand before the pope, but every time he tried, every tactic got him thrown from the Vatican into the street. He made so many desperate attempts he was finally threatened with a long stay in the Vatican prison if he tried to see the pope without high references. His family would remain enslaved and his mission a failure if he could not get behind those closely guarded walls.

Adrian stepped across a stream and sat against a mossy boulder, his favorite thinking place. The sun set without his notice. The night and her sounds crept up but were as far away in his consciousness as the sky itself, powerless to free him from anguish.

The nightly forays he and Johanna made into the city were, from his point of view, unsatisfying from the start. Each trip escalated arguments about where they should look for her father while Adrian wanted to stop at every Christian order to petition cardinals and bishops about his family's slavery. Plus, every night Johanna was sidetracked by the poor who overflowed the streets.

"Can we continue once without stopping at every door?" Adrian would ask, harshly.

"Let me see to the old woman first."

Often they snuck back out of the city before sunrise without having looked for her father or seeing any clergy. Exhausted from the arduous work of caring for the destitute, each had begun to resent the other for their unyielding demands.

Adrian watched the burbling water of the stream as he remembered their last conversation.

"This is not the way to find him," he recalled saying to her that morning. They hurried out of the wide arms of the Leonine gate, opening the city to the world at sunrise.

"This might be exactly the way to do it," she had said coldly, the hood of her robe close to her face. "Where else would he be except with the poor?"

"Can we at least do something that I want to do for once?" he demanded. "Spend one night in a way I want? Does every decision start and finish with 'little brother'?"

Johanna gave him a look, one he had only seen her give to enemies. "You do what you want. I don't care any more."

She turned to the naked old man prone on ground, unconscious and shivering at the gate. The look slapped his heart like a palm to the face. He left her in the city and they had not spoken since.

Now he was forced to consider a course of action he thought impossible.

Adrian looked at the water dancing over the rocks, the air filled with brook sounds. Johanna's colony had commingled so completely that he felt like a foreigner among them. And no matter how busy and involved he got, Adrian never overcame the feeling he was in the way even as he helped the village take shape.

*I must live where I can pursue my duty. I came here to free my family. That is my first obligation and I have failed them. I have to move to Rome and find a way to get to the pope.*

He dipped his hand into the stream, drank the cool sweet water. Then heard a sound that did not come from the forest.

He looked up. A silhouetted figure stood inside a moon shadow cast from a large tree on the other side of the stream.

The figure gestured to him and he stood and approached it warily. It was a woman in a dress and scarf beckoning him.

"Who are you?" he asked, looking for signs of an ambush.

"One who needs forgiveness," the woman said, her voice distorted against the rush of stream water.

"Forgiveness from what? Come out from the shadows and show yourself."

The figure hesitated, then stepped into the full light of the moon. It was Johanna, wearing the dress he bought her in a faraway village long ago. But it was more than a dress that changed her appearance. Even in the moonlight Adrian could see her face, always soft and clear, was even more pronounced from a light ash rubbed beneath her eyebrows and onto her eyelids, darkening and deepening them. The blush of berry juice had been used to redden her lips. She stood before him transformed, a beautiful exotic woman wearing a brightly patterned Viking sash around her waist, her head wrapped in a deep forest green pagan scarf wound into a short turban, tied at the side of her temple. Her boyish manner and expression had vanished with a simple cosmetic touch. Adrian could not believe the beauty before him, bearing the likeness and carriage of a royal maiden from a country not yet founded. He stepped forward to get a closer look. She reached out, her hands around his neck and kissed him. She held him with a tenderness he had not felt in months.

"I love you," she whispered. "I can't bear to see you be so sad knowing I am the cause. I apologize for my selfish ways."

He wanted to throw himself down, beg forgiveness for his foolish heart, but she put a finger to his lips and led him from the stream.

"Shhh," she said. "Walk with me? As my lover?"

When she watched Adrian leave the camp, Johanna was chilled by his expression. *He is not leaving me, but his heart is.* She hurried to the wagon, grabbed the sack she kept hidden. Once in the forest, she opened it to reveal a kit she put together over the months on the road. The dress, Bennito's shiny brass vessel she planned to use for a mirror, the sash and scarf, bequeathed from a dying woman in the Saracen raid, the little colored ash pots she picked up after watching the women apply the mysterious creams. She secretly coveted their transformative powers. She planned to surprise Adrian when they got to Rome, found her father, freed Adrian's family, settled into their lives together, their hardships left behind. She longed for the night she would leave her role as a man forever and reveal her true feminine self to him on a romantic evening he would never forget.

That fantasy dissipated when Adrian walked away. She needed to use everything she had to keep her man from leaving for good *now*.

The task was more difficult than she ever imagined. It took frustrating, disastrous hours to get right what appeared to be a simple application of ash, crèmes and powder. She looked at her reflection in the brass vessel after the first attempt, repulsed at the clownish puppet looking back at her.

She washed her face and started over again. This time she gazed upon a ghostly ghoul with blackened eyes and exaggerated, blackish lips. She remembered watching the women, thinking how easy it looked. Now Johanna was panic-stricken. She could not ask for help, this had to be done on her own. Could she not even make herself into a woman? Had she completely lost that side of her nature? Had she gone so far in her refusal to give up her role to ever come back, losing Adrian in the bargain?

When Adrian roughly called to her that evening, every quality of personal authority and inner strength she had created to that point, dissolved. Could she let go of everything she had become? Could she surrender her role if it was the only way to hold onto Adrian?

An hour later Adrian and Johanna, holding hands as lovers, fell in step with others entering Rome in the early evening, blending in with other lovers in the crowds, making their way through the massive doors of the Leonine gate.

"The city feels different," he said. "Do you feel it?"

The streets were illuminated with the fires of revelry as another side of Rome came awake. Johanna and Adrian passed musicians, magicians and lovers who strolled with them along the streets.

Johanna kept fussing with the tight fit of the dress hugging her hips, across her buttocks. The turbaned scarf, everything made her self-conscious. Adrian took her hands away in his and kissed them.

"Relax with who you are. You are a truly beautiful woman."

She felt herself blush, shy and awkward at the compliment.

"We've never been down into that quarter, have we?" she asked, her head tilted against his shoulder.

"The poor cannot afford to come to this neighborhood," he said.

They were swept along into an unfamiliar part of the city, bright, noisy, appearing as a large carnival and every nook was a sideshow. They passed an alley where a crowd had gathered around a man holding the largest snake they had ever seen. It coiled up his leg, behind his back and over his shoulder, its forked tongue flicking in and out next to his face.

"Only the Snake can save you," the man said, flicking his tongue out like his pet. "He sheds his skin for your sins. Pray to him."

Johanna and Adrian left the man's sermon on how the divine snake had come to replace all other religions in Rome.

They came to a wide boulevard and another crowd, gathered around a man with a lighted torch who stuck the length of it down his throat, then spat flames several meters into the air in a fiery arc.

"A New Church is at hand," he proclaimed. "All who want to know God must be cleansed with his Fire. Fed by His Flame."

"That food is too charred for my taste," said a man in the audience. People laughed and the fire-man begged alms from the crowd. Johanna and Adrian inhaled a sweet smoke of cooking foods that wafted over the street, coming from vendors' charcoal braziers.

Johanna had Adrian wait by a trio of musicians who sang about Jesus going to the underworld to meet Homer and Odysseus. She went to a stall, bought half a chicken roasted in garlic for Adrian, a baked onion covered in a crunchy cheese for herself, and some honeyed grapes for dessert. She squeezed Adrian's arm as the song ended.

"Here's a good spot to watch the world pass by," she said. They sat on a low wall and ate, smiling at each other like children.

"How is it that we've managed to miss this part of the city?" asked Adrian, as two tall African men passed by in brightly colored robes with jangling ornaments around their necks, hands and legs. An aromatic blend of incense blew in behind them and lingered in the air and Johanna and Adrian inhaled jasmine, pepper rose and gardenia.

"It's like the whole world decided to walk down one street in Rome," agreed Johanna. She took his hand, excited. "Let's come here every week. We will get away together and walk with the world."

"Can we come like this, as lovers?" he asked. She blushed again and nodded. Adrian pulled her to her feet, took her in his arms and kissed her right there in the open, disregarding the passing crowd who took no notice of yet another pair of lovers overcome by passion. Johanna resisted a moment, frightened by their public display. But then abandoned herself and sent her kisses right back.

"Johanna," he said suddenly, and pulled back from her with an earnest look. "I've been so angry. I've become bitter with a hateful sin."

"You do not sin."

"I do. Johanna. My only love, I am filled with jealousy."

She looked at him in disbelief.

"Jealousy and envy. I am ashamed."

"How can you envy a ragged girl who pretends to be a monk? I am the sinner not you, brother. I am the one who is ashamed."

"A ragged girl who commands the love and devotion of hundreds. A ragged girl who is more a monk than I."

"I tell you again," he said. "Mine is the sinful heart."

"I would drop this charade tonight, but as a ragged girl I would be helpless. I would end up lost, wandering here on this street with men waiting to prey upon me."

"This jealousy is a false tormentor," said Adrian. "I love you for your bravery. For your persistence. I was raised my whole life on lies. I know that women are neither fragile nor incompetent. I have seen it in you, in Veleda, all the women in the colony. Old voices keep telling me I should hate the way you have chosen, but that way has made me love you more. I swear by our God, Johanna, I always will."

She took his face in her hands and kissed him. They held each other in the midst of the passing people and knew this was the night and these were the hours and feelings they would hold onto. If anything happened to separate them, this would be the night their memories would run to embrace.

They paused outside a tavern to watch a woman dance sensually before a large crowd. She was tattooed on every inch of her body, including her face, tongue and the palms of both her hands in intricate colored shapes, figures, scenes on her arms and legs, across her back. The faces of two lovers, colored in bright reds and pinks and blues were portrayed in profile on each of her bared breasts. Each breast and lover moved with her, the two embracing in a bawdy kiss when she took hold of each breast, pressed them together, bringing the scene alive on her skin.

"I am the Painted Goddess," she intoned, whirling in a diaphanous skirt so short only her sex was covered, though she moved her hips to ensure a flash of it. She chimed tiny cymbals on her fingertips, her head and neck moved in short, staccato turns, this way and that.

Adrian nudged Johanna. A tattooed man snuck in and out at the back of the crowd and lifted valuables from the rapt watchers. "Venus and the Virgin have been made one in me," she said. "Come, for just a few pennies you can see their stories live upon me."

Adrian reached out, grabbed the tattooed man's arm as he eased by, and surprised the thief with a fearsome look and a vice grip. The man panicked, shook free and ran, bumping into the crowd, and scattering his stolen goods when he tried to escape.

"Thief!" rang out throughout the crowd. The crowd turned into a gang and descended on him. The tattooed woman saw what was happening. She stepped in the opposite direction and disappeared into the crowd. Johanna and Adrian walked from the tumult around a corner and found themselves on a quiet avenue.

Johanna clung to his arm, Adrian walked erect, his chest out slightly, his chin held up and he seemed to roll and sway, almost strutting down the street.

He had never acted like this before. It was strange and yet the most appropriate affectation in the world. He never felt so much like a man, proud this beautiful woman walked beside him, on view for the world to witness as his.

"This is how I always want to be with you," said Johanna.

He was about to speak, but a cry made them stop still.

Ahead, beneath the torch of a tavern, three Roman soldiers assaulted an adolescent girl. They groped her breasts, squeezed her behind and reached between her legs. She squirmed and tried to get away, but they laughed and pushed her like a toy from one soldier to the other. Johanna started for them and Adrian gently held her back.

"Be cautious," he said. "See the odds first."

The girl broke away and one of the soldiers followed. He easily jogged beside her, jeering at her helplessness. She ran past Johanna and Adrian as the soldier reached out to grab her.

Johanna stuck out her foot and tripped the big man.

He stumbled, slid hard on the stone street, and scraped a wide swath of skin on his legs before he slammed into a wall.

"This way!" she called.

The girl, disoriented, stood there panting. Johanna took her hand and pulled her to the busy boulevard where they had come from. She pushed the girl into the crowd as the other soldiers yelled and gave chase. The three lost themselves in a pack of celebrants dancing shoulder to shoulder. Johanna held the girl's hand to reassure her, pulling her through the giddy masses. The three of them wove in and out of the throng as the soldiers shoved everyone out of their way.

"Over here," said Adrian. They ducked down another street. Near the gates of the city, Johanna, Adrian and the girl waited in the shadows behind the drapes of a closed market stall. They watched the soldiers pass, bent on retribution but not able to find the audacious couple who dared interfere with their games. The cursing guards pushed their way along until they were out of sight. Adrian, Johanna and the girl slipped through the city gates.

They left the volatile, bright night of Rome for the stillness of the countryside.

"Slow down," said Adrian when they were back at the settlement. "Not so fast, child."

The girl voraciously consumed a piece of flat bread spread with goat cheese and olives. Beside the fire, the girl ate and then gulped from a water skin.

Johanna came out of the shadows, her face washed, dressed as John again. When Johanna draped a blanket over the girl's shoulders, she looked up and tried to place where she had seen this monk.

Johanna felt the sleeve of the girl's ragged dress, at one time an exquisitely fashioned tunic made of the most expensive material, unbelievably soft, almost liquid to the touch. It was material she had only heard about, stuff woven from the spittle of worms.

"Who cast you into the street?" Johanna asked.

"Did you go to the church?" asked Adrian.

"That's where I was thrown from," said the girl, swallowing water. "I was the ward of Archbishop Sergius. *Ward.* I was his slave."

"Sergius," said Johanna. But it could not possibly be the same man. "Was this Sergius once a priest who came from England?"

"My home," the girl nodded.

"Did you travel from England with him?" she said and the girl nodded again. Johanna held her arm to prevent her from taking another bite. "Did a man join you on the journey? A large man with a beard?"

"No one joined our misery. No one escaped it, either. My mother is buried on the road here," she said and burst out crying. She held out the pouch with the Archbishop's Seal and dropped it into Adrian's hand. "This is all I have to show for my misery. Take it. The gold stinks of him. Sergius gave it to Gaetani to buy the senator's land."

Johanna and Adrian looked at each other, but before they could ask another question, the sound of galloping horses brought all three to their feet.

Alerted by the hooves, the colony came awake; everyone rushed from their tents drawing weapons. Johanna picked up a dagger, slipped it into the folds of her robes.

"Veleda!" she called.

A line of heavily armed Roman cavalry stopped at the edge of the camp fire. Johanna thought they might be after the girl and threw Adrian's cloak over her as Veleda came to them, her bow aimed at the Romans.

"Who sends you?" Adrian called. The horsemen ignored him.

"Answer him or answer our arrows and swords!" yelled Johanna at the men. The sweet coziness of the world she and Adrian had in each other's arms not three hours ago was a far-gone memory.

The sound of more horses approached and the soldiers parted to let a Vatican carriage roar into the encampment. A liveried eunuch climbed down the driver's bench and opened the gilded door.

A monk stepped out. He put his arms inside the sleeves of his robe, calmly surveyed the agitated camp of the armed Vikings and pagans until his gaze found Johanna.

"Brother John. You and your followers receive an honored guest," said the monk.

"Who are you?" said Johanna. She heard Marozia, standing just behind her, shiver with recognition upon seeing the man.

"I am Gaetani, assistant to your guest, the Archbishop of Rome."

He opened the carriage door and Sergius, in full religious raiment, emerged. Helped by the hand of Gaetani, the archbishop stood at the top of the steps, remaining above the crowd. Gaetani knelt at his feet. The entire settlement, awestruck by the presence of a holy personage, followed Gaetani's lead and dropped to their knees. Sergius looked over the colony, passed a brief blessing over the barbarians with the sign of the cross. The braid of his white chin whiskers fluttered in the light breeze like the tail of an irritated cat.

*The Woman Pope*

"Bless you, pilgrims," said Sergius. He held up his hand in the manner of the saints painted on the old icons; the last two fingers bent downward, the index, middle finger and thumb straightened. The lanterns, fixed in glazed sconces at the corners of the carriage, glowed brightly behind him, shedding light on his shoulders and head like a faint halo. "In the name of the Father, the Son, and the Holy Spirit."

# CHAPTER XXVI

JOHANNA PUSHED THE girl down into the kneeling crowd. Pulling her own hood over her head, Johanna felt a shadow fall over her. Sergius stood above her. She dropped to her knees before the Archbishop of Rome.

"Rise, good brother," he said and touched Johanna's robe. "Your name is renown in the city because you have honored the poor."

"Your Grace."

She got to her feet but kept her head down as Adrian watched her seem to shrink in the archbishop's presence.

All the months, the sleepless nights spent thinking about this moment, the wild fantasies about what she might do, what she would say, how she would extract the truth of Halbert's fate from him. Not only was she driven to find her father, but if he had caught up with Sergius' caravan only to fall victim to Sergius, Johanna obsessed on revenge. In vivid daydreams throughout the journey she tortured the evil priest, wielding instruments of pain over every inch of his flesh. Johanna visualized walking him to the door of death, then rejoicing in his expression when his soul began its descent into hell.

She always had to catch herself, to think of his rehabilitation, his evil ways turned toward love. But try as she might these were weak, emotionless fantasies, stamped beneath the feet of her real craving for the worst kind of harm.

Now, at his side, all thoughts of revenge were swept away. The memory of that night aboard ship paralyzed then reduced her to a mute shell staring at the ground.

"Join me in my carriage," Sergius said and led her to the jewel-trimmed vehicle. "Come, John, we have business."

Johanna stumbled at his words. The very ones he used to command her to his quarters aboard his ship. Sergius caught her elbow and stopped her fall.

"I have him," said Sergius to Adrian. "I will take care of your brother."

They continued to the carriage where the door was opened by solicitous Gaetani, who helped her into the sumptuous interior.

Johanna was doused by a numbness that made it impossible to turn, run, or even speak, much less revile Sergius.

Inside, the curtains were drawn and a scented oil lamp sputtered, keeping Johanna in partial shadow across the bench. Sergius reached inside a cupboard, retrieved a bottle.

"Metheglin?" She shook her head. He shrugged and filled a goblet.

"You have traveled far to our city?" She nodded. He waited for her to continue, to tell the story and make the small talk. She said nothing. Sergius frowned and took a sip. "Do you love the church, John?"

She nodded again.

"So I have heard, but I am puzzled. Why have you stopped here and not come to the city and your order? Are you offended by some slight?"

"Offended? We were turned away at the gates of Rome."

"By whom?"

"The Roman army."

"You were not allowed to enter?"

"They were given explicit instructions by your grace."

"That is a lie," he boomed, his voice filled the cab and made her flinch. "That is an intolerable lie. I will deal with the perpetrators who have kept you from us."

"We heard that lie from every official and churchman we petitioned to enter the city."

"Unfortunately, I am surrounded by incompetents," he said, and his voice dropped back to normal. "Well-meaning men who act on their own without my consent."

"They claim to have been told this lie from your lips."

"Bring your people inside the safety of Rome tomorrow," he said, ignoring the observation with a wave of his hand. "I will provide my personal escort, and the church will right this wrong."

"Thank you, reverend signore. You are kind, but we have already paid Theodoric to live here."

"Theodoric, the senator? "What is wrong with you, John?""

She tensed, her hand sliding for the knife in her robe.

"The man is a treacherous sinner often rebuked by the church," Sergius continued. "No one informed you, son?"

She shook her head. His face relaxed, he stroked his white chin whiskers. Sergius reached over and patted Johanna's knee. She blanched so hard he was taken back, but dismissed it as a nervous response to the presence of the Archbishop of Rome.

"I understand. It is upsetting to be fooled. But you will come to Rome, I will petition Pope Leo for the return of your money and matters will be settled. We have a need for dedication like yours."

Pleased at his resolution, he leaned back, finished the mead in a quick series of little sips. Johanna tried to contain herself.

"Thank you, your grace. We will do as you say. Oh. Will you be housing us in the Vatican?"

Sergius' head came up and he nearly gagged on the liquor.

"What?"

"We are over four hundred souls. I know you must have a plan and a place you can feed and clothe us, am I correct?"

"I -- You are a resourceful lot."

"I know you would not want to see us wander Rome penniless. As beggars the city would rise against us. And if your petition for our lease money falls on deaf ears we'd have no where to live and our community would be hated."

"You will organize as you have done here, using your skills to fend for yourselves. The church will support you with prayer and guidance," Sergius said, closing the conversation.

"Our souls nourished, but our bellies will lack?"

"Stop this protest, right now," he said, pointing his finger and leaning into Johanna. The congeniality of equals was gone, replaced by the stern superiority of a lord to a servant. "You will leave this land tomorrow, do you understand? Look at me, boy."

*The Woman Pope*

Sergius squinted in the dark at Johanna, who remained under the hood. She felt the knife within the folds of her robes slip from her fingers into the crack of the bench at the carriage wall.

It occurred in a flash to Johanna that she might have fallen into a trap. She was overcome by a terrible dread that Sergius knew who she was all along. This pretense was to bring her all the way in so he could lay her bare in her most vulnerable state and exact his own revenge.

"Something about you," he said and reached out to push the hood from her face. Johanna pulled away, fumbled for the knife between the seats, hoping she could get him to tell her what happened to her father before she cut his throat. He put his hand on the hood to throw it back and expose her face. She could not reach the dagger. Her fingers felt the blade, but it was jammed too deep between the seats. She jerked her head from Sergius' hand, then felt his grip dig into her shoulder.

"I said look at me," said the archbishop in a low growl.

Johanna began to tremble. Everything faded around her except the image of Sergius on deck, a huge broadsword raised above his head.

At that moment a hard banging erupted at the door.

"I am not to be disturbed!"

"Not even for an old friend?"

Sergius froze, then pulled the curtains back. Theodoric and his private army had surrounded the carriage and the archbishop's guards. Sergius whispered out the opposite window to the driver.

"Drive. Ride away, fool."

"Please don't leave us yet, Sergius," said Theodoric. "I humbly extend an invitation and would be honored if you'd accept."

The whole carriage rocked violently on its wheels. The door was hammered with heavy blows. The lock broke away and the door was flung open off its hinges and crashed into the dirt. Sergius looked away from Johanna and tried to muster the composure of his office. He walked calmly down the steps and faced a mounted Theodoric who wore an armored breastplate, a plume-tufted helmet and a scarlet tunic held at his shoulders with golden clasps. He was dressed for battle.

"Theodoric," said Sergius, aware of the eyes upon them. "This outrageous act, this violence to the Archbishop of Rome will not go unpunished by Pope Leo's hand."

Theodoric dismounted and walked to him. Johanna got out of the carriage and instantly Adrian was beside her, leading her to one side. She was dizzy and leaned on him.

"I pray you're right, archbishop," said Theodoric with a jovial bow. "But you ride onto my property in secret. You come to persuade my tenant to abandon land you yourself desire."

"That slanderous accusation will cost you dearly," Sergius said.

Theodoric turned to Johanna. "Tell me, John the English. What was the good archbishop's conversation with you?"

Johanna stepped forward, face away from Sergius. The senator folded his arms, cocked his head.

"Did he tell you to leave the land and our lease? Did he demand you and your followers come to the city to be protected by the church?"

All eyes were on her, but she stood there in silence a long tense moment. Finally, she nodded. Theodoric's smile returned in full as a loud murmur spread through the colony.

"After all you've paid to me, John?" asked Theodoric innocently. "Is that the wise course?"

"He will not be robbed by you," said Sergius.

"Oh, I robbed them for twice what the land is worth," he said to Sergius. "Only the monk was willing to pay the price."

"You see? Fraud was his only plan," said Sergius, vindicated. Theodoric took several coins and dropped them into Johanna's hand.

"It was done to keep you, archbishop, from forcing the sale of this land," he said. "Brother John. I give you back half what you paid me. Live here. Protect us by being Rome's eyes and ears. Rome will eat you alive if you bring your followers inside and he knows this. Tomorrow the archbishop, you and I have an audience with the Pontiff to find out why the Archbishop of Rome needs property he has no authority to own."

Theodoric walked back to his horse.

"This was your sole purpose here," called Sergius at his back, furious. Theodoric was handed the reins and he turned to the head of the city's churches.

"You have been here a short time, yet act as though you are a bull and all of Rome is your cow to mount. May I suggest, Archbishop, that you prepare yourself for the experience of being gelded," said Theodoric. He mounted, patted his gelding broadly and he and his guards rode off. Sergius turned to Johanna with undisguised hatred.

"You betrayed me. Damned me by your answer and I swear you will feel the sting of this."

Sergius went to his carriage, whispered to Gaetani who nodded and got up on the bench with the driver. The man cracked the whip and raced the horses from the camp. The carriage roared off the property as quickly as it had come.

Moments later a scream shook the air. A pagan and a Viking followed the sound. They dragged the broken body of the carriage driver back to the camp fire. He had been pushed from his seat, trampled and crushed beneath the carriage wheels for not getting Sergius away from Theodoric.

Johanna looked at the body, her mind racing over the coming meeting. When Sergius recognizes her, she will be revealed before the most spiritual man on earth, Pope Leo. He will call her a sorceress and have abundant proof when she is unmasked. Her life will be reviled in front of those she loves. She'd be torn apart as a witch, a charlatan who dared challenge the holy Archbishop of Rome.

Johanna tried to pray, to ask God for help for her final, humiliating end. Adrian glanced over and saw Johanna's eyes roll up in her head.

"John," he said as she hit the ground, eyes fluttering, mouth open, as if yanked into the beyond by a dark spirit.

# CHAPTER XXVII

THE VATICAN COURT was filled with a thousand churchmen dressed in the brightly colored robes of their orders. Some wore their poverty with ragged garments tied at their waists with rope while others were grand as royalty, and expected to be treated as such, wrapped in layers of expensive embroidered cloth. But today, from bishop to acolyte, rank was set aside in the excitement and every beard in the room pushed rudely to view the proceedings.

Pope Leo the fourth sat high up on the marble throne, his white bushy eyebrows arched above penetrating gray eyes while a massive white beard fanned across his chest. He dressed in white robes sewn with pale rose jewels. One hand fingered his whiskery bib, the other held the massive golden crozier of his office.

"I have related everything, Holy Father," said Sergius, kneeling before the papal throne. "I am slandered by accusers who hate the church and thus hate me. I am the victim of a conspiracy. Theodoric and this foreign heretic, this deceitful monk, plotted the schemes you heard. They created lies no one can possibly believe of your servant the archbishop. If there is a man here who can uphold these falsehoods, I will say nothing against him."

Sergius lowered the tenor of his voice to bring all the gravity he could to it.

He turned and pointed dramatically at Theodoric and Johanna. "But if it be otherwise, then by my right I would demand the immediate excommunication and exile of the two sinners who accuse me."

The whispers in the great hall made the pontiff raise his crozier for silence. Johanna, next to the senator and Adrian, was so afraid she could not stop her teeth from chattering.

"Step closer, youth," gestured the pope with his free hand.

Johanna left Adrian's side and came before the man. She dropped to her knees, clasped hands together and was awestruck in the presence of the man closest to Saint Peter, the nearest mortal man on earth to Jesus Christ Himself. Some said the pope was not mortal at all but upon his divine elevation to the Chair was transformed by the Hand of God and lived on as a demi-god even after the passing of his flesh. Johanna could not believe she was here, alive to see this day and this man she once had hated and now revered. He looked down upon Johanna with wrinkled brown eyes shaded by huge fans of white puffy eyebrows.

"Raise your right hand," said the pope. "Swear before God what you have told me is true."

"Yes, Holiness," she breathed, drenched in a cold sweat. She raised her hand. "The archbishop commanded us to leave the settlement we had already leased. Only when Senator Theodoric interceded did I know his real intent. I swear by God this is the truth."

"This is a serious accusation," replied the pope and looked out over the assembly. "Are there others here who can attest to this?"

"There are, Holiness," replied Theodoric, stepping forward with a short bow. "Respected men, signores Cologna, Orsinius, Pantagruel and Venicchi. Each has received similar threats from the archbishop."

The named men stood across the hall in a group and debated nervously among themselves, gesturing with frantic motions. Gaetani stood close on one side of them, arms folded inside his robe.

"Step forward, honorable merchants, give testimony," said the pontiff.

They murmured and nudged each other. Finally, Pantagruel, the old vintner, stepped to the Chair, took off his black peaked beret, bowed and genuflected on one knee. Sergius glared until he saw the expression on Gaetani's face.

"We have nothing ill to say of the archbishop, Holy Father," he said. "We know of no threats, to ourselves or anyone else."

"He never intimidated nor approached you to purchase your land?" asked the pope.

"No, your Grace," he said and glanced at the other men. "Never."

"Holy Father!"

"Quiet, senator, you had your opportunity. Thank you, signore Pantagruel, gentlemen." The pope turned to Johanna and Theodoric. "Words alone cannot condemn the archbishop who is our extension, heart and hand."

"He has intimidated and silenced these men with threats even now," said Theodoric.

"Theodoric, watch your tongue or I'll have you dragged from this hall to the depths of the Vatican," said the pope.

Theodoric started to speak, but held back. The pope let the threat sink in and sat in a stony silence and let the tension build beneath the surface of the hall.

"Yours is a most serious charge without evidence," he said, finally. "We ask each of you to forgive each other in the name of Christ. It is our Savior's wish that we bury our hatred and look with love on our brother. Swallow this bitterness and forgive each other. Do this for the good of your souls. Do this for us. Do this *now,* senator."

Theodoric sighed but made no move.

"Senator Theodoric," said the pope, warning.

Theodoric stood, defeated. There was nothing left to do but give a hollow apology to Sergius, whose face was a perfectly constructed replica of the unjustly accused.

"I understand what must be done, Holy Father," said Theodoric.

Johanna could not believe what she was seeing. The liar who betrays his own faith, a manipulating seducer and murderer without conscience was about to slip from justice untouched. Sergius was being raised up as an innocent man and people would think Theodoric a cruel politician intent on destroying the reputations of the righteous.

The governing roles of these two forces were not easily understood by the common people. Most could only grasp that Sergius was a living symbol of religion and Theodoric was that for man. The two embodied church and the state, but at any time when both rose and dared to challenge the other's authority, it was man who lost the battle.

It was too much for Johanna. Sergius had destroyed her world with lies, poison, and if her father was dead, murder. Before she could think better of it she was on her feet.

"There is proof, Holy One," said Johanna.

The whispers of the crowd echoed across the high ceiling of the hall. The pope called for quiet. Everyone in the congregation looked at the little monk before the pope.

"What is your proof, son?" the pope asked.

Theodoric faced her, uncertain what the little monk might do and concerned their case might be harmed even further. Johanna pulled out the coin pouch Marozia had given her, held it aloft for all to see.

"The archbishop's bribe. In this pouch is the gold he was to use as bribes to force Theodoric to sell the land to him."

A rumbling outburst came from the spectators. Johanna then turned and pulled a shaken Marozia out from the crowd to stand with her.

"This child was his slave and was present when Sergius gave instruction to get the land 'by any means,'" said Johanna. She threw the pouch at Sergius' feet. It was embroidered with his official seal.

The gold spilled, rolled over the marble floor and those around it scrambled to pick up the rolling pieces. Sergius looked at the scattered money, his face ashen. Theodoric's mouth opened. The pouch was brought to the pope who pounded his crozier to quiet the noise at the sight of gold.

"This is not mine," Sergius said. "And I've never seen that lying whore in my life."

"Are you sure?" she asked. She pulled Marozia farther out into the hall to be seen. "Did you not bring this child from England? Did you not share her with others as a gift? And did you not brand your property like cattle before throwing it away?"

"If the whore claims that she lies," bellowed Sergius.

Johanna walked the girl to Pope Leo, dropped the strap of Marozia's dress. The scar on her shoulder was clearly in the shape of the Archbishop's Seal. The pope examined it against the pouch.

"Is this the truth, girl?" asked the pope. Marozia nodded, broke down in tears.

"Sergius' bribe and his seal. Indisputable proof, Holiness," said Theodoric and gestured at the money and girl while looking at the crowd for approval. The hall murmured in disgusted agreement.

"Silence," said the pope. He stood and pounded the heel of his jeweled shepherd's hook on the floor. This unprecedented move stunned everyone in the hall and it became still. He waved the staff over their heads and Johanna and Sergius got on their knees. "Why have you kept this until now, son?"

"I prayed I wouldn't have to let the archbishop be brought so low, Holy Father."

"You withheld the truth."

"Only in hopes he would not force it from me."

Pope Leo looked down at the extension of his heart and hand with grave disappointment.

"The money and your seal convicts you. Our trust is broken. You will do penance for this crime."

"But Holy Father."

"You will be contrite and humble yourself before God," the Pontiff roared. Sergius dropped his head to his chest. The pope held up the gold scepter and made his pronouncement. "Look upon this fallen man and take his lesson. Ambition kills what is precious. It leads us down the darkest path. Learn from Sergius, who was archbishop and who may rise again after he has searched his heart and atoned."

Outside the Vatican Hall Johanna and Adrian walked down the long steps, followed by a churning mass of excited observers.

"John!"

They turned to see Theodoric approach.

"All of the city has heard the news and is calling for you. You've freed them from Sergius' tyranny. Look."

He pointed to a crowd gathered around Sergius at the stairs of the Vatican court. Johanna watched as they stripped off his robes, his hat, and shoes until he stood naked in the street. They jeered his thin frame, tugged hard at his long chin whiskers, laughed at his blotchy genitals, scarred a sickly yellow from burns, and he then was spit upon from every angle. A sackcloth was thrown at him, and he bent to pick it up. He put on the rough, itchy cloth and calmly took the blows of ridicule.

"You are the beloved of Rome, and they want you to serve them," said Theodoric, and clapped Johanna on the shoulder. A mob of citizens surrounded her, calling her by the name they had heard the Senator give her.

"John Anglicus!"

"John the English, our saint!"

People stuffed flowers in her arms, hugged her. A mass of ecstatic strangers engulfed her in a crush of loving arms and kisses. She yelled over the crowd to Theodoric.

"My people are on your land. I have to go to them!"

"Your land is here, John Anglicus. These are your people now, the citizens of Rome!"

"I cannot do this! I have to find my --" she began but was lifted into the arms of the multitude, over their heads and swept away into the crowd.

Theodoric laughed so hard tears rolled down his cheeks. The Senator watched a phenomenon in the making, one he helped create. He could not help think of the monk's theatrical toss of the money at Sergius' feet. It was a brilliant move even he would not have had the presence of mind to produce. He knew he had chosen wisely.

A political obstacle in the way of the Vatican had been removed without the use of an army or poison. All done *gratis* by a charismatic little monk who wanted nothing in return but to continue to pay him for the land. Theodoric would have paid an assassin or poisoner ten times the going amount for the elimination of this impediment. The senator called to Johanna as she was borne away over the heads of the mob.

"Many are called," he laughed. "But few are *taken*!"

Adrian approached the senator and bowed.

"Sir," he said. "You now have what you desire."

Theodoric regarded the little brother's confidante.

"I suspect you too have a desire," he replied. "Your name is Adrian?"

"Yes, Senator. But this desire is not for myself. It is for the lives of my family who have been loyal to Rome but who are now enslaved by Rome's enemies," said Adrian and looked the senator in the eyes

Theodoric measured the incorruptible gaze of this intense monk, and sensed why the little brother had chosen him as his closest ally.

"Walk with me, Adrian, and tell me what you desire."

# CHAPTER XXVIII

ROME, FROM A distant hillside, glowed inside the walls in luminescent amber firelight. Celebratory fires blazed, reflected against the low clouds above the metropolis. The city shimmered in sultry heat waves that made Rome appear as a mirage, an apparition ethereally hovering between the seven hills. A flash of lightning came from the clouds and streaked across the sky in jagged fingers. The brilliant white forks surged down into the peaks of the mountains to the north.

"A thunderstorm tonight," said Adrian.

"It will feel good to ride in the rain, brother," replied Galt, the huge pagan who had converted to Christianity and become a good friend to Adrian on the journey. The two men checked the bags of supplies collected from Theodoric's store rooms and glanced at the celebration. Flares shot from the turrets on the walls; the burning arrows arced into the sky.

"Galt. Why do you think your gods abandoned you?"

"They got old. Became weary and could no longer fight the One True God and so He killed them. Is that not so?"

"I don't know," he sighed. "I only hope our Everlasting God has no enemies waiting behind Him."

"I hear the company, brother," said Galt and pointed out into the dark. But instead of a company of soldiers they were expecting, a carriage from the house of Theodoric galloped up the hill and out of the dark. It stopped beside them, the door flew open and Johanna got down and ran to Adrian. He saw the panic in her eyes and knew that because of Galt she forced herself not to grab and cling to him.

"I was told by Theodoric he granted your wish."

"He was generous, brother John, yes," said Adrian. More rumbling came from the dark and when they looked they saw several dozen of Theodoric's private army race across the last of the valley before the final climb to the settlement. Adrian led her away from Galt to give them privacy. Johanna could barely contain herself.

"Your family will be safe, thank God. But when do you think you will return? Adrian?" she asked.

He stopped and faced her.

"I never thought I could fall in love with anyone but God. Johanna, I can't serve him and burn so hard inside. I go home to save my family. And when I come back I must return to my vows."

"What are you saying?"

"Please. After what happened with Pope Leo and the crowds and...You've been called to God, you have gone beyond me."

"I will never go beyond you, don't say that."

"And what was once a disguise is now who you are."

"I don't want it. I give it all up. Take me with you. I will do whatever you ask. I love you," she reached out for him, but Adrian took hold of her arms and held her at a distance.

"The world has moved between us. But if continents separate us, you will always be with me. Know that."

"No, Adrian!"

The thunder of hooves built until the first line of cavalry rode out of the dark. The soldiers were armored, ready for the campaign ahead, and stopped before Galt.

"I have to help my family," said Adrian. "You have to help Rome."

"Come back to me. Please. I need you with me. I can't do this without you, I'll fail."

She pulled away his arms and embraced him. He pulled her off.

"With God you cannot fail. I won't forget you. Not in this world or any other, I swear," said Adrian. He turned from her and walked across the embankment to Galt and the waiting company of soldiers. Galt led a sturdy-looking courser over and Adrian mounted the horse. Adrian turned a final time toward the little monk and saluted her with a nod and a wave, then rode off with the soldiers.

Johanna was stunned beyond feeling and unable to react, to yell, to cry, to scream or even open her mouth to give an audible farewell. She was helpless to anything but watch the man she had crossed more than a physical continent with gallop out of her life.

≈ ≈ ≈

Johanna was swept away not only into the crowds of Rome, but into a world few people knew existed.

She followed Theodoric down a long corridor deep inside a palace belonging to the church, then turned down another hall. In the crush of that first day, Johanna told herself she would divide her time between her settlers and the incredible duties, opportunities really, offered to her by the mother church. But she could not foresee what it meant to be instantly famous in a city that thrived on myth and the fantastic.

"Brothers, stop that," she said and hurried to two monks rolling on the marble floor of the corridor. They struck each other, pulled at the other's hair and beard. The new celebrity monk was on his way to a reception and the two men had come to blows over who would open the door for Johanna. The senator laughed.

"What is wrong with them?" she muttered to herself.

Johanna stopped before huge double doors intricately carved, painted with flowers and winged cherubim.

"They want what you have."

"What is that, senator?" she asked.

"This," he said as the giant doors swung open to reveal a hall as large as an outdoor coliseum.

Heads turned to see the already legendary monk who had led hundreds of barbaric pagans a thousand leagues to Christ. The city's titled and wealthy strained to get a glimpse of the little brother.

Every eye was on her in the doorway, and she was petrified. She felt they saw what she really was, too. They must know what simple peasants and warriors did not. She was certain that hers was such a poor disguise that only the humblest were fooled. She was led to a banquet table that easily held a hundred guests.

"Little brother, sit by me," called a merchant over the echoing murmur. He stood on his seat at the banquet. His smile came at her from a demi-mask made of solid gold. The room erupted into laughter at the man's daring. Startled, Johanna walked toward the man, but her arm was taken by Theodoric who guided her to a place beside Sbrinja.

Johanna was seated next to a beautiful, dark princess exiled from Constantinople. She had black, shining, wet-looking hair coiled in scalloped layers in a high pointed pile on her head. She was dressed in the most opulent gown Johanna had ever seen, swirling pastel blue stripes against a milky white. It barely touched the edges of her brown shoulders and plunged in a deep scoop across the plain of her breasts, so low it allowed half of the chocolate full moons of her nipples to rise over the horizon of material. Johanna had not been this close to finery and wealth since dining at Sergius' table and felt breathless, vulnerable.

"Little brother?" asked the princess after they were introduced. Johanna looked around the palatial room filled with royalty, high ranking clerics, merchants and famous soldiers, every one staring at and whispering about her.

"Yes, Highness?"

The princess leaned close and nonchalantly let her bosom press into Johanna's shoulder. Johanna was caught full force by the princess' perfume. The woman smelled like a secret, a forbidden promise inside a profusion of oils and musky flowers Johanna could not identify.

"Is it true you built an entire town for your savages and domesticated their wild ways?" she asked in a heavily accented Italian.

"No, Highness," Johanna shook her head with a smile. "I am afraid you have been misinformed."

"Our humble brother would never attest to such a thing," said Theodoric beside her. "Nor would he ever say he has worked tirelessly for his colony and the wretched of this city, ministering to the sick every night."

"Senator, please," Johanna said.

"Nor would he tell you that he has concluded his continental quest by toppling the Archbishop of Rome in one stroke, a man hated for bringing misery to rich and poor alike."

"Senator, that is not true," Johanna said.

"Of course it's not, brother, I apologize," he said and winked at the princess, thus the whole side of the table. The guests saw the gesture and responded with knowing smiles as they grabbed at hunks of grilled meat from heaping platters on the table.

Johanna spent the rest of the evening denying the stories, speaking to men and women gathered four deep around her. Those who could not get close enough to meet the monk became drunk on wine and the excitement of their new guest. The great hall echoed with laughter and loud voices competing to be heard. A parade of faces and voices passed in front of Johanna and her unease faded. She was thankful no one seemed to think she was anything but a young monk.

"This way, John of England," Theodoric said the next morning as he led her down steps to his waiting carriage. Several high born, titled women fluttered toward them from across the street, their ladies-in-waiting hurrying behind. The women called to get Johanna's attention, but Theodoric opened the door and quickly helped her into the coach. He loaned it to Johanna for her beck and call, though she would rarely get the chance to use it alone.

"The governor's palace," he said through the window curtains.

They raced through the city, pulled by six horses adorned with gold braids in their manes and woven through their tails.

"The governor of Rome?"

"Today I'm going to introduce you to the real city. Far beyond anything you saw last night."

"If you like, I could introduce *you* to a Rome I do not believe you ever had the pleasure of seeing, senator," she said. He laughed.

"You are familiar with the wretched of Rome, but you don't know her invisible heart, the political and social infrastructure, where this city truly lives."

"Where does this place exist?"

"The door opened slightly last night. Today you will step through and enter an unseen land where unspoken bonds and the strictest competition exist between every person of power."

"You say this place cannot be seen?"

"It's a shadowy nether world."

"What do these persons do there?"

"The Vatican is the base for some of the wealthiest families on earth, some of whom vie for control of entire countries in the west."

"What does the realm of God have to do with that?"

"With power? With kings and land and wealth? John, every grand and smiling face you meet from today on, whether priest or prince, is part of the labyrinth. Every person you pass in the hall is bound by the politics of secrets. Secrets you will never hear outright. You may catch pieces, yet never know exactly what they are talking about."

"Why?"

"Do you really want to know, son?" he asked. "You are a young man and so devoted."

"I wish to know the truth of all things."

"Perhaps one day you will. But so much is hidden," Theodoric said and settled into the cushions of the carriage. "And the rest is illusion."

# CHAPTER XXIX

THE LONG ROMAN summer, so humid, rank and malarial, finally cooled into autumn. With it came golden fall colors and soft angles of sunlight on the heels of shorter days. Every morning Johanna awoke in a different villa's luxurious surroundings. The wonder of luxury had long worn away and she longed for simplicity and privacy.

Johanna had asked for a small room in the Vatican. She had been deep inside Rome for more than six months.

She threw off her nightshift and slipped into the dark brown robe with its peaked cowl, cinching it at the waist with a hemp sash. Johanna adjusted her breasts, bound against her skin day and night inside a thin linen strip she dyed close to her natural skin color, knowing any slip might show more flesh than could be explained.

She washed her face in cold water from a bowl on the bed stand, then put her hand beneath her bed and withdrew the secret object. Considered by many clerics to be sinful as an icon, Johanna nonetheless scrutinized her reflection in the little brass mirror she held to her face.

The youthful freckles had gone and her face had a narrow, sculpted look in its thinness. She pressed at the skin on her cheeks. Her eyes still sparkled hazel, but she thankfully detected a slight but sustained bagginess under them, plus the faintest of lines at the corners. Whether the lines had come from squinting daily into the sun as she made her way toward Rome, or from rich foods from tables of the wealthy, or because of the strain from months of scrutiny by the city's elite, she did not know.

Johanna was glad any kind of change moved her appearance away from girlishness.

She still received looks of bewilderment and often outright surprise when she entered a room, but the power of her presence quickly dissolved every silent question.

Johanna tossed her head, tried to see her hair from another angle. She kept the fine light brown hair cut in a coarse and jagged bowl around her head. The bleached streaks of blond streamers from the summer sun had faded into a darker shade for the fall, and the tonsure was a wide and deeply mown circle on the crown of her head.

She turned from the mirror, got down on her knees at the window and said her long series of prayers. She thanked the Lord again for returning Adrian safely to Rome after his long absence to free his family. And even though he had refused to see or speak to her, she prayed God would end their unbearable feud.

She rose, looked out her window and saw how another autumn had come upon Rome.

"Six months," she said aloud. She could not believe it had been so long since she had seen Adrian. It had been a dizzying whirl of events and appointments to see important people who clamored to meet her. She opened the door to call Anastasius to get her carriage.

"John!"

"Brother John! Over here."

A horde of personal attendants from famous houses across Italia swarmed the hallway. All waved sealed letters urgently requesting a private meeting with the monk.

"I've come from the Duke of Tusculum."

"Hear me first, brother, please!"

"I've a much better invitation for you."

Johanna turned on her heels, went back inside as hands reached out with their letters even as the door closed.

≈ ≈ ≈

"Should I contact Hbramas' order?" asked Anastasius.

*The Woman Pope*

"No," she said as the carriage pounded over the road. "It is enough to know where he is."

Johanna looked across the carriage at the young monk. She had been courted by many for the position, but decided on the quiet and intense Anastasius. Late one night she could not sleep and wandered the cavernous Vatican halls. She heard laughter in a room off the main corridor and saw Anastasius bent over a book, his shoulders shaking with a private mirth, a candle lighting one of the Vatican's many cubbyholes. In him she found a fellow seeker of wisdom who could not stop his search just because the day had ended.

"Should I send the usual?" Anastasius asked. "Food, clothing?"

"Not too soon. In a week or so, yes."

Every morning she sent runners to Adrian, every evening a message returned with his refusal to meet her. She had heard stories of an intense battle for Adrian's village that lasted weeks. Then Adrian awoke one morning to find the Saracen's gone, his village and family free. He returned to Rome to pay for the victory of his prayers.

Once back in the city, he went directly to a religious school led by a revered holy man, Hbramas. Adrian offered his discipleship as he had promised God he would return to a monk's life. What better place to fulfill his debt than where a simple man's teachings soothed the unrelenting ache of his heart?

Johanna's carriage slowed as it came to the Vatican entrance.

*I can not let him go, but can not beg, either,* Johanna thought to herself as she walked down the tapestry-hung corridor to her rooms. "Please keep me informed of all you can, Anastasius."

"Of course, brother."

"And continue the search for my father as well."


Johanna refused much of what was offered by the wealthy, who loved the miraculous little monk. Within a week of her entrance to the rarefied social strata of Rome, Johanna's awe of the Eternal City faded. Her humble politeness turned into an open critique on the lives of the rich. Fed only by the hunger for money, power, gossip, revenge and squandering their senses on petty pleasures, Johanna thought them all pathetic. She often caught herself and had to remember the words of her father, 'judge nothing until the end.' Still, the rich needed and, as she soon discovered, craved her leadership.

"Please, brother John, please," pleaded Theodoric's wife, Althea, during the first mad bloom of her fame. "Come dine with us. Rome's most illustrious playwright is presenting his latest work for a few select guests tomorrow. They say Phormio is brilliant, better than Terrance and it will be a pleasant distraction from those wretched souls you deal with every day."

"I have come to Rome for those 'wretched souls,' and not to be entertained, Lady Althea, but thank you."

The senator's wife begged until Johanna relented, but with conditions.

"I doubt your guests will consent to them."

"We'll do anything," said Althea.

"Every member of your dinner party must do exactly as I ask, without question and regardless of rank. They are to be stripped of their positions for the night."

"Brother," declared the beautiful woman, licking her lips. "For the honor of your presence we would gladly whip each other naked and senseless if that is what you demanded."

The senator's wife's tone suggested that absurdity would be exactly to her liking. She could only guess at the predilections of this woman and her decadent circle. Johanna awakened one night to the sounds of moaning, of several voices in pain or ecstasy, she could not be sure. Johanna thought she was dreaming but later saw identical scrapes on the wrists, ankles and necks of Althea and her friends.

One morning as guest of the senator she passed the open door of a bedroom and stopped dead in her tracks. The odor wafting out made her head spin. The empty room was awash in a musk she recognized from the Viking longboats when she caught lovers after their sexual business. But this was a scent so thick with the smell of the expended glands of men and women and blood it made Johanna dizzy.

Althea claimed ignorance and an incredulous shock when Johanna confronted her, yet had the same bemused smile on her face as she wore now.

"Tell them to be ready at sunset," said Johanna.

"So early? Some often don't wake until then." Althea saw Johanna bristle. "But I will have them ready, don't worry."

The senator's wife was ecstatic. It was the socialite's coup. A messenger dashed out with invitations. The most beautiful woman in Rome would again dazzle the city by possessing what everyone desired. Althea spent the rest of the day between skin treatments to repair the small abrasions from the rough sex, and her two daily massages, one to keep her muscles supple and the second for sexual release, all the while receiving messengers with their enthusiastic acceptances from the guests invited to the adventure.

Theodoric was happy for his wife when she told him the news over dinner. Though he took no part in her games, he condoned them the way a parent allows his child the gifts and attentions of others.

"You are so beautiful when you are busy," he smiled as he cut into the roast duckling on his plate.

"I feel a new world is about to come alive," she said, unable to eat. Several times throughout the meal she whispered new ideas to her lady-in-waiting behind her chair.

"It goes without saying," he said, lifting the crisp skin from the breast and dipping it into the garlic and raspberry wine sauce. "I trust you will be discrete in front of our new friend."

"Have my actions ever been otherwise?" she said with mock dismay. They had to laugh, thinking of her famous escapades in the past.

For Theodoric, her games of sexual intrigue kept Althea content, too busy to do anything dangerous. Such as brewing a plot to overthrow him. Other wives had been successful in bringing down their powerful husbands, some by way of disgrace, others by opening the door for an assassin at night, hired by a lover who promised more than husband or in-laws could provide. And with the right poison, some did the deed themselves.

Theodoric encouraged his wife to take lovers of both sexes. In a society where a hint of prurient interest could bring public torture and death, sexual wantonness in the spoiled elite she was a part of was a way not only to flaunt, but to gain a higher level of excitement from the fear of being caught.

On occasion Theodoric watched their games as an invited guest, seated in a special box seat above the proceedings. He looked on and was thankful. He loved his wife very much and was relieved she had a hobby she could throw herself into with such enthusiastic abandon.

Theodoric dipped another mouthful of duck into the sauce and brought it to his mouth. The sweets and sours rose and fell with every turn of his tongue and he savored each contradictory yet compelling taste. He was content. And this new little twist might even hold Althea's attention for a while.

Hours before the scheduled performance of the play, Johanna led Althea and her party, a small band of the city's most power-ful men and women, into the poorest and most dangerous section of Rome, Hell's Quarter. That evening would become another Roman legend, joining the others before it as gossip made its way through the chambers of the wealthy until strands of the story finally drifted down and settled onto the street itself. The following day the deeds of Little Brother John the English were on the lips, distorted with every telling, of nearly everyone in Rome.

The main guest in Althea's party was Phormio, a dandified poet and professional sycophant. Obese and perpetually squint-ing, he wore a bright red and blue silk scarf his trademark attire, tied around and knotted with a flourish on top of his oversize head. Known for satirical verse plays, he poked gentle but re-spectful fun at the rich for their lack of sophistication. As the company left the lights of the street lanterns and headed into the darker section of town, Phormio boasted he had never heard of the area they were in, much less passed through it.

Johanna, carrying a covered bucket, stopped the company and crooked a finger at Phormio. She led the snickering play-wright into a hovel where, once inside, the smirk fell away, and he made a face. The smell overwhelmed him and he gagged, steadying himself against the wall. He pulled out a perfumed handkerchief and put it to his nose.

"Never smelled that before?" she said and set down the bucket. She opened it and ladled a thick soup into a bowl, handing it to the poet who was riveted, his eyes fixed next to the candle glowing beside the child in the corner of the room.

"Feed her," said Johanna. He crossed the room and fed soup with shaking hands to the emaciated eight-year-old girl. She had just a thin painting of skin left outside the bones of her languid face, her wide eyes out of focus, dying.

"Do you think," Johanna asked when the poet finished his task and set the ladle down, "the world of this child has a place in your art?"

"It's not what I know. I have never seen this world before."

He looked at Johanna, opened his mouth to speak but the child made a weak cry. She threw up all the soup she had been fed onto the front of the playwright's tunic, then went into a long seizure, her little body jerking in spasms on the bed.

The poet backed away, speechless as he watched the child wrench in a heap. Johanna bent and comforted her. Phormio turned to the wall and wept, face in his hands.

After the company left that hovel they were marched directly to another. Two brothers, wastrel noblemen, were made to carry an old man between them into a church so that he could light a candle for his dead wife. The drunkards thought it a jolly turn and sang a tavern song.

"Sixteen liters were drunk, if memory serves right, after the seventeenth serving of wine," they sang as they carried the man down the street, "The ugly barmaid became a goddess in heat, and when she lifted her dress, became mine!"

The brothers watched the old man pray from the back of the church and were quiet.

Outside, Johanna told the two nobles to carry the man back to his house, but they laughed and walked into the street away from the party.

"Enough of this pretense. This penance has gone on long enough for me, brother John. Please, rub the others' noses in their guilt. They like it, but I think I'd rather have a taste of the communion wine," said the elder, Caius, and winked at his younger brother.

"I know the tavern where they serve a good vintage of the holy drink," Porto the younger added. They left the group and staggered down the street, singing at the top of their lungs.

"When she lifted her dress, became mine!"

Later, Johanna sat with general Moldavus, a rugged, harsh man famous for his tactical skill and ruthlessness. Johanna had him act as midwife to help deliver a child. The band of wealthy participants stood awestruck, not one of the men ever having seen a birth.

"How does it feel to see where your soldiers begin their march?" she whispered after the baby's head emerged and took its first breath. The party applauded, moved by the wonder of it.

The officer's eyes narrowed and he grimly endured until the baby was out. She made him tie the umbilical cord then cut it with his dagger. The general, weaving slightly, dried the infant off with a cloth, then passed the newborn to its mother who took it to her breast. Johanna and the general stepped outside.

"Your lessons are for children, monk," the general said. "They are for the uninitiated, not for someone who knows this world."

He walked away, slipped and fell over on his face in the street. He was helped up on wobbly legs, woozy as a drunkard and nauseated.

Each person who played a part that evening had their stories passed on. At every opportunity the teller of the tale swore forever afterward that the mighty had been shaken to the root of their beings in a pivotal moment.

The debut of Phormio's play to be performed when they returned was forgotten. But Johanna's bravado burned like a wildfire through the wealthiest chambers of Rome.

"The gall of that monk," said the exiled princess from Constantinople the next week as she stepped from her bath wearing the smile of someone whose boredom has just been broken.

"Then what happened?" she demanded of her maid.

The maid leaned in to whisper the details in her mistress' ear, while on the other side of the city in another palatial villa...

"To his daring," four gossiping royals laughed and raised their glasses as they lounged naked on the big bed together. The young cousins, two teenage brothers and two older sisters nearing spinsterhood at twenty-five, drank wine and relaxed after a tipsy, rather lifeless dalliance that had become routine.

"Did you hear what happened to Caius and Porto?" asked the youngest sister, stroking the chest of the older male. The others perked up with more interest than they showed in that afternoon's liaison.

She recited the tidbit as heard from Marca, the woman who was both her astrologer and perfume supplier. It was reported that the two royals who walked away from the church were unable to accomplish their mission to drink themselves into oblivion, try as they might.

"Caius and Porto left several taverns sober as owls and mystified," the sister said. "They found themselves at their family home where they tried to reconcile with their father, from whom they had stolen and humiliated, but the man had let go of his sons in his heart."

"Who was their father?" asked the male cousin. The younger sister shrugged coyly to warn that she could not speak the name.

"They were so devastated they left their drunken ways," she continued. "And enlisted as sailors. They sailed away to help the poor off the coast of the unknown southern continent, hoping acts of charity might curry his favor."

The others on the bed nodded knowingly.

"A good story," said Althea to Theodoric weeks later. She worked at her loom while the senator sat at a table beside the fire, overseeing his young son's attempt to master a Latin verb. "But the truth is they got very drunk after leaving us. They were severely beaten in a tavern they had no business being in, and when it was discovered they came from wealth, they were hauled off and held for a large ransom."

"Isn't Lurentius their father?"

"Why, love, you have been thinking about this, haven't you?" she smiled. "Yes. And you know Lurentius. When he received the ransom he had the emissary beaten and sent back to the kidnappers. He pinned his three word response to the dying messenger."

"Which was?" asked Theodoric.

"'Kill them both,'" said Althea. "The captors cut the brother's throats, but of course that's not the version making the rounds."

Theodoric looked lovingly at his wife. She was serenely striking in the fire's light. Her long blond hair was down and her eyes flashed blue and gray. One bare white shoulder revealed a red welt, a thin whip's lash that plunged down exposed skin and hid beneath the material covering her breasts.

"And the good general? Did he really faint?" he asked.

"You really think that savage Moldavus would faint at a birth? I have heard tales from people who should know that he has personally consumed his share of newborns before and after battle. I watched the old man trip as he walked away from the scene, bored to death. His bad knee made him go down. He was carried away from the party."

"I suppose the Phormio story is a myth as well?"

"Actually," said Althea with a curious smile. "Phormio has dropped out of sight. He did seem different after that. Haven't been able to find out what happened to him."

The audacity of the little monk was unknown to the dissipated upper classes, so used to sycophants like Phormio groveling with transparent flattery. Johanna's open contempt was a balm. After that night they stood in line to have her terrible favor heaped upon them.

Many came to know her in other ways. She condemned then ignored some when they offered what she knew was a bribe for her spiritual counsel. Others learned that a selfless deed quietly brought to her attention worked better than charity puffed with fanfare.

It became a mark of distinction to host an elegant function and have her as guest, only to be publicly berated. In the midst of an event, the little brother would bring the activities to a stand-still, scalding uests with her tongue, shaming host and hostess and pointing out that what was provided for a few guests might have been sustenance for an army of the poor.

Dramatic and mesmerizing, Romans loved it as their forefathers loved a good show with gladiators facing off in the Coliseum.

The highest rungs of society rushed to bare their backs to her tongue, eager for her to lash their spiritual flesh. They begged for atonement for their transgressions and John the English, who could not be forgiven the transgression of her disguise by the one she loved most, had more than enough whip for each and every rank who came before her.

# CHAPTER XXX

BEFORE A CROWDED Vatican court, on an overcast October morning five years after the colony had been turned away from Rome, a mass was performed by the pope. The aged Leo took a bishop's miter and placed it on the head of the priest kneeling before him. The old man made the sign of the cross, then bade the priest rise.

"Our new archbishop," said the pope and presented the new shepherd of Rome.

A stunned Johanna looked out on her congregation.

Her posture bent under the weight of the high tiara. She clasped her hands together and looked down, prayers mumbled on her lips.

During the procession outside the church she blessed the delighted crowd who pressed close and called for Good John The English's favor.

She looked for Adrian in the sea of faces and reaching arms.

In the black robe of his order, cowl pulled low, Adrian was there, not far away, but she could not see him. He noted to himself that her face looked older, had matured. He also noted how that soft brow of hers now carried a heavy weight across it.

"I love you," he said aloud, knowing the words were buried in the voices calling for her attention. He slipped away, disappeared into the throng of well wishers.

"Take me to them, Anastasius," she said, exhausted from shaking outstretched arms, blessing crowds and babies. The first duty she gave to herself was to perform an outdoor baptism at the colony.

Two hours later she stood before those who made the pilgrimage with her so long ago. Johanna turned to Veleda, herself transformed. The wild-woman was dressed in the fashion of a Roman matron and was a mother of three girls – four, three, and her infant being baptized.

The wind blew down from the high hills, the sky grew dark with clouds and the first breath of a coming storm threatened the suburban congregation.

"The little one's name, Veleda?" asked Johanna. Veleda beamed at her proud Viking husband standing beside her. The big red-head held the other girls on each massive arm.

"Johanna," she replied. "After you, John."

Johanna looked at the baby and lost her fight with tears. She dribbled baptismal water over the blinking infant and prayed.

*"Oh, Magnum Mysterium..."*

Afterward, families celebrated with a feast and singing and dancing. Johanna held Veleda's baby and swayed to the music, rocking the sleeping child to the sound of flutes and drums. Veleda and her girls stood beside Johanna and children of the community and their parents, excited and proud the archbishop was there. John was theirs. The parcel of land was no longer a primitive camp but a thriving village with wood homes, brick and mortar buildings on flagstone streets where they once slept on the ground in animal skins.

The curious from the city came to the village and were proudly told their home was founded by the youthful Archbishop of Rome.

"We'll have God's house to shelter us," Veleda pointed to the stone church being built in the village center.

"I'll miss being under His big roof out here. So will you, wild-woman," said Johanna. They laughed.

"I'm glad you came. We all wish it were more often," said Veleda. Her face had softened in five years, along with her sinewy frame. She looked healthy, more comfortable with the body and the faith she now carried. Johanna noticed gray was beginning to streak through the coiffed black mane of Veleda's hair.

"Where's Adrian?" Johanna asked, looking toward the musicians, trying to make the question sound offhanded. She drew the baby's face close to her own so that she might smell that amazing infant pink flesh smell and feel the soft new skin on her own. She had been waiting the whole day to ask that one question and she tensed for Veleda's answer.

"In the city," said Veleda. "He never leaves his order."

"A shame," said Johanna. She wanted to cry out her loneliness, but instead turned it into a reprimand she knew would reach him. "He should be here for this."

"He gave his blessings, but holds some secret pain," began Veleda. Her sharp eyes widened looking over Johanna's shoulder. "Basilea, don't touch that!"

Veleda's oldest daughter had taken a parchment sheaf from inside the carriage and stood in the doorway, fascinated with the writing. When her mother yelled she dropped it and ran away. "Forgive her, father, she's a good girl but hasn't yet learned her place."

Johanna started to praise the child's curiosity, but stopped, was suddenly weary. She handed the baby back, hugged Veleda and was helped into the carriage by Anastasius, her secretary and confidante. A crowd had gathered at the carriage; they called out to Johanna who waved back as it took her from the village.

At the gates of Rome Johanna stared across the bouncing carriage at Anastasius, who finished his report.

"I'm afraid there's nothing to be found of Halbert, your father."

"Do not stop searching," she said a little harshly, though she knew there was no need for her emphasis. "Even for a moment."

"John Anglicus!" came a familiar voice outside the vehicle. Theodoric galloped alongside the carriage. His son Lucien, now nine years old with a mischievous smile inherited from his father, rode a red spotted courser beside him.

"I have word that when you dine with the Holy Father tonight, your fortunes will rise again," Theodoric called.

She was about to speak when the window glass shattered, spraying both her and Anastasius. A rock crashed through the opposite window, bouncing off the roof and onto the floor, just missing them. Theodoric called the guards at his flank.

*The Woman Pope*

"Get the assassin!"

"No. No punishment," cried Johanna, waving them off.

"But if it had --"

"I said no," she demanded. He shrugged, and called off the guards. But Theodoric remained behind the carriage until they passed through the Leonine gate.

≈ ≈ ≈

"You demon! Sergius!" cried Halbert from the street. He picked up another rock as the carriage clattered at full speed, long out of range.

He staggered on his feet. A low beggar now, haggard and drunk, hair matted into unwashed locks at his shoulders. Five hard years had melted his robust frame into a gaunt thinness, his skin hung off his bones while dark smudges ringed his eyes. He was about to throw the other stone when a water-seller grabbed Halbert and spun him around.

"That's not Sergius, you filthy sot," he struck Halbert across the face and sent him to the ground. "That's our beloved John Anglicus."

"What? Who's that?"

"The archbishop, you old drunk. I ought to beat you to death right here. People would cheer if I did."

"I-I," stammered Halbert, struggling to his feet. "I didn't know."

The man, disgusted by the filth and smell, pushed him. Halbert stumbled and fell heavily again on the stone street.

"Your Sergius will bury you soon enough."

"Do not curse me with that, I beg you," said Halbert.

"Why not? Sergius the Cadaver buries all the outcast scum like you. He's the Archbishop of the Dead and you will meet him shortly," said the man and walked away.

"Wait." Halbert dragged himself to his feet, the drink dissipating in his blood, overpowered by a sudden force of adrenaline and memory...

He recalled how he once tried to get to Sergius, plotting with Mullung to find a way to kill the man who robbed him of the only person who had made his life worth living.

Troll Mullung, sighed Halbert as he stood up to go after the water-seller. He remembered his friend from what seemed like a lifetime ago. Years before, after they saw Sergius' elevation to archbishop, Halbert nearly reached his goal of revenge, but the attempt cost him dearly.

Despite Mullung's warnings, Halbert could not be dissuaded. All else except finding Johanna meant nothing.

Mullung agreed to help but only if he created the plan of attack. Mullung knew his friend must make this attempt or die in the process. With a fox's cunning, the dwarf snuck into a Benedictine monastery and stole robes for their disguise.

Once inside, the two friends were able to find out where Sergius was quartered. They left the monastery and headed for the Vatican. Mullung adjusted the shortest robe he could find, but nevertheless it threatened to trip him at every step.

At a service entrance, Mullung offered a monk his back to help unload a wagon. When the duty was done and the man turned, he and Halbert stole into and through the bowels of the Vatican complex.

"This way," whispered Halbert. They heard voices and stepped behind a large tapestry. A young monk with deep wrinkles on his face exited a room protected by two Vatican guards. As the monk closed the door, Halbert glimpsed Archbishop Sergius removing his robes. Halbert gestured to Mullung to stay while he approached the guards.

"I have an urgent message for the archbishop," he said, his hands clasped before him, his hood low. "From Pope Leo."

"Where is it?" asked the one guard. "Let me see the scroll."

"It is not written," said Halbert. "It is far too important for anyone's eyes."

The men glanced at each other, unsure.

"If he does not receive this news immediately, it may be too late to save your lives," said Halbert. "You must act now or face the archbishop's wrath."

The one who spoke got a nervous look, shrugged and opened the door. Halbert stepped forward, the length of the chamber before him.

"Who is that?" a voice sounded behind them. The guards turned to see Gaetani returning to the room.

"This monk has an urgent message from the Pope," said the guard.

"Pope?" began Gaetani, suspicious. "What is this about?"

Halbert leaped at the door and pushed his way between the guards.

"Assassin," Gaetani croaked.

Halbert rushed into the middle of a large chamber room and looked around, a metal spike in his hand. The room was empty.

"Where is he! Where is the monster!" Halbert bellowed.

An instant later he was tackled to the floor from behind by the two guards. They took the spike away, stood him up and beat him. Halbert took the blows almost as a salve, their pain no match at his losing Johanna.

A little black blur named Mullung rushed into the room.

"You steel tufted turds!" he called, kicking at the armored guard. "Take this from someone your own size!"

Guards came into the room with short pikes at the ready. They pulled Mullung off one guard, woozy after taking several good kicks to the face and groin. The two friends were placed side-by-side, their arms held back. Halbert smiled wanly at his partner, his guide, then both were beaten until they lost consciousness.

Gaetani stood over the two men. "Take them down."

They were dragged away, taken to a dungeon in the Vatican. Gaetani spoke to the remaining guards.

"I'll follow with instructions as to their disposal," he said and walked to a door at the end of the room. He followed the corridor, eyes aimed at the end of the hall, to a partly open door that had steam seeping out of it. Gaetani peeked inside.

Sergius was in a fog of steam and sat on the edge of a bath. He was attended by a eunuch who stood beside him at the patterned marble tub. Gaetani noted the young eunuch's robe was pulled down around his feet. Sergius' fingers had lifted the man's small penis so he could view the mutilated remains of his emptied scrotum.

"I see by the rather fresh scars you came late to the church. Is that right, my son?" The young man nodded. Sergius could tell that the eunuch had been castrated as an older child by the church, an adolescent, with the blessing of his parents. Though publicly frowned upon, Sergius knew the practice still existed; the sacrifice was exchanged for an easier life, though a passionless one, than he would have known on the street.

"Your Grace," said Gaetani at the doorway.

Sergius continued inspecting the genitals. "Speak."

Gaetani brought several monks from the order Halbert and Mullung had stolen their robes, into the dungeon to witness the torture.

"I'm not here to kill these two," he told the monks. "I am much too soft at heart and do not have the stomach for it. My only job is to extract the truth behind the attempt on the archbishop's life."

He picked up tongs heated to a glowing red on the coals. Mullung and Halbert passed a look between them.

"Sergius stole my daughter," Halbert said.

After several hours, those were the only words he was able to get Halbert to confess. Gaetani mistakenly thought he meant the girl Marozia, ward and plaything to Sergius. For a brief but crucial moment, he felt sorry for the man. To know his child had been trained by Sergius to be a courtesan and his spy, and then thrown to the street to die, would be more torture than the hot iron his back had taken.

"I do not care what you do with the impostor monk," said Sergius when Gaetani reported to him. "But bring the troll to me."

Gaetani freed the would-be assassin in the presence of the monks, and stripped the man of his robes. Mullung watched as his friend was led from the dungeon. They stopped at the door when Gaetani signaled.

"Never come this way again," warned the priest. Halbert used the last of his strength and looked up.

"Be always brave, my friend," said Mullung.

"Mullung," Halbert gasped. He was yanked from the doorway by the guards. It was the last time they saw each other.

The guards threw Halbert naked into the street, half dead onto the paved stones.

Mullung was carried and set on the floor before Sergius. The archbishop looked at the tiny man, his mouth gagged with leather straps, his feet bound. Sergius' eyes lit up.

"Why, you have no hands, my son," he said. He stepped up and studied him as Mullung squirmed on the floor, trying to kick him. Sergius untied the gag.

"And you'll have no cock when I get my jaws around it."

Sergius smiled at his audacity then signaled the guards. "Strap him to the table."

Once bound, Mullung called out a string of curses at Sergius, who had a guard lift a heavy leather bound chest onto the table. Sergius held out his arms and the eunuch behind him lifted the robes over his head. He stood naked except for the archbishop's miter on his head, a plainer version of the high ceremonial hat. Mullung saw the scrawny frame before him, his genitals yellow and purplish with wrinkles and scars, and strained harder against his bindings.

"Do not worry," said Sergius, and opened the latch on the black chest. "You will not be violated that way, my son. I do not want to ruin my robes and so the precaution."

Sergius lifted instruments from the chest and set them on the table. When Mullung saw them, neatly lined up over a blood stained cloth, he stopped straining. Out of the chest came sharp edged saws, picks, gouges, vices, pliers and blades of which Mullung could not have imagined at his most wicked. All of the finest steel, shining with a brilliance Mullung had never seen on metal, almost liquid in their brightness.

"You are wise to be still," said Sergius. He placed a comforting hand on Mullung's brow, smoothed the rough hair from his forehead. He spoke softly, with concern, as if he and Mullung were old friends and he was a physician administering to the little man. "You will give an excellent reading. If you cooperate we will try and finish soon. Will you do that, friend?"

Mullung glared, then dropped his head. A minute passed before he made the slightest nod, not taking his eyes off Sergius.

"Very good. We will all be grateful," Sergius smiled. He reached for the first instrument, a foot-long, razor sharp dagger. When he saw it held up, Mullung fainted briefly. He returned to face consciousness and Sergius waiting patiently for him.

"All right, my friend. Let us take a peek into the future and see tomorrow. Shall we ask what the Fates have in store for us? Give a good reading and we will end this business as quickly as possible, I promise. The entrails of a troll are the best, as I am sure you have heard. Your innards will tell my tale, divine what will become of me.

"Let us put the gag back in place. I am sorry, believe me, but this way is best. Do not move, little man . . . Stop it. Do not squirm like . . . I know, I know, it hurts. That is why you should not . . . Shhh. Don't. . . Here. Oh, yes. Here we are. Yes, look at this. This, oh this looks good. Yes, this bodes well indeed. Listen to me...Do you see the length of this bowel? I will tell you what this long section means if you -- Listen. We had an understanding, did we not? If you continue to...Oh, little man, little man, little man. Stop your struggling. Look at the shape of this piece. Quiet. I am afraid this is going to take longer than I thought."

≈ ≈ ≈

Halbert survived. The mercy of the street came in the form of a hod carrier and his family. They found him near death, dragged him home, nursed his wounds and fed him until he recovered. The good people softened Halbert's heart for a while.

One evening he walked out of the family's little room and surrendered himself to the underbelly of the city. In wine and spirits came no relief, but the waters of Nepenthe allowed him momentary forgetfulness. He spent his days searching for Johanna and gathering the means to lose himself at night. He never spoke of his little friend, Mullung, a guilt for which he could find no words. He talked instead about the brilliant daughter who once shared his life.

"Forget this 'little brother'," he would say, dismissing the famous monk's exploits with a wave of his bottle. "Listen to this story if you want to hear about daring, if you want to hear about goodness."

Halbert told the stories so often that he came to believe the breathtaking details and detours he created in each tale. The favorite monk of the people paled in comparison.

So when the information was revealed by the water-seller after the holy carriage had passed, Halbert knew Sergius' fortunes had been reduced. At that moment he experienced the closest thing to joy to enter his heart in over five years. Standing in the street, he wiped his bloody mouth and went after the water-seller, who continued on his away. The man heard Halbert's approach and got ready to strike again when he heard the drunkard call.

"Tell me, please, sir. I have just one question," pleaded Halbert. "At what cemetery does the Archbishop of the Dead send off his souls?"

# CHAPTER XXXI

SERGIUS UTTERED A few words over the dead.

Not prayers for their souls, but curses under his breath. He made a vague sign of the cross then signaled the burial crew to dig. Sergius, priest to corpses, moved to the next open grave and pulled his black robe close against the rain.

He squinted at the desolate cemetery around him, a garbage strewn hill far from the city. Crosses and fetid stacks of bodies marked the hellish site he was doomed to walk until his penance was complete.

At the next pit, he performed the same empty motions and moved on, but at the third grave he was so overcome by the smell he put a rag to his nose.

Sergius heard a rumble and turned. In a flash he was taken off his feet and sailed backwards down into the freshly dug grave.

A heavy weight crushed him, the air knocked out of his lungs, he felt the bones of a corpse crack beneath his back. The body's decomposed hand emerged from the sheet next to Sergius' face.

"Do you know who I am? I am death. Your death, Sergius. Look at my face and see your fate. I have come for your life."

"Have mercy!" said the priest beneath the raving ghoul.

But this could not be a ghost, it had weight, smelled of sour wine and was very much alive. Sergius could not focus his eyes out of sheer terror, but knew it could have been any one of dozens who searched him out over the years to try to extract revenge for the pain he caused a family member or loved one. Demoted to the most menial status, Sergius was watched carefully – had it been five years already? -- to prevent an escape and yet his occupation made him vulnerable to attack from those lives he had touched as archbishop.

"I am the dead man you left in England to be crucified. You stole my Johanna. Now, if you want to die quickly, tell me where she is."

Sergius turned from the man's foul breath and screamed when he saw the corpse's skeletal hand beside his face. Halbert wrapped his hands around Sergius' throat as the priest's memory was taken back to the voyage from England, which seemed a hundred years in the past.

"It was an accident, I swear! On the passage. There was a fire."

"Liar," Halbert said and applied pressure, but allowed the purpling man to spit out a response.

"I was burned badly. I can prove it. There was panic. She fell over in the night. We searched for hours but she was lost. I was so distraught, I ended my horrible ways. I sent guards back to escort you to Rome. But they never found you. Please."

Halbert squeezed slowly, relishing each increment of pressure, and watched Sergius' eyes bug out from his head. Now that he had heard the story, true or not, he would be able to rest. He would savor this moment over and over, remembering how he made Sergius' eyes burst from their sockets. How the man gagged silently, his face racing from a screaming red to a blackish purple.

Halbert wanted to be able to recall the look on Sergius' face when he expired. The feel of the evil man's flesh in his hands, the abject dread on his face. It was too delicious for words and for the first time in years Halbert was filled with peace. As tears came down his cheeks he thought he would take this man's life, pray for Johanna's soul and finally leave this city forever. All that can be done will be done today, he silently reasoned. It's time, finally, to leave this city of ghosts.

In the midst of his exquisite pleasure, he was suddenly jolted with a thunderbolt of pain. Halbert was dragged down into a painful darkness and thrown into a deeper pit than the grave they wallowed in.

The shovel came flat down on the madman's head. Sergius, pressed between attacker and corpse, gagged and flailed. Several hands reached down and pulled the big man off.

Minutes later, beside Gaetani, Sergius felt his wrung neck and regarded Halbert face down in the grave. Gaetani held the shovel. Though the rain began to fall harder, Sergius was contemplative and did not seem to feel it.

"Johanna was a most remarkable woman. I miss her company," he said and took the shovel from Gaetani and dug it into the earth. "Miserable dog, join your wretched daughter."

Sergius shoveled mud into the grave until Halbert was completely buried. His strength gave over and Sergius tossed the shovel into the grave then leaned on Gaetani.

"When will this torment end?"

"You will be relieved of this burden soon," Gaetani said. He took his master's arm and guided him through the garden of gravestones.

"You do not know that," said Sergius, bitterly.

"I swear your fortune is already changing, master."

"Tell me."

"I cannot, I fear. Your indulgence for one more day will make all the difference," he said enigmatically as he led Sergius away.

Five minutes later, the mud that covered Halbert moved. The surface shivered over the water in the grave. It slowed and was still again. The rain came down, covering the cemetery in fitful sheets. An emaciated three-legged dog, a gray mongrel with black spots, limped along sniffing for any morsel no matter how rank, even from the dead. The dog came near the edge of the open grave and flinched as if struck. Tail between its legs, it saw nothing but loped toward the leafless trees to escape the baleful presence it could only sense.

Mud and water rippled again at the grave. With a bellow of anger, Halbert burst through half an arm's thickness of mud.

He stood up gulping air and immediately coughed. Rain ran down into the grave in rivulets. He gasped for breath in the muddy pool. The corpse that he and Sergius had fallen upon had risen up on the tide of water and floated beside him.

≈ ≈ ≈

Halbert staggered through the storm holding his head. He walked an hour before venturing a look back to the city below him. He spat a silent curse, felt his brain fizz like the bubbling waters of a spring and, before he could sit, blacked out and collapsed face down in the road.

Later, the rain slowed to a drizzle and a fine mist rose from the ground like a fog. Half hour more, Halbert's body shivered as he lay in the mud. A break in the clouds opened up a blue ravine in the sky and the sun shone through in a single beam on the far hills.

"Is he dead, mama?" came a little voice above Halbert. The hand of a child on the unconscious heap, patted his head as she would the sleeping family dog.

Two hours later Halbert sipped steaming beef broth from a wooden bowl. He was dry, clean, and his body warm beside a fireplace. Two girls clung to their mother across the room and stared at him. The mother rocked the youngest, feeding at her breast as she watched the big man come back to life.

"Have you come far to Rome?"

"Too very far. And now I am afraid I've had enough and wish to go home," he smiled. "I thank you for you kindness, it saved my life."

"Will you go back to family?"

"I lost my family when I desired to see Rome. My daughter..." he stopped. "Well, I'm going back."

"Rest with us a while," said Veleda, a shawl modestly pulled over her breast and the baby's head. "We have plenty of family to share."

Four year old Basilea watched the big man sip his bowl while tears rolled down his cheeks into the broth. She left the safety of her mother, walked over and stroked his knee, comforting him the way she had seen others do. Halbert saw her empathetic face and had to smile. She looked at her mother with enthusiasm, to show Veleda how well her comfort had worked.

"What's your name, little one?"

"Basilea," she replied and pointed to her sister. "She's Dora."

"Basilea, I will tell you and Dora a story if you like."

She looked at her mother, who nodded. Basilea was swept up onto the man's knees.

"I will tell you a true story about an amazing creature. A bug that prays," said Halbert.

"Bugs cannot pray!" protested Basilea, laughing, and looked at her mother and sister for confirmation. "That's silly."

"Oh, this one can. Now, listen," Halbert began in a hushed voice. "A little girl, just about your age..."

≈ ≈ ≈

The high ceiling of the Pope's private dining room was bright with torches and bathed the gathered bishops and cardinals in a golden sheen. Everyone in the room talked loudly, eating dinner at a table big enough to accommodate the twenty men around it.

Pope Leo sat at the head of the table and spoke to churchmen on either side as they cut into huge wheels of cheese, pulled apart loaves of bread so hot sweet steam rushed up toward the ceiling. The churchmen laughed and belched, lifted goblets of wine poured from tall jugs carried by servants. They gorged on roasted geese brought in on platters by young boys. The men grabbed barehanded at stacks of ham steaks smothered in a pepper sauce.

However, the plate of the pontiff was empty. He glanced at the kitchen door, his mouth watered from the smells and sounds of ravenous feeding around him. At the kitchen door a hungry derelict sat on a stool and ate from a heaped plate while a watchful priest stood over him. The priest saw the pontiff's look.

"Enough. You are only to taste, not finish." He pulled the plate from under the man's face, walked it to the pope who smiled at the belated food and raised his glass for a toast.

"To our new archbishop. May God give you a steady hand for your trials, a compassionate heart for your judgment," he said gravely. Then, with a wink. "And a beard to grace your wisdom."

Everyone at the table laughed and drank and chided Johanna, who sat quietly at the far end of the table. They coaxed her to stand.

"Thank you, my brothers. To be part of your family is a blessing, one you may discover not to be so sweet," she threatened, facetiously. She pointed a warning finger around the room. They laughed again and cheered, their fondness for the popular youth was evident in the hazing they gave her while she tried to make her speech.

"Little brother," said a cardinal from across the table. "The sweetness comes from knowing you wear a bishop's robes but prefer a beggar's shoes!"

It was one of the rare times when every churchman in the room was relieved by another's elevation; they knew at least one among them was not engaged in secret machinations to gain more power. Johanna was aware of this and was glad to have larger battles to fight without their foolish intrigues.

"May your elevation bring peace to our troubled city," said another cardinal. All murmured their assent and the room quieted, though with a sense of unease. Rome, the grandest city ever built on earth, was crumbling daily, its splendor and influence long a memory in its glorious past. Who knew what would become of her tomorrow?

"I raise my glass to you," she said. "But I raise it higher to the souls we serve, and highest still to God Almighty--"

A shriek from the kitchen door froze every guest in place. Clutching his stomach, the food-tasting derelict staggered to the table despite the priest's hold on his arm.

"I am slain," said the derelict. All turned to Leo, still chewing. Every eye went to his plate: it was empty. The pope spit the food out, pushed his chair from the table and rose slowly. Fear scalded the room.

"Poison," someone whispered.

"No," said Leo in a hushed voice, incredulous.

"Call the physician!" said Johanna breaking the silence. The pope collapsed in his seat and churchmen rushed to him. Johanna pushed her way through and Leo grabbed her arm.

"Who would do this to an old man? I am afraid to die, John," he said. His eyes widened as a terrible wave swept over him.

The churchmen wept and cried out to heaven. Bishop and cardinal pulled at each other's clothes, their own hair. A profound sickness quickly came over the pope, racking his body. They watched his skin burn with redness that swelled into a taut, glistening purple as if he were being strangled from within and might burst. He wretched and the bishops and cardinals screamed. They hit at each other as if to drive away the unreality of the scene.

"Holy One," she said. "Repent, let the Lord take you in His arms."

"But I am the pope," said Leo. "I am the pope."

"He knows who you are, Leo," said Johanna, firmly. "Is that all you will tell Him when you stand before His Face?"

Leo grimaced with pain. Then, like a guilty child, "He might be angry with me, John."

"Only if you hide what He already knows."

"You've been my son, opened my eyes, but I'm a sinner. From the Chair I've done many wrongs. Oh, John, I've all eternity to fear."

Three cardinals began to chant.

"*Omnia vincit amor, et nos cedamus amori.*"

"I'm summoned to judgment this hour. I see what awaits me. I've done much wrong. I took gold and land in return for favors. I have known many women. They've borne me a dozen children, but especially Ellysa, she is the mother of two of my favorite sons."

"The Lord forgives you," said Johanna. Pope Leo grabbed her collar and pulled her close as the poison dug into every organ.

"John. Change this Chair's destiny. I know you can. Give them hope... Do what I, do what others have not done. Do...Oh, God. Oh, God, Oh, my God!"

The pope's mouth foamed a bloody red. He convulsed with the shudder of a body being forced to give up its all. The room filled with the highest religious leaders in Rome watched as Pope Leo IV died in Johanna's arms.

≈ ≈ ≈

A Vatican carriage raced through a rainy night to the gate of the walled estate. Johanna got out and approached the armed guard.

"Let me pass. I will see the murderer. I will have the assassin before me." She disregarded his drawn broadsword and called out at the mansion. "Theodoric! Poisoner. Coward. Show yourself!"

The gate opened. Theodoric stood on the other side, his beautiful nine-year-old son Lucien in his arms. Johanna heard Althea's heartrending wail inside the villa.

"My, God, Theodoric," said Johanna. She was galled and mortified by her horrible accusation. "Forgive me. I --"

"My little man begged for his father's plate tonight," Theodoric said. "He wanted to sit in his father's chair at the head of the table. To command the slaves as they served the food. He wanted to show me he was a leader. He wanted to be his father. My son. My name. My life."

Johanna stepped closer and looked at the boy. His features were at rest, but the pain he suffered twisted his mouth into an unnatural gape. Theodoric stood, drenched in the rain, the inconceivable act lay upon his blank face, his eyes stripped of light. She smoothed the boy's hair, blessed them both, and put an arm on Theodoric's shoulder. She spoke to the guard, sent him for priests, for relatives, and a physician with knowledge of sleeping droughts for Althea.

Johanna got back in the carriage and called to the driver to hurry, providing the place he was to ride as swiftly as possible. She told him the exact address where they would find the murderer of the senator's only heir as well as Pope Leo the fourth, Vicar of Christ.

# CHAPTER XXXII

SERGIUS READ TO several priests gathered in his small damp room. They chuckled in the candlelight, listening to the bawdy tales of Scheherazade from one of the last books in Sergius' vast library not sold or given as a bribe. His company that evening included other fallen priests who had remained to serve at the outermost edge of the clergy. Some were there out of a desire to repent while others, like Sergius, had no choice and were closely watched.

Sergius read the story of a powerful jinn, a demon who kidnapped a beautiful princess on her wedding day, flew her to his hideaway where he took lustful pleasure from her every night, only to vanish each day to do some other terrible deed. The princess had managed to steal his magic sword and waited to hack the demon to pieces as he returned that night. When the demon stepped through the door of his home...

"Sergius?"

The door was kicked open with a crash and the priests looked up in guilty surprise. Johanna led several guards inside and they took Sergius by the arms. Johanna stood before him and slapped Sergius across the face with all her might.

"All the evil you have ever given birth to dies tonight."

The guards dragged him from the room as the priests cringed.

She led the way as Sergius was walked down the steps to make sure he was stored in the deepest cell of the Vatican's dungeon. The floor was flooded with an inch of rain water that had turned into a noxious filth. He would have to stand on a rotted wood cot to escape it.

"What is the charge, brother?" said Sergius. "What have I done?"

"You have accomplished all you've set out to do," said Johanna. "You've caused all the misery possible for a man to cause. Now you will be rewarded for all your work."


A month later, Theodoric found himself in the same dining room where the pope had been assassinated. The same bishops and cardinals were there, but this time there was no grief or mourning but instead fierce arguments washed the room in an almost tactile hatred. The moment had come to see who had collected enough power to claim the Chair. The men yelled at each other and clashes broke out around the room.

"The city's destroying itself. If it goes on another month this city will be taken. A pope must be chosen now, today," said the cardinal who had chanted last rites over Leo.

"I say after Sergius' trial," said the bishop whose patchy scalp was evidence of his pulling out his hair at the sight of the dying pontiff. "We must wait until then."

A disgusted Theodoric stepped up to a table full of plates, glasses and leftover food. He grabbed the edge of the table and turned it over with a *crash.*

"You want to wait because your brother Petrus comes from Gaul to fight for Leo's place. Did you not think I would find out?" he walked slowly around the room and glared into each face. "Or any of your schemes to become pope? You, Cardinal Portius. Your nephew from Tuscany, you truly believe him to be next in line for the papacy? You've paid others enough to make them think so. He is eleven years old, fool. You, Bishop. Your father has been mentioned. You, your uncle. You, Cardinal Voltas. You didn't think I'd hear of an army of cardinals, all your kin from Germania, entering the city? And you, Bishop Rossi, trying to raise yourself to the Chair by offering barrels of wine as a bribe? *Wine,* for the Chair of Saint Peter."

Theodoric spat at the bishop's feet.

"Not a man in this room is fit to wash the robes of a pope much less wear them."

"Who is, senator?" asked a cardinal. The room went silent, waiting while Theodoric pondered the question.

≈ ≈ ≈

She left the stuffiness of her room and walked through the quiet pre-dawn streets of the city. When she finally stopped to rest, Johanna realized she was in the same quarter Adrian lived with the holy man, Hbramas, where the revered man and his disciples made their home.

Johanna looked for a quiet place. A stone church, ancient and poorly tended, stood across the street.

She prayed in the deserted chapel, on her knees before the altar, and tried to release enough anguish to let her heart be filled with the Spirit she often sought but seldom found since living in Rome. She knelt at the bench, tried to clear her thoughts and meditate to the place of peace but was nagged by a prickly suspicion. The real reason she could not call God into her soul, she thought, was because she had been in control of all around her for so long that it was impossible to surrender herself to anyone or anything.

A noise at the door. Johanna slipped out of the pew and into the shadows. How foolish of her! This was surely one of Hbramas' chapels frequented by his devotees. What if it were Adrian? What could she possibly say to him? How could she face him after so long?

Two young lovers entered and lit candles at the door. They approached the altar, were wary and skittish. Kneeling together, the very young man, fourteen at most, took out a ring and placed it on the girl's finger. In a halting but sincere voice, he spoke his vow to her.

They seemed somehow familiar to Johanna; she thought perhaps they came from the settlement.

"You have no one to celebrate your love with you?" asked Johanna softly. They jumped to their feet, ready to run, but Johanna held up her hand. The girl recognized the Archbishop of Rome.

"Father, our families hate our love so we must keep it secret, though it cannot stay hidden anymore," she said. She put a hand to her protruding stomach and began to cry. The boy slipped his hand in hers.

"Come, kneel," said Johanna, smiling. "I'll marry you."

"We do not need anyone's blessings," said the boy, facing Johanna. The girl was horrified and squeezed his arm.

"Darius. Do not speak to his Grace like that."

"No, Maria, we will not do what they want anymore," he turned to Johanna. "The church has given us no choice. We leave tonight to make our own life. Forgive my rudeness, Holiness, but God knows our hearts and His is the only permission we need."

He bowed his head in apology, then took his lover and walked away, the girl glancing fearfully back at Johanna. They exited through the side door and left a saddened Johanna behind. She fell asleep trying to remember where she had seen them before.

Hours later she rose, surprised to find herself lying across the steps of the altar, jarred awake by turbulence outside the church.

She opened the door and Johanna was met with driving rain and chaos in the streets. The news of the pope's death had caused a panic. Without a pope the people believed not only the city but their very souls were vulnerable to Satan, who waited for such an opportunity. Johanna watched as hordes of people pushed at the door, begging for information, surging toward a lone monk who stood in their path.

"Is there a successor yet?"

"Has the devil come to take us?"

"All your prayers will be answered soon," said the monk, holding up his hands.

Johanna caught her breath. It was Adrian.

≈ ≈ ≈

Gaetani stood at the door of Sergius' cell and wept, rubbing his face and so accentuated the deep wrinkles between his red eyes.

"Your plot has cost my life," Sergius said without emotion. "Had you come to me..."

"I could not," Gaetani said, straining to keep his voice low. "I counted on your innocence to protect you. With a new pope you would have risen again, up from the outcast to your deserved position."

Sergius snorted a laugh. "You have certainly changed my position. My trial is today. I will be hanged, briefly, for the enjoyment of the crowd, before I am drawn and quartered like a thief. This is my last day on earth, my friend."

"Sire, if I could change places with you I would, gladly!"

Sergius thought a minute and reached his hand out, gently touching the hood of the priest.

"I believe you would, loyal brother. I want you to leave me now."

"I don't want to leave you."

"Return to my room. The last bottle of metheglin I own is tucked below two loose boards under my bed."

"You want me to bring it to you?"

"I want you to stay in my room and enjoy it, brother,"

"I don't understand."

"I want you to drink the mead for me. Now, listen to my instructions, then listen to your heart. From both of them you will be set free from your guilt."


≈ ≈ ≈


Adrian tried to calm the panicked crowd pushing at the doors of the church.

"We don't know when he will be chosen," he said. "But please remain calm --"

"What will happen to us?" cried a woman, desperate, her hands clutching his robe. "This city will fall without our Leo."

There were angry shouts, someone threw a stone that glanced off the wall next to Adrian's head. His words were drowned by confused people determined to make someone suffer for their loss. The crowd pulled and screamed at him as if he willfully withheld information about the pope's death.

"You have not lost your God. You have only lost a man," came a high, familiar voice. The crowd turned at the shocking words, and saw Johanna step outside to stand at Adrian's side.

"Leo was St. Peter's heir, yes, but he also was just a man. He has gone to heaven. Now go back home and pray to God to deliver a new pope to us. Go, I tell you."

"Protect us from evil, Archbishop. Help us!" cried a man and lunged toward her. His sudden movement gave the jittery crowd permission to converge.

"Stop it. Get back."

Her shouts were lost in the hysteria, and she and Adrian were crushed back into the doors by waves of crying mourners, flagellating themselves and their neighbors with sticks. Adrian got the church doors open and pulled Johanna inside as the mob was about to consume them.

They hit at arms and legs trying to get in, and finally locked the door as the pounding fists rattled the wood. They stood silent and listened to the rage on the other side of the doors.

Then they faced each other and looked into eyes they had not been this close to in more than five years.


Adrian stepped back. She steadied herself against the wall.

"Adrian," Johanna breathed.

He considered the girl-woman he had gazed upon long ago aboard a ship on a faraway shore; intense, full of self-knowledge and subservient to no one's wishes or dreams but her own.

Her eyes, still piercing, were heavier at the edges. In the middle of her forehead faint worry lines had dug themselves into her countenance. But her face refused to relinquish the beauty he saw that first time. Her lips remained full as ever, her face retained its fine nobility along with the sleek lines of her jaw and chin. Beyond the short hair and tonsure, beneath it all, Adrian could see no man, no monk, no leader. He saw nothing but beautiful Johanna.

He resisted the pull of feelings and recalled the hours he had prayed and denied himself, working so hard for the poor – to forget -- until he lay down exhausted each night. Still, the woman before him would be the only woman he would love for the rest of his life.

"Brother," he whispered.

Johanna looked across at the only man whose spirit matched hers. His gaze remained an intense reflection of her own, but crowned by the wild tangle of curling brown hair now slightly strung with strands of an early gray woven in his beard and along his temples. Johanna sucked in her breath. This man's moral righteousness made her shallow brethren in the Vatican seem like spoiled, anchorless children. A man whose will was stronger than all of them combined, whose mind had the capacity to go beyond the codes of their tiny worlds. Adrian was the only man willing to embrace ideas no one else could see, much less understand. How had it been possible to let this boundless spirit go?

After several seconds of contemplation, she knew she could not. Johanna stepped forward.

Adrian stepped back. He could not do this. It had been too hard and hurt too much when he walked away the first time. She deserted the settlement, took up with the wealthy in Rome and remained in a disguise, a *lie*, living as something she was not. For a long time Adrian hated Johanna for what she had done to them, to him.

He put his hand in front of him, as if to push her away.

But as he looked at her, the wall he had worked so hard to build over the years began to shift. Everything he could not escape stared back at him. He thought a long moment, and knew he had no choice.

Adrian had to surrender; he let go and crossed the space to her. They embraced, touched each other's face. The embrace and the tears washed away the dust of the past and left clear images of who they were in each other's arms at that hour, at that precise second, never more alive than at that moment. They stood together inside a rare conjunction when life shuts out nothing and

*The Woman Pope*

allows one to see, hear and feel everything. Johanna and Adrian were lifted out of themselves and for a brief epoch that lasted as long as a blink, became part of time's trinity: all of what time is rushed through them. It tumbled from the future, flowed from the very moment yet to come, into the present and drifted into the past even as their eyes remained locked onto each other.

Adrian became afraid. He pulled away, his eyes filled with fear and suspicion. She took his arm.

"Adrian, no," she knew that despite his fear he felt the same as she. When they touched, all the reasons to remain apart vanished. There was nothing but old delusions and she would not allow them to distort the love she knew was real.

"Johanna, what was once a disguise is now who you are."

"No, I reject it. Don't you see that?"

She saw the true light that shone inside him and when he felt that from her gaze, his fear evaporated. He reached for her again and she put her face on his chest.

"I have lost my way, Adrian. I've killed, made men suffer. I had hoped the Eternal City was a holy place, different from the rest of the world. But Rome is just the world in small. Its sins are less disguised than I and I want to be free of them."

He stepped back to look at her.

"Will you leave everything and come with me?"

"Yes! That's why I'm here. As soon as Sergius' trial is over I will leave Brother John behind forever."

His expression fell.

"And then as soon as the new pope is elected," he said. "Then as soon as the poor are seen to."

"I cannot leave this second, no. Adrian, if I vanish they will think I killed the pope and I'll be hunted down while Sergius is set free."

"If you were Johanna, John would never be found."

"That's not fair. You know I must see this man taste justice."

"Let others give him that taste. He tasted yours that day with Leo."

"That's hateful to say. What I did that day was right."

"The truth is never hateful, only true."

"Don't judge me."

"I say the same to you," he said and they stood there. Once again the distance appeared between them.

They could not go back, they were the same people and yet so different, from two different worlds.

"Why do we torment each other, Johanna?" he said. "I only want to serve God and have a family with a woman as she is, not as others would have her. You cannot be her, you know you cannot."

"I can if you let me," she said. "I'm sorry, Adrian. I know my disguise has always pained you greatly."

Johanna's expression changed. She gripped his hands so hard he thought she might hurt herself. He knew that expression.

"Adrian, listen. I pledge myself to you forever, beyond my last breath. I do not need to see Sergius suffer. I do not need anything but you. Please, let's leave, now. Take me away with you."

A long pause hung in the church; it held its breath and waited to hear Adrian's answer. He wondered if he could do the same thing he asked of her. Could they leave without a word? Could they take to the road again as beggars, the world forever threatening them?

He searched the face that was everything of value in his life.

Adrian took her in his arms and they kissed, sealing her word to his in a silent pact as final as death.

"What if we can not find your father before we leave?"

"I'll make sure someone will tell him where we've gone."

Never was Adrian more grateful for her than at that moment. He kissed her again, long and with tenderness.

Then the doors burst open.

# CHAPTER XXXIII

A DOZEN ROMAN guards, led by Anastasius, rushed into the chapel. The lovers leapt to their feet as he approached and bowed.

"Holy Father, you must come right away."

"What is this, Anastasius? I am not going --"

"You are elected," he said, in disbelief. "Raised to St. Peter's Chair. Praise God."

"Impossible," she said and looked at Adrian. "I cannot. This is --"

"We are given no choice. The entire west is tearing apart," he said. Johanna and Adrian exchanged looks for a tense moment, a silent communication passed between them.

They gave each other a nod. Then turned and ran.

"If we're separated, meet me at the settlement," shouted Adrian as they shot down the aisle for the side door. The stunned guards were not sure what to do, but reflexively gave chase.

Johanna and Adrian reached the side entrance at a run when a chapel priest stepped out from the sacristy. Before they could stop they slammed into him and crashed into the door. It broke open and all three tumbled out into the alley. Two of the guards were on Adrian before he could stand while the others surrounded Johanna. She reached for Adrian, but was pulled away.

"Adrian!" She was marched off between the men.

"John! John! Joooan!" he screamed. His words drowned out in the roar of the crowd. The street, filled shoulder-to-shoulder at the front of the church, watched her led away by the armed escort.

The crowded street at the Vatican roared. Thousands waved at the high balcony where the word would come. They waited for the new pope to appear and give his promise of safety for the city.

Behind those closed doors of the balcony, Johanna was ushered into the presence of cardinals and bishops and an impatient Theodoric. Every man dropped to his knees except the senator, who stood with his hands on his hips.

"Blessed is the heir to St. Peter," hailed a cardinal.

"This is an error," she said. "Any man here is worthier."

A half dozen attendants entered the room with rich robes and the high, conical miter and gold scepter of the pope. They approached Johanna but she waved them away.

"I cannot accept this. I will not accept it."

"You are called by powers greater than yourself," said Theodoric.

"The cardinals must re-convene and ask God to choose another."

"This choice has always been far too important for cardinals," he said. She realized he was the only non-member of the clergy in the room, and the only man wearing armor for battle. He knew some secret and it included everyone in that room.

"The family who has put three Holy Fathers on the Chair before Leo does so again for the good of the Holy Roman Empire."

"That is a blasphemous lie!" she said.

What the senator had said was not only impossible, it was so sinful it could not be seriously contemplated. Yet his unflinching look, combined with the averted faces of Rome's holiest men, struck a place that put panic in her heart. She called to the man closest to her.

"Cardinal Beldoni, tell him."

The cardinal looked away, put his hands inside his robe. She turned to a bishop.

"Put his wicked tongue right, brother."

The bishop looked at the floor, mute. She scanned the room and every man there except Theodoric avoided her gaze.

"All the robes you see here, red or purple, owe their position to my family," he said. "They cannot deny the power that has made their simony possible."

The room stirred at the suggestion of this dark sin few ever mentioned out loud.

"St. Peter's Chair cannot be purchased," she said. "It is God's Will on earth."

In her time in Rome she had learned much about manipulation and the crafty arrangements of power. Johanna had long known she was being played by those powers. A seemingly anonymous gift to the poor might appear, then shortly after a wealthy merchant would show up innocently, without word of his deed, to ask her blessing. She let those things pass because no one profited except the wretched. But it was impossible to imagine that God's mother church could be run like a market, men ruthlessly vying for position with deals and bids and secret negotiations.

"That's good, John Anglicus, and right," Theodoric said. "And that's what you will tell the people."

He signaled the attendants. They surrounded her to wrap her in the papal robes, but she stepped away.

"The Chair be damned. I refuse."

"If you hold your followers in your heart, you must choose this path or they will suffer, every soul. See for yourself."

Theodoric went to the window. She followed and looked out. On the hills outside the city, two armies collided and fought. Johanna could hear the cries of battle as they reached her as a tiny rumble on the wind.

"The Saracens are the first to hear of the pope's death," said Theodoric, standing behind her. "They're fighting amongst themselves today, one warlord tries to wrest control from the other before they attack the city. They know Rome is without a pope, is rudderless and in turmoil. Tomorrow the winners will gather like vultures, readying for attack. Anyone outside the gates will perish."

"My people," she said, thinking of families on the hillside. "You cannot leave them out there, Theodoric."

"We can not save everyone, there's no room."

"They are farmers now, with wives and children, not warriors."

"There is no choice. They will sack the city unless a strong hand steers our course. You are called, John, loved by the people and you must lead them *now*," said Theodoric, stepping in close to her. "You must become the prince of the wise."

Johanna looked at him, at the warring armies. Caught, she had walked like an insect into his trap. Forced into making the hardest decisions of her life from a scheme she instinctively knew was as old, well-made and ancient as the city itself. Her face flushed with the shame of her knowledge; each man there knew she had no choice.

"I accept. Now call them in. Let them have shelter, please."

He snapped his fingers and signaled the attendants to approach with the robes. "Of course, after you give benediction to the people. We must hurry, peace has fled."

≈ ≈ ≈

Adrian struggled with the guards in the alley of the church. The crowd that had followed them edged closer, curious who they arrested. Was it the future pope, several wondered to each other. The guards were outnumbered by dozens, became nervous and waved their swords. The crowd crept closer, unafraid of half a dozen armed men. This gave Adrian his chance. He yanked his arms from the distracted soldiers and sprinted into the oncoming mass and disappeared.

Adrian fought through ever-mounting crowds for an hour before he was able to get close to the Vatican. He pushed past weeping men and praying women. He stepped over throngs of people on their knees, hands clasped. Finally, Adrian squeezed through the masses until he stood next to a Roman soldier. When he put his arm to get his attention, he was struck by the man's shield and was thrown to the ground. Adrian rolled beneath the mob and was almost trampled by hundreds of feet.

*The Woman Pope*

The crowd around him went wild. He got to his feet and followed the crowd's gaze. The blow to his head added to the sight before him and Adrian could only stare, stunned.

On the balcony stood Johanna, dressed in the office of the pope. She had difficulty making the sign of the cross. She blessed the crowd three halting times then backed away from jubilant masses that overflowed the square and filled up the streets beyond. Johanna stepped backward and was met by the waiting arm of Theodoric. Adrian could do nothing but gape at the pope of all Christendom.

≈ ≈ ≈

Surrounded by an entourage of eunuchs and monks, Johanna was hurried by Theodoric along a hidden corridor deep in the Vatican. The only sound in the hall was the echoing tap of leather sandals on stone and the swish of material from their robes. Weighted down with forty pounds of flowing fabric and embroidered vestments, she tugged at the golden girdle around her waist and the thick, uncomfortable jewelry wrapping her arms. Her head throbbed from the heaviness of the three tiered, gem-encrusted coned tiara balanced on her head. The jewels flashed red, gold and green and reflected their colored lights on the walls as they passed.

"First, you must condemn Sergius for the murder of Leo," Theodoric whispered. "He must be executed today."

"How can I do that? I'm not the temporal law."

"But you influence it. The world must see you act swiftly and command control. Excommunicate him. That will seal his fate at his criminal trial."

They turned a corner and stopped. Two guards stood at attention with their backs to a door. Johanna looked to Theodoric, who nodded. In unison the guards turned the handles of the massive doors and the secret corridor opened up.

Johanna walked through the entrance, out from behind a tapestry into the immense space of the papal court. It was filled with clergy. A single crisp note of a bell rang out and the court fell to its knees. Johanna and her party swept through the room in a tense silence. She paused at the stairs which led to the Chair of St. Peter and gazed upon a throne that looked more for a king than a simple fisherman.

≈ ≈ ≈

Veleda squinted, breathed evenly and pulled back on the bowstring with reawakened strength. Her eyes locked on the screaming Saracen who charged her. His war cry to Allah was cut off when her arrow found the bull's-eye of his open mouth.

The settlement was filled with Saracen attackers and the settlers fought hard, in fact fought enthusiastically against the odds. Veleda's Viking husband slashed two invaders with his sword, killed both with a single blow, then he turned for more.

At Veleda's house, the front door was smashed open, hammered by a heavy axe. A Saracen warrior stepped inside. He grinned when he saw Veleda's children cower in a corner. He took a knife from his belt, crossed the room and stood over the terrified girls.

He raised the knife then heard a most curious sound: a bird whistle. He turned toward it and the side of his face was crushed by the flat bottom of an iron cooking pot. The blow was so swift he dropped dead on the spot of a broken neck. Halbert stepped from behind the door, pot in hand, took the man's weapons and faced the girls.

"That poor fellow has lost his appetite," he said and winked to calm them. He pulled up a floorboard in the center of the main room, eased them down beneath the floor and replaced the plank. Then he walked out the front door and rushed into the fray.

≈ ≈ ≈

Adrian had pushed out of the crowds and walked along the edge of the city, headed toward his order. He had lost her again. He needed a quiet place to think, to plan his next move. He heard a distant commotion that broke through his thoughts. When he recognized the sound it made his spine tingle with a current of fear. He ran all the way to the northern gate and stopped. In the distance he could make out an army flooding the settlement. He grabbed a pitch fork from a hay pile and ran.

≈ ≈ ≈

On the floor of the papal court, Sergius was prostrate at the foot of the pope's throne. A cardinal stood to the right of the chair and read the charges from a sheet of parchment held up by a young page kneeling in front of him. The cardinal's monotone voice echoed through the hall. From the stone floor, Sergius ventured a glance. He caught Johanna's eye and when Johanna saw his expression she was unnerved.

There was no way he could know who she was, but it was more than that. This was the second time the man's life had been destroyed by Johanna. He deserved the harshest justice, she reasoned, yet the task was repellent.

The charges ended and Theodoric nodded at Johanna. She held the golden crozier in her right hand so tightly her knuckles were white.

"This crime demands the highest penalty, Sergius," she said. "Rise. Are you prepared to pay for your sins?"

He stood and remained in profile to address both the pope and assembly, his hands clasped in prayer before him.

"I have been wicked, yes, Holy One, and have caused suffering," he said in a surprisingly strong voice. "But in this murder I am innocent. Spare me this final cruel touch by your hand."

His words rocked her. They were a variation of her words aboard his ship long ago. The same words she spoke to red-haired John, her namesake, who saved her life.

"I call witnesses, brothers Bandini, Gullus, Wickham, Othene. Please tell the Holy One," he said and looked into the crowd. The named priests stepped forward and knelt.

"Speak," she said.

"Your Grace, he was with us all day. He's done much good work to atone in God's eyes. As God is our judge, the priest had no part in this."

"He did not have to attend the murder to be the one behind it," she said. The hall rumbled agreement. "That's the mark of this poisoner. He leaves his victims and appears elsewhere when they suffer."

"But your Grace--"

"Holy One," interrupted Theodoric. "Here's a man who knows Sergius as a good customer."

A little old man stepped from behind the senator, bowed, but was too rickety to kneel. He was the local dispenser of herbs, curatives and sometimes darker potions.

"Did you sell Sergius poisonous herbs?" Johanna asked.

"I-I-I," he began, but was overwhelmed by the place and audience. He nodded sheepishly, stepped back and tried to blend in with the crowd as voices rose in the hall. She raised her hand for silence, then stood and pointed the scepter at Sergius.

"The accused is convicted of this horror. Judgment can only be thus. Sergius, you are hereby excommunicated from the church, separated from God. It is, as all know, the harshest punishment. May God have mercy upon your soul. Take him to the court of the city for his trial."

"Conviction without evidence!" a shrill voice rang out. The words seemed to come from no distinct place, but rolled through the hall in mid-air, disembodied.

Everyone looked around trying to locate the ghostly cry.

"That's the way of the new pope!" said the voice, the words slightly slurred. "He condemns the innocent!"

A young monk was the first to notice. He gasped and pointed. All looked to the high, domed ceiling.

Gaetani, Sergius' devoted disciple, stood on a rafter beam directly above Johanna. The priest clung precariously to a piece of rope connected to the beam. He swayed, drunk on the last bottle of strong mead and his love of his mentor. What was there left to do after the miscalculation of his great plan? Certainly he could not let his master die because of his mistake. The mead in Sergius' room provided the courage needed to perform this final service to the man he adored.

"I bought the potion from that lying poisoner! I took the life of the evil pope, Leo!"

He pulled a leather bag from his robe, let it drop. It sailed almost twenty meters to the floor in front of Johanna. A priest picked it up, passed it to the old man who smelled the contents and gagged.

"Poison," he coughed. Then added, "Not mine."

Theodoric signaled the guards on either side of the hall. Johanna watched a fear begin to register in many eyes.

"Sergius should be on the chair, but was caught in the lies of this anti-pope. Sergius is innocent!"

The first guards at the rafters edged their way out to the man.

"Bring him down alive," whispered Theodoric to the lead guard.

"Sergius is beyond reproach," continued Gaetani.

Johanna felt a pat-pat-pat on her shoulders. She looked down saw the drunken man's tear drops had splashed onto her robes. "If anyone should be killed it should be me, for my deeds."

Gaetani saw guards ease across the beam toward him.

"Sweet Sergius, Innocent Lamb of God. We will meet again in the arms of Christ our Savior. Until then, live. Let them have me."

He looked down at Sergius, made the sign of the cross, then tipped over into the air as if diving into a lake.

Johanna watched the priest fall, his arms out from his side; head first, his robe flapping like the wings of a terrible bird. She could almost make out the deep creases, the tree of wrinkles scored into his forehead as they grew larger and their branches reached out to engulf her in their deadly shade.

# CHAPTER XXXIV

BEFORE SHE COULD react, Johanna was pulled from the chair, thrown to the floor just as Gaetani's head met the marble seat of St. Peter's Chair with a sickening crack.

Shrieks flooded the great hall from the sight of a man crumpled impossibly on the throne. The first row of spectators was splashed with blood. Cardinal Longa, one of the men closest to the scene who did not faint, voiced the crowd's unspoken feelings.

"Demons are among us," he said, loud enough to send a chill through the hall. Everyone stared at the twisted body on the sacred chair. Johanna looked into the face of Sergius. Longa saw Sergius still clinging to the arm of the pope. Why, the *accused* saved the pope from being crushed! He pointed to the pontiff and priest together on the floor. "Look. Sergius saved the life of John Anglicus."

The frightened faces of bishops and peasants approached Sergius. The man who moments ago had been convicted as a murderer was now viewed with new eyes. Clergymen reached out, touched his robe and begged his forgiveness. The event was instantly understood to be a divine intervention for a wrongful indictment. God had reached out to touch a man so pure of heart that, despite his conviction and certain death, he never thought of himself, but to protect the Holy One. Several went to their knees saying as much and to ask for his mercy.

"Sergius saved the pope from death," said a bishop at Sergius' feet.

"Sergius the Innocent," said another.

Theodoric helped Johanna up while he gave orders. A blanket was tossed over the body and it was carried away between two guards, a trail of blood dribbling across the floor. The rumble in the hall escalated to a roar with cries for Sergius' charges to be recanted.

"Rescind the sentence."

"What?"

"Rescind the sentence if you want to hold onto these people," hissed Theodoric. "Speak, John, if you want to retain their loyalty."

Dazed, Johanna called for order and got no response. Screams were let loose and arms flailed across chests, hands beseeched heaven. She pounded the crozier on the floor. Nothing. The great bell sounded and its peal reverberated around the hall. Theodoric sent the guards around the hall to restore the peace.

"I said quiet," roared Theodoric.

Several minutes later, after lashes from guards, the din quieted.

"Exonerate him. Quickly," the senator whispered.

"You'd watch the man who murdered your son become a hero?"

"Listen. If you do not take charge and command them you will see Sergius rise to the Chair in your place," he said.

A numbness overtook Johanna and made speaking difficult.

"Sergius, the charges brought to me against you are in error," she said, finally. Johanna looked away, unable to face him. "You are...free...of any...sin. For...forgiven. Go in peace."

Sergius dropped to his knees, clasped his hands. Voices rang out around the hall. The surprised priest was set on shoulders and taken by ecstatic priests, cardinals and bishops out of the court to the street, praised for his amazing feat. Johanna turned to Theodoric, the shock wearing off.

"Take me out of here," she said. "Before I tear these robes off."

Theodoric signaled and she was swept from the hall by the papal entourage in a flurry of vestments.

The moment she stepped into a chamber off the main corridor, she turned on Theodoric.

"That viper is now a hero!"

"I feel the same," replied Theodoric calmly. "But you saw the tide turn yourself. The man saved your life in the presence of the entire court, John. They would not forgive anything less."

"It was a ploy. He planned this."

"A ploy that worked," he said, not unimpressed. "We must be patient. Wait to strike him down. If you don't recognize his act publicly, the people will hate you and love him even more."

"This is wrong. In the blink of an eye they have forgotten all the evil he's done."

"That is Rome," said Theodoric with a shrug.

It brought an odd smile to the senator's face. It was a comfort to the man to know that gods may change, power and reigns and regimes many change, but some things Roman forever remained constant.

He left with the entourage and Johanna was finally alone in the dressing chamber. She put a hand to her throat, the thickly embroidered material clamped at her neck so tightly she could feel her pulse beating against it. She felt strangled by the cloth and undid each layer like the burial gowns of royalty. She stepped away from the door and caught sight of herself in a mirror.

"Holy God," she breathed before her image.

It was an unreal vision cast back to her. She did not resemble a pope. Or a man, or a boy or a person of any sex. She looked like a doll. A painted toy cherub in the finest garments, fashioned after an ideal, a vision of how the artist hoped to represent the link between ethereal heaven and coarse temporal earth.

Johanna nearly tripped over the cascade of material as she tried to sit on a wood stool. More alone than she ever had been, separated from her father, from Adrian, from her own life and despite the clothing, the title and all it entailed, she felt separated most from God. Johanna got down on her knees.

She prayed until her mind emptied.

Hours later Johanna stood. She looked down at herself and discovered she had only gotten off the first layer of vestments. She struggled with a series of fasteners up the side of the next layer, when she heard voices, then pounding on the door. Theodoric entered with several perspiring centurions who filed nervously into the room. The captain, blood on his face and arms, knelt before her and saluted.

"Holy One. Saracens attack. The Saracens have taken the settlement on the hillside. We fear the Muslim dogs will ride next for the gates of Rome."

"You must leave immediately," said Theodoric. "To the summer villa until we can put down the --"

"Call a company of Vatican soldiers, have them meet me at the steps," she ordered.

"John. You cannot convince them to leave merely by your presence."

"I will meet them with more than my presence, senator," she said and picked up the heavy, jewel-laden crozier. She pushed past the men and Theodoric took her arm.

"The pope belongs to the people. I cannot let you do this."

"I am doing this for the people," she said and pulled her arm away.

She ran down the steps and found the papal carriage. Instead of getting inside, Johanna climbed onto the driver's bench and looked around at the confusion in the streets. Citizens hurried toward the Vatican, for the safety they thought it offered. She spotted one of the Vatican officers leading a platoon of cavalry.

"You. Gather your men and have them flank my carriage," she said and pointed the papal crozier so he would receive her authority. The officer saluted, called out orders.

"You cannot help them, John," Theodoric said as he ran up to the carriage. "You will not live to see the end of this day!"

"Do you still not know who I am?" she said. "These robes mean nothing."

The carriage sped off with her on the bench next to the driver as he whipped the horses to a gallop.

# CHAPTER XXXV

VELEDA'S HUSBAND, EXHAUSTED and bleeding profusely, glanced up from his grim work to look over the settlement. It was filled with men and women in combat. His eyes searched the battlefield for his wife. With no strength left to fight and cursing his weakness, he dropped one of his arms. He immediately fell beneath the blows of four Saracens who stabbed at him from all sides.

Across the settlement Veleda caught sight of her husband. She raced through the confusion, let an arrow fly, taking one of the attackers to his death. Running as she re-armed her bow, she was struck from behind, and the blow threw her forward on her feet.

Veleda stumbled but remained upright. She took several steps, then fell to her knees. She reached a hand behind her and felt the handle of a Saracen hatchet buried deep in her back. Its owner stepped up to reclaim his weapon, took hold of the handle with one hand, put a foot on her back for leverage to pull his weapon from the infidel.

A yell made him turn.

Adrian, running flat out, completed his lunge and pierced the Saracen from gut to back with the sharp tines of his pitchfork.

He lifted the man off his feet and pinned him to a tree like a bug. The attacker writhed, his feet not touching the ground as Adrian took the dying man's sword and turned to Veleda.

It happened so fast he did not have time to think. A mounted Saracen rode by and leapt onto Adrian, knocking him to the ground. They rolled in an embrace until Adrian was on his back, the Saracen above him, straining to cut his throat with his scimitar.

Adrian held his own, but felt the stronger man press for the kill, the blade inching down toward his skin. He wanted to cry out, beg the dark man to give him one brief moment, to let him run to his love, to say good-bye to Johanna. Adrian would promise to return, he would swear to any god the man wanted if he would grant him this one wish. But there was no reprieve. The warrior smelled of the rusty, metallic aroma of blood of those killed. Adrian could see every pore, every mashed whisker of his killer's beard, the bushy eyebrows that connected in the middle of his forehead, every speck of dirt that streaked the man's panting face, the facial muscles taut, his teeth bared and grinding, his lips pulled back in his relentless pursuit to slay Adrian.

In that moment Adrian was granted his wish. Adrian was removed from the man's clutches and left the battle behind.

He found himself transported back to the ship where he first met Johanna. Playing like children, he chased and caught her from behind and tumbled with her into the thick ropes coiled in a corner of the deck. The girl in his arms, her face beaming at him, ready to receive his kiss.

In the next instant Johanna's inviting lips faded and became the scowl of the man that would take his life. Adrian felt his muscles weaken, the battle to keep the blade from his throat lost.

The steel edge touched his skin and he felt its sharpness. In a moment the blade would sever the cords and arteries in his neck. The warrior was pressing so hard the steel would surely pass through the softer flesh and reach the bone of his spinal cord. Adrian closed his eyes, took a final breath before letting it all go, giving in to this grim warrior's overpowering strength.

A massive jolt above him stopped the weight of the blade. Adrian opened his eyes. Did the man plan to torture him first? The arms of the Saracen shivered and trembled like an old man's. The warrior's head jerked strangely. Adrian felt the power of the man's arms evaporate. Droplets of blood fell on his cheeks and he thought they were his own until he focused on the face of his killer. Two red streams trickled down from the Saracen's nose and splashed onto Adrian. Beyond the man's glazed eyes Adrian could see the blade of an axe lodged in the top his head.

Adrian pushed and the twitching man rolled off him. The man kicked at the dirt with convulsions.

As Adrian witnessed the man take his final breath, which should have been his own, he was yanked roughly to his feet. He stared into the face of his rescuer.

A big, bearded man stood before him.

"Halbert?" he said, blinking.

"Adrian?" Halbert squinted. "Impossible."

"You live?"

"So I do. Not for much longer I'm afraid," he said and hugged Adrian. He saw something over Adrian's shoulder. "Hurry."

He put a sword in his hand and turned Adrian to face three Saracen soldiers running at them. They met the attackers and fought.

Halbert held the arm of one and swung the man around, right into the sword of his fighting partner. Adrian slashed the third soldier's back while Halbert slashed the first. The Saracens were felled. Halbert and Adrian took their swords, leaned on them like crutches, leaned against the others' back for support and took a moment to breathe.

"It's better Johanna died at sea than see us end here," Halbert gasped for air and wiped his face.

"Died?"

"I'm sorry to tell you, son. She loved you very much."

"She is alive, Halbert."

"Adrian, no. Do not live like I have, gnashing your teeth on that cruel illusion."

"She lives and rules Rome," Adrian turned to look at the old man. "She sits on the Chair of St. Peter."

Halbert grabbed Adrian by the shoulders and would have hurt him if he had found a lie in his eyes.

"She…Yes, you know it, don't you? She is alive! You're telling me what I have always felt," he said. More Saracens bearing swords and lances ran at them. "Live, Adrian! We must fight and we must live!"

They turned and redoubled their fighting as the battle furiously intensified around them.

*The Woman Pope*

"Joooooooan!" yelled Halbert. He waved the sword in the air and ran at the lance men, turning the sound of his daughter's name into a war-cry.

≈ ≈ ≈

Two hundred mounted Vatican soldiers flanked either side of Johanna's carriage. They fought Saracen horsemen while riding at full speed to the settlement. Johanna urged the carriage driver on, waving the crozier over her head as they raced toward her former colony.

Nearing the entrance, a Roman and a Saracen horseman clashed with their swords, riding neck and neck alongside the speeding carriage. Johanna took the reins from the driver, whipped at the animals and glanced over in time to see the Saracen block the Roman's sword with his shield. The Saracen reached over with the large circle of metal and used it to push the Roman from his seat. The Roman fell from his horse and struck the ground beneath the rear wheel, his leg caught in the spokes of the carriage.

It snapped off the man's leg and instantly broke the wheel. The carriage swerved wildly and Johanna lost the reins as the vehicle shot out of control. The back of the carriage swung out to the side and caused the coach to loose its balance and tip. The speeding carriage tossed Johanna and driver into the air while it turned sideways and flipped over. The heavy wagon crashed to the ground, rolled over and over and broke apart at full speed. The carriage disintegrated.

Pieces shot in every direction in an explosion of wood and metal. The momentum slid the coach along the ground for a hundred lengths, creating a dust storm. Johanna rolled along in a cloud while the gilded doors, soft plush seats and all shattered materials flew by. Sharp shards of metal and slivers of wood spun every way, stabbing two men to death. A round wheel of jagged glass the size of a dagger blew out of the vehicle's window and penetrated a Saracen's stomach. He opened his mouth to scream, but was crushed beneath the chassis of the tumbling carriage.

Johanna continued to roll amid the destruction. The vehicle came apart; doors, frame, roof, wheels, axles, floor boards, finely painted siding, glass sconces, harnesses, benches, hinges, nails, pillows and drapery. Every piece of the carriage turned into deadly flying debris tossed about in its own storm.

Finally, it all came to a strangely peaceful halt inside a cloud of dust. Johanna lay a moment, dazed by how fast and yet how slowly the whole experience had happened.

She looked through brown dust swirling everywhere from the carriage, and as it settled found herself in the middle of the battle.

She spied the crozier that had flown from her hand. She ran, picked it up, clubbed the neck of a Saracen and dropped the man in the dirt. Then she turned and ran into the settlement. Johanna entered the village fighting.

≈ ≈ ≈

The Saracens soon became aware of the fury coming from a little, ornately dressed priest. Eyes turned to watch him swing the jeweled crozier like a seasoned soldier. When they realized who it was, the attackers became nervous at the sight of a warrior pope. This was not some rarefied cleric with soft hands and an aversion to blood, but a veteran warrior fighting alongside peasants who also fought like hardened soldiers. These farmers seemed to rejoice at a chance to clash.

The Saracen commander watched a huge blond peasant take a pick axe and split the head of one of his men as easily as a melon. These peasants fought hard and fought dirty and when two hundred Roman horsemen followed on the heels of the destroyed carriage at the entrance of the settlement, blowing horns and curses, the Saracen commander knew the skirmish was lost and called a retreat.

Johanna turned from beating the head of a Saracen and had just enough time to raise the crozier before a sword blade aimed at her face clanged into it. It shattered the staff's gold outer casing and knocked her to the ground. The sword's owner wheeled his mount around for another pass. Johanna glanced up at him.

It was the Saracen commander.

Driven by the blood he had spilled that day, he charged with no thought of his own retreat, but only to leave the field with the life of the infidel's religious leader. Johanna got to her feet and readied herself. His sword poised above his head and about to swing, the wild dark man suddenly looked up, surprised.

Johanna instinctively dropped to the ground as another horseman passed beside her from the opposite direction. Between her and the Saracen she was almost trampled by the horses of the opposing riders. The men swung for each other. The Saracen missed and was slashed across the chest. He toppled from his horse, rolled to the ground and came to a stop in a dusty heap before Johanna, dead.

She turned to her deliverer. The sun was at his back and made it impossible to identify him. She shielded her eyes to catch sight of his features but instead caught the sun's flash on his raised scimitar.

"Thank you, friend. Do I know you?" she called.

The rider turned his horse and brought the beautiful Arabian beast close. She looked up at the one armed Muslim leader she had wounded years before.

"It's possible. With Allah all things are possible," he said and laughed. He spurred the animal, brought his horse to a gallop and called out to his men. Johanna watched as his band of marauders routed the competing sect of fleeing Saracens.

"Wait!" She wanted to stop him, wanted to ask a thousand questions but he disappeared into the fray, calling out praises to Allah with his sword waving in his one arm.


Two hours later the battle was over, the sounds of retreating horses and the calls of fleeing men replaced by the wails of the wounded and dying. .

Johanna wandered across the carnage and, about to bend and care for a fallen Viking, froze. A chill passed through her when she saw Veleda on the ground near by.

She got on her knees and held friend in her arms. Johanna grimaced at the blood and the hatchet still lodged in her back. Feelings shut down from the battle came rushing over her. It was like holding Bennito again.

"Veleda," she said. The once wild-woman was barely conscious and her eyes labored to come into focus.

"I go to see who has won," she smiled.

"Won?"

"The Old Ones or the One God."

"You know the Lord. Let Him be your comfort."

"Yes. He is mighty this Lord. But John, He is not fair," she said.

How far she has traveled, thought Johanna, and stroked Veleda's cheek. She seemed proud that she had taken a warrior role once again. Being a mother and having a family had softened the hard edge of her heart, but the years also removed another edge, the edge of a seeker. She had always loved the fight.

"Shhh. He's more than we can ever know," said Johanna. "Go. Let Him take you over the last bridge."

Johanna began last rites, but Veleda, eager to move on, hurried over the temporal span of bridge and into the realm of the next hunt. The wild-woman breathed a final, ragged breath while Johanna prayed for her soul.

"Johanna."

She looked up. Adrian stumbled toward her and fell, bloodied. Johanna let Veleda down and rushed to him. Grief could come later.

"Adrian!"

She kneeled and held him. His arm was slashed and he was cut and scraped over most of his body. He looked as if he had been trampled by a hundred mad horses.

"Your father. He. . ."

He lost consciousness. Johanna tore the lining from her white robe, now filthy with blood, dirt and sweat, and wrapped his arm. He came to and she pressed his wound to stop the bleeding. He groaned.

"My father, " she asked. "What did you mean?"

His head jerked slightly, his eyes fluttered.

"He is here." He passed out again.

She looked over his shoulder, then laid Adrian's head down. She stood and searched the field in a slow tack from left to right. Her gaze stopped on a tree at the edge of the battlefield and she squinted to make out what was beneath it.

She ran as fast as she could.

"Father!"

Halbert lay against a tree, an arrow poking out of his side, cut and wounded in several places, eyes closed, mouth open. She tripped over a body and fell. On her hands and knees she crawled across the ground until she reached him. He did not move. She put her head on the ground and swore.

"I hate you, God! I hate You! You've taken every one from me! I only wanted You. Praised you every day, even before I was touched by Your Hand. I gave You everything in my heart. But now I take it back! I take my love back, damn You!"

She threw her head down and wept, so bereft she could not catch her breath, choking on her own tears until she thought she would die right there, slain by anguish.

"Don't blaspheme, little one."

"What?" She could not trust her ears. She looked up. Halbert was hurt, but alive and smiled at her.

"The god you have found must love you very much to bring you back to me," he said.

She crawled to him, he opened his arms. He took a huge breath and folded his daughter into his arms as if he held the only thing that could sustain his life. Johanna savored the touch; the moment was as close to being perfect as any miracle.

"Forgive me, Lord. I praise Your name. The God of us all. Your Will be done."

"He brought you to me, I praise Him with you," said Halbert and he began a song they used to sing when she was a child. Adrian staggered to them and sat beside Johanna. She put an arm around the two men she loved more than life and, though death was all around, she was filled with a peace she had only known when taken into the Spirit.

≈ ≈ ≈

Theodoric walked the battlefield and was sickened. Ringed by his personal army, he stepped over bodies. Veleda's children were brought to him and looking at the oldest he remembered his son.

"Take them to my wife," he told an aide. Theodoric continued through the village. It had been a long time since he had been in battle but the familiar feeling of nausea and disgust filled him as he surveyed the worst that men could do when they faced each other.

He called for more burial wagons to be brought out, then turned his attention toward a strange sound wafting across the field. What he saw shocked and surprised the man who prided himself on his cool-eyed understanding of the workings of the world.

The new pope sat against a tree, nestled at its trunk between the monk Adrian and another man he did not know, surrounded by heaps of moaning and mortally wounded men and twisted, dismembered corpses. The three had their arms entwined and were singing.

# PART 4
## CHAPTER XXXVI

"THIS MAN LOOKS more like the Halbert I remember," whispered Adrian. In her private dining room a month after the battle, Johanna, Adrian and Halbert sat at a candle-lit table and ate lemon-roasted fish from the Tiber, garlic fried in olive oil from the settlement's gardens and braided bread baked in Vatican ovens, served with red wine from Pantagruel's vineyard. Halbert talked of his adventures before and after reaching Rome, as he pushed food from heaped plate to mouth. Johanna, dressed in the linen robes of a pope at rest, smiled at Adrian. Both privately noted not only how quickly he had regained his robust frame but how his stories had taken on a familiar ring with repetition.

"Your health returns, brother," she said solemnly and put her hands in her lap. It took a moment before the phrase registered and Halbert stopped and tried to recall when and where he had heard it. He looked at Johanna's stern facade. After a few heartbeats her expression cracked and they burst out laughing, so much that Halbert, his face reddened, clutched the healing arrow wound in his side.

"Ow. This is the kind of pain I can stand. A contented pain. So happy for you two I can withstand anything now. To you both," he said and raised his glass.

"Halbert, if what you say is true, may I ask you to withstand a great labor for me?" asked Adrian.

"Whatever you desire, son."

Adrian rose, brought crutches over and stood by his chair. With effort and a touch of consternation at having to leave his dinner, Halbert stood.

Adrian helped him through the main hall then turned down a corridor Halbert had not before noticed. Adrian stopped at a long shelf just before the corridor turned and to Halbert's surprise pushed aside a wall tapestry and revealed a door. Adrian led Halbert through the door into a dark passageway. It ended at the bottom of a set of stairs. Halbert stopped midway up the steep set to catch his breath.

"Are we walking to England?" he said, feeling the wound at his ribs bleed through the bandages. He was now clearly irritated at having been dragged so far from the table.

Adrian urged him up the flight to a door. On the other side Halbert found himself cooled by a breeze. They were on the roof, looking out on the city in the warm Roman night. Adrian led him across the roof to an altar; a small covered table set with lighted candles and strewn with flowers. Adrian knelt, his head bowed before a confused Halbert.

"Halbert. Good father, I brought you here…" He trailed off.

"I hope it is worth the blood I'm losing," Halbert grumbled.

"I brought you here to ask for the hand of your daughter. I love her with all my soul. I ask your blessing."

"I'd give no one else my blessing, son," Halbert smiled, and placed his palm on Adrian's head. The roof door opened: Johanna appeared in the doorway in a loose fitting white dress, a cloth veil fluttering behind her. She looked like a spirit from another world. She approached and kissed her father's cheek.

"Father, will you please marry us?"

"I'm no priest nor a Christian."

"What does the pope need of a priest?" asked Adrian.

"I should not be the one."

"Who else on this roof or below it knows our love better?" asked Johanna. "Will you call the god Jehovah you once worshipped to join us?"

He thought a moment, then nodded. Johanna and Adrian knelt before him and said a prayer under the stars. Halbert looked out on the city. It seemed a new place at this height, its savagery and hardness softened by the cool breeze, its usual cacophony hushed, as if all of Rome were listening.

Later, in the bedroom, Adrian prayed frantically while he knelt at the side of the bed. He was more frightened now in a different way than at the height of battle in the settlement. The door opened and Johanna stood in the doorway in a nightgown. When she crossed the room they held hard to each other to steady themselves. They kissed, and shook with nerves.

Adrian let her down onto the bed and slipped off her gown. He took off his robe and they lay side-by-side. They remained silent, reveling in the other's nakedness, for the first time completely undisguised. But they shivered so badly they had to pull a blanket over them, clinging to each other.

"Can we go slowly?" she asked, not knowing if she could.

"Only if you'll let me hold you like this forever," he said. Uncertain, lacking knowledge, both wept more than once that night. Johanna was in pain, Adrian was clumsy. But they did not give up and for their persistence the lovers gained a deep understanding of the act of love; both strove to give pleasure rather than receive it.

"That feels nice," she said, and touched his cheek, giving him a clue as he moved. "Yes, love. Soft, just like . . . that."

≈ ≈ ≈

Every night was a sensual education. They lost all shyness, grew bold and tried to inflame the other's senses with a new touch, a different turn of the other's body this way and that to create a new sensation. Johanna had never seen the scar on his buttocks, and they laughed at how he got it during a boyhood prank. He had never seen the small, wine-colored birthmark that was hidden deep in her inner thigh. His little kisses on it made her sigh and made him bold. They memorized every inch of skin on the other and every parcel of land they owned had a precious view and was ripe to explore.

"You..." she began, but caught her breath when his touch sent a jolt through her. "Adrian!"

Late at night they snuck like children in a stranger's home through the rooms of the Vatican. Starving after hours of love-making, they sat in the kitchen and stuffed themselves on fresh fruits and pastries left in the massive pantries, and gorged on the leftovers from the papal meals.

They crept through the Vatican and found themselves in immense spaces of dark rooms holding candles for light. They examined the artwork, tapestries and treasures that had been saved from looting in previous ages. Some rooms were stacked with furniture created by local artisans, gold framed triptychs taller than themselves, statuary, and paintings from all over the world.

Every night the lovers slipped down corridors and found halls that led nowhere, while others took them into secret places.

One night Johanna pulled Adrian through a dark corner in the northeastern section of the Vatican. They had entered a concealed space, like a tunnel through the bowels of the building that led into a secret passageway. Adrian stopped, blew out the candle, pushed Johanna up against the wall and pressed his lips and his weight against her. Both panted as Adrian took Johanna where she stood, unable to wait until they reached a bed.

≈ ≈ ≈

Theodoric dropped the purse into the monk's hand. The brother was escorted off by Theodoric's bodyguards. Theodoric headed for the stable to take his morning ride.

"You have something delicious for me, don't you, love?"

His wife, dressed in a sky blue diaphanous gown, rode her favorite courser at a brisk canter back from her exercise.

"Don't I always have something delicious for you, Althea?"

She got down from the horse, her dress sliding nearly up to her waist. Theodoric noted the strength and shape of the muscles from her calves to her backside, as well as the new welts laced across her thighs. He was proud to have such a beautiful wife, a faithful wife and loved her so much he had to struggle with not to give her everything she asked for. Althea walked with a bouncing step to her husband and slipped her arm through his.

"I see your good brother Carlt has beaten my brother Bonicchi to the punch," she said. She lifted Theodoric's hand, inspected his manicured fingernails, then licked his index finger.

"Sweet," he said, kissing the top of her head. "So beautiful, so clever, but you've never known how to choose spies."

"You are so good at everything," she said. They walked in silence a ways. "You are going to make me beg, aren't you?"

"Have I ever made you beg, my dear?"

"Yes, you have, and rightly so."

"I would never do so unless it was for your pleasure."

"Then tell me. You know secrets, the big ones, die with me."

Theodoric laughed. "That's true and this is a big one."

"Yes?" Althea eyes were hungry and she licked her lips. This would be gossip worthy of whatever it was going to cost her.

"It seems our John has fallen in love."

"That is news! Who is the lucky girl? Do I know her?"

"It appears John the English loves his own, like your friend Gormandi and his crowd."

"Even better. There is so much more to work with. This is excellent, thank you, my beautiful Theodoric. Whatever you desire tonight will be yours. You shall have it all, ecstasy for each and every sense," she said and slipped her hand beneath his tunic as they walked. Her voice purred in his ear. "You do not even have to ask, I know what you want. I will have the dark ladies and their Assyrian boy, the one you've been eyeing, bought for you, plus I will arrange other surprises. But go on. Continue, love, continue."

# CHAPTER XXXVII

"WHAT DOES THIS have to do with the church?" asked Johanna. Two men knelt before her while behind them servants held up gold bars from chests placed before the papal throne.

"It has everything to do with Rome," Theodoric replied. "And this decision cannot be separated from the Chair."

"That's not what the Church teaches and you know it."

"It's how the Church retains its authority, John. If you pay attention, it's a lesson this Chair teaches us all," Theodoric nodded to one of the kneeling men, who gestured behind him.

A little boy of eight wearing grand clothes in the style of a miniature duke, was ushered before Johanna. She laughed out loud at the adorable child dressed like a man. She had an overwhelming desire to take him on her lap and smother the child with kisses. Instead, Johanna bit her lip and tried to frown.

"And who is this fine gentleman?" she asked Theodoric.

"He is to be one of your cardinals, father."

"And one fine day he shall be a righteous one."

She looked again at the gold set before the Chair, then at the boy.

"In name only, of course," the senator assured her. "For the title alone we'll finish the wall and recruit a thousand men to guard the southern province."

"I assume this holy child has been in service to the church all his young life, suffered with the poor and spent years in cloistered meditation on the gospels he knows by heart?"

"The boy doesn't yet know how to read, as I am sure you can guess. But that's not the point here, Holy Father, is it?"

≈ ≈ ≈

Johanna slumped into the papal throne and looked out over the court.

*Almost two years*, she thought. Two years seeming to last the single turn of an hour-glass. The court had continued every day with the same wealthy men in their expensive cloaks, wearing tight Phrygian skull caps topped with bright plumes of exotic birds, intricately sewn bangles shining off them. Johanna held up her hand to Theodoric.

"It is right to let them marry. Look at how much love they have between them. It is not for their family or any one to keep them apart."

She looked at the bottom of the throne to a girl, a beautiful child with curly jet hair and violet eyes just blooming into adolescence. She was on her knees next to a boy her age, his face too young for a beard, his eyes wild with apprehension. The children passed furtive looks.

"If Guillania marries Stephanus against her father's wishes, we lose the Colognas and two powerful clans in the east," said Theodoric. "What the children want means nothing."

Two bishops whispered in Johanna's ear, indicating each family in the court, their association to the Chair, the Vatican and Rome and tried to explain the dizzyingly complex web of allegiances each represented.

She stood, frustrated, and looked at the kneeling children. Johanna made the sign of the cross over them as their eyes beseeched her.

"Go in peace, but you must honor your families."

She left abruptly through a door behind the Chair so she would not be able to bear the cries of the young couple at her back. Theodoric caught up as she walked the private corridor.

"Holy Father, we have much important business today," he said and took hold of her elbow. She yanked it free and whirled on him.

"For whose benefit? I have done nothing but grant you favors for two years. Tomorrow comes soon enough for the pope to follow your orders."

The senator watched the rippling flourish of robes as they moved down the corridor.

$$\approx \approx \approx$$

Johanna locked the door. She walked to the wardrobe in the corner, partitioned off from the rest of the room by tall screens illustrated with stories from the bible. She removed the tiara and set it on its stand.

*Lord, You raised me up to the Chair to become this?* she prayed. *To wear a robe worth enough to feed a hundred families? To become a pawn in some ancient game? I served the poor when I was one of them. Now that I have power I am useless.*

She worked the fasteners under her chin and felt her breath come easier. It was always the same. A heart-felt challenge from her and then a debate, but she was always outnumbered and ultimately there was no choice. The men knew her every argument and came back with answers so polished with logic it seemed they had been passed on to them centuries before her arrival.

She stared at herself in the brass mirror, trying to see through the image shining back at her. She felt nauseated.

She removed the embroidered robes and undergarments, undid her breast wrap and stood naked before the mirror. She stared intently, studying herself for the first time in years of secrecy, looking at her posture and turning to inspect herself in profile, gauging the changes evident everywhere in the reflection. Johanna assessed her long, shapely legs, but when she squared her shoulders noted that her small breasts had become larger, heavier, more rounded in the last two months, much like the rest of her. She had lost the thin frame of youth and a fuller body had taken its place. Its maturity was a pleasant surprise. Johanna bent to feel the heft of her right calf when she was suddenly grabbed from behind. She gasped, terrified.

"What are you doing back so early?" asked Adrian, playfully.

"Don't ever do that," she said.

"Your Holiness, I apologize," he said.

"I'm sorry," she said catching herself. "You scared me. I, I'm not feeling myself."

He put his lips softly on her neck and kissed. Adrian caressed her forehead, brushed back her damp hair.

"Tell me about this sanctuary again," he said.

"It's near the ocean on a hillside. The life is simple. The brothers pray and do good works. It's a quiet monastery and every brother is kind. They'll welcome the four of us."

"The four?"

She took his hand, put it on her stomach.

His eyes went from belly to face. Speechless, he could do nothing but hug her. Then he slipped down her body, gently put his cheek to her rounding belly, kissing it, making circles over it with his tongue to mark the place. He put his ear to it. After a moment his head jerked up.

"I hear it!" he exclaimed. "Listen! What a roar!"

"That's only my hungry stomach, you great good fool!" She laughed.

"Nonetheless, this child will roar."

"I want our child to have a peaceful life. Perhaps at the monastery our path will become clear," Johanna smiled, then frowned and sat up in bed.

"Do not worry, love," said Adrian.

"I'm so useless and impotent here --" she began, and without warning gagged. She hurried to the next room where Adrian heard her become ill. After she finished he led her back to the bed. He got a cloth and a bowl of water from the sideboard to cool her forehead.

"My turn to be nurse," he smiled. "My God. I'm going to be a father."

# CHAPTER XXXIX

IN THE POPE'S boudoir Adrian and Johanna slept late, stuck to the bed and each other in the humid stillness of a Roman August, her second as pope. Johanna woke first and got up. Walking across the floor she caught a glimpse of herself in the brass mirror. Five months and she was already heavily filled with their child. The solid bulge of her belly excited and frightened her as she wrapped her arms around its curve. Despite the illness that dogged her every day, she gazed at herself with pleasure. She finally looked upon the real Johanna.

Noise broke into her thoughts and she went to the window. Below, people hurried from building to building clutching their valuables. Fires burned across the city with black funnels of smoke pouring into the sky. She smelled a desperate unrest, sour with fear. Johanna saw a group of foreign soldiers looting, carrying food out of a business that sat within the shadow of the Vatican. She watched as the owner was beaten and thrown to the ground at the door of his establishment.

"Leave him alone," she yelled, but they ignored her and ran off. She could not believe it. Too far away to see that she was anything but the pope yet they ignored the Vicar of Christ's personal reprimand.

The city was tearing at the seams no matter the tactic, no matter the proclamation, and no matter the political decision she had reluctantly acquiesced to. Theodoric claimed the appointments would ensure peace and stability. Yet crops failed, enemies camped outside the walls and the only import that came through the gates was dread.

*None of our good works to the poor have had any effect, Lord,* she thought.

Knocking pounded at the door.

"Adrian," she whispered. But he was out of bed and slipping into the adjoining room as she threw a robe around her. The knocking continued until Johanna opened the door a crack and stood behind it to hide her belly.

"John, the court cannot wait another -- you're pale, are you ill again?" asked Theodoric, dressed for battle. He had been prepared for war every day for the last three months.

"It's not serious, but I have to rest."

"Rest when Rome is not cursed with plagues," he said. "Goth's are destroying cities not fifty leagues away. Do you realize how weak we've become in just the last month?"

"I am aware of our plight."

"I am surprised since we rarely see you."

"I am very aware of the situation you and I have helped create."

"What are you talking about?"

"You know what I mean. You don't need me for your purposes. Why not dress a statue in my robes and continue as you have?"

He attempted to flash his renowned smile.

"If nothing else, John, come soothe the people. They need to know you are praying on their behalf. They need to see you in control of the world, not a casualty of it. Come to St. Peter's and exorcise the city's demons. The people will see you and regain the faith that is fading."

"How dare you," she said and her cheeks reddened. "Day after day you demand I make decisions in ways that fill your pockets. Now you presume to tell me what the people need? I know what they need, Theodoric, and it has nothing to do with your personal empire."

"You are wrong and I will not discuss this foolishness."

"I will come when I am able," she said and closed the door. He banged on it behind her.

"Rome cannot wait, John." He pounded again on the door then stomped down the hall.

She listened until his footsteps were gone. Johanna pounded back on the door. She knew she had lingered too long in this role but her health cursed her. The nausea and swelling of her limbs should have gone after the third month, she knew that from listening to midwives, but every day she was as plagued as the city by sickness.

"Rest," said Adrian as she sat at her wardrobe.

"That's exactly what I intend to do, brother," she said with a conspiratorial smile. "Would you like to rest with me?"

"Of course I would, but please," he pleaded. "We must leave the moment you feel up to it, love. Halbert and I have prepared everything for the journey."

She nodded solemnly, then, as she had done every day for six months, she took Adrian down the length of a side corridor and entered the Vatican library to 'rest.'

"Thank you for having me again, Holy Father," said the spice merchant, Philipus, with a bow. A refined and generous Roman and so soft spoken that every word seemed a whisper, Philipus bought books from every corner of the known world, from lands of the rare spices he traded and imported. Philipus gathered books and writings from ages so long past that reading those ancient pagans was believed by many superstitious clerics to corrupt the soul.

"Philipus, always a pleasure for my head and heart," said Johanna.

She went to her area, a portion of the library set with works Philipus had previously brought, spread out on a large table and piled with codices, manuscripts and books. Beside the oversize chair for her to sit were pillows and ointments and herbs to help ease the pain that would inevitably come for her.

Months before, Halbert had joined them and the three entered the library in the morning, went their separate ways until the afternoon meal when husband, wife, father and Philipus met and talked about their explorations into the worlds of the books.

After the meal the company parted and she continued reading Virgil, Pliny, Lucian, Aristotle, Cicero, Horace, Epictetus. Johanna read Xenophon's account of the trial of Socrates to the others, and was filled with wonder at the beauty of human reasoning and imagination from these long dead men, saints despite their lives without Christ.

Johanna looked up from her book and saw Adrian gaze out a window, contemplating a passage he had just read. She saw at Halbert at his table, book closed in his lap, sound asleep, his expression clear of worry, glad to be in the same room with his daughter and son-in-law.

She knew this was what she had always desired. To be on the path for the search for truth, shaking down fabrications, seeing through interpretations the rest of the world accepted as solemnly as the Gospels. This, and to be with the men she loved most. She could not have been happier.

≈ ≈ ≈

"Holiness," said Theodoric as he waited for the pope to come out from one of his too-frequent reveries. "Can we continue?"

"Of course," she said and sat straighter. "Proceed."

"Thank you so much for your attention."

Theodoric continued to speak when she felt a terrible pain burst inside her, like the talon of a hawk dug deep into her gut.

"Ahh," slipped out. She clutched her belly. The noisy court went dead quiet.

"Your Grace? Are you all right?" asked Theodoric. She adjusted her robes to cover her movement.

"Fine, senator. Fine. Gentlemen. Continue."

The attack passed, subsiding like a bad dream.

"Holiness," said Theodoric, irritated. "What is your decision?"

"I beg your pardon?"

"Just say 'yes,' John," he whispered, angry. "So that we may get to our dinners at a decent time tonight."

"It has always been the politics of land," said Philipus at lunch one day. "Charlemagne's sons are old and his legacy has faded since his death. Their Frankish kingdoms in both the East and West and the Kingdom of Lothaire have dissolved around them."

"I have met Louis the Pious and Charles the Bald," said Johanna. "They are kind but..."

"Well intentioned men but weak soldiers," said Philipus. He looked out the window and hesitated before he spoke. "Sometimes the best men do not have the ruthlessness needed to rule."

"Is that what you think of me, brother?" she asked. "Come, you know your honesty is expected."

"The Chair, whether you are the one who sits on it or not," he said. "has little to do with the education of the spirit or inquiry into the soul. Nor does it help the poor. I am afraid that for as long as anyone can remember it never has. I believe you understand this now, yes, Holy One?"

She had feared those very words since her first day on the Chair, and immediately knew their truth. Despite great and compassionate men who came before her, the pontificate had for centuries been little more than a puppet for emperors, kings and royalty. The Chair held the power to crown the next leader who would command the west. The pope and the church legitimized whoever became emperor and along with that tremendous influence it drew every man of ambition, every seeker of power and every perverse desire to try to gain what it could from that power.

≈ ≈ ≈

"I am afraid for you," Adrian said as they ate dinner with Halbert. "And the baby."

The pregnancy had strained her body so hard she was no longer able to go out to the street and comfort and poor, or even visit the library without suffering fits and searing pain. Philipus was kind enough to send her favorite volumes so that she might read from bed. Her fingers, feet and ankles swelled to an almost grotesque thickness. She had daily, massive headaches, and she wept with pain each time she had to urinate.

One morning before light, Halbert and Adrian carried Johanna, at six months along, down through the secret passageway to leave the city. But as they eased down the steps Johanna began shaking violently and vomited. In such a state they had no choice but carry her back to bed.

Another two months had passed with more setbacks in Johanna's health, more excuses to Theodoric and, at seven months pregnant she could not leave her bed.

Halbert stared at his shiny spoon. Adrian tugged at his beard, full but trimmed nightly by Johanna and kept neat.

"We've had a good life here," said Johanna, smiling weakly from bed. Suddenly, she burst into tears. Adrian got up and put his arms around her.

"Heaven's house on earth," Halbert said and set the patterned silver spoon down as if bidding goodbye to a friend. He leaned over and wiped Johanna's cheek with his napkin.

"Everything is ready," said Adrian.

"Has Anastasius found horses?" she asked.

"I secured a good team for us," said Halbert.

"We could not ask Anastasius. No one can know anything," he said and went to the leather bag he had stowed beside his chair. "Any who knows you must be completely surprised when we disappear. Believe me, Theodoric would pry any information from them."

Adrian pulled scrolls from the bag, spread them on the table. One was a sailor's coastal map of Italy and the western Mediterranean, another was a crude approximation of the coast of Gaul. He outlined his plan, setting their dinner cups on each corner to keep the map flat. He recited the spare points of the journey they were to make so solemnly that it was as if their escape was a death march and not the only hope of survival.

"We leave tomorrow," he said. "Anyone looking for our trail will have few footprints to follow."

"How shall we go?" Halbert asked.

"We can not walk the road we first took here," Adrian said, his finger ran along the winding lines on the map leading out of the city and into the hills. "It's crowded with armies and merce- naries waiting for the right moment to challenge Rome."

"The coast?" asked Johanna.

"We'll sail north at the shore, here. No more walking for you," he said to Johanna with a wan smile. "On water we can make the monastery long before the child is due."

They discussed the details of what was needed to take on the journey, then went off to bed, all three depressed.

Johanna and Adrian tossed and turned in sleep. Adrian woke in the night to find Johanna moaning. When he reached for her, she was soaked in sweat.

"My Lord God," he prayed. "Why is the child hounding her so hard every day? Can't You ease her pain a little? Please?"

At daylight she could not get out of bed and could barely move her arms. It was clear the plan had to be delayed. Halbert and Adrian stood outside the bedroom door.

"We cannot do anything more," said Adrian. "She needs a physician."

The lines across his forehead, once just traces on a smooth face, were now a dark wavy pattern the length and breadth of his brow.

"Any fool who sees her, much less a physician, will know exactly what ails the pope," said Halbert.

For days they sat and tried to keep the sweat from pouring off her skin. They forced water into her, soaked her for hours in cool baths. Her belly cramped, every joint in her body ached and her head wanted to burst like a dropped melon from the pressure inside it. It was harder to keep the nosy servants away, their sus- picions grew into wild rumors that came back to them via Anastasius. Every story made them afraid.

≈ ≈ ≈

In his villa south of the city, Theodoric pushed himself away from the remains of a small stoat cooked in a creamy mint and garlic sauce. He smiled at Althea who laughed at a joke told by their new confidant, the man who now graced their table every night.

"Thank you for your generous cup, senator."

Solicitous, a praise for each course served, his own sought-after metheglin brought as gift to host and hostess, Sergius raised his glass in a toast.

"Long live Pope John Anglicus," he said. "Long live all who prosper from his blessings."

"To darling John," said Althea, raising her glass.

"To you both, my best companions," said Theodoric. "But, good Sergius, I believe you would prosper more if you attended court."

"The pope has forgiven me, senator, but will never let me near his court."

"He can't do anything. Come with me. You and I have much work there."

Sergius raised his glass. He then openly and lasciviously winked at Althea. She nodded in his direction and a sensual blush burned across her cheeks.

Those two fit perfectly, thought Theodoric. Althea had recognized a like-minded soul in Sergius the first night he came to dinner. Since the death of their son, her games meant more to her than anything and she threw herself into them with a fury.

Theodoric had watched as she led the famous priest from the table that first night, took him by the hand to her special friends waiting in her play rooms in a separate building at the far end of the villa. Later, when Theodoric took his usual seat above the activity and out of sight, he watched with fascination as Sergius astounded Althea and her playmates with new games of his own device. His novel approach set a frenetic tone rare for the beautiful but jaded group of powerful men and women. The twists of Sergius' mind sent Althea and her friends to breathless new heights of lust and pain and made their own routines seem naïve and innocent. By the end of the evening Theodoric saw each man and woman cast a wary respect and fear on this man who was able to cause more agony, inflict more tortured but delicious ecstasy with his long braided white chin whiskers than any in the room could evoke with leather, metal or other instrument. They recognized in him a master, a genius of pain.

Althea came to Theodoric that night weak as a baby, stumbling into bed with tiny cuts and abrasions all over her sweating body. She slept for eighteen hours.

As Theodoric watched her sleep that first night, his wife's exhausted but beautiful face painted blue by the moonlight, he was overcome with a cold dread. What if Althea left him for Sergius? Or, even worse, conspired with him? It would be a relatively easy plot. They could have him killed by poison or assassin, then move together with Sergius in front, Althea directly behind as an unstoppable juggernaut to the Chair.

Sergius' presence commanded power and though his body was skeletal, he elicited desire from Althea and her kind. Being horribly scarred, the sight of a naked Sergius baring himself to the others was disgusting, yet he made them fall on their knees to pay homage to him, and several of the young men and all the women of Althea group slathered with lust for the old man.

When Sergius persuaded them to participate in the violation, torture and ultimate murder of the Assyrian slave boy Theodoric favored, they all shivered with forbidden sensations.

Theodoric wanted to stop the sacrifice as it neared its frenzied conclusion, but his tongue was mute, spellbound by the horror that played out before him.

Night after night Theodoric watched some of the most powerful people in Rome risk their lives in the hunt for the rarest combinations of carnal sensations, the heights of which were reached only when each man and woman had the real possibility of losing their lives in the process.

Theodoric looked down upon his sleeping wife and feared for his life. He had to force himself to keep from strangling her then and there.

He told himself he had nothing to fear from sweet Althea as he smoothed her damp, tangled hair. She was without ambition. *To conceal the pain of our son's death she had put her heart into her games.* The real thing, the cold, cutting blade of power was not to her taste. At least not now.

Even so, the following day Sergius' first visit, he engaged another spy. Someone to keep an eye on a relationship that would no doubt develop after that night. If Althea turned on him, remote chance or not, Theodoric wanted her close by, in his bed and within his two hands' reach.

# CHAPTER XXXX

ADRIAN MOVED ALONG the dark passageway, one hand on the wall, the other stretched out on his right. He felt for the place where the stone staircase curved then descended to the ground floor. On the other side of the wall was the main corridor in the Vatican and all who walked it were unaware of the secret parallel passageway. He found the steps and hurried down winding stairs, careful of the slippery mold growing in the damp. His mind raced with a rising panic he could no longer hold in check.

Time had run out.

Another month had passed with sickness and false starts until it was clear Johanna was not going to get any better. Sick or not they had no choice but to leave. Now.

A sliver of light hung in the black distance. Adrian fixed his eyes on it as it grew larger with every step until it became the outline of a door. He slid the bolt and pulled, momentarily blinded by the intense afternoon light bearing down on a secluded courtyard.

Adrian crossed the hidden square and thought about Rome in the last weeks. While they waited for Johanna's health to improve, the city sunk to its lowest depths. The land had been squeezed dry by drought, diseased by tremendous clouds of grasshoppers and Romans had been cursed by an epidemic of the yellow sickness. Foreign armies battled the forces of Rome and her allies from the Western Kingdoms in every direction. Incursions threatened the city every morning and death camped outside the gates every night. Meanwhile, inside the protective

Leonine Wall, roving bands of thieves terrorized the streets while citizens were fed a daily ration of oppression.

Adrian walked to a covered carriage beneath an olive tree, a sleepy team of four horses tethered in the shade beneath it. He could see the hills outside Rome above the top of the courtyard wall, brown and barren in the sweltering heat.

Every day they let pass, another way of escape collapsed. There were rumors from Anastasius about Johanna's church officers forming an insurgency within their ranks. Was there a plan to have the pope and his male lover removed? Or would the senator simply have them quietly taken away and killed? An exasperated Theodoric demanded she appear before a council that evening to see if she was fit to continue on the Chair. Who knew what decision he had made, what fate he already planned for her?

*Today it must happen or not at all,* Adrian thought. He took one end of the muslin tarp on the carriage and shook, snapped it like a sheet and sent dozens of grasshoppers flying. Adrian did not bother about the ones on his clothing and stuck in his beard as he stretched the muslin over the wooden arches, curved to make a billowy tented space. He got inside and examined the parcels on the floor. Books wrapped in rabbit fur, extra clothing for three people traveling to far shores. He brushed insects off the bags of grain, dried foodstuffs, checked the skins filled with water and wine. He looked over a cache of weapons: swords, hardwood staffs, long daggers with both straight and serrated edges, unstrung bows with four quivers full of arrows with sharp heads of steel.

After the inventory of weapons, Adrian sighed at the thought of how they might have to be used. This journey already felt harder than the first. Foreign armies on the hillsides, amassed from every part of Europe to stake out a claim on wounded Rome. Adrian did not relish the thought of trying to get past them or the organized pirates at every port, making the coast just as perilous.

He hopped down from the wagon, tied the flaps of muslin against prying eyes and went back to the secret entrance. Slipping through to a stairway hidden by tall shrubs, he re-entered the gated door and went back up the passageway, taking the steps one at a time, climbing steadily until the steps ended and he followed the incline rising between the floors of the Vatican.

At a familiar door, Adrian slid his body between the tapestry that hid the entry and stepped through the wall directly into the pope's bedroom. Halbert, dressed for travel, jumped with surprise and grabbed the hilt of his dagger. The old man wore a forest green tunic, had at least two other knives in his belt, and was covered in perspiration.

"As soon as the sun goes down," he said to Halbert, who nodded. They looked at the door to the adjoining bedroom, waited for Johanna to come out.

In the bedroom Johanna had awakened from a long nap and was immediately aware that her illness was gone. She had never felt better. In her mirror she looked normal.

"You two should have left months ago," called Halbert, fretting at the door. "I could've followed."

"No," Johanna said smiling as she came into the main room. "We'll never do that again."

"You look...well," said Adrian.

"I am. I feel wonderful."

"Thank God," said Halbert. His daughter looked years younger, her skin clear and rosy and she had the smile she had worn when she was happiest.

Adrian stepped over and put his hands on her shoulders. "We must go right after sunset, when it is cooler, and dark. For your health."

"My health is not important," Johanna said. "But I know what is."

She went to the window. Outside was chaos. In the distance a band of looters ran up the stairs of a church while overhead the rising smoke of fires set by rioters sent ash into a dull gray sky. It broke her heart to see her city gone mad while she was pope. She felt responsible. Despite her exhaustive arguments and the outward appearance of authority, the real powers which had run the city for hundreds of years had beaten her. Now she was leaving. The poor, with no one except the ideal of the pope, would suffer most. The poor, she knew, always paid the highest price. They would pay hard when the pope vanished.

"Come and get ready, Johanna," said Adrian. "It's a gamble to even wait until dark."

He held a faded dress up to her, and smiled.

She put a hand to her mouth. It was her old favorite dress, the one he bought her and worn once long ago when they walked the streets as man and woman, undisguised, holding hands and kissing passionately, without fear, in view for all of Rome to see. Despite her gladness, she was about to protest that she would never fit into it in her condition, when he showed how the dress had been widen to fit her. She hugged Adrian.

"Father, bring the wagon to the western gate at dusk, to the little alley near the doors. I will meet you both there."

The men looked at her as if they had not heard right.

"Meet us?" said Adrian. "You are going with us. Now."

"I am going to perform mass at St. Peter's first and bless the people before we leave."

"Johanna, no!" said Halbert.

"No!" said Adrian.

"It will be the last time John is seen."

"The risk is too great, child," said Halbert.

"The risk is greater if I just vanish. The people, their misery is so harsh, father. Look at them. Murdered, robbed, their lives crushed. Listen to me, both of you. We go to safety, but they haven't got a choice. They need a small comfort from someone they believe in."

"Johanna, please," begged Adrian. "This small comfort will cost your life and the child's."

"Daughter. Johanna. We must leave together if you want to live!"

"I will be brief. Theodoric will be so glad to have me in public he will leave us alone. It will buy us time on the road. Tell Anastasias."

"Johanna, I am your father and I forbid it!"

"And as your husband --"

Even as the men stood in disbelief they saw the familiar determination on her mouth, the resolution in her eyes. Both stood over her in the chair. They pleaded; what good would this thankless gesture bring? Who would care? Think of the child. She expended no energy to refute their arguments but simply smiled at the two loves of her life, and took their hands in hers.

Debate was useless and, finally, they knew it. She would give a last gift for the poor and that was that. She could not remove the danger of invaders or pestilence, Johanna told them, she could only give herself.

"Go quickly," she said. "The city is falling."

She opened her arms to her father who hugged her and wept as if she were already lost. She patted his cheeks then tugged lightly on his left ear, the old signal when she was a little girl. Halbert remembered the gesture and cried harder. It was her signal for him to set her down from his shoulders, to let her walk on her own. She pulled his ear close.

"Remember what you told me the last time we parted?" she whispered. "That we will never truly be apart? I know it now in a way I could not then. Let me go. Let me act upon my heart. I love you. You have been the best father. We will be together always."

"I love you, my daughter, my child, my Johanna," he said. "God has seen us through so much. I cannot do anything but trust His wisdom."

He went to the hidden door Adrian used earlier and turned back to his daughter. Adrian knelt beside Johanna and held her gently around the stomach. She placed her hands over his head a long moment, ran her fingers through the curls of his hair.

She had known this beautiful creature as a boy and as a man. She saw again the arrogant young sailor on the ship with a noble carriage and a keen belief in himself. The earnest seeker of God walked beside her in the mountains and plains on the way to Rome. The romantic Adrian walked proudly with her, hand-in-hand when she wore his gift of the dress. He stood beside her Chair and supported her as she agonized over decisions.

He had done what no other man on earth had been able to do: let her be who she needed to be, and let go of things that were important to him for her sake. *He is my perfect mate, Lord*, she prayed. *You know how grateful I am for letting us be together.*

Johanna bent and kissed the top of his head.

Adrian rose, the front of her robes marked with the stain of his tears. They leaned into each other until they were face to face. They kissed, crying, lips to lips, eye to open eye. Adrian tried to speak, to put his love into words and his fear that he could not live without her if this gamble failed. It was not his heart but words that ultimately failed him. She put her hand over his mouth and looked into his eyes. She scanned every place in their blue depths, speaking to them with her own. No words were said, but Johanna nodded several times and acknowledged an unspoken communication that moved Adrian's heart to a deeper place than any human speech.

Finally, he turned and went to Halbert at the door. The men gazed upon her, unable to change her mind, unwilling to leave by their own accord.

"And you both think *I* am so stubborn!" she smiled, folding her arms in mock petulance. She pulled back the tapestry and opened the hidden door.

"I'll meet you at St. Peter's gate," she said. "Before the sun sets."

They had no choice. They looked back at her until the passageway turned and they finally had to leave her sight.

Johanna's heart could take no more and she had to stagger to the bed to sit down.

≈ ≈ ≈

Adrian and Halbert walked down the dark corridor and more than once had to stop to compose themselves. Halbert paused at a secret door that led into the main corridor.

"I forgot my traveling cloak, son," said Halbert. "I left it in the alcove here."

Halbert opened the bolted door and they exited into the bright corridor. A few steps along the marble floor, Halbert located his cloak hanging on a peg. They turned to go back to the passageway and heard heated voices argue around the corner. It was so intense father and son-in-law edged over and peeked around.

"The pope must know," said an old bishop, his fists clenched. A group of two bishops and three cardinals stood in the center of the corridor.

"The pope is sequestered with his lover and will not come out if Satan was at the gates of Rome," said a fat cardinal, his red robes stained from neck to waist with sweat.

Adrian grabbed Halbert's arm when they saw the source of the churchmen's debate. Laid out side-by-side on two pallets at the bottom of a grand marble staircase, surrounded by their weeping house slaves, were Senator Theodoric and his wife, Althea.

Their clothes were dark red, almost black, dried and clotted with blood, their throats cut to the bone. The faces of the powerful couple were unrecognizable. Their heads to the ends of their hair were caked in thickly coagulated red clumps.

"Look at the feet," Halbert said, pointing to the lengths of rope which bound their legs at the ankles. Halbert whispered his surmise that Theodoric and Althea had been hung by their feet from a tree or perhaps a high wall and left to drown in their own blood.

"Murdered," breathed Adrian. "Rome will surely fall over the edge when we leave and this becomes known."

So shocked they did not notice who was also there, calmly inspecting the victims.

Sergius stood behind the two pallets, his back to Adrian and Halbert.

"Assassins," hissed a bishop at Sergius' side. "The snakes are already crawling all over each other to get to the spoils."

"Another great sadness Rome must endure," said Sergius. He caught sight of a smudge of blood on his right sleeve and tucked the offender into the other.

"They were found an hour ago," said the bishop.

"That freshly killed?" said Sergius. "A shame. Two powerful, beautiful people. He was brilliant and she was, well, Althea was delicious."

The bishop looked at Sergius curiously for the remark, but the high ranking favorite of the senator and his wife evenly met his gaze. Movement caught Sergius' eye over the bishop's shoulder and he focused his attention on the far wall of the corridor. Two men unknown to him passed out of sight into an alcove. Their appearance struck Sergius as strange. They should not have been there. The younger man was dressed like a Vatican laborer and the older one dressed as a forest man. Yet he was left with such a powerful flourish of curiosity that Sergius left the bishops and followed them.

He walked several paces and stepped into the alcove. They had disappeared into the air, seemingly, as there was no other route out.

Sergius looked around the tapestries hung about the room for the door they'd taken to exit. There was none. He shrugged and was about to retrace his steps when he stopped, turned to the tapestry on the wall and, purely on a turn of mind, pulled back one corner.


Sergius came out of the dark corridor to the doorway of the courtyard. Peeking out from the shadows, he squinted into bright sunlight. The two men were at a covered wagon filled with supplies for a long journey. He tried to get a better look at the strangers who had moved through secret passages even he did not know about. He was surprised to find that door behind the tapestry, but more so at discovering an alley at the end of a dark passage where none was supposed to be.

Sergius blinked and tried to identify them. The younger man was not a common worker as he thought. It was clearly Cardinal Benedict, known as Adrian, the pope's confidante and most likely his lover. Their "brotherhood" was common knowledge; the two were inseparable. The information was less titillating than the gossips made it out to be since Sergius knew countless men of rank, including past pontiffs, who found comfort in the arms of their own sex. But why was the Cardinal dressed as a pauper? And who was that man with him? Another lover? Or was there a conspiracy gathering here?

"Please safeguard her, son," said Halbert. "I could not bear to lose her twice."

"Do not worry, Halbert. We'll all be well into the country by tonight."

"Thank you. Now, can you fill the gourds with water for the horses? I filled ours but forgot who was most important."

From his vantage Sergius watched the old man hug the cardinal and send him off. When Adrian left, Halbert's eyes filled with tears and he was overcome. The old man turned and faced partly in Sergius' direction.

Sergius felt as if he had taken a sharp blow. The left side of his mouth began to twitch as recognition struck him so hard he felt the sting of it across his face.

Johanna stood naked before the mirror, amazed. So undeniably a mother-to-be. She had removed her clothes and bathed herself from a basin to prepare for the mass. The sickness had receded and she was so thankful she felt well, so much better than normal. She felt...free. She reached for her papal robes a last time and as she did she froze.

From the corner of her eye she caught an image in the mirror. The image leered with a skeletal thinness, hands on either side of its face as if to keep it from exploding with emotion. Johanna wheeled away the mirror. Impossible, she told herself. It must be another trick of her sickness like her other fevered delusions. But this delusion came full into her vision even as she waited for it to disappear. It did not go away but stayed and licked its lips like a wolf whose dinner was laid out before it.

Sergius, mouth agape, stared at her naked body.

# CHAPTER XXXXI

SHE THREW THE robe in front of her and backed away trying to cover herself.

"How dare you!" Johanna screamed. "Leave me!"

"I cannot believe it," gulped Sergius, hands to his cheeks, his eyes all over her.

She saw him take in her body, his eyes flooded with revelation and every suspicion coming together in one great crash. The priest had to steady himself in the doorway.

"I said leave or I will call the guards and have them --"

"Have them what? Tell them what?"

She tried to pull the robe over her nakedness but only succeeded in exposing the swollen breasts and the high-carried mound of her extended belly.

Sergius laughed at the sight of her.

"Will you tell them a woman with child is pope? Oh, the gods. No prayers ever sent to them could match the treasure uncovered before me."

She turned and ran from the room and got to the door to the corridor. Anastasius would be close by and together they could subdue him and figure out what to do.

Johanna grabbed the handle, but before she could get it open Sergius stopped the door with his foot and easily pushed it closed. She backed up into a man-tall iron candle stand and nearly tripped on it.

"My sweet, sweet Johanna. You have come back from the dead to haunt me. And to save me," he said and reached for her. "Let me embrace you, my long lost lover."

She grabbed the frame of the heavy iron stand and tipped it over. Sergius had to stop its fall before it toppled on him. Johanna took the moment and ran through the nearest door. The effort tore at muscles in her lower stomach and the pain made her lightheaded as she hurried into the first room she found. Johanna was all the way at the rear of the pantry before she realized where she was. There was no exit. Sergius came at her, smiling. There was no weapon in sight and she was surrounded by sacks of grains, flour and vegetables. Serene, his demeanor almost humble, he took his time as he approached. Sergius removed a small dagger from the folds of his robe.

"I will call my guards!"

"Do what you like. However, they will be busy with Theodoric and Althea."

"Theodoric?"

"She was a beautiful woman who strayed too close to the ledge of desire. I am afraid she called my bluff in our last game this morning and, well...The senator would never let me live after what he found. He was not supposed to return so early. So I sent them off together. That was the right decision, was it not?"

"You killed them?"

"Their business in this life is finished. It is we who have something much more important to discuss. You must help me, dearest. Imagine my dilemma. Do I execute the impostor to the Chair and become the next pope for the deed?"

She was at the wall with nowhere to go and only a sack of flour beside her. Sergius leaned in within an arm's reach so that she could smell the wine on his breath.

"Or should I unmask the greatest fraud in the history of the church and be remembered forever? Which honor would you choose if you stood in my place?"

He extended his weaponless hand and his smile faded.

Sergius' mouth turned into a grimace and he bared his teeth, the pretense of humility gone. He grabbed for her neck to bring her face-to-face with him.

She ducked, reached into the barrel and threw a fist full of flour in his face. He bolted upright and choked, his face a powdery cloud. In the instant he reacted she leaned forward and pushed the priest over a sack of wheat. She ran from the pantry.

*The Woman Pope*

She had to find a weapon or die.

Johanna raced into the kitchen looking in cupboards, shelves. Nothing. She searched the room. Sergius was about to emerge, she heard him cough and spit out the flour.

She caught the glint of a knife's blade on the side table and went to it. She reached for the handle and was suddenly scorched with a fiery sting. She pulled her hand away and saw the back of it had been slashed, but so expertly as to barely break the skin. She covered the wound with her other hand and saw Sergius standing beside her, a white-faced ghost, dagger in hand.

"Johanna, my Johanna," he said as if they were on a leisurely stroll. "It is like that night aboard ship. That was a night, was it not? Though you left before the celebration. I took, well, I believe more than a dozen men and women joined you in the ocean that night. For your sins. They did not survive as you have. Did you know that? I have carried the scars from that night all these years. The pain you caused has served me well."

She picked up a rag from the table and tied it around the cut. To her surprise, Sergius did not lunge at her but instead moved away from the door and, inexplicably, gave her a point of exit by stepping to the table and pouring two glasses of wine from a thin flask taken from his robes. He lifted one glass and faced her.

"Join me?" he asked. Painted white by the flour he was a death frost, the blanched mask washed his features until only the reddish skin around his eyes was visible.

"You murderer. You thief of life."

"Flower, we must not fight. Today we celebrate," he said and raised the glass. "To you, Johanna, who unmanned me and who is now by me unmanned."

He laughed at his joke then sipped, unconcerned when she ran from the room.

The pain in her stomach slowed her and before she got half way across the sprawling chamber room she was grabbed from behind by her hair.

Sergius yanked it without emotion, her head jerked back and she cried out. He pulled her, the crook of his arm around her neck and the blade of his knife to her throat.

He walked her across the chamber to the double doors that led outside.

"What god can I give thanks to for this triumph?"

They passed her crozier on its stand, its heavy casing and jewels restored after the battle. Sergius tucked the knife into his belt, picked up the crozier and carried it with him.

"What deity brought me the one person I have thought about and wept over for years?" he asked. His voice dropped. "There is none. No god would *dare* answer the prayers I have prayed."

He guided her outside. They came out onto the rooftop, a lush garden area five stories above the city.

Theodoric and Althea dead. Two of his enemies gone. Now, to have the pope who ruined him turn out to be the girl who so deeply scarred his manhood, to have her in his grasp, it was too much to have hoped for. He had to fight back tears.

Near the edge of the building, Sergius swept his hand out over the vista of Rome.

"Johanna. Look upon this city. Plague, hunger, hopelessness. This has been your reign. Today you relinquish it to me on this, the sweetest day of my life."

He edged her forward, pushed her into the waist-high railing at the edge of the roof. She used both hands to brace against him and keep her swollen belly from being dug into the thin metal slats. The rickety fence, meant as decoration and not a barrier, wobbled against their weight and was the only thing between her and a five story fall.

"You. A woman, *nothing*, yet you rose beyond me," he said. "I will always remember you, and I swear you will remember me. You will beg for my mercy as I introduce to you a death far more exquisite than the one I gave Theodoric and his wife."

He pressed her again into the railing and raised the crozier overhead in a victorious wave. With his gesture Sergius proclaimed himself the new owner of the crozier. He shook the heavy rod over his head and over the woman pope. With his other hand Sergius took the dagger and steadied the blade on the flesh beneath her chin.

Every humiliation flashed before him: His genitals mutilated by her hand. The scorn suffered in front of Pope Leo. Torture at the hands of peasants. Years in misery with the dead before Gaetani's sacrifice. Those images moved as one continuous scene, driven before him by the galloping chariot of memory.

He realized he held the knife to the chariot driver's throat.

In a flash his blood heated with an idea. It charged through his brain, boiled his blood and surged into his scarred shaft. An erection was released with a hardness he had not experienced for so long the sudden swelling frightened him. The blood rushed through his withered glands and pounded with insistence at Johanna's backside.

Sergius knew exactly what he was going to do.

"Yes, we will consummate the exchange of power with an intimate ceremony."

He set the crozier against the rail with one hand, keeping the knife to her skin, then pulled the back of her robe up and exposed her buttocks. He noted it was rounded by pregnancy but still as firm as the rest of her body. Sergius took the dagger from her chin and placed it on the neckline of her thin robe.

Johanna said a quick praise to God and waited for the blade to pierce her.

In one long expert slice, Sergius cut down through the material and ripped the entire robe in half. He pulled it away and Johanna spun around, completely naked before him once again. He stared at the swollen ball where a flat stomach had been. He took a half step back, then pulled the knot of his satin sash loose and opened the front of his robe.

"Look at me," he smiled, his hand on her neck. "Look upon your good work."

His penis hung before her, lifting itself away from his leg. Its ropy veins bulged, band despite its deformity it rose, engorged.

Johanna could only stare and hold her stomach. Sergius turned her away to the railing. He placed himself along the crease of her backside. With his foot Sergius kicked her left leg to one side, forcing Johanna to spread her legs as she held onto the rail while she focused her remaining strength on keeping the unborn child from being crushed between the bars.

Johanna knew his intent. For a moment she thought this rape might be a blessing in disguise. For no matter the unbearable disgust and violation, it would at least give her a few precious minutes to plan while he took his anger out on her flesh.

But as she felt his hardness pushing against her, the truth of who he was struck with a cold clarity. His design was clear in the way he touched her.

In that instant, Johanna of Mainz lost all hope.

She felt the knife against her throat as Sergius positioned himself. Johanna felt herself go dizzy with a fizzing whiteness and had to breathe through her mouth in gulps to keep from losing consciousness. He was going to sodomize her at the same time he murdered her.

"Flower, what do we have here?" he panted. "I believe I've found a place no man has been. And I've found my home, Johanna. Take me in. Open for me alone."

Sergius was going to cut her throat while he ripped her insides at the same time.

"This is how you will remember me," he said in her ear, his chest to her back. "I will still be taking you long after you have left this life."

Her life would end and he would spill his triumphant abuse into her corpse, humiliating her both in life and in death. It was the perfect manifestation of his most perfect moment.

So excited by the genius of his plan he could not swallow but kept panting and licking his lips like an animal that smells blood.

"Call to your people. Call out the truth as you die. Tell them you are mine. Tell them my little flower dies a second time," he said trying to work himself into her. "Tell them this time she dies for me!"

She braced herself at the rail and put her hand on the crozier as she sucked in breath. She felt the pressure of him and prayed to God to let the end come soon.

"Yes! Slowly, love, slowly! You must feel everything before you die. No, no, welcome me at the door," he said, and pushed.

She was so panic-stricken she could not summon the calm needed to bring the Spirit to her. She gripped the top of the crozier and called out as Sergius forced himself into her.

"Lord God!"

"Scream, Johanna! Call to Him! He is with us! Take me into you and He will answer! You will finally see Him!"

Bent behind her, hunching his pelvis, his lips at her ear, Johanna gripped the crozier and slid her hand down several inches. The texture of its gilded sides crept along her fingertips through her arm and up to her brain where in the midst of panic it finally registered. Johanna looked up, took a breath and gripped the crozier just below the crook.

She let out a scream that made Sergius flinch with surprise.

She was not going to die without taking this demon with her.

Johanna yanked the jeweled staff with all her might. The heavy staff struck the side of his head and Johanna heard the thump. The blow threw him off. He tried to slash his knife but she dropped to her knees before his hand could draw the knife across her throat.

He stumbled back two steps.

Sergius reached out and got the fingers of one hand around the crozier. But she held fast and pulled the staff out of his grasp as he slashed down again with the knife. The blade grazed her right breast and drew blood but Johanna got it away and took back control of the crozier.

She held it cross-wise from her chest like the staffs she had used long ago. Sergius bared his teeth and lunged at her belly with the knife. Johanna lurched forward at the same time and slammed the crozier down onto his hand. The precious stones on its crown ripped into skin and bone. Sergius screamed, his hand filled with an unbelievable pain.

Johanna stepped back and held onto the railing for support. The blood from the thin cut on her throat ran down her neck and merged with the blood on her grazed breast. She looked at this man who had doggedly tried to kill everything of value in her life. He had afflicted every part of her for so long it was impossible to remember a time without a bitter memory of him. His face wore the same expression as when he stood on the deck about to cut her in half with a broadsword. The servants aboard ship, the adolescent girl, all the serfs and families he maimed or killed came together in a vision of pain floating above his head, the violence of his life a dark halo.

"Broken!" he cried. He was a man like no other she had ever known, a force without a soul driven by cruel desires, guided without conscience or remorse, in perfect at-one-ment with evil.

"Sergius," she said, soft. "Let me return to you what you so love."

She stepped into him, fully cognizant of higher voices from inside that were loudly calling out to her. But she refused to listen and whirled the crozier.

The solid metal bar cracked the side of his head with such force it dropped him to the rooftop floor. He held his bleeding temple and began rolling and kicking. The pain was so intense he could not remain still, but had to stand, stomp his feet, and scream as he turned around and around. Johanna brought the crozier up over her shoulder.

"In the name of my father, who's heart you broke open and filled with years of misery."

She swung and landed a blow on the other side of his head.

The sound of a dull, thick contact, then his head whipped to one side. He reeled, wobbled on his feet and fell to his knees. He tried to stand. Twice he tried. Three times he struggled, slipped on his blood. He crawled to the rail and grasped the unsteady bars. Sergius pulled himself up and draped himself across the waist-high bars, his left hand still clinging to the knife. He raised his head and looked at her.

"In the name of the sons, whose mothers and sisters you have defiled with your touch," she said and swung again, this time for the center of his face. His head smashed against the rail and his nose flattened to the side of his face. The entire front row of his teeth were broken and clattered to the floor of the balcony along with a hail of jewels knocked out of the crozier.

Johanna stood over him and watched the priest struggle with his agony. Rivulets of blood ran down his face creating bizarre patterns against the white flour mask. He took hold of his nose and pulled it with a gristly snap back to its original position so he could breathe through it again.

The skin of his cheeks had been peeled back like bark of a tree. Instead of looking like an adult man, his age fell away and he looked like the child of some terrible disease. His braided chin whiskers, once white and exotic, were dyed red from blood.

Johanna started to swing again, but stopped.

The sight of him caught her off guard. His hideousness found the place she had been trying to conceal until she was finished. Try as she could to hide it, his torn face found her compassion.

She looked at him with a double sorrow. Sorrow for his condition and sorrow for her inability to be truly Christ-like and turn away from the violence she surrendered to. Did he really not deserve mercy? He had finally been savaged and could not do anything else. He was finished.

"Forgive me, Sergius. God Almighty, have mercy on us both."

She let the crozier drop and walked away.

She would escape the city with Adrian and her father, sneak away in the wagon, she thought as she went toward the door. They would sail from the coast and find comfort in the monastery with the good brothers. They would work, debate, grow vegetables, pray at vespers and she would make absolutely sure their child would never know the emptiness of compromise or the depths of regret she had found herself cast herself into.

Johanna limped across the rooftop.

"Would you let a man die without confessing his sins?"

She slowed but did not stop, then turned to look at him over her shoulder. He was on his knees, one arm on the rail and the other pressed to his face. He ran his tongue over the blood on his lips, his eyes riveted on her. She could see the thrill of the taste in his eyes. He seemed to revel in his pain. He crooked his finger to summon her as he leaned against the rail.

This bloody work was helpless, she told herself. She watched the unrecognizable face, jaw limp and broken, and his gaping mouth a dark hole with stumps of teeth. She should walk away. She should walk away. She knew beyond all else in her brain that she should walk away.

Johanna did not.

She approached, warily. His struggle to breathe in ragged panting breaths was proof that Sergius had only enough time left to whisper a last confession or, more likely, a curse. She picked up the crozier and, using it as a crutch, hobbled over and leaned on the staff.

"Confess, brother. There is still time."

"Closer, Johanna," he gasped, coughing blood and trying not to move his broken jaw. "Hear me. There is no more after this."

Johanna bent to listen with her right arm tucked under a swollen belly. She looked into his eyes and saw that, despite his misery, his eyes were all over her, excited by her bloodied naked body, pregnant, out in the open under the light of day. Everything about her excited him, the enlarged pink nipples, the curve of belly. All of it streaked in red. Seriously injured and still he ogled her. She became incensed and started to turn from him, when he suddenly hissed, raised the knife he had managed to hold onto all this time and reached out a long, arcing arm.

The blade cut across the distance between them and aimed at the center of her left eye. But as his arm came next to her head she held up the crozier, ready for his trick. It blocked his feeble jab and knocked it out of his hand, but the force made her stumble. Right into his arms.

Johanna fell forward into him at the rail. They were face-to-face, she on her knees pressed against him, Sergius weakly pushing back while pinned to the rail. The whole side of the flimsy railing creaked and squealed under the strain, and bent dangerously over the side of the roof.

Johanna and Sergius stopped the struggle. They knew it was about to give way. They gazed at each other. For the first time since she had known him, Johanna saw fear in his eyes. He blinked once with apprehension and then the rail parted and gave way at his back.

The entire front portion of rail tore away from the rooftop and dropped over the ledge. It clattered along the wall as it fell five stories to the ground.

Sergius was tipped backwards over the edge. He reached his arms out to grab Johanna, fingers grasping to stop his fall. He never took his eyes off her as she reached out. But not for his hand. She grabbed first thing she could; the long white rope of his chin whiskers. And stopped his fall.

It took all her strength but she held him in place. He leaned awkwardly back over the edge, only half his body and the length of his braided beard kept him from thin air.

"Pull," he hissed. His neck stretched forward while his backside hung over the balcony edge, arms held out from his side.

She tried to lean back but despite his skinny frame his weight was too much.

"I...I...can't," Johanna panted. "I can't! I'm sorry!"

She grabbed the braid with both hands, but felt herself pulled forward over the edge.

"Then come with me!" he screamed, and his arm reached out to take her with him. But the only thing he was able to snatch was the braid from her hands.

The moment he took hold of his own whiskers the mistake registered.

For a split second he hung in the air, then Sergius fell.

He sailed down five stories to the street with half an arm's length of braided beard whipping above his head like the red tail of a kite.

Sergius lived inside an extended moment, much like Johanna's long fall from ship to the sea. In his mind he pumped away behind her, hands around her belly, squeezing with all his might, gleefully watched the agony on Johanna's face, her head tilted up, lips stretched back to their limit. Sergius felt his lust rise to fullness in his penis and it gave him strength to penetrate her again and again until he felt his loins finally...

His body met the stone street head first.

The force on his skull sent a starburst of blood in every direction for several paces. A thin sheet of blood and bits of his brain splashed the ground, the walls and two old women walking by, and threw a red spray over them. So used to the violence in the city the black-clad grandmothers did not cringe. Instead, they angrily stepped up to the dead man who lay exposed to the waist, his skull mashed in, yet somehow retained a full erection at his death. They spat on and cursed him for ruining their dresses despite the fact that most of the contents of his head had been strewn onto the street. One grandmother wiped her shoe on his chest. Then the women walked away careful to avoid the splatters on the street.

Johanna stared down at the scene for several moments. A sharp pain struck and she cringed. Johanna looked down: A puddle formed at her feet.

"He tormented everyone, Heavenly Father! Murderer! Torturer!" she shook her fists at the sky. "He is repaid by my hand! I took justice for all who could not!"

Johanna, exhausted, sat on the roof ledge.

"Lord God. I have lost what I have sought most; Your path. I've wandered farther from You the more I seek to find You."

Remorse spread across her face and filled her body.

"I have searched. For my father, for my lover. Searched for myself. And lost You along the way. Forgive me for that. Forgive my proud and reckless life."

Sounds of shouting reached her. The discovery of Sergius' body drew a horrified crowd around the fallen saint.

"He saved the pope and then gave his own life," she heard someone say.

"He's a martyr to Rome, to the church."

Johanna turned from the voices, rested her head on the roof floor, and prayed. She waited for an answer and in the silence closed her eyes and slipped into a restful peace. The contractions stopped. Johanna again felt better than she had in months.

She felt a breeze. It cooled the air and the sudden change in temperature blew the humidity from the rooftop. With her eyes still closed she reached up toward the sky.

# CHAPTER XXXXII

WHEN SHE OPENED her eyes she found she was returned to a painful world. She stood and leaned unsteadily on the crozier. Johanna forced herself to walk across the rooftop, bruised, naked and feeling wetness run down her legs.

She sat at her wardrobe and cleaned off blood. She stained four bowls of water, then bound her cuts. She put on the simplest robe of her office, plus a wide brimmed papal hat to conceal her face. Johanna went to the door and called Anastasius.

When he saw her the young assistant was appalled.

"Now is not the time show yourself. Not like this."

He pleaded for her to rest but she insisted he give the signal for the procession to St. Peter's. He did so reluctantly, then returned to help Johanna to the Vatican entrance.

Descending the stairs Johanna looked out on the crowd being kept at bay. The surge of an oncoming contraction made her lean on Anastasius but at the same time she was refreshed by the usually cool breeze that continued to blow throughout the city.

It was suddenly clear to Johanna how much she had experienced. Not only cruelty but wonder, loss and enlightenment, despair, grief and anguish as well as revelation, fulfillment, hatred, pettiness, longing, love and power. She had not only experienced good and evil but at some point along the way had been both. *What have I not known?* she asked herself as she gave out her blessing to the hordes near the Vatican steps. Was there not a sensation, emotion or feeling she had not gone through and learned from? What more could a Creator bestow upon His created?

It was then that she felt the breeze dry up. The air became still once more.

The frenzied pitch of the people on the street was such that a nervous Anastasius spoke to the army General Moldavus, the commander Johanna had made deliver a baby years before and who now ordered the papal guards to surround the pope.

Moldavus and Anastasius stood at the top of the Vatican steps and watched the pope ride the donkey into the crowd. The animal was her gesture to the people that, though pope she was as they were in that no matter the spiritual powers she had, she was one of theirs.

The pope signaled and the procession waded tentatively into the masses, citizens amazed that the rumor of their guardian was true. News had spread that John Anglicus was among them once again. He had come back from the precipice of mortal illness to dispel the demons torturing the city. The squares and boulevards were filled to overflowing with residents trying to get a glimpse of the pope. Many cried out, waved and begged to be reassured they would be saved from evil. Townspeople climbed over walls and hung off rooftops, called and whistled at the sight of John the English.

Anastasius saw apprehension in the general's eyes. The general gazed up at a sky almost white with a thick haze, the blue squeezed out of it. The odd cool breeze had died away as suddenly as it sprang up and the stultifying humidity crept back into the air. Moldavus called to the captain of Theodoric's personal bodyguards.

"Bring my carriage around to the back," he said, and the man saluted and left. Anastasius could not believe it.

"You are not leaving, are you, General?"

Anger flashed in Moldavus' eyes at the insignificant monk who dared question him. They looked at one another knowing there was going to be trouble today and knowing the general was about to take the easy way out.

"I will be back."

*The Woman Pope*

"To clean up the mess and take glory for doing so?" asked Anastasius. The general thought to grab the insolent but perceptive monk by the neck and squeeze until the young man's eyes burst, but instead walked away.

Anastasius hurried down the steps after his spiritual master, Pope John Anglicus.

≈ ≈ ≈

"Halbert, hurry to the gates," said Adrian and handed him the reigns of the carriage. He could not wait another minute and got off the moving wagon and untied one of the horses.

"No, Adrian! We cannot separate now! She'll be here soon."

"I cannot leave her alone. If anything happens I can help."

"You cannot get through that mob, son."

Adrian reached into the wagon and withdrew his red cloak.

"They'll part for a cardinal," he said and threw it around his shoulders.

The horses stamped and snorted, sensing tension in the air and hearing the noise rising on the streets. The men did not speak but their fears passed between them.

"She is gone, isn't she?" asked Halbert, his voice small as a child's.

"As I've often heard you say," Adrian replied. "Judge nothing until the end."

"I borrowed that from the wise St. Augustine," said Halbert.

"Go," Adrian said, mounting his horse. "If I do not come back with her you'll have to get to the coast on your own."

"Adrian."

"And do not look back," he yelled. Adrian put the horse to a gallop and rounded the corner of the courtyard.

≈ ≈ ≈

The pope fell from the donkey.

The mother and daughter followed.

The cardinal carried the fallen pope.

And like every moment, every hour, like every year since that day,

It all happened in the blink of an eye.

≈ ≈ ≈

"Adrian," cried Johanna.

He tripped on a body sprawled in the road and they fell to the ground. They looked up and saw the street blocked by delirious thousands. The fall hurt her belly so bad she knew she could move no farther.

"Johanna," he said. "I'm here and will not leave, my love."

She felt his love as he kissed her cheek and stroked her hair. His caring for her in spite of his own fear made her feel better. Johanna sighed and took his hand from her brow and kissed his palm. He smiled. In spite of it all, her lips felt so gentle on his palm.

"Adrian."

The contractions began in earnest. Her eyes widened and she clutched hard at Adrian's collar.

"I am here," he said.

"It's coming. Help me, oh God, help me, please."

She reached her hands beneath her robes and Adrian's followed. A final yell and she pushed with all her might.

The crowd closest to them watched in confusion. The past year the city had lost everything to pestilence and plagues. They had pleaded for the pope to save them but nothing helped. And now what was this?

The mob hushed each other and strained to see what was happening.

"Look what the pope brings forth," said a man who stood before Johanna and Adrian. He began to yank his hair until only a few wispy strands blew about his bloody head.

The crowd swelled forward in a tide unable to believe what their eyes witnessed as they stood transfixed on Pope John VIII.

Mouths hung open, speechless. Thousands of eyes bulged, staring.

Johanna lay with her back against the wall, her hands on her knees. Panting, her eyes locked onto Adrian who knelt between her legs, arms beneath her robes.

There was no one else, no place else on earth and no need to escape. The dust and humidity evaporated and the buzzing flies and flying grasshoppers vanished. Shouts gave way to a hushed calm. Johanna clasped Adrian's arms and the destination of their journey was now in clear sight. Despite the years they had walked together, passing through cruelty, blood, ignorance, hatred, betrayal, all the greed and evil from the world of man it was always love that drove the engine of their hearts. It was what carried them to this spot and to this day and this moment. The world fell away and for a moment they were alone.

Adrian, freed of everything, thought how perfect it was to be here with his wife. He looked up and smiled. Johanna returned his smile, weak and pained as it was. Adrian thought back, remembered the first moment he had seen her. A girl of sixteen furiously fending off the crude hands of sailors hauling her up the side of a ship. His heart fluttered at the sight of her, the long hair whipping around her head as she fought and her strength as she kicked at her tormentors, eyes flashing intelligence and passion.

Johanna fighting, embattled, striving. It was who she had always been.

The girlish laugh and her luminous smile flashed when the wave washed him across the deck, and ignited his heart. He felt their first kiss again, her lips solidly pressed against his. He recalled the devastation of their parting, the memory of Johanna in his arms once more after the miracle of their reunion. He remembered the first touch of her breasts and their forbidden thrill. In bed as man and wife years later they laughed about it.

Adrian had known on the ship he would never meet another woman like her. Across a continent and the years there was not one person who came even close. Adrian had watched her perform miracles, turn rabid barbarians into gentle seekers who followed her across the known world. She built her own city when Rome turned her away, dealt with the powerful as if they were less than peasants, and treated the sick and the hopeless as if they were the rightful sovereigns of the kingdom of earth.

Adrian looked across at his love, breathing hard though the strain was not enough to completely drown the smile of her accomplishment.

She was a mother.


The crowded street recoiled at the sight, astounded. After a moment's silence, the Pope was heard to groan. Then came a tiny wail. The sound of life rose above the stillness.

"Shhh, babe. We are almost home. Adrian, he's beautiful," said the Pope, holding the newborn.

Adrian bent and kissed the baby's wet, fluid-covered head. He saw the cord disappear between Johanna's legs and took the dagger from his belt while he held onto the flesh. He waited for the pulse to fade before he hastily tied and cut the cord as he had seen Johanna do many times.

"He is so beautiful, a little miracle. Oh, I love you, Johanna, I love you both," said Adrian, touching them.

He felt the crowd surge toward his back and Adrian suddenly stood up.

He slashed the dagger at the crowd to hold them back and noticed a woman and her four-year-old child were beside him pushing at the crowd. A mother and her child were their only allies.

"Get back!" he yelled, waving the dagger.

"The pope is a woman!" a man screamed, pointing. His face and arms were bloody stripes from his fingernails used to gouge his skin to release his sinful thoughts. "She has tricked God Himself!"

The blur of grimaces and moving arms and legs in the crowd around them suddenly came into Adrian's sharp focus. There was a candle shopkeeper wearing his apron, a dandified clerk in his ink-splattered tunic, a skinny wife of a ragman, a thief-turned-beggar with no right arm and no left hand, a lascivious bathhouse attendant, a fat fruit seller, a bricklayer, messenger, landlord, field hand, horse groomer, butcher, tailor, seamstress, maid, whore, cobbler, tanner, fuller, smithy, thief, idiot, jongleur and a thousand others. Every image Adrian gazed upon was breathtakingly clear and frozen in place, just before they all exploded at the same moment, driven by a single purpose in the presence of such profane sorcery.

Every person crowded along the little street who witnessed the event went completely and utterly mad.

Rakes, staffs, stones, arms, voices and fists began to fly, creating a dusty whirlwind. Adrian fought with a fury that sent the first wave of the mob back. A metal rake swung down at him and Adrian caught it. He pulled it from the stableman's hands and struck the man across the knees, sending him to the ground, screaming. Adrian whirled the rake around his head and clubbed and gouged anyone within reach to keep them from Johanna and the babe. He butted a woman on the side of her head, cracked a stick-wielding arm, ran the rake down a man's face and jabbed a knife-wielding butcher in the throat. Adrian's fury matched the insanity converging on him. He struck and maimed and sent a dozen men and women to their deaths and did not stop even as the crowd pressed in to try and kill his family.

Suddenly, he felt a pain burst through his back with such violence that it took his breath away.

Adrian looked down at himself. The long blade of a curved harvesting scythe dug all the way through his back and the sharpened tip poked out of his stomach.

There was a collective gasp from the crowd.

Everyone quieted as they waited for his reaction. This powerful warlock who had fended off so many, why, he might pull the blade out and call demons down into the crowd. He might laugh at the attempt to wound him and curse the people for their pitiful strike against the forces of hell before he cast a final spell and destroyed them one and all.

But Adrian looked around, his pale blue eyes dazed as he tried to focus on each person in front him. A red foamy dribble formed at the corner of his mouth.

"Adrian, I love you," said Johanna. Her voice was not desperate, but was firm, assured.

"What?"

"Look at me, Adrian," she said. "Forget about them. Forget the madness around you. Adrian, look at *me*."

Adrian's head jerked around and he kept blinking and squinting until he was able to focus. Johanna, with her back against the wall at the corner of the street a few paces from Adrian, held their wet and crying son.

"We will meet you there," she said. "Do you hear me? It's alright, you can go. We will meet you there."

"Johanna," he began.

"Shhhh. Go. We are right beside you."

Adrian opened his mouth, then nodded. He had been given permission to let go of the struggle. Adrian dropped to his knees with a bewildered look on his face. He reached his hand out to Johanna and their newborn and fell forward into the dirt. She reached out for him, smiling. He reached for her and fell forward. He landed on his face in the dirt, dead.

Anastasius suddenly broke through the crowd. Johanna saw the young man was about to join the mob, lose all logical contents of his mind and go mad with them.

"Anastasius! Brother, take the baby," she yelled at the overwhelmed monk. He stood there with the crowd, staring at this impossible blasphemy come alive on the street. "I said take the baby *now,* brother!"

The sound of her voice snapped Anastasius back. He looked upon his master, the pope, who was a woman, a mother, and could only gape like the others.

"I said take the child and quickly, Anastasius! Here!" she said and held the baby out. Her command was enough for him to react and he took the infant from her but his eyes never left Johanna. "Go, take care of my son, my good brother. Run."

He looked down at the baby who gripped his finger with a tiny fist. The monk noted the back of the infant's hand had a large, wine-stain birth mark. When he looked back at Johanna it was to do the only thing he could do at that moment. He obeyed.

He pushed his way through the crowd whose eyes were focused singly on the harlot from the book of revelation. The

　　　　　　　　　　　　*The Woman Pope*

whore of Babylon had taken the shape of the pope and not only cursed the Eternal City, but had caused the commencement of Judgment Day.

The permission given to Adrian and Anastasius was the permission the mob also needed. They leapt upon the creature and her dead consort and went at them like the grasping talons of a swooping bird of prey.

≈ ≈ ≈

In the narrow alley Halbert pricked up his ears.

Noise so wild and deranged sprang up that he shivered at its ferocity. He waited at their pre-arranged spot near the western gate but with the outcry he could stand it no longer. He hopped down from the wagon and ran.

Tears running down his face, Halbert fought his way through a crush of people, knocking them out of his way with his fists and yanking others to one side by their hair. They were not people at all but rabid animals. As Halbert struck blows to part the crowd, he saw Johanna's loyal assistant, Anastasius, push his way in the opposite direction holding the bloody robe of a cardinal. Halbert slowed his pace knowing he must be close and looked at the fury ahead of him. He could not believe it.

Moving through the frenzied crowd he passed blood-stained hands waving shreds of garments over their heads. The owners of the red flags were screaming at and beating one another and speaking in a single incoherent voice.

Halbert pulled one screaming man aside. He took the man's closed hand, pried it open and recognized the cloth in his bloody hand as a shred of the pope's robe. Halbert smashed his fist into the man's mouth, sending him to the ground.

Holding the strip of cloth Halbert screamed with the others. He lost himself and simply stood and wailed, his voice mingling with a roar that filled the entire city.

Beside him in the sweating melee was a rug dealer who beat a dead man with a brick. Next to him a beautiful high-born woman with tangled golden hair wearing a green silky dress splattered with blood, on her knees with her hands around the throat of an unconscious man who had been clubbed and trampled. The smell of fresh blood and tens of thousands of mashed grasshoppers was so thick the odor seemed to eat the oxygen from the air. The crowd had gone into a massive, all-consuming blood-lust, a frenzy to make something, anything pay for the unrelenting tide of misfortune which had so long chewed their city, their lives and their souls.

One group of Romans was in front of the narrow wall near the corner of the street. Their faces and arms and hair were stained a deep red and this group of twenty or more men and women were rooted in place shrieking at the sky, driven completely insane by what they had witnessed and what they had done.

Halbert stopped in the middle of the chaos and shook his head, trying to pull himself out of the choir of madness. He took hold of the skin on his left eyebrow between his fingers and pinched. He squeezed so hard it brought more tears streaming down his eyes but the pain brought him back to his senses. He turned around and around lost and alone in the turbulence. Then Halbert pushed his way forward through the moving arms and legs to the wall at the corner of the narrow street.

At its junction was a dust-covered white wall splashed in stripes of blood. The blood ran along the ground to the corner and went from top to bottom and ran out into the road itself. Halbert knew this was the place. The place where the journey ended.

There was nothing left. Nothing where his daughter and son-in-law should have been. Only the scuffling of demented feet on dirt turning black with blood.

Halbert dropped to his knees in the midst of it all and began to pray. For several minutes he was left untouched by the dementia around him.

His heart stripped bare, the old pagan called out to his Johanna's God.

Halbert stopped asking why, for it was too much and too late for an answer. He left all thoughts of his daughter and focused on the unfathomable Creator of all things and it made him calm. His prayers brought him back to who he was from the time he was a boy; a seeker and a lover of wisdom and the praises he sent to the god Jehovah centered him.

"Thank you, Lord of my child," Halbert whispered.

He looked up with a soft smile aimed at the haze-whitened sky. A man stumbled over him and fell to the ground beside Halbert in a fit of heaving convulsions brought on from an egg-sized stone lodged in his eye socket.

Moments later arms, sticks, clubs, ropes, knives, hammers, blades, rocks, bricks and the raging whirlwind of a city that had lost all faith rolled over Halbert. A human tornado, snarling and insane with grief blew over and buried the praying man beneath its wrath.

# EPILOGUE

NEARLY SEVEN CENTURIES later, on the same narrow and unremarkable street, most Romans unknowingly walked passed the crumbling wall where Johanna and her family perished.

On a cool but still humid morning in mid-September, 1644, a traveler from Sweden, Lawrence Banck, stood on the same spot. The young man looked around for some clue. He knew it could not be the statue that many had whispered was pope and child. What he looked upon was the Virgin and baby Christ, was it not? He stared at the statue, hoping it would reveal a secret. True, there was no halo of divinity around the child, and the mother did not appear like other Madonnas, but it was similar enough to the thousand others around Rome that it was impossible to grasp a different message.

Finally, he gave up and dropped the flowers near the nondescript wall. He crossed himself and hurried away, over to a crowded St. Peter's, blending in with the other anxious worshipers flowing into the doors from the street.

Inside, as an invited guest, he marveled at a private ceremony which had just begun.

It was not the coronation itself, but an important ceremony that had been performed now for hundreds of years. A line of cardinals waited at the bottom of a high platform where steep steps led up to a red marble chair. The new pope, Innocent X, walked up the steps to the throne-like seat. The chair was unusual in that it was pierced through the middle. Like a commode, it had no center.

The pope-elect got to the top of the steps, turned to his brethren, who were now literally and figuratively lower than him in the church hierarchy. After a terse silence in which the new pope seemed to glare at each man in the hall, he lifted the hem of his robes over the edge of the chair and sat. This was the signal for the churchmen waiting beside the platform. In a single file they passed beneath the chair.

Directly under the raised platform, head bowed into praying hands, he glanced straight up, crossed himself and passed on for the next to view. Each cardinal stepped under and inspected the exposed genitalia of the seated pope-elect. Satisfied the prince of the wise had the requisite equipment, they crossed themselves and moved on.

After his turn, one of the cardinals stepped away from the line and hurried out from under the platform and whispered to a waiting priest. This priest gave a signal to yet another priest in a doorway at the end of a long corridor. The man nodded, slipped inside and gave order to the monks who stood manning the signal fire and the bird cages.

From a corner of the rooftop of the Vatican, a white plume of smoke suddenly appeared. Then, to the delight of cheering crowds below, white doves were released into the sky. All who saw it breathed a sigh of relief, assured of the continuity of the Chair and of the protection it bestowed upon the city.

Inside St. Peter's, the line of churchmen continued under the chair. The new pope stared ahead, visibly disturbed, trying to maintain a sense of dignity while dressed in heavy bejeweled finery, wearing the three-tiered cone tiara and holding the holy crozier, the staff shaped as a shepherd's hook, as the spiritual shepherd he was elected to be.

The new pope believed, as did most others, that the reason for the ceremony had long been lost. The idea that the Vicar of Christ could ever be anything but a man was just an old argument to keep a useless ritual alive. Many of the elders could not explain why, as part of the election process, they had to look upon the genitals of the pope-elect. There was nothing written about this in the scriptures, nothing in any of the teachings of the church to indicate such a prescription. Quietly, internal petitions had been circulated to have the ceremony withdrawn.

It was argued the ceremony was an obscene act of pure humiliation for those beneath, shaming the men whose powers were being eclipsed by the one sitting above. It was argued back that the exposure of the elected one's privates insured a small, if momentary, humbling of His Holiness. The memory of his manhood being inspected and inwardly gauged by subordinates would come to mind with every witness who had an audience with him.

Every time the argument against the ceremony reappeared over the years, its purpose had to be invoked by the select few whose job was to guard the memory. These keepers of the secret quietly took their brothers aside and told them about an incredible sacrilege that took place long ago. An unforgivable event, though cloudy and contradictory, was still in the thoughts of many. They reminded those who would disband the ceremony of the sacrilege in the form of the bust of *Popessa Iovanna*, Pope Joan, hanging in the hall of popes. Despite being given another pope's name, her feminine face was unmistakable as it looked down as prominently as any other pope in the hall.

The elders also disparaged the statue of woman pope and child erected without their consent near the site of the carnage, even though the official description was that of the Madonna and Child. It was not enough to quash the whispers feeding the city's hunger for myth and legend.

Forgotten by most clergy, the name of the woman pope was kept alive mostly by women. Her memory was as strong and as subterranean as the rites, dates and beliefs of the old gods that had merged into the doctrines of the church. Even if the priests dismissed and sometimes vehemently chastised the stupid, superstitious peasants for their pagan ways, the idea of a *popess* was still held privately and held dear.

In whispered discussions inside the Vatican, church fathers held out the hope that in time the humiliation, the disgrace and the shame would be quietly erased from memory and from books and, at last, from history itself.

Over the course of years, alterations to the records were made. There were well-meaning but duplicitous monks and conspiracy theories along the centuries, but in the end the final historian, the inexorable cataloger of all events, Time, put his hand upon her and walked Johanna from memory into the shadowy labyrinth of myth.

≈ ≈ ≈

Maria had her youngest daughter firmly by the hand and hurried down the narrow street. She approached the wall and saw there was nothing to mark the spot where so many had died. Yet certain marks still lingered after two and a half decades, dug into the wall. Stick figures and shapes. Not words, the peasants and tradesmen could not read, but the markings were the stories of the illiterate who had been there as witnesses that day.

Maria also saw the remains of dried flowers and handmade trinkets scattered about the area. Conical papal crowns made of twigs, a mother rag doll cradling an infant doll and other objects marked the place many in Rome came to honor, though just as many avoided. She had heard that early every day a woman in the employ of the church came and swept everything away without a trace.

Maria glanced around and squeezed her daughter's hand. The little girl, taking her cue, dropped the flowers clutched in her hand.

"Is this where Gramma died?" the six-year-old asked, squinting up at her agitated mother. The child knew her mother was on edge when she worried the double mole near her left eye with quick, itchy strokes of her finger.

"No, this is where we saw the woman who was pope died," replied Maria. "Gramma brought me to see her when I was younger than you."

"Who killed her, Mamma?"

"People. The people killed her."

"People did not like Gramma?"

"No, I just told you Gramma did not die here," said her mother, feeling memories come up and wash over her. Maria heard footsteps and looked up. An old woman approached the wall. She took her broom and began sweeping without regard to their presence, brushing the flowers and other leavings into a pile. Maria led her daughter from the spot. "I will explain it to you again at home, so you won't forget."

"That woman was not supposed to be a pope, was she?"

Maria did not respond, but walked down the road as she had done a hundred times. She wanted to answer the child's questions while the girl was still curious, but it was impossible to escape the dread. The images of that day were burned into her psyche: Her mother screaming, trying to pull the mob off the pope and her dead cardinal, watching helplessly after being thrown from the two lovers, the red chorus of flailing arms moving in and tearing them to pieces.

Like hundreds of others that day, her mother left her senses. Her family found Maria first, crying in a doorway miles from home. Days later Maria's mother was discovered wandering aimlessly on the other side of the city, carrying on a conversation with someone who was not there.

Something had broken inside. It was too much to grasp and Maria's mother was sent to a place beyond this conscious life, never to return.


As she walked now with her own daughter, Maria could not escape the memories of that day. She recalled the awe she felt as she sat on the ground before the woman pope, who spoke words she could not remember, but could still clearly see the smile and feel the pope's gentle touch on her face. The smell of blood and mashed grasshoppers so thick in the air as well as a presence, an almost palpable *otherness* that was upon the woman pope, one Maria had only rarely experienced since, a moment here and there during Mass the few times she managed to let her mind be free of everything but God.

Her resolve never to forget became even stronger in the years to come. Maria lived a long life and made sure her many children and grandchildren were taken down that narrow street, on the very spot it happened, and made them vow to pass the story down to every one of their own.

≈ ≈ ≈

Anastasius The Librarian opened the window to let in the light and watched, three stories below, as a young mother walked her little girl along the early morning street. He turned from the window and sat at his desk with a single candle before him. Though it was just after sunrise he already felt weary, but this was the only time he could work unobserved and he stretched to push himself awake. He opened the copy book he had taken from its secured cabinet in this most private section of the library.

He sighed and rubbed his watery eyes. He felt the wrinkled skin on his face, as worn as the rest of his body; his back so bowed and aching he walked in a perpetual stoop, the dark lustrous hair from his youth gone a thin steel gray, and he blinked at the milky film over his eyes that made them nearly useless.

Anastasius had to use the enchanted glass to make the letters bigger, transform them from black blurry squiggles into the words he copied in his books. The glass was an astonishing piece of magic he only dared bring out in the privacy of the library. It had been given to him by a Persian scholar two years before. The old man had got down on his knees to thank Anastasius for letting him in to the library to study after several requests to suspicious priests and bored bureaucrats had failed.

The Persian, Anastasius remembered -- though many spat the label 'Saracen' at him -- had traveled the five hundred leagues twice in his life to visit Rome. The first time as a soldier bent on converting infidels, the second time as a scholar in Rome to drink the waters of knowledge. He was to be deported from the Eternal City because the Emperor was again having trouble with Islamic forces rampaging on the continent. But when the learned man with one arm spoke of the 'little brother' of long ago and the times they had shared, Anastasius secreted him into the library, took him aside and told him the rest of the story. It was this man's appearance, not to mention his extraordinary gift of the magic glass, which dissolved any remaining excuse. The old Mohammedan's anecdotes of John Anglicus prompted Anastasius to do what he had been urged by others to do for many years.

Anastasius pulled the candle close and set his hand under the magic glass to check the progress of his condition. The glass made everything large and come into focus. What he saw was not good. As if he needed visual evidence. Anastasius took his hand away and felt it continue to tremble. He was ancient at forty-three years of age and not long for the world. This last work would take all his remaining strength and hurry him toward the rest he inwardly longed for.

He placed a single piece of parchment beneath the glass and began his first entry. Seated in the dusty chronicles section, Anastasius worked in secret where the church histories were kept. This was also the place they were added to and, sometimes, this was the place where certain elements were covertly altered. Perhaps a name or a date was inserted to shed a cleaner light upon the men and events involved. Sometimes entire lives disappeared from the records when political winds changed. Biographies of the apostles, saints and the lives of the popes were here in the most important area of the library, though few but the most scholarly clerics knew it existed.

By this time, Theodoric was long dead and all but forgotten. Roman families quickly shifted alliances and tore apart what the senator and generations of his family had built. Already the story of *Popessa Johanna,* barely twenty-five years after it happened, had been set aside as current events pushed it into the past, forgotten by some, dismissed as legend by others. This was the most important reason Anastasius was compelled to write. Set down by his respected hand, it was vital that the genuine report be sent into the future to explain what had really taken place.

He began the entry with straightforward facts. Scraping his quill across the rough page of grayish lambskin parchment, he noted that in:

"A.D. 854, Lotharii 14, Johanna, a woman, succeeded Leo, and reigned two years, five months, four days."

Was that the right year? he wondered. Or was it 855? He shrugged and knew it was good he was starting now before the years blurred completely. He dipped the quill into the ink again and thought about his approach. Working through the morning, he wrote the history from the days when he was the famous little brother's assistant, through the time of his celebrity to his elevation to pope, and onto the inconceivable moment when he looked upon the pope for the last time, as a woman, as he cradled in his arms the newborn he would carry to safety. Really, did anything else in his life matter, before or after that moment?

He paused to rub his cramping fingers, his thoughts on that day lived once again as they had, in some small way, every day since it happened. But he did not have time to linger. He concentrated on phrasing the next sentences. How he ran through the maddened streets with the child. How he raised the popess's son in the church, teaching him the scriptures in Latin and Greek.

*Ah,* he thought to himself, the quill held just above the paper. *That part of the story will have to wait until Adrian, our beloved Pope Adrian III, and myself, are long departed before it can be revealed.*

He put the quill point back to the parchment and suddenly felt a burning sensation streak up his left arm.

It quickly snaked its way up and buried itself in his chest where, to his surprise, it disappeared. He began again but a moment later that same sensation struck his heart and exploded. Anastasius' chest was on fire from the inside and the monk stood up, knocking over his chair.

"I...Lord...wait!" he began. "Please. I must finish before You..."

But his vision was blasted with thousands of falling stars in pastel lights and he was enveloped in a cloud of white that drew the aged monk from the library.

Anastasius found himself standing in a doorway he had never seen before and, afraid to look, he closed his eyes. When nothing happened he slowly lifted his lids and saw what was on the other side of the door.

He smiled. It was simply fantastic.

Through the door was a mist-covered forest with a wide, inviting path running through the middle of it. But that was not the fantastic part. Not only could he see clearly again, but he had the eyes of a child. Every shade of forest green gleamed, and trees and rocks and flowers were as sharp as they could be. Anastasius looked upon the intricate grandeur of every object as if for the first time. He inhaled and took in an incredibly luxurious, almost tactile forest perfume carried on a gentle breeze. When he inhaled the scent again and filled his lungs, he stood up straight for the first time in years. Taking in the fragrance of the forest he felt the tight curved bow of his old back crack at every vertebra, let go of its arthritic constriction and become relaxed and supple.

The breeze filled the doorway in front of him and Anastasius gladly stepped through it. His task in the library a vague memory he no longer had any connection to, his pains released and now at last the child he'd never had time to be, the young boy hurried down the path at a full run.


## THE END

# ACKNOWLEDGEMENTS

It has taken several years for this book to reach print, for reasons good and bad and in the end I hope every one has made this book a better book and me a better man.

The people who have made contributions here, as you will note, are all women. Their interest, suggestions and encouragement are all part of the good things in this novel, however, I take full responsibility for not listening when I should have if mistakes and shortcomings are found.

Many thanks to Judy Braha who introduced me the original idea years ago in Boston. She started me on this wonderful journey by directing a play in which one of the characters was Pope Joan.

Thanks to Carol Givener and Meredith Strang who edited the manuscript at different times; I gained much from their observations, both emotional and scholarly. To Heidi Duggal, posthumously, who revealed, among many important things, which New World herbs and vegetables would not be growing in ninth century pre-Europe. To Debra J. Rigas, a talented editor for this final version as well as being mother of our talented musician daughter, Layla Angulo.

And finally, I thank my wife, Virginia Feingold Clark, who has been much more than an anchor of support. Virginia has been there to gently remind me to let go of the past and free myself of any resentment and smallness that I would occasionally slip into when this book seemed, at times, to slip away into myth and legend itself. She has shown me the spirit I have tried to create in Johanna, and for that I will always be in her debt. I acknowledge her deep contribution to my life and dedicate this book, with much love, to her.

# ABOUT THE AUTHOR

Nelson Clark lives and writes in Los Angeles, California. He has completed a dark contemporary mystery and is working on another novel. Comments, observations and rants just might reach him at thewomanpope@gmail.com.